TASA'S PATH

Jeffrey J. Michaels

TASA'S PATH

Printed in the United States of America
First Printing – February 2009

Original cover portrait by Lane Brown
Cover artwork and design by Andrei Bat

ISBN #   978-0-9969371-0-8

Let us walk awhile and perhaps you will learn something.
Perhaps you will learn something of your own truth.

Dedication

To Jill, who liked the story even before it was finished, and still laughs and cries every time she reads it.

To the mystical beings who walk amongst us today. The blood of the dragons is still strong.

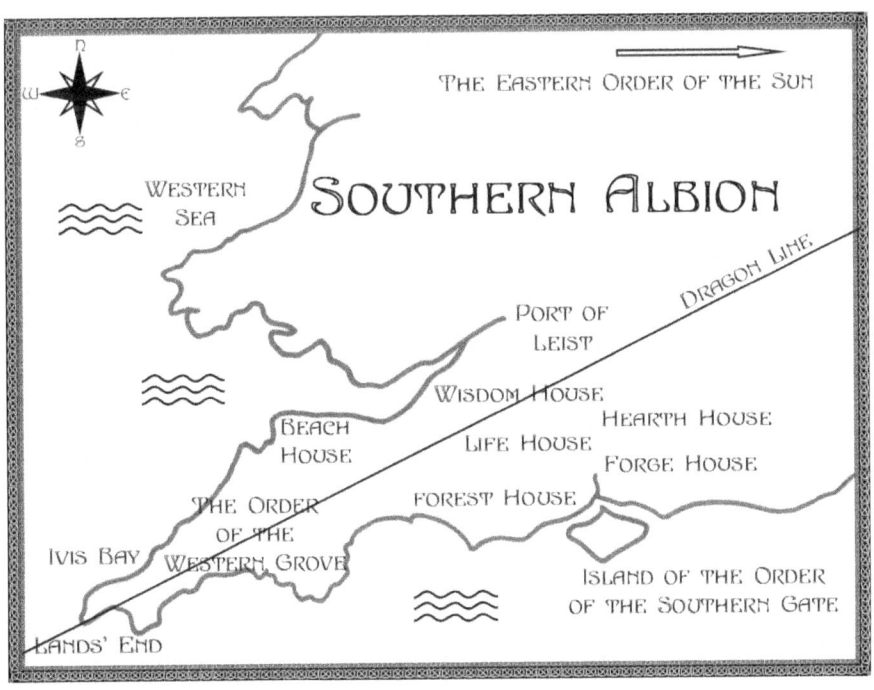

THE EASTERN ORDER OF THE SUN

WESTERN SEA

SOUTHERN ALBION

DRAGON LINE

PORT OF LEIST

WISDOM HOUSE

HEARTH HOUSE

BEACH HOUSE

LIFE HOUSE

FORGE HOUSE

THE ORDER OF THE WESTERN GROVE

FOREST HOUSE

IVIS BAY

LANDS' END

ISLAND OF THE ORDER OF THE SOUTHERN GATE

PENTHE HOUSE REGION

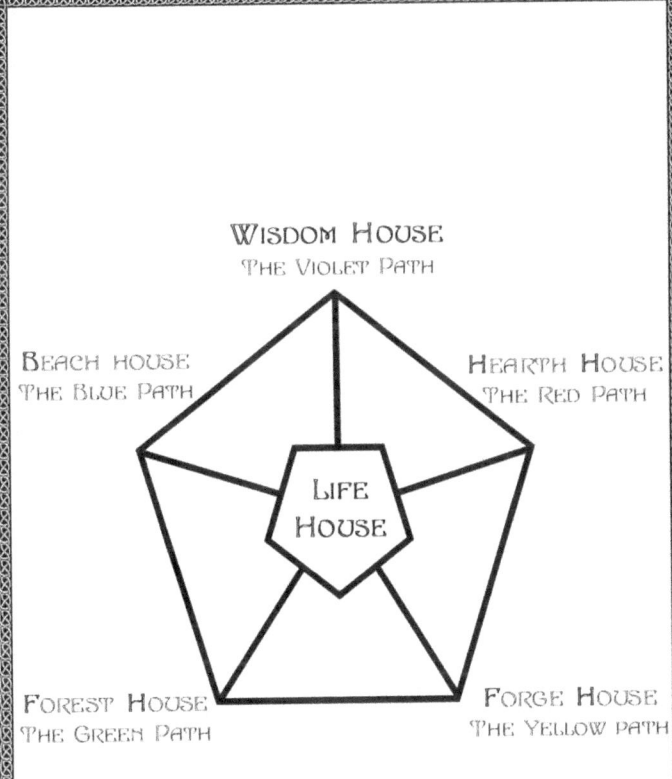

WISDOM HOUSE
THE VIOLET PATH

BEACH HOUSE
THE BLUE PATH

HEARTH HOUSE
THE RED PATH

LIFE
HOUSE

FOREST HOUSE
THE GREEN PATH

FORGE HOUSE
THE YELLOW PATH

PENTHE HOUSE
THE HOUSE OF FIVE DOORS

Table of Contents

1 - Voices in the Dark...1

2 - There is a Truth about Dragons 12

3 - Perilous Passage.. 20

4 - Green and Growing 33

5 - An Irregular Decision.. 42

6 - Reds and Greens.. 46

7 - Of the Blood of the Dragons 55

8 - Little Men in the Forest 64

9 - Dragons and Dreams 67

10 - A Song in the Night 71

11 - Temple in a Storm.. 76

12 - Rite of Passage 85

13 - A Return to the Sea..91

14 - Things Being Relative 94

15 - To Wonder at the Truth of Things 110

16 - Speaking of Changes 115

17 - Tracking Mariel..120

18 - An Agreement of Dragons................................133

19 - Different in a Different Way............................. 141

20 - Smile on a Stone..146

21 - Good Together 149

22 - A Simple Song 154

23 - A Crew Begins to Form 161

24 - Changing Course..173

25 - A Time for Truths...177

26 - Letter from Home 185

27 - A Quiet Edge..193

28 - The Changing of the World.............................. 200

29 - Reasons to Believe... 207

30 - Tea in a Temple with a Dragon.........................212

31 - A Dragon's Eye View 223

32 - Tasa's Journey... 230

33 - To Be Bound to Dragons.................................. 239

34 - I of Stone and You of the Forest...................... 248

35 - Gathering 260

36 - The Leavings.. 264

37 - Handfasting.. 274

38 - Salt Water 288

Addendum - Penthe House...................................... 293

1
Voices in the Dark

RUMORS FLOATED IN THE NIGHT. The child heard them from her leafy perch outside the window. Island breezes blew soft and did not disturb her refuge, nor did the words blow apart. Tasa knew the sounds, understood the sentences, but full meaning of the conversation hung just out of reach of her comprehension. Arriving late in the day, the two strangers did not find Tasa's mother to be a welcoming force.

Inside Tasa's mother's house, the woman dressed in white spoke. "We sense your daughter from afar. She is strong, and we will need that strength. Tepes is weak, chained, yet it appears he has influence still. The dragons have been…absent for too long."

"Tepes! Do not beleaguer me with old tales of the blood dragon!" Tasa heard the latent anger in her mother's voice. "How many years, nay, centuries have we gone with no threat from ancient horrors? Do we need to scare ourselves? Is there true reason for fear?"

The dark-skinned man said, "There is a certain diminishing of some humans, men who are lacking in the blood of the dragons. They are moving from the eastern dark mountains across the land to the west, and also south."

Tasa listened to the man's voice and stayed quite still. It was not a common sound on the island, the deeper tones of a man. She knew men. Here on Solaine, their island home, there were men that sailed the azure waters. Mostly they lived on other shores, neighboring isles. Some lived on the sea itself. They brought supplies and traded for oils, wines, and cloth. Some would stay for a while, months, but not years. The women of Solaine sometimes would smile in certain ways and the men would stay. Sometimes there were sons. They often left the island with their fathers before their voices deepened.

"Are they here, these diminished men? Are they near?" Tasa's mother asked. Her tone was different with the man, but still held defiance.

From the branch where she perched, Tasa could see a portion of the room they occupied. Her mother stood near the fireplace, the man near the door. The woman dressed in white held the center of the room and spoke again. "It does not appear that your island is in their path. Not as yet. They seem to prefer darker lands. Your bright days will not easily suit their..." Again the woman dressed in white paused, as if uncertain of the truth of her own words..."transformations.

"Sister, you are remembered well, and we offer you welcome should you chose to return to Penthe House." The woman in white's voice held the same tone of authority that Tasa felt when her mother gave instruction at the great house in their village.

"I have never left Penthe House." The words were sharp, intense. Tasa felt the challenge as her mother spoke. "Penthe House is here as well as Albion. Speak what you mean."

The woman in white took an audible breath, calming her own sharp retort. "You have done well here. From what I have briefly observed, the women of this island are a strong force for balance. They know Gaia and seek to follow her will." Tasa felt the woman in white's reluctance to speak plainly. She sensed that the words to come were themselves unpleasant, the addition to an old argument. She listened closer as the woman in white lowered her voice.

"We at Penthe House...in Albion," she amended, "have felt a growing fear in the eastern lands. The stories that arrive on our shores, you recall, we gave little credence to them at the beginning. Many journeymen, those who are long lived and strong in the blood of the dragons, now speak of these things. The weight of their words lends a sense of reality to what is unreal.

"We, at Albion, may choose to recede from the world for a time. We cannot be involved in great battle. Our role is ever to be healing. We hear and carry hope that the giants are being moved from their own slumber. They too are reluctant to act. They well recall the Age of the Battlecrafters and do not wish to see their rise and return. We know that the giants are the ones to act now, just as they did in the days of Tepes' wrath. Being giants, they are slow to come to this decision.

"We, at Albion, desire to bring together those younglings who carry the strongest potential to serve Gaia. The ones that possess, not just the blood of the dragons, but also the fire. We come here now, seeking Tasa, though I know that your refusal is certain.

"We…" She paused once more, longer, and when she began again it was with a deep tenderness and pleading in her voice. "*I* desire that you also return to Albion, my sister. What is now lost to us, let us find it together again. I have come all this way to ask these two things and nothing more."

The silence drew out. Tasa often sat silent for hours in wind-twisted trees and sheltering caves along the southern rocky shores. She remained still in this early night. She remained quiet. She did not fully comprehend this conversation. Penthe House? Dragon's blood? What was this about? Tasa sensed deep sadness and regret flowing from her mother. Suddenly a strong wave of anger touched Tasa's mind.

"Nothing more?" Tasa's mother had a tone when she was angry. It made others quiver in fear. Young Tasa rarely felt that anger directed at her and pitied any of the women of the island who behaved in such a way as to elicit that response.

"Nothing? Just my child? My child and that I abandon my home and community? And for what reason? This old and vague fear of yours? And *now* you call me sister? Where was that word when I took my leave?" Tasa observed her mother, pale hands placed upon her hips, teal-blue eyes ablaze and flaxen hair whipping about her face as if it had life of its own. Tasa often wondered at the physical dissimilarity between her mother and herself.

Tasa became aware of a gentle voice deep in her mind. "You are not alone," it said. It was the voice she sometimes heard in the quietest of moments.

The moonless night deepened. The shadows around the house were stark and defined by light cast from inside the house. Tasa looked down from her shadowed limb and observed the dark-skinned man. He had moved from inside the house to out, and Tasa had not noticed. Few people could get so close to her presence without her first sensing their approach. As a child Tasa was a masterful hide and seek player.

Now the man stood near the base of her tree. He pulled a long pipe from his tunic. Tamping some leafy mix into the bowl, striking a stone against a stone for a spark, he caught the leaves afire. The voice in Tasa's mind said, "He brings fire with skill. He breathes smoke with ease."

The light from the glowing bowl grew bright in the dark night. The man stood in shadow, away from the light of the window. He must have slipped away from the two women before the conversation turned personal. Tasa noted that he was away from the light, but not out of reach of their words. In the shadows, but aware of the light.

The woman in white spoke further, though her tone shifted from one of authority to one of remorse. "Sister, please hear me. You know me well. You know this is not my usual conduct. You know that these words are difficult for me to speak." She paused, taking several deep breaths. "Sister, I am sorry. Truly and deeply. I have been in sorrow since the moment your ship left the dock. I was caught in pride. I expected you to relent, to return. I wanted to be right and for you to be wrong. My heart was lost in my search for power. My heart was lost. I come to you now seeking to find my heart." Tasa imagined she could hear tears on the woman's face.

Tasa's mother's anger was unabated. Her words snapped and cracked like a whip. "You come to me with tales of fear. You ask me to act out of fear. You speak of your sorrow, but not of your love. You offer me nothing except to leave what I now am and return to *your* fold. And why? Because YOU have sorrow? Have I not had mine own sorrow? Have I not lost mine own heart?

"This island was nothing when I came here. I asked for a bare island, and this is where Gaia has taken me. Now we are fertile, and we are growing. Now Penthe House is alive on this rock in this blue sea. Penthe's principles are alive here. Alive and open, welcoming and not closed. Accepting and nurturing to *all* women. To all who come to these shores.

"The principles we learned together are still good. The wisdom still strong. *We* did good together. Now *I* do good alone. I have heard no tales of terror from the north lands. No journeyman lands on my shore with fear to tell. I left because *you* wanted to exclude those lacking the blood of the dragons. You now wish to completely recede from the world? Then go. You have already receded from my heart."

The dark-skinned man sighed and blew smoke into the darkness. He pulled a long breath, causing the embers in the pipe to glow bright again. Firelight danced along his strong hand, fading into dark at his wrist. Tasa thought of her own sun-darkened skin as she noted the muscles in his hand. She thought of her mother's flaxen locks and of her own deep black, straight hair. This man, this journeyman who brought the woman in white to their shore, his hair was also deep and dark black like her own. But where Tasa's was long and straight, his cascaded across his shoulders in graceful waves.

The woman in white spoke again, "Sister, I have made many mistakes. I came a vast distance seeking to adjust some of them with my presence. I came seeking to lessen the distance between us. I fear that too is a mistake. My words still come from my own soul. I have failed to communicate my thoughts clearly. I have raised your anger again. I have increased my sorrow. Perhaps it would be better to speak further tomorrow. I will stay tonight and hear your soul if you wish."

The night air remained soft, the breeze fading away. Tasa heard her mother's voice clean and clear, the quiet edge slicing any tentative ties the woman in white sought to create. "To speak further on the morrow, on this matter we are in agreement. Tonight go. We will speak again before you leave Solaine." Tasa's mother spoke in a dismissive but dignified manner. No kinship existed in her tone.

The blue door of Tasa's home opened and closed as the woman dressed in white passed out into the deepening night. She disappeared into shadow as she took the path to the communal house above the bay. She walked alone.

Moments passed, and the blue door opened again, Tasa's mother stepping out into the night. She gave a low whistle, four notes and then a fifth. The dark-skinned man responded with the same notes only reversed. Tasa's mother walked into the shadows where he waited, but she left the door open.

"You!" Ire hovered just at the edge of her voice, a fire that never quite ignited. "What were you thinking, to bring her here? She brings an old argument and new fear. She wishes to take joy and happiness away from me. Is this some kind of retribution from you towards me? Why am I followed by other people's pasts?"

The dark man allowed a moment of silence. The night remained quiet. Then he said, "I was thinking, 'The Woman in White wishes passage to my home seas. Who better to sail her there?' I did not do this thing without regard for your feelings, Kila. The words she speaks are true. There is trouble descending upon our age."

"And so, you believe that my Tasa should go to Albion and recede from the world? You think I too should return? And what else? Take everyone here along? We all board your ship and vanish away from the world of humans? Are you afraid too? What is happening to this world that all the brave beings I once knew seem to cower at legends and forest tales? The New Men are ever afraid of the dark. Have you reverted and become one of them?" She mocked, spinning her hands about, pointing at his broad chest and waving her arms in disbelief.

Despite her mother's stormy behavior, the dark-skinned man remained calm. "I believe you should listen and hear, Kila." Tasa could not recall anyone using her mother's name. Here on Solaine everyone referred to her as Mother Blue. To Tasa's mind it was because she almost always wore clothing of a brilliant blue. Now this man spoke her name easily and in such a familiar way. Tasa knew her mother's name. She now wondered if she herself had ever spoken it aloud.

The dark-skinned man continued, "I believe that you should do what you always do: learn, consider, consult, then make up your own mind and do what you will." It was his turn to mock. He did so gently.

Tasa heard her mother laugh. Not the hearty laughs she shared with everyone, not the soft laugh she gave to Tasa when they accomplished chores or walked the island paths together. A gentle laugh, like the touch of a feather, almost a breath. And Tasa heard the dark-skinned man laugh his own gentle laugh in response.

He said, "It would be good to be together again on the waves, Kila." Tasa watched as they moved closer to one another.

"It might be at that. That thought is the reason I told you to stay away. I have responsibilities here now. I cannot, will not, leave. And you must. I know there is another who is waiting for you. And your Woman in White, you must take her away with you." Tasa's mother stepped away from the man and towards the door. "You are free."

"What about Tasa?" the man asked. "Is she…?"

"I will introduce you properly someday. Next year perhaps. Be here for the solstice. Perhaps…" and she paused in the same manner that Tasa had noticed in the woman dressed in white. "If you are then free, perhaps stay until equinox."

"Which solstice?"

Tasa's mother laughed that same laugh. "Your choice. One of the next three, but if you miss those, I will not be a welcoming force." Then she whistled that brief tune and stepped through the blue door. The dark of night returned as the wooden door closed.

The dark-skinned man whistled the reverse again, softly, almost silent. Then, speaking into the night and seemingly to no one, he said, "You are a quiet one."

****

The next day dawned bright yellow. Tasa gazed from her bedroom window down the hillside to the bay. Summer was upon them, though through the year the weather rarely altered. Warm, relaxed breezes arrived at the small harbor from across the azure sea.

They called it the Ringing Sea and sailors spoke of the lands that circled around it. It was the only water Tasa knew besides the tumbling streams that flowed from springs and small caverns down the northern mountain. In the seaside village life held a constancy that Tasa never questioned.

Her books and maps told of other places. Visitors told of strange lands. Some of the denizens of the island came from distant countries and during informal gatherings they would sometimes speak of their place of origin. Many did not. There was a sense amongst the population that whatever had gone before in their lives now was vanished. They may acknowledge a previous life, but most spoke of the day of their arrival as if that also was the day of their birth.

Tasa's questing mind was also a respectful mind. She may want to ask, but rarely did she pry. Her books told her much, and many of the journeymen and their crews would bring new volumes to her. She tried to read them all, but many were deep in their subject matter, and she did not comprehend fully the meanings. "Someday you will know," the voice in her head would say. When she felt frustrated, the voice would speak calm words and say, "I will remember these things for you."

Tasa now watched her mother walk the dusty path through the olive trees and past the grape arbors. She moved towards the village by the bay but paused to gaze down at a ship resting just offshore. Tasa had never seen one quite like this. Sails and deck and hull, all the same components that made up other ships, but there was a sleekness to this one, a sense of life about it. It seemed more a creature of the sea than a vessel to traverse the waters. A bright, vital light seemed to emanate from the twin hulls. The deck gleamed brighter, richer than other weather-worn wooden planking on the smaller fishing vessels.

For Tasa, the strange words in the night had left this day abnormal. Tasa was curious and did not sleep her usual hours. This day, awake much earlier than normal, she watched from her window and wondered. For just a moment Tasa thought her mother would turn back. Her mother had not asked where Tasa had been when she walked through the blue door later in the night. She had said nothing to her mother about last night's conversation. The island was safe. Tasa was clever. She was trusted. Night held no terrors.

That preceding night, Tasa never really fell into sleep. Far too many questions wandered through her young mind. For nearly twelve years she lived only one reality. All others fit into pages and scrolls or tales that were told. Tales of distant places and times, but also of fantastic beings like giants and dragons, but surely these were simple stories, meant to amuse and nothing more.

Now this woman dressed in white and this dark-skinned man came to change everything. Tasa knew that color white. She knew her own mother possessed a robe made of the same material. She knew where it was stored in their house. She had never seen her mother wear it. Only the deep blue one and once in a while, during planting and harvesting, a robe of deep green.

Down in the harbor, just at the end of the dock, a man dove into the water. It may have been the dark-skinned man, but even Tasa's well-trained eye could not see for certain at this distance. She noted that her mother, still standing at the bend of the path leading into the village, also watched. The man who dove swam out to the sleek, bright ship in the harbor and hauled himself aboard by the anchor rope. Tasa watched her mother resume the journey down the path away from their home, slowly at first, then with a swifter step. Tasa watched her mother hurry, as if she might be late.

****

Tasa and her mother spoke later that same long summer day, watching as the sun's rays sloping across the land created deep, slow-moving shadows amongst the rocky hills above their dwelling. They sat in their small, stone-tiled courtyard sipping cool water flavored with lemons Tasa picked earlier.

Together they watched the bright ship as sails spread outward like wings, catching wind and western light. The sleek vessel looked beautiful as it slid across the sea and away from the island. The same wind that blew the ship from port rustled trees in the golden twilight. The same ancient wind that twisted the tree branches that now made up their chairs. Leaves scampered across hand-painted tiles, dancing in spirals at their bare feet.

"You may one day travel aboard that swift craft, Tasa."

"Where would I go, Mother?"

"To a place of deep greens. Sometimes it is a place of deep whites and then it is cold."

"Like in the caverns?"

"No, child. You have never known cold like this. But there is warmth there as well, even in the coldest months."

"What will I do there?"

"You will learn, like the women and girls who come here to this island. You will learn about life and living."

"Why can I not learn these things here, Mother?"

"There is much to learn away from home. There is wisdom in travel. No place is safe, but some places are safer than others. Gaia calls to us and we go; you know this part. There is more to this world, and I cannot teach you everything, though you have learned much."

"Who will take me there? Will you also travel with me to this green place? Will it be the dark-skinned man that carries us across the sea? Will I go to the one who called you sister?"

Tasa's mother turned to look at her. One tear rolled down her pale cheek, though Tasa could see the track of one that preceded it. "You see many things, Tasa. More things than most. You are quiet in your knowledge, and I forget the way you see and know. No, child, I will likely not be traveling along by your side. Yes, the dark-skinned man who brought you to me will also carry you away from me. I am needed here no matter what comes our way."

"How will I know what to do there? How will I live without my mother to guide me?"

"There are many mothers in Albion. There are many mothers and many daughters at Penthe House. You will be well cared for, as I was before you. It is a place of refuge for some, but it is more. It is a place of the First Men, those with the blood of the dragons. It is a place that should be without fear. My own fear is that it will become a place where the fearful are no longer welcome. It is why I must remain here. The ones in fear need a place to go. This island can be that place. You must journey there, to Albion, to Penthe House, and learn your path. I will need those skills, if you choose to return to your home, return to me." Thoughtful silence drew out between them.

Tasa asked, "When will I leave here, mother? The ship has sailed."

"I am not yet ready to lose you to the future. For a while you will still be my child, but today you have passed a threshold. You do not yet know it, but this day you have stepped into your future. It is a future I did not anticipate. I sense now that much may be asked of you, Tasa. I know your heart deeply. I know that whatever will come, you will do the best thing you can do. It is not a lesson that came easily to me. You seem to have been born with it intact in your heart." Tears rolled freely from her eyes. Tasa stood and walked to her. Though she was long and lean and no longer a child, Tasa sat in her mother's welcoming lap, and they held each other loosely in the fading light.

"Will I return to you?" Tears now rolled from her own eyes.

"That is an unwritten future. I desire that it be so, but we cannot see this clearly. Amir will return. The dark-skinned man. Master Amir and his swift craft will return. Then he will again depart. You will go. I will remain. Remember me, child. Remember my love. Always love Gaia and listen to her voice. Once, dragons gave us guidance. The dragons are gone now; we must listen more carefully."

Tasa loved her mother and trusted her words. In her heart, Tasa also knew that dragons were near.

2
There is a Truth about Dragons

THAT SUMMER PASSED, and the winter was noticeable only for the shorter days and longer nights. Tasa liked the night. Stars stretched down to the sea, and she spent much of her time simply sitting in contemplation. When her mother would allow it, she spent nights near the shore. Several women kept homes near the edge of the water.

The memory of the night of the mysterious visitors faded a bit. Tasa chose to wait, to not press others for any information beyond her own senses. Much of her life was quiet in this way. She watched. She listened. She waited.

From that night on she took closer note of the population of her island home. In her childhood years, Tasa was told it was an island for women, a refuge, a haven, a place to gather strength and gain balance. Once the women grew strong, they then were nurtured and given time and space to grow.

Tasa attended her mother's classes and willingly helped the many women who lived nearby. In the past, the village at the edge of the sea was a place to visit in the company of adults. After the peculiar visitors in the night, Tasa began to venture there alone.

As an only child growing up on a distant island, Tasa read many books. As new residents arrived, she would ask if they carried any scrolls or maps or bound pages. It was she who began to gather them together in one place.

Tasa witnessed the many vessels that came and went from the docks at the bay. Her awareness expanded as she watched the men of the ships. Some seemed dull or pale to her eyes, while others, usually the captains, seemed to glow when they moved a certain way or spoke about their journeys.

Tasa liked when she heard the tales of travel. She did not feel a great call to the sea or distant lands. She did wonder about the world in her own quiet way. And she pondered her mother's talk of the travel she would one day partake. She watched for the return of the dark man, Master Amir her mother called him, and his gleaming vessel with white sails like wings.

She read the books, looked at the maps, searched for the words her mother used. "Penthe House," she said, and "Albion." Far to the north and the west she found them, an island, much larger on the map than tiny Solaine and with no direct route from here to there.

She spoke to the captains. Shy at the first, but bolder as they smiled and answered her questions. Some knew of Albion, but few carried personal acquaintance with anyone who sailed there. "Our boats are good for the Ringing Sea," the sailors would say, "for island hopping, for days asea to be sure, but nay so much for a journey such as that, such as Dagda Nicholaus might take."

Every time the boats went to sea, Tasa would request from certain captains and crew, the ones that had a glow about them, to return with a new book or a map or scroll and they often did. In this way, the island gained a large library, for Tasa's mother set aside a building as a storage space for her child's mounting volumes.

One bright day a man, tall and straight and dressed in white clothing, wandered into the library and began crafting shelves and organizing the books. Upon close inspection he did not look old, though his long white hair at first gave that appearance. He said he was of the order of a particular dragon and little else about himself.

Tasa was most often silent around him at first, watching with wide blue eyes from a distance. All the while she would watch, the man would talk to her. He would speak of what he was doing and the volumes he was shelving, giving histories behind the writings or tales of the authors' lives. He would describe the order of his work and talk of writing and the making of paper and ink, and scrolls, and quills and brush.

Occasionally he would speak of his dragon, for that is how he described that venerable being, "his" dragon, or "my" dragon, or "our" dragon, when talking of his order. It seemed that the dragon in the man's stories was a student, a disciple of sorts, following in the way of another Ancient Dragon.

"The one that gave us history," the man would say, and Tasa was not sure what he meant. She did not ask for clarification, only listened as the man talked. He spoke of the dragon as being like stone. At least that was how Tasa's young mind first heard the dragon's name. In later years she understood the name to be Wollston.

One day as she was perusing the shelves, Tasa began to find books there that she knew had not come from her collection, nor from members of the community. A short time later she found the library being staffed by a number of pleasant strangers. These new ones quickly adapted to island life and became welcomed by those that had lived there for generations. Of the men and women who staffed the library, most of them dressed predominately in shades of white. Not the brilliant white of the painted buildings, nor the white of the clouds above the sea, but an off-white, like the parchment of a new scroll or the grayish white of a marble tablet.

"The problem with books," one of the women said, "is that you can't know the difference between what really happened and what the author thinks happened. If you are there to see it, things might appear very different to you or me than the one who is telling the tale of distant events." In this way, Tasa began to trust her own sight and hold back her opinions until she felt that she had several versions of the stories and histories to piece together for her own vision of what may have happened. "Even that is a slippery way," the woman said when Tasa spoke of her philosophy. "Now you are just making up the story to fit your viewpoint. Certainly, you've added to your knowledge, but you still don't know. Is it true? Perhaps, but only to you."

"What if it feels right in my heart?" Tasa was quite young when she asked that question but remembered the words of the woman's reply well. "If you can sense what is true in your heart, then you are wiser than those who ponder great thoughts all day long. The heart is more powerful than the brain, never forget that. Always include the brain though, for it well balances the heart."

Later that day, Tasa sat on the rocks near the clear blue water. Her eyes were closed against the bright sparkling of summer sunlight as it danced on the wind waves of the sea. She lay back upon a sun-warmed, sea-worn rock. Her mind was soft and peaceful. Daydreams came easily in moments like this and Tasa enjoyed allowing her thoughts to drift.

Tasa heard a voice near her. "It is true what the librarian says." Squinting, she looked around and did not see anyone. The sun was brilliant and the white rocks at the edge of the sea gleamed bright. The voice seemed to come from near a large rock just at water's edge. A dark rock, different from the sun-bleached ones of the southern sections of Solaine.

"What is true?" she asked, watching the rock. Suddenly the dark rock opened its eye and looked at her.

"Many things are true. What is true to you?" The voice was resonant, but not deep. Tasa did not then notice the subtle change of subject.

"Is my truth different from yours?" she asked.

"I don't know what your truth is and so I am unable to reply. Do you, for example, believe that rocks can talk? Or do you believe that other things that can talk may sometimes look like rocks? Do you believe it is appropriate for a rock to talk? Or do you believe that you are asleep and only dreaming?" Young Tasa jumped a bit at that last comment for she had just that moment been wondering if she was dreaming. She looked hard at the rock, black and shiny, and saw clearly that it was no such thing. Her heart beat faster. It took a moment to realize what she was truly looking at as she traced the outline with her eyes.

"Maybe..." she started slowly, "maybe I believe that dragons can hold very still. If I did, that would be my truth. If it was, would it be yours also?"

"Why yes, child, it would indeed be my truth and so now we believe something together." There was laughter in the voice. "I believe that you live on a most beautiful island."

"I believe that too!" Young Tasa was excited and enjoyed this game. "Now we believe two things together! I believe that..." she paused, considering, "that dragons must be very wise."

The thing that was not a rock laughed openly now and Tasa saw the teeth of it. Her eyes widened a little. She wondered if she should be alarmed. "I believe that dragons must be very wise as well. But I also believe that dragons can still make mistakes. At least, that is what I have been told. The one who instructs me assures me that he is capable of seeing things differently than other dragons. Does that mean the others are making mistakes, or perhaps it is my teacher who is mistaken?"

Young Tasa sat for a long time staring at what was not a rock, considering the implications of what would happen if a dragon should make a mistake. What did dragons do actually, she pondered, that they might possibly do poorly?

"Perhaps," said the black thing that was not a rock, "I am not really believing something then. Perhaps I am only believing what I am told without question. That does not in itself seem wise. So, you and I see how a mistake can be made without ever taking an action."

"I have never known a dragon," she spoke after a long interval. The eye in the thing that was not a rock looked at her the whole time, not blinking, yet also not staring. "I do not know if I can believe they would be capable of mistakes. So, I do not believe that, but I also do not disbelieve that thought. I too, have been told things to believe that I did not question."

"What does your heart say?"

Tasa looked out to sea for a moment. When she looked back the dragon was gone. "I believe in dragons," she said softly.

A voice from the sea whispered back, "We believe in you, Tasa."

****

"You prepare to leave us," the woman said. The man dressed in white, the one called Caraphino, stood near. The woman was often near Caraphino, and she was called Parla.

"I do prepare, but I am not certain what to do to be ready. My clothes are packed for the sea voyage, but mother says that I will be provided special robes and clothing when I arrive, so I need not bring much. I have some books I desire to bring along, but mother says there are books and scrolls in Albion and no room on the swift craft for me to carry as many as I wish." Tasa sat at a low table, her brow furrowed. In front of her was an empty, battered, old leather satchel awaiting purpose. Spread across the table lay an array of maps, scrolls, bound books, and loose pages. Some of the pages were blank and Tasa held charcoal sticks and brushes in her hands. Nearby was an ink pot with several well-used quills.

Caraphino ran his hands among the writings upon the table. He had watched Tasa carefully selecting the works from the shelves for most of the morning and through the noon meal hour. She had been placing various works in the satchel and then removing them only to try another combination. Finally, he said, "The question to ask yourself, Tasa, is this, 'What will benefit me in my travels the most?' Is it the tales of old from 'Epimetheous' Scroll of Memory' or perhaps 'Days of Early Light' from the remembrance collection of Conadais the Elven? You recall he is differentiating himself from Conadais the Giant with whom he disagrees about the formation of the Dragon Council and also from Conadais the Dragon with whom he disagrees about the formation or even the existence of a council of giants.

"Or do you wish to carry more pertinent information such as Pescator's 'Guide to Survival and Sustenance Upon the Waters of the Ringing Sea' wherein he describes how to catch and prepare such delicacies as eel eye pie or..."

Parla cut the man's lecturing off, shaking her head and raising an eyebrow at him. Turning to Tasa she said, "Or none of them at all. You are a well-read being, dear girl, and you will undoubtedly continue to be such a person, but I recommend that you carry less, remember more, and read what is available in the places you find yourself. The ship you travel on will offer you much to do and learn about. Knowledge is not found only in books."

Parla rummaged about and pulled a few articles together. "Here. A map will do you well. I suggest you copy this one from Pirireis. He is said to have traveled with the great one we now call Dagda Nicholaus in the days when the humans were young. Make several maps, dear, one for the entire voyage, that is here to there, and also one for just getting to the Pillars. Then maybe one more for just the landmarks that you may see along the way. Add the ports you may stop at to the first and third. This way you can keep track of where you are and perhaps the captain will even share with you some navigation skills. Add to the maps as you travel. This way you create something useful, and maybe when you return, we can hang them upon the wall. We will call them 'Tasa's Travels' or maybe 'Tasa's Passage' or...hmmmm. Well, time to figure that all out in a few years. Just remember, while you are onboard the ship you are just a passenger, so stay out of the way, but if the captain seems to be at ease, it never hurts to ask questions."

"I am not always at ease with asking questions," Tasa said. "I much prefer to watch and wait to see what can be learned only through looking and listening."

Parla laughed. "That is what you do, and you are good at it too. When we first arrived here on Solaine we did not know if you could speak! Now, my goodness, you ask so many questions of us it is difficult to keep up with your mind. Do not be shy on board; only do not be in the way. It is hard work to sail a ship. Or so I have read."

"You get to experience something I may never do, Tasa. A map is a tool, but it is different to actually travel. Still, this time of year the sailing should be smooth and easy. I will miss you these next few years." Her voice lowered, and a tear formed in her eye.

"I will miss you too, Parla," Tasa said. "And the library, and you too, Caraphino. I learn so much from you both. I do not know really why I must go away to continue to learn. I know that it is viewed a privilege and I feel like I should feel honored. Only I do not. Solaine is my home. It is everything I need and more. There is so much to be learned right here, and there are experiences to be gained just from life on this island. I think maybe I should just remain here. I do not believe mother is of such a determined mind that she will disagree."

Parla looked at Caraphino with some consternation at Tasa's words. He winked and smiled. With her head down and her hands on several piles of books, Tasa did not notice their shared, silent communication. Caraphino stepped forward then and laid a hand on Tasa's head. A gentle light emanated from his palm. "It is true, Tasa, that it will not take much to alter your mother's mind on this matter. But it is what *you* want that truly matters now. What do you desire in your heart?"

Calm fell about Tasa then. She had felt scattered, but now a sensation of peace gathered within her. She had felt undecided, but now saw that she could gain much direction in this voyage and likely more in her time at Penthe House. She could return in just a matter of years and be of great benefit to her mother and the women who arrived and lived on Solaine. She wanted to be useful, not important necessarily, but someone who was capable and not a burden to others.

She thought of her life until now. It was a fine life thus far. She did not feel anyone was inconvenienced by her presence. This was not always satisfying and sometimes it left her lonely, but at least she was not in the way.

"What I desire is to learn and grow. If it means I must leave Solaine, then I will do so. I will be quiet and simply observe. I will remain out of the way as you say, Parla, but I want to learn to help where I can, to not be a burden. I hope I have not become a burden to you."

"A burden? Goodness, dear Tasa. You are a joy to us! Without you first beginning this collection of knowledge, we would not have a purpose," Parla said.

Briefly Tasa wondered what they had been doing before they arrived at Solaine, but Caraphino spoke again saying, "It is because of these qualities that you have been recommended to Penthe House. Well, these and more. You have great potential, Tasa, but it is up to you to find your path in this world. It may require a journey to be able to find your true home."

Tasa went quiet at these thoughts. For a time, then, she worked on her maps, making little notes about things along the way. She drew small pictures at the edges, places upon Solaine that she frequented, views and sights she enjoyed. Near the water's edge she drew a black rock where none should be. Within the rock she sketched one open eye. She listened for the voice in her mind and heard only silence.

3
Perilous Passage

THE SWIFT CRAFT MALI CARRIED HER FROM HER HOME. The voyage began in calm blue waters beneath a brilliant yellow sun. The impending autumn equinox brought the sense of harvest to the island. Soon grapes and olives would be carried to presses, grains would be brought to the mill, and fruits would be plucked from trees and stored in cool caverns around the village. Tasa had wanted to stay long enough to taste the first fruits of that harvest, but her mother said that it was necessary for Master Amir to leave before the equinox and that it was the right time for Tasa to depart.

She bade farewell to her mother at the docks of their island home. As the swift craft sailed from Solaine she was able to see the entire island for the first time. A high mountain in the north, green with a forest that climbed to near the peak, Solaine became less hospitable: rocky, dry, and mostly barren, as the island came to a craggy end in the farthest southern point. From the deck of the Mali, it did not look very large. And the sea itself kept growing until it stretched without interruption in her sight from one horizon to another.

Having been to sea before in small fishing vessels she felt no fear of the water, but this was the first time so far from the sight of land. Her journey now would be to travel from the northeastern end of the Ringing Sea out and across the ocean northward to the Albion Isles. She read maps and seafaring accounts from her books, but the reality of the sea differed greatly from parchments and ink. Her library was large, but the sea larger.

This journey was in response to a formal invitation to attend Penthe House on the island of Albion. The invitation came from a small delegation of women, each wearing the various colors of one of the Houses of Penthe, though Tasa was unaware of the significance at the time. They explained briefly what she would gain in experience and in knowledge. They made things sound wonderful and exciting.

There was no real choosing, however, and no true discussion with her mother. Only an expectation that Tasa would attend Albion's Penthe House.

Tasa recalled the visit from the woman dressed in white two years earlier. She recalled the odd conversation in the night. She did not question her mother about that time, only asked, "Is this then the time we spoke of before? The time where I will travel away from you?" Her mother only nodded.

At the docks Tasa was introduced to Master Amir. "He is the owner and builder of the craft," said a man called Troylis. "I am her captain."

Boarding the ship, Tasa looked all about. The Mali was quite different from the smaller fishing vessels that could be seen frequenting the island. Larger and sleeker, with great sails that swept from her sides as they departed, she cut smoothly through the surface of the sea, and it felt like flying. For the first day, life aboard the swift craft Mali was lovely.

Nervous and excited, Tasa listened well to the safe conduct instructions that Captain Troylis gave the small group of passengers. It was good that she paid close attention to Captain Troylis. After the Mali sailed around a long peninsula the weather rapidly turned gray and black. Wind-driven rain fell heavy against the gleaming deck. By night the sea pitched high waves and the Mali rolled and tossed heavily.

Captain Troylis called all passengers together in the main cabin at the center of the Mali. "I'll not be sweet with my words. This crew, this good vessel, we have traveled many leagues and I have seen some desperate times. This is one of the worst I've seen in the Ringing Sea. We cannot make a port in this storm. The Mali is a worthy vessel, stronger than most. We'll stay the course. Master Amir knows his craft. Stay inside. Use the straps on your beds to keep yourselves from being tossed about. I believe it will get better after we clear the Pillars."

Tasa looked at the map she had copied for herself. She knew the Pillars marked a narrowing of the sea just before the ocean itself. She did not know for certain, but they appeared a long way off.

Despite the warnings, rough waves swept two careless passengers off the craft the third day out. Tasa heard the cries of "Man overboard!" From below deck she heard the sound of boots running to and fro above her tiny cabin. Later she learned that only one had been recovered from the sea. The decision to abandon the search was difficult, but the weather was so wild that they could not even be certain they were in the same vicinity as the poor castaway.

The voyage took on a somber tone after that. A human life was lost, but also time. Captain Troylis was quiet and grim as he struggled to navigate the waters. Contrary to his words things only got worse as they left the vicinity of the Pillars, tall cliffs to the north and also the south that framed the passage between sea and ocean.

Keeping to the interior passageway that ran the center line of the swift craft, Tasa had taken it upon herself to run supplies to passengers too sick or frightened to leave their cabins. The sea shook everyone. It was not pleasant, but Tasa, lean and light, was capable of remaining steady, often anticipating the waves. In her travels to and fro along the corridors of the swift craft she often stood braced upon the stairs at the back of the pilot's cabin listening to the two men.

Deep in the stormy night, she heard Captain Troylis speaking with the tall, dark-skinned man called Amir. "We've been too long at sea already. This passage out of the Ringing Sea should only have taken a week with stops. We're gone near two now. This is no interior storm, Amir, but a cyclone 'pon the ocean. We'll not easy return to the Ringing Sea, but we'll be the safer there if we do.

"Truth! I expected this weather to lighten." Captain Troylis spoke through clenched teeth as the swift craft dropped to the bottom of a trough. "Everything's intensified. The shape of these waves and their speed..." He paused and looked at Master Amir. "I am not afraid to speak my mind with you. We are in danger. Greater than any we have faced."

From Tasa's vantage point she could see that Master Amir's face never lost its composure. His voice even, he said, "I know you wish to return to the Ringing Sea. The wind is strong against that course. This sea is too fierce. We barely discerned the northern gate, and the south pillar not at all. Like as not the waves would drive us hard upon the shore. It would not be a shore of our choosing and these lands are rocky. I'll not lose my life and I'll not lose yours either. Our cargo is precious to me."

"What then? Head west? Into the storm?"

"West and north. This cyclone is a tricky beast, but the edge is that way. We are in it deep, but it must blow out sooner or later. Still, I grant you, this is a challenge. We have seen much together. The crew is strong. We will talk about this one for a long time."

Tasa, crouching against the back wall of the steering room, lost her balance as the ship lurched to one side. She found herself sliding into the pilot house and up against the captain's legs.

"Here now!" Troylis caught the girl and righted her. "What are you doing away from the safety of your cabin, child?" He spoke with a touch of anger in his voice, but Tasa sensed his concern. Amir glanced over his shoulder, his long hair tied back with leather straps. His eyes narrowed. The side of his mouth rose. Tasa could not be certain, but it seemed he smiled at the sight of her.

Tasa pulled at the flap of a pouch. "I've brought bread and tea. Some fruits also. Mister Carcher says he can't cook. The crew is so busy, and I felt you all needed food." Tasa looked Troylis in his eyes and saw them soften.

"Brave lass. My thanks and Master Amir's as well. Passage way is rough enough. You stay off the decks now. No one allowed out there but crew. Head back and stay safe. We'll get us all to a safe harbor."

"I know that, but I'll not stay hiding when there is a need," Tasa said. Amir looked at her again. The deck heaved, and she braced herself steady.

He beckoned. "Step up here, Tasa." She moved closer to him and saw the storm through a window. They were perched atop a wave taller than many of the hills she had scrambled about on her island home. She felt the Mali tip and begin a long rough slide into the deep, shadowed trough.

Master Amir gripped a large wooden wheel and leaned heavy to keep it steady. Troylis gripped a strong oak railing with one hand. He circled Tasa's waist with his powerful right arm and held her close, bracing his legs for impact. The shudder as they hit the bottom nearly tore her from his grasp.

The Mali dove beneath the waters and slowly rose again. Outside on the deck she saw men dangling from safety ropes, swinging wildly about as they struggled to regain their footing. She could see men hauling ropes ever tighter, pulling heavy, wet canvas to the masts. The sea pounded over the decks, sweeping them about. If not for the ropes and harnesses, they too would be lost at sea. Tasa marveled at their bravery.

"They do what they must," Amir said. "The same as you bringing food. Always do what you must."

In front of Master Amir, Tasa noticed a circular case of polished oak with a glass covering. Inside was a spinning crystal. Amir saw her gaze. "It is our guide. It senses lines of energy and gives direction when there are no stars or visible landmarks."

The captain's voice was close in her ear. "It is a constant thing, or should be. It should not be spinning." Troylis held her still, but loosely. His voice quivered. "This is unnatural."

Amir tapped a second dial. Inside, the stone wobbled but did not turn. "Follow the compass. North and west." Amir affirmed his decision to Troylis. "And happy to have your help, Tasa. Heed Captain Troylis' warning. Stay the inside passage." His tone was one of dismissal. The swift craft Mali tilted as she rode another wave upwards.

Gripping the railing, Tasa moved to the cabin door. "Yes, Master Amir. We will be safe. I know this," Tasa said as she slipped out the cabin door. And she did know it, but there was no sense to the knowledge, no logic, only a feeling. As she closed and secured the door, she overheard Troylis speak.

"She says she knows. Is she too a kin to the dragons?" Master Amir's answer was lost to the roar of the storm and the thickness of the sealed portal.

Their sojourn was to have taken three weeks, four perhaps if they choose to stop along the way for some trade. Those weeks passed and then another and still the storm blew hard against them. The crew battled for control of the craft against the raging sea. Supplies were rationed. Nerves were ragged. Passengers, women and men, wept at their helplessness. Sleep and rest were all but impossible. Many fainted away for hours at a time, awakening with a cry of fear. Eyes were red and faces gaunt.

Tasa did not completely comprehend the severity of the conditions. Her short life held no experience by which to measure. She only felt the anxiety of all on board. She saw the waves rise high above the sides of the swift craft and break hard across the bow. She felt the endless pattern of upward movement followed by severe plunging back into the hurling sea. Masses of heaving water washed the ship, pulling anything that was loose off the deck, to be lost in the endless expanse. As the weeks wore on, loud cracks and booming noises punctuated the constant sound of storm winds as mighty masts and spars fractured and broke away to be hurled at the hull, smashing repeatedly against their fragile shelter until torn completely away, pulled into the ocean.

With most of the passengers and many of the crew weak with nausea and bruised, battered, and broken, few remained to assist in the operations of the journey. Tasa did not like the exaggerated motion, but for the most part, she was able to keep her body under control and also her balance. She sought out Master Amir and Captain Troylis to see if there was anything she could do to assist. Better that, she reasoned, than sitting below amid the panicky and seasick passengers.

Troylis accepted her offer without question. He had been giving her useful tips on moving about and remaining safe, as she first acted as a steward bringing food and water to the beleaguered crew. As the storm took its toll Tasa sought to do more and more for the others. There were many injuries as people were unexpectedly tossed up and down. She had some training in healing from her mother and other women from her home, yet this was all beyond her experience. Master Amir never panicked and always worked to get them to safety. Tasa took his example and kept going the best she could. She did what she must.

She often wanted to find a dark corner and simply dream of her beautiful sunny home. "That," she thought to herself, "will not help us survive. Dreaming does not bring me home." Yet thoughts of home kept arriving unbidden. She could picture the stony southern land, recall the warmth and breezes. The days spent in daydreams…

The voice in her head said, "Dreams may keep hope and home alive. You are not lost. You are sought. I seek you and am also tossed by the winds." The voice had been absent for some time, but she remembered it well from her youth. Where had it been? Where did it come from? Before she could focus on the voice, the ship would heave once again.

Tasa suffered many scratches and bruises in the course of her work aboard the Mali. Her youth and strength held. The voice, though weak and distant, strengthened her hope.

Out of necessity, Troylis finally posted her as lookout. It was an act of desperation. He needed all strong and trained hands just to keep up with the damages his ship was taking. He and the crew were battered, some broken, all exhausted. There were two ways of acting as lookout on board the Mali. The main one was to climb the tall mast and keep watch. This was an impossible task in most storms. Now there were no masts left to climb.

The other was different than on most other ships. The Mali had a spherical room at the tip of one of the twin hulls. Bulging slightly out and away from the rest of the craft, slightly higher than the deck, this place was sheltered, but still forward, offering an unimpeded view of the seas ahead. It did not give the elevated advantage of the mast, but was protected by thick glass and metal braces, allowing an observer to keep watch so the pilot could concentrate on the task at hand.

Tasa, secured in the forward observation bubble with meager provisions, quickly learned how to use the communication tube and a long glass that let her see distances as if they were close. It was not truly possible to see very far except perhaps when they were at the peak of a wave. The motion of the craft was so irregular that Tasa often kept the long glass in its protective holder, secured with a strap to the wall. It was rough duty, but she held fast, strapping herself in and searching the horizon as best she could.

At times Tasa thought that they may be within arm's length of land, and she would never be able to see it for the darkness and the spray. She often doubted her abilities and worried that she was failing the crew due to her inexperience. There was no relief for her, and she slept little in the exposed bubble. She spent the long daylight hours willing land to appear in front of her eyes. Night brought some relief for her tired and strained eyes, but little sleep. She noted that Master Amir did not seem to sleep, so Tasa fought to remain alert as well.

At the end of the fifth week of the storm or perhaps the sixth, just at the moment before sunrise, she believed she saw a light. Part of her mind wondered if she'd fallen asleep and was dreaming. Her sight was a blur, her surroundings a deep, dark haze. The voice in her head spoke and she strained to understand. "Gaze now. Look for fire. You know fire. Seek. I am fire and we are close."

She focused all her attention at one spot on the window. Suddenly it appeared again, weak flickering light, looking to be atop a tall stone castle or towering fortress of some sort, and another brighter, seeming to be floating out on…No! Over the water. A signal fire was blazing against the stormy darkness and rain! She fixed her eyes on that. More, she fixed her mind on the illusive flame. She tried but could not see it through the long glass. Tasa pressed herself against the curve of the bubble, bracing her body so as not to lose sight of the land.

She began calling out her observations through the talking tube. Captain Troylis sounded weak and far away. He questioned her at first. They could not see what she saw. Was she certain? Tasa heard Master Amir's voice speaking to Troylis. "Certain or not we will heed her vision." The constant upheaval had rendered her ability to sense direction battered, but she thought, she believed, that she felt the Mali alter just a bit. And there it was, the signal fire now burned off the front of the craft. As they turned, the sky ahead seemed to come alive with a long column of flame rising from the sea into the roiling clouds. In those moments the force of the wind dropped, and the pitching waves steadied.

The Mali struggled towards rough and rocky shores. It took another day to come in close to the coast. The structure Tasa thought she had seen was gone from view. It was replaced by a wild shore and Tasa felt that they were being pulled forward into the land. The sea shattered against jagged cliffs. To her vision there was no harbor or safe landing, only high, rough walls of dark rock. She was too exhausted at that point to be scared.

The harrowing approach ended as Captain Troylis found a sheltering bay hidden amidst the cliffs. The Mali careened past more craggy rocks jutting from the surface of the sea. Then, once in the bay, stability of a sort returned. There they anchored and rode out the final elements of the storm.

Tasa had ridden out the last of the storm at the prow of the swift craft. She witnessed the full fury suspended in her clear post, all alone.

In time a reasonable calm returned to the sea. Under rigged sails, the Mali limped into a port some distance away, itself battered and filled with debris and shattered ships. Crew and passengers quickly received the care they needed. Amir himself pulled Tasa's exhausted form from the battered bubble and carried her in his strong arms to a house where women dressed in white or violet robes offered care and comfort.

"It is Tasa," Amir called out to a woman nearby as he lay the girl on a bed. The woman, small and dark-haired, hurried over and bent to see Tasa's face. "Oh my! Dear child." Tears formed in the woman's eyes. "You are safe now, Tasa. Safe in Albion." She turned to Amir. "And Kila?"

"She remained on Solaine."

"Her own private world," the woman said.

"It is her home now. She does good there. We will talk of this later on. Our concern is Tasa."

The woman had been applying cloths, some warm, some cool to the many bruises on Tasa's face and torso. The cloths were scented and pleasant. She poured a bitter liquid gently into Tasa's mouth. Tasa felt consciousness slipping away. This woman, clothed in a robe of deep violet, seemed familiar somehow, but Tasa's mind could not focus.

"Sleep, child," the woman said. "Rest. I will be with you now."

****

Days later, the sun shining gentle autumn rays through heavy clouds, there was an impromptu celebration held in the recovery ward of the House of Healing. Tasa remained dazed, ensconced in a deep, soft bed. A small band of bandaged sailors gathered near her. Captain Troylis commended her in front of the remaining crew.

She learned that several had succumbed to the rigors of the voyage. Some went for their final rest into the savage sea. Captain Troylis presented Tasa with a yellow and green scarf, two sides bordered with white. Tasa did not then realize that it was the scarf of the Order of the Southern Gate. Tasa did not then realize that women and men trained for many years before earning the privilege of owning such a scarf. Tasa did not realize that it was Captain Troylis' personal possession. Tasa was just happy to be off the Mali and on land.

Master Amir had been there at that time and, during a brief meal of warm soup and warmer bread they all shared near her bed, she found herself staring long at his face. She had often seen him on board during the voyage, but the circumstances of the journey left them unacquainted. The harsh journey kept everyone busy, and socializing was not a priority. It was a voyage that they all survived, not one of bonding. She noted now that his eyes always seemed to be looking off into some distant land or even a time past. Maybe he looked into the future, she pondered, for she had heard of such ones.

Master Amir's skin was a deep brown and reflected the light of the sun shining through the window. His eyes were bright blue and clear. Within his eyes, Tasa saw, a light shone. Every time his gaze swept over her, Tasa felt a strange thrill, as if this man held the power to see her true nature, her very being.

Amir saw to it that Tasa was well cared for. When she recovered enough to travel, he chartered a vessel and personally saw her to the port nearest Penthe House. This journey was brief and the sea smooth. Amir kept Tasa busy working lightly with ropes and sails, teaching as they traveled.

When Amir docked the ship at the port of Leist, she heard him speak to the harbor master. Their late arrival to Albion was explained by Master Amir as "some slight delay at sea." Tasa marveled at that phrasing. Master Amir was so calm in his tone and never once had he seemed overly concerned throughout the ordeal. Though she knew the storm was uncommonly fierce, she wondered if, in fact, the sea was often difficult and if all sailors were masters of understating their experiences. They parted at the Port of Leist.

****

The treacherous sea journey from Solaine to Albion concluded six lunar cycles ago. Tasa spent one month in the House of Healing recovering from the ordeal before traveling on to Leist. She spoke little of it to anyone since then.

Another month was spent at Hearth House, this before her official entry into Penthe House and her yearlong path through the six houses. She did not begin her acolyte duties then, only spent quiet time with the children and younglings that were in the care of Hearth House, also called the House of the Red Door.

Reflecting on her recent past, Tasa believed her arrival timing into the Order of Penthe was perfect, even if her passage to Albion on Master Amir's swift craft was less so. Like all of the girls, she began her acolyte path at Hearth House. For Tasa that meant arriving in the first of the cold months. Here she spent the winter solstice within, training. Cooking and cleaning and fire-stoking water for bathing and laundry, and everything she did seemed designed to keep her warm and cozy and out of the cold. She acclimated well, making many new acquaintants.

Tasa did not have many friends on the island she once called home. She was not unfriendly, only private. Many of those on her sunny island were older, many were younger. Few were of the same fifteen years as she.

****

Time passed and Tasa departed Hearth House after two lunar cycles on the third day of the full moon. By tradition, Tasa walked the acolyte path to Life House, the symbolic center of the lands collectively known as Penthe House. The distance was not great. She and three others, bundled in cloaks and boots, followed a path cleared of snow. There she met with the Mother in White. This was the person in charge of the Order of Penthe House.

This was not the same Woman in White that once visited her mother on their island, the one that said, "Sister." Tasa dimly recalled seeing her here at Albion, at the House of Healing, wearing robes of violet. Diminutive and dark haired, Tasa did not recognize her visually at the first. Only when the woman spoke did the young girl recall the deep night and puzzling conversation. Her mother never spoke of that night and responded only obliquely if Tasa questioned her. Tasa learned to keep questions to herself.

This other Woman in White, the woman who directed all the others, this one called Mother White, was older, her hair silvered with age, but young in her bright eyes. Tasa felt apprehensive about that first meeting. Others, especially those that were in their second or third years at Penthe House, spoke of the Woman in White's stern voice and furrowed brow, strong discipline and difficult lessons assigned.

Tasa brought a gift of cookies, baked fresh by her own hands in the ovens at Hearth House that morning, and the Mother seemed to like them quite well. Their discussion was brief: a simple review of her progress, some talk about her physical recovery from the journey, and Tasa was excused to walk her path through the snow and ice to her next assignment, Forge House.

****

That first meeting with the Woman in White was almost two lunar cycles ago. Like Hearth House, Forge House was a place of fire and warmth. Unlike Hearth House, it was noisy, and the work was heavy and hard. The acolytes of Forge House were often dirty with soot or dust from shaved metals. After work there was more work, for they were assigned the task of laundry and clean-up. In the mornings they must be found wearing clean work clothes. In the evenings the acolytes were charged with cleaning the dirty robes of their own and those of the older adepts who sought Forge House as a path.

Yellow robes of Forge House now hung down Tasa's lean form, bright in the early morning sun. She wore her dress robe today. Tasa always tried to keep one robe separate and cleaner than the rest. Today she was entrusted with making a delivery of sharpened tools from Forge House to Forest House. This was her first visit to the House of the Green Door. She wore a green sash that indicated her level as an acolyte of Forge House on the verge of moving to Forest House. In the past she had similarly worn the yellow sash on her red robes as an acolyte of Hearth House whose next assignment would be Forge House.

This robe and sash ranking confused her at first. Differing robes and colors and houses all held meaning. Differing combinations gave visual evidence of who belonged where. All acolytes were bound to two houses at once so that they could learn the interconnectivity of all disciplines. Soon, she knew, she would trade her yellow robes with green sash for the green robes of Forest House and the blue sash of the house by the water, the Beach House. She would dress thus for two lunar months and then switch again upon arrival at Beach House.

Beach House was also called the House of the Blue Door. Tasa recalled her own house on her home island of Solaine and the brilliant blue color of the painted wood door. Tasa also recalled her mother's blue robes. There was much in the stories told by the girls who had been at Penthe House for more than a year about Beach House that reminded her of home. The lessons were about living with the sea, but also living on it as well.

For the most part, Tasa embraced all the new experiences here in Albion. Although it was still two months away, she already felt some apprehension about her time to come at the House of the Blue Door. She secretly hoped that she would not have to learn boat craft when she arrived at Beach House. Tasa's memory of the sea journey to Albion was not a pleasant one.

****

In Tasa's first days at Penthe House in Albion, the memories of the perilous storm arrived without warning. As her time at Penthe House lengthened, as other matters entered her mind, the dreams of storm-tossed life faded away. Today she was away from Forge House and walking her own path, finding her own way through the forest. Today she was stronger and healthier and felt a purpose in carrying the tools from one place to another. It was spring in this greening land of Albion and although she had learned much, Tasa knew there was much more to learn. She now recalled Master Amir's parting words to her as he helped her find passage inland to Hearth House from the busy Port of Leist.

"You are a quiet one, and yet you see. There is much one can learn in quiet, but there will come a time for you to speak your own truth. There are many truths in this world. In time I would share some of my truths with you. For now, you must discover your own path. Perhaps you and I will journey together again. I would count that day as an honorable one." His eyes held her transfixed as he spoke. He had one hand on her arm and the other held her hand. She looked upwards at him and felt his presence, his true self. She felt strength. In his eyes, she saw his light and wondered, did she have a light of her own?

4
Green and Growing

ON THE MAP SHE HELD, the path was a straight line. Tasa felt glad that it was, in reality, an ever-changing path. She understood the need for marking it as a straight line. It was simpler to draw. Some maps were like that. She was beginning to understand the wisdom of the ever changing. Life, she was learning, is never simple. Her home island remained warm in winter and kept cool in summers, the weather temperate and never varying much. Here in Albion every month seemed to be a different climate.

On this pleasant spring day, Tasa shifted her load of tools as she shifted her thoughts back to the house ahead of her. The pack across her shoulders was quite full and the sacks she carried in each hand helped balance her. It was all very heavy. She had not been weak when she left her island for Albion, but after two months of carrying small children and sacks of flour and buckets of water at Hearth House, followed by two months of constant stoking of the metal-working fires at Forge House, her muscles had grown considerably.

Tasa looked at her reflection one morning not long ago. She was not yet a woman, that was certain. Long and lanky still, and not the body of an adult, that was what she saw in the reflecting glass. Yet her body was different from when she departed home. Straighter somehow and taller maybe, more solid perhaps, and if she moved her arms just right her chest and ribs did not seem thin so much as lean. Tasa made fists and raised her forearms above her head the way she had seen the young boys do in the orchards of her island home and yes, there was quite a bit of definition, as they said.

She felt stronger in other ways, the kind of strength that she sensed about Master Amir. Although she knew he was powerful in a physical way, it was deeper than that. She felt stronger in her body, true, but it was more a strength of confidence, of being able to accomplish things on her own.

The cycle of the full moon began tonight. Tasa knew that she would be advanced to Forest House in six days. The thought made her happy. It had been nice to be warm for the winter, but she missed being outdoors in the fresh air and sunlight.

The spring equinox was passed. Plants were showing signs of growth again. It had been strange to her that everything seemed to die completely in the winter months. On her island home everything had a dormancy cycle, but it did not seem so...dead. She had seen snow before, on the mountain tops, on other larger islands, from quite a distance actually, never on Solaine. Not like Albion, however. Not so much and not something to be lived through. She liked it at first when it fell and then with the candles and fires at night during winter solstice celebrations. After a few months of constant whiteness and wetness she felt quite sad, sad all the time and about nothing in particular. Except for the pines, there was no green to be seen and little sun. Then the rains began.

Now, today, she was feeling much better. The sun shone brightly and seemed to recall that it was supposed to cast warmth. Tasa turned her face upward to that fresh sun.

"You're the quiet one." A voice came from the trees and Tasa jumped a bit. She was happy for the heavy load. Without it she may have really jerked in surprise and then she would have felt embarrassed. Her heart raced. Her eyes looked through the branches in the direction of the sound.

Suddenly a figure, a girl about Tasa's age, seemed to appear right in front of her. Reclining on a thick low branch, she was nearly impossible to see, despite the fact that Tasa had been looking right at her. The forest girl swung her legs about and leapt lightly to the forest floor. No noise was made when she landed. A little somersault and a skip and suddenly Tasa had another being standing next to her.

The girl was dressed in browns and greens, some leather and some rough cloth, with belts and pouches and little sacks tied all around. A little shorter than Tasa, she seemed older somehow. She had the size of a young person, but more the shape of an adult. Deep brown eyes peered into Tasa's blue. Tasa peered back. The stranger from the trees had cat-like whiskers.

"My name's Mariel. You're Tasa, right?" Tasa nodded affirmatively. "You'll be at Forest House soon. I've been watching. You'll do okay. You spotted me quick and not many can." Mariel jerked a thumb over her shoulder at the trees along the side of the path. "I'll teach you how to find the right plants for cooking and the right ones for healing." She patted some of the pouches. "And I'll teach you to see in the woods. You'll do okay. You're already quiet." Mariel leapt high, higher than Tasa thought anyone should be able to leap. Mariel slipped into the branches above the path and, with barely a rustle, vanished from sight.

Tasa stood looking about for a moment but could not find a trace of Mariel anywhere.

She began walking once more, pondering the encounter. At least, she thought, I am not lost. The map she carried was vague as to distance and time spent walking. Hearth House and Forge House were close in proximity. Even the White House, what they called Life House, was near to them. Forest House was a different matter. She had been excused from her normal fire-tending duties for the entire day. In addition, the adept that woke her with the instructions had done so even earlier than usual. The expectation seemed to be she would be gone for most of the day.

Forest House now came into view in pieces. Well designed to exist with the growth surrounding it, much of the structure itself was still living trees. The longer she looked, the more she saw. Windows in tree trunks and winding stairs that started above the leaf line and walkways suspended between branches and suddenly she saw activity and people moving all about. They were all dressed in similar colors as Mariel. Some wore more green, some more brown, and a few even wore bright red swatches. Few wore robes and then only those upon the ground. Some carried bows and quivers and staffs. Others had packs of tools similar to the sharp and polished items in Tasa's heavy sacks.

She stepped inside the shade of the large tree at the end of the path. The coolness of the forest washed over her, and she realized how warm she had gotten walking in the bright sun.

Closing her eyes, Tasa let the feeling of warmth fade. When she opened them again, she gasped in shock. A long and lean form dropped lightly to the ground in front of her, a young man, all swathed in a bright and glorious green with a brilliant red shirt under his vest. He bounced high and then bowed low, doffing his pointed red cap. Tasa leaned back at a slight angle, keeping one foot behind the other to maintain her balance.

"Greetings, Forge House!" The green-clad man smiled broadly. "What brings a master of the smithy here to the home of wood?" His speech was ebullient, and he bounced back and forward as he spoke.

Tasa stared at him. She had become used to people acting in different ways and enjoyed the variety of personality traits of those she worked with. For the most part, everyone remained mild and kept to their own business, sharing dreams and thoughts at meal times or in those between times of work and sleep or sleep and work. The denizens of Hearth House and Forge House seemed to match her personality, unassuming and quiet for the most part.

Most of the new acolytes were slightly shy and unsure of their place and Tasa was no exception. The adepts and other more experienced denizens of Penthe House were mostly respectful of this and sought ways to make the new ones feel comfortable. She had begun to assume that every house would be the same. Now, here at Forest House, people were dropping out of the trees in front of her and being very bold. Not to mention very mistaken. How could this one think she was an experienced smith? She wore acolyte robes. She was barely old enough to stoke the forge fires. Perhaps he was simple.

"Brought us some fresh tools, did you?" He leaned close to her face, and she leaned back a bit farther. "Well, the tribe of the Greensmen will be happy to see you! The Oakmen too!" He spun on one foot and waved in an indirect direction. All the while the smile never left his face. Or his eyes, she noticed.

Those eyes of his danced and sparkled like the sun through the spring leaves of the trees. His smile seemed to originate from the depth of his green eyes. He wore a short beard and a trim mustache, not whiskers like Mariel, but a real beard of hair, red hair. Pretty red hair. He placed his hat back on his head. Tasa noted the shoulder-length loose curls and thought of her own hair. Black and not very exciting, straight and long, it now hung in a plaited tail down between her shoulder blades. His hair shone like the summer sun setting across the Ringing Sea. And he had those green eyes.

"Coming to us soon I imagine!" He touched the green sash around her waist without seeming to care whether she wanted him to touch her or not. She felt her eyes widen in surprise at his boldness. He seemed to not notice. "I'm Red Robin, or at least that is what they call me here abouts! Sing like a bird I do!" He hopped a little dance step. "Well, it was a pleasure to meet you! We will see more of each other I am certain! Maybe we can sing a song together! I'll even give you some words to use!" He laughed at that and gave her a too familiar pinch on the chin.

Turning quickly, he bounced and skipped off, calling after someone he knew. Or at least it seemed as if he must know them for the familiar way he called out. Yes, "familiar," that was the word for him. He was far too familiar with her and Tasa felt a little put out at the green-eyed, red-haired, handsome Red Robin and his too familiar ways.

****

"Perhaps you would like to bring those inside." A soft voice came from a doorway. A doorway that had not been there before, Tasa was sure of it. A woman stood tall and lean in the shadow of the portal of a building that Tasa had not noticed before. Set back and deep in the shade of a spreading oak, it was hard to see even after she realized that it was there. So many things seemed to be hidden or hiding at Forest House. And just what was a man doing here anyway? The Order of Penthe House was primarily populated by women. It was a shelter in some ways and men were not forbidden exactly, just restricted. At least that was what she thought.

The Orders of the Eastern Sun, the Western Groves, and the Southern Gate were where men and boys grew and learned. That was what she had been told when the adepts of Penthe House spoke with her on her island home. That is what they told the boys when they asked if they could go too. In the four months that Tasa had officially been here at Penthe House, she had not seen a single adult male. Until today.

"Those are for Forest House, are they not? Or perhaps you are simply taking your tools for a stroll?" The voice was soft, and the woman smiled and dipped her head. Her eyes never left Tasa. Her green eyes. Tasa shook herself and moved towards a bright green door. The woman stood aside and Tasa entered.

"You may set them down over here." She indicated a little stone alcove to the side of the door. The room was high, and the polished wooden walls gleamed in the light of many candles. Tasa thought that the building she saw outside didn't seem to be big enough to accommodate a room this size. The green-eyed woman's voice was fluid and melodious and Tasa found herself wishing she would speak again.

"Don't let my son bother you. He means no harm." Sunlight shone through several high windows and Tasa wondered how it reached the inside of the building when it wasn't touching the outside. A shaft of light fell on the woman, and she turned to smile at Tasa. Red hair cascaded about her shoulders as a leather tie came loose. Tasa thought again about her own uneventful hair hanging straight and boringly black. The woman's green robes shimmered in the shaft of light.

"Robin is here to select some for training at the Bard Lodge. We have many talented young women who would just be wasting their time training in the traditions we teach. Do you sing or play, dear?" Tasa shook her head no.

"Hmmm. Yes, well, I see that you will be on your way to be a forester soon." The Woman in Green's voice chimed bright and clear. "This is your first year, isn't it?" Tasa nodded yes.

"You do speak sometimes, do you not?" Tasa nodded yes, then became embarrassed and sought a word or two of acknowledgement. The red-haired woman in green spoke first, "Yes, well, 'Do not waste your words' I say and here you are doing what I ask without having heard the instruction. I must say if you fulfill all your duties so swiftly under my tutelage, you will do exceedingly well." Her mouth curved in a slight smile while her eyes twinkled with amusement.

"Come, let us get you some refreshment before you return to the hut or the house or..." she paused, furrowed her brow, and looked deep within Tasa's eyes, "or wherever you are supposed to return to." She led the way down steep steps that spiraled below ground.

A gathering of long wooden tables appeared at the bottom of the stairway. A few young women and girls moved about setting places and bowls of bright fruit in strategic spots. Shorter padded benches were neatly lined up on either side of the tables, awaiting the moment of mealtime. Tasa could smell the aromas from the kitchen at the far side of the room. She realized how long it had been since morning and her single bowl of hot grains.

Tasa was not a morning person. It was not her pattern to eat in the morning. It was not her pattern to do anything in the morning. At Hearth House they quickly realized this and set her appropriately as the night sitter. Her tasks there included keeping the children sleeping quietly and quietly getting them back to sleep in case of disturbing dreams. This was not a common occurrence as most of the children felt very safe within the realm of Penthe House. Most of her nights, then, were spent studying and practicing her mending arts by the late fires with only one or two others even awake in the hours of darkness. Some held the task of fire tending in the various rooms and others prepared the morning meals. Tasa enjoyed the solitude.

At Forge House she was required to rise early and stoke fires and gather fuel. This meant that she must retire to her cot at the peak time of her personal energy. It was quite maddening at first and she never really fell into the habit. Eating so early was very difficult for her. The result was she often felt hungry in the early afternoon, for Forge House ate twice in the day with only a brief break of thick bread and warm, dark, thick tea during the work period.

The work they accomplished was noisy and, out of consideration for others in the realm, the forges were closed down before the sun set. The fires needed to be stoked early to maximize the time allotted. Early to bed and early to rise was the motto of Forge House acolytes. It was not a motto Tasa recited enthusiastically.

The Woman in Green turned to one of the place setters and gave quiet instructions. Younger than Tasa and slim, the place setter smiled and skipped into the kitchen. Her brown hair also hung in a long braid and bounced in a wave as she leapt and landed in rhythm. She wore a long skirt that was slit up each side to the knee, revealing thin legs clad in high leather boots. A slight movement and Tasa wondered, was that an animal peeking out of a deep pocket in her tunic? Dressed in Forest House greens and trimmed with Beach House blues, the girl vanished through a wooden passage.

Everywhere the wood gleamed and shone with light reflected from candles and braziers. Sunlight emanated from holes in the ceilings. The smoke from the fires ascended through similar holes from which the light descended.

"Come. Sit with me. We will share some food. I don't know about you, but I can never eat much in the morning. It is one of the privileges of being the Lady in Green and the Mother of Forest House that I can request food at any time. Even when I am up late into the night."

Tasa stared at her. She had begun to think that she was the only one with nocturnal habits.

"Maybe I am too forward, but you do look hungry." The Lady in Green smiled at Tasa and kept at it until Tasa finally smiled back. "I knew you could do it! Now, if I can just get you to make some utterance, a squeak or peep or..."

Once she started smiling, Tasa found herself feeling silly. The sparkle and lively dance of the Lady in Green's eyes made her comfortable and for the first time in a long time, Tasa let loose a little giggle.

"A giggle!" The Lady in Green laughed and clapped and Tasa snorted a laugh and then ducked her head in an effort to regain the rigid iron control that she kept at Forge House. The laughter had been let out, however, and was not about to be stifled. Together the two women looked at each other and laughed out loud. The place setter returned with a tray of food and joined in without knowing why they were all laughing. Cooks and workers emerged from the kitchen and also smiled and chuckled, making little jokes, and soon the room filled with laughter and giggling.

Slowly they gained control and the silliness lost momentum. Wiping her eyes, the Lady in Green said, "I just love to do that! It makes the day so much brighter!" She took Tasa's hand and held it in both of hers. "You must learn to laugh freely if you are to be around me!" Tasa found herself wishing very much that she could be around this marvelous person.

The tray of food held wooden bowls of stew and warm bread with honey and a sweet tea with a sweet cream and some raw vegetables. Tasa ate to her fill and then some. The place setter returned with a tray of sweet dark cookies and some cakes and tall glasses of cold, golden juice and Tasa found room for more. All the while they ate in silence, except for the occasional, "Mmmmm."

"Thank you!" Tasa said. The Lady in Green leaned over and put her arms around Tasa in a warm embrace.

"Your first words to me and they are expressions of gratitude! My dear, I do not even know your name, but I like you very much!"

"Tasa." Tasa spoke and lowered her eyes. "My name is Tasa."

"Tasa, a lovely sound and one that suits you. You are quite beautiful, and I hope you are looking forward to your time with us."

"I am," Tasa replied.

The Lady in Green sent Tasa home with a letter for the Mother of Forge House and a small sack of tools to fix, adjust, and sharpen. She also gave Tasa a small leather bag filled with treats and meats "for the journey back" and she winked.

"To those closest to me," she said as Tasa took her leave, "I am called Mother Meg, and you must call me such, but only when we are alone and together. I wish that when we meet again you will call me such, but if we meet in a group, I will be Forest Mother, understood?"

Tasa smiled, nodding yes. On the winding path back to Forge House, a voice floated out from the trees saying, "You'll do alright here, Tasa of Quiet Nights. You will be alright."

5

An Irregular Decision

FORGE MOTHER CALLED TASA INTO HER WORKSPACE late the next day. Forge Mother's yellow robes were stained and torn and spotted with small smoking holes where sparks landed during the day. In fact, they were not really robes at all. They were more of a thick coverall with short sleeves and long slits around the legs. When she moved, the heavy fabric swung away from her legs and Tasa saw the corded muscles of her calves, noting that they matched the mighty arms and shoulders of the extremely tall woman.

Forge Mother pulled a thick, sweat-stained leather strap from around her forehead and dropped it into a pool of water inside a stone pillar. Large, callused hands scooped water up and splashed it over her short hair. She let it drip down her neck and throat. Tasa thought she could hear hissing, as if something hot was cooling rapidly. Forge Mother's broad shoulders blocked the view of the pillar and metal basin within.

"Have you enjoyed your stay here, girl?" Forge Mother's voice was deep and booming in the small space.

"Yes, Mother," Tasa replied.

"You are polite, girl, I give you that. I think you have not so much enjoyed as endured." The woman laughed large and Tasa did not find room to join in. "You are a good worker. You have an uncommon good eye for the flames. You're quiet and I like that. Hearth Mother sent a good recommendation along when you came to us. I had my doubts." She scooped more water and stripped off the dirty yellow work clothing. Tasa was a little uncomfortable with the familiarity, but Forge Mother seemed to have no problems with disrobing in front of her acolyte. "I always have my doubts.

"Forest House wants you sooner than your required time." Tasa's eyes went wide at this. "It is irregular. I don't like irregular." Strong arms washed strong back and water riveted down well-defined muscles, pooling in dirty, sooty little puddles on the stone floor. "Do you want to go?"

Forge Mother looked at Tasa, her eyes warm and direct, light shining in them like the fires themselves. Tasa felt hot under her gaze. She did not know how to answer without giving offense.

Forge Mother smiled out of the corner of her mouth, one eye closing slightly. "Normally I don't care much for girls like you. You think too much. There is something strong about you that I like. You can say yes without hurting my feelings, girl. If you say yes, the Forge House fires will be the poorer for it."

"I *have* enjoyed my time here, Forge Mother." Tasa meant the words and they surprised her. "The work with the forge fires is pleasant. At times I feel I have an affinity with the flames. I do not feel a calling to the craft of the forge, however. If you wish I will stay my full time and there will be no complaint on my part. The lessons are good lessons and I hope that I have learned them thoroughly, so that my life will reflect well on your teachings." Tasa spoke evenly and looked Forge Mother in the eye.

Tall and strong, straight and mighty in her stature, fearsome to the new ones that entered into the House of Stone, something softened in Forge Mother at that moment. She walked to a tall closet, one of the few things made of wood in the room. She carefully removed a fresh, clean robe from within, allowing it to flow across her body from head to foot. With a wave of her hand, she beckoned Tasa to follow her as she walked behind the closet and through a passage hidden from obvious view. They entered a dark, windowless, stone walled room.

After lighting a few candles, Forge Mother motioned Tasa to set a fire in a small stone ring at the side of the dim room. As flames rose and light spread, the Forge House acolyte could see more details. Rough, spare furnishings and a few accoutrements were arranged in a straight and efficient fashion. She noted that there was no mirror. The only thing in the room that seemed to be well kept was a large wooden desk and a matching set of shelves. Writing utensils and manuscripts lay neatly in select piles on the desk's smooth and polished surface. Bound volumes and well-wrapped scrolls were stacked neatly on the shelves.

Above the desk hung a painting of a large man with a mass of thick silvery hair. Images of ships and the sea surrounded him and in his hands he held a large book with a circular symbol visible on the cover. Tasa thought that if she were to get close enough to the painting, she would be able to read the title of the book. Forge Mother indicated that she should take a seat in a large, unevenly padded chair and, pulling a sturdy chair from the desk, sat near Tasa.

"Every tool for its own purpose, I say." She looked at Tasa, squinting slightly with one eye. Tasa felt like she was being appraised. She had watched Forge Mother receive shipments of stones and gems, carefully selecting the ones of highest quality for the various tasks and projects the house was working on at any given moment.

"Given time, I could sharpen you into something useful for the House of Stone, girl. I will not do that to you. You are a tool for another purpose. It may be that you are not a tool for the Order of Penthe. Don't take my meaning to be that you have no value." She reached over and opened a drawer in her desk. From it she removed a leather pouch and from there she poured a single stone. It gleamed in the firelight and seemed to glow from inside. Forge Mother held it out for Tasa to see.

"It is too beautiful. I would never be able to diminish the look by setting it in jewelry or a binding for a book. It would be a disservice to the stone and to those that would look upon it." She sighed, and her eyes shone with the light from the gem. She had a faraway look that Tasa had never seen on Forge Mother's face. Normally hard and grim, Forge Mother now looked soft and almost beautiful. Tasa noticed a strange light in Forge Mother's eyes.

Tasa felt bold suddenly and asked, "Where did you get the beautiful stone from?" Just as suddenly, Tasa felt bad for asking such a personal question. Forge Mother glanced at the painting above her desk and quickly wiped the back of her hand across her eyes. Had that been a tear?

"This? Oh, from a long time ago, from someone far away. I was younger. Not as young as you, but..." She shook her head and quickly deposited the gem back into the pouch. Turning her back to Tasa, she opened the drawer of the desk and gently placed the pouch inside. Grabbing quill and ink and a short piece of parchment, she began writing. Tasa sat in silence, wondering at her question. How did she dare be so…familiar?

"It is only five more days until you would move on. I'll not delay a work in progress. You get good marks from me, girl. It is still early and if you hurry you can get gone from here and on to Forest House before dark. Here is your mark of passage." She held out the parchment, waving it about a little to help the ink dry.

"Thank you, Forge Mother." Tasa spoke quietly, allowing a bit of excitement to rise in her chest.

"Go quickly, girl." Tasa stood. Without knowing why, she gave the Mother of the House of Stone a bow.

"And Tasa," Forge Mother spoke quietly now, "in your travels and in your life, please do not mention the contents of the pouch to anyone." She smiled as Tasa nodded affirmatively.

"Go."

6

Reds and Greens

IT WAS A CLOSE THING, BUT TASA ARRIVED at Forest House with her small, worn rucksack of personal items just as the last rays of the sun cast deep shadows through the grove. Small lanterns were all about and hung high in the branches along the pathways close to the buildings. Mother Meg squealed and clapped with joy at the sight of her and after reading the letter from the House of Stone.

"Bria!" she called. "Bria, our Tasa has returned to us!" Tasa recognized the girl from the day before. On her shoulder sat a little sparrow. The bird flew upwards as Bria skipped out into the grove and the three of them stood beneath a bright yellow lantern. Tasa thought the lantern swayed a bit but felt no breeze. She looked up into the trees.

"Come on down, Mariel!" said Forest Mother without looking up and Mariel dropped obediently from above. "Now let me see. She is taller than both of you by a bit, but I think that between the two of you we should be able to gather some clothes for her to last the next few days, just until the official robes arrive on third moon day.

"Highly irregular! You don't know how surprised I am that Forge Mother released you to us early. She does not like irregular! Now Bria and Mariel will get you to your room. It is Bria's room right now, but she will soon be moving on to Beach House. I will miss you so, my dear!" She stroked Bria's cheek. "Now Tasa will be at my side, and I wish for you two to be friends. Together you may serve Forest House well in the future! Go now and return to meet me in the commons at my office when you are settled."

Bria and Mariel each took one of Tasa's hands, Mariel scooping up her little rucksack of personal effects. They skipped off into the early evening shadows all together.

It was dizzying. Tasa felt great concern after only a few moments. Hearth House and Forge House both were neatly arranged with straight paths and squared buildings. More gardens at Hearth House and more stone walkways rather than wood at the House of Stone, but essentially, they were regular and easy to move about. Fences guided a person and kept things in order.

Here at Forest House, there were no straight lines and no easy way for her to know which way they were going. Up a little ladder of twigs and sticks tied tightly in bundles and across a short bridge of rope and vines, along a thick winding branch, down a smooth pole and through an arching thicket, between a hedge and a large stone, and suddenly they arrived at a circle of huts of stone and thatch. They entered one of the huts. Inside, Bria lit a small candle set in a carved stone holder and that was their only light while they were there.

Not much here, thought Tasa, but that was typical of an acolyte hut. The cot was wide, and the blankets looked thick and warm. A small fireplace was nearby with a goodly supply of wood, and a little table stood with three chairs. Against one wall was a small shelf with a few books scattered on mostly empty shelves.

Bria went to a little wooden box and opened it, pulling out some clothing. "Here, try this on. It is a little big on me; it might be just right on you." Tasa pulled her yellow Forge House robes off over her head and slipped the green shift on. She wriggled a bit to get it over her shoulders, but once on it felt soft and warm. "A little tighter than what I normally wear, but it feels good," she said.

Mariel dug around in a pouch that she carried slung across her shoulders. Tasa hadn't noticed before, but Mariel was barefoot. Now she handed over some leather sheaths that were vaguely foot shaped. "Here. I never wear these, rarely anyways. I've got another pair that I haven't even touched. They should fit you fine." And they did, forming to Tasa's feet like her own skin and feeling soft and comfortable right away. Tasa was glad to be out of the heavy shoes that she had worn at Forge House.

"Let's see!" Bria spoke brightly as Mariel gave Tasa a spin. The shift spun out slightly at the hem just below Tasa's knees, but otherwise clung to her body neatly. Her feet made no noise on the rough floor as she stepped in a tight circle. She felt very light and free and smiled and giggled a little. "Thank you! Thank you!" she exclaimed over and over, and the three girls hugged each other, celebrating their new friendship. Tasa suddenly felt pretty.

"Nights are still cool. I've got an extra cape with a good hood. I'll bring it by before morning." Mariel smiled at Tasa. "You look like you belong here already. You'll do alright!"

Tasa reached into her pack and pulled out a scarf. "If it is to be cool, then I may want this." She tied it about her neck. It was her gift from Captain Troylis.

The path back was no less confusing than the way there and Tasa expressed her concerns.

"I was confused at first too!" confessed Bria. "More than once they had to send someone out to find me!" She laughed at her own struggles.

"You'll catch on." Mariel dismissed the worries. "You spotted me tonight above the lantern. You'll do alright. Bria does alright. Most don't see me easily. You'll do alright."

They arrived back at the commons. In the brighter light of the office Tasa could see the slim blue stripe at the end of the sleeves and the hem of the green shift she now wore. She had not thought about it, but there was no sash to her garb. The robes of every other house wore the sash of the next house in their path. Forest Mother looked up and caught her noticing the thin striping.

"In the woods we try to blend in. There is not much natural bright blue in the shade of the groves or the bole of the trees. We are forgiven this and allowed to modify with the understanding that it is not an exception, just an adaptation to our needs." The Lady in Green slowed her speech and turned to face Tasa fully. A curious look passed over her eyes. "Now child, tell me where you acquired this very particular bit of cloth?" She fingered the scarf gently.

"Captain Troylis gave it to me. I helped while I was on board. I spotted land and gave the cry, Forest Mother." Tasa was unsure of the tone of the question. It was the first time that she had not seen a smile on the Lady in Green's face as she spoke.

"Hmm…yes. It is not everyone that receives a gift like this for spotting land, dear. I must question the harbor master before it is time for you to walk your path to Beach House. This will surely raise some eyebrows from Mother Marion. And amongst the three of us it is 'Mother Meg' dear." Her smile returned and Tasa, though still uncertain about the question, felt better about the conversation. "For now, my dear acolyte, it may be best to keep this scarf some place safe and unseen." Tasa's mind whirled with questions, but Mother Meg turned, and they all followed out of the offices.

Between there and the kitchens Mariel vanished, and Bria leaned close to Tasa when they noticed her absence. "She likes to be sneaky, and she really is pretty good, but she's not as good as she thinks. I spot her all the time. I just don't let on." Bria laughed, light and pleasant.

Another meal of cakes and sweet bread with honey and cinnamon, some warm soup, and a hot potato with cheese and broccoli made Tasa feel warm and comfortable. A spicy tea with lots of milk made her feel alert. Mother Meg and Bria spoke of the way of things around Forest House. Tasa was surprised at the way that Bria conversed with Mother Meg, just as if they were equals. She found herself drawn into the conversation and quickly lost any reservations about speaking freely.

It surprised her that Mother Meg wanted her to take Bria's place as one of her personal assistants. To that end, the orientation process for Forest House that every acolyte went through was to be handled by them privately. "There's not that many new ones this turning anyway. I find that it is more pleasant to pair the new ones up with someone that may be their friend. Don't you think that is a nicer way than to be put into a room with everyone else and treated as if you are all the same?" Mother Meg laughed a little, but Tasa did not sense a great deal of mirth.

Later Bria explained that Forest House was different in many ways and all of them because of Mother Meg. "The policies here are not something that was agreed upon in meetings at Life House with the All Mother," she said, "but it is also not something that you should ever, EVER bring up to anyone, and especially Mother Meg. Her policies are hers alone and we all keep to them while we are here. Quiet and unobtrusive, that's the way to keep Mother

Meg happy and," Bria added, her dark eyes flashing, "you definitely want to keep Mother Meg happy!"

They were strolling arm in arm through the compound late in the night and Tasa was feeling a little sleepy. She had gotten up early and worked a full day at Forge House. Much had occurred that left her in a state of high emotions. Now, dismissed by Mother Meg, they were casually returning to the acolyte huts for sleep. Bria assured her that they would be able to sleep a little late in the morning and Tasa felt happy about that and about many other things.

A figure dropped from a low branch and startled them. It was Red Robin.

"Ho ho!" He sang the syllables in pleasing notes. "A new one and already at mother's beck and call!" Robin bounced backwards. "Let's get a look at you…" His voice trailed off as he recognized Tasa from the day before. "My true eyes! You have certainly become more in a short time than I observed a short time ago." His voice was softer and his manner less exaggerated. He looked at Tasa directly and she felt a little embarrassed under his gaze. As if sensing her discomfort, Red Robin bowed low and removed his hat.

"My Lady." He suddenly spoke very formally. "Allow me to re-present myself to you." He stayed bowed and did not move. It was as if he was waiting for something and Tasa did not know what. Bria had been as startled as Tasa when Robin dropped out of the tree but having had more experience in this kind of behavior, recovered quicker. Still arm in arm, Bria now nudged Tasa. They looked at each other and Bria nodded towards Robin, her eyes silently communicating something that Tasa did not receive. With a little trepidation and a little annoyance, Tasa thought about his request and spoke softly.

"You may present yourself to both of us, Red Robin, and you may do it in the daylight and not when we are at a disadvantage or when you have leapt upon us in the dark." Tasa tightened her grip on Bria's arm and began walking away. She was not certain that she was moving in the correct direction, but she moved with intention and without looking back.

When they had traveled some small distance down the path, Tasa felt Bria shaking. She wondered if she had been truly scared by the encounter and turned to look at her face in the light of the growing moon. Bria looked back and could contain herself no longer. She burst out laughing and, not knowing exactly why, Tasa soon joined in.

"I can't believe you said that!" Bria exclaimed. "No one *ever* talks to Robin like that!"

"Well maybe someone should have done so long ago. What does he expect when he just drops in on people unannounced? That we will be grateful for having a scare? And did you see how he looked at me? What nerve!" Tasa's indignance cut through the laughter and Bria stopped walking and turned her new friend to face her.

"Many of the women here in Forest House would do anything to have Red Robin look at them in such a way. He is quite a skilled bard and is sought after as a mate by many. None have been able to catch his eye for long and many have to put themselves in his path to do just that. He just put himself in your path, Tasa, and that is no little thing around here." Bria was smiling slightly as she spoke. "There is much about you that I think is unseen."

They walked a few paces more and Tasa asked, "Do you think he is still bowing?" Together, they laughed all the way home.

＊＊＊＊＊＊＊＊＊＊＊＊

One cot meant that Bria and Tasa shared a bed. It was wide and long, and the girls were both slim, so there was no hardship. The night was peaceful and deep. The sun was high in the sky when Tasa awoke. Bria was already gone. On the table lay a neat pile of clothing and stockings and a new leather pouch like the one Mariel carried slung across her back.

At a central hut in the acolyte circle Tasa found water and bowls and soap and cloth for her morning ablutions. Soon she was dressed and ready, but for what she did not know. The day was cool and this early in the spring she thought it wise to wear the cloak and hood that Mariel had given her. She secured Captain Troylis' scarf in her new leather pouch and promised herself that she would learn more about that as soon as she could. For now, she must find her way to the commons, and it seemed she must do so alone.

With a little logic and remembering the direction she traveled from Forge House and the direction that she left the commons with her new friends and a little luck at hearing some laughter through the trees, Tasa found her way not quite exactly to her goal, but to a path that seemed wide and gave her some hope that she would not be completely inept at the ways of tracking and trailing.

Eventually she homed in on the Forest House commons and walked into the clearing with a slightly false sense of confidence. Waiting near a tree, near the entrance to Forest Mother's offices, was Red Robin. She walked directly towards the door and did not turn her eyes in his direction at all. Several young women seemed to be doing little but busy work in the clearing and they stopped now and watched Tasa out of the corners of their eyes.

Red Robin bowed as she approached and spoke. "My Lady. May I present myself to you this fine morning?" He did not bow low, and he kept his eyes on her as she approached. His green eyes.

Tasa didn't miss a step and replied, "I said you may present yourself to 'us,' meaning my companion and I. Perhaps it escapes your notice, but I am alone at this time." And she walked past him and through the door. She walked past him and his long red hair and green eyes.

The day passed swiftly, and she found herself very busy running this way and that with messages and assignments from Forest Mother. Bria was with her for much of the day and several times they spotted Robin roaming about. Each time they separated, and it became quite an exciting game of hide and seek for the girls. Late in the afternoon Mariel joined them for a cool drink of water by a pool.

"If you keep it up, he'll just get bored and lose interest in you." Mariel was lying still on the spring grass by the swift little brook that flowed out of the pool. "He likes easier games."

"Why would I want him to be interested in me?" Tasa asked.

Mariel brushed a cat-like whisker and raised the brim of her hat, looking first at Bria then regarding Tasa as if she had turned colors and grown a third arm. "You are different, I'll give you that." A little smile tugged at the corner of her mouth. Tasa liked that she made her friend happy.

At dinner time a hush spread through the tables when the trio of girls walked in. Surreptitious glances from all corners made Tasa feel very self-conscious. Mariel said, "Don't mind them. They all fall over when Robin walks by. They don't understand why you would treat him the way you did."

Tasa thought a moment and asked, "How do they even know?"

Mariel laughed and said, "They probably know up at Wisdom House by now! It's the grapevine and you're big news. The acolyte that said 'no' to Red Robin. Some are telling it that you punched him in the nose."

It was a strange feeling to eat knowing that everyone around had been talking about her. Tasa was not one to seek attention. Quite the opposite. Finally, she asked Mariel how she knew what everyone was saying and how she knew that other houses knew.

"Why, I've been telling everybody! It's a great story!" Mariel laughed. "You're like a heroine in one of the old songs! Like Brigid, a mighty woman of power, that's what I've been telling. Punched him in the nose!"

Tasa did not know how to feel then. She was angry that Mariel would say such things, but at the same time she felt good that anyone would think she was like Brigid. Then again, she felt foolish, for of course she was not like the heroines of old. She was an acolyte of Penthe House and not even halfway through her first year! For no logical reason she turned and punched Mariel in the arm. Hard.

Mariel grabbed her arm, gasping at the sudden pain, but did not cry out. After a couple of deep breaths, she smiled at Tasa and said, "See! Mighty like Brigid!"

****

The remaining four days of the full moon cycle passed swiftly, and the time came for the change of houses. All the fresh, first year acolytes walked the path to Life House and there received counsel and their new assignments. Most of the second-year girls simply walked the path to the next house in the Order. Some had been following the acolyte path for several years and now received the robes of an adept, taking permanent residence in the house of their chosen Order. Tasa and Bria attended the session at Life House and Tasa was officially recognized as an acolyte of Forest House and given the green robes with blue trim. Bria received her Beach House blue robes with the violet sash of Wisdom House. The new friends parted with tears as if they had known each other a lifetime.

Tasa found herself in an unusual position. She was not exactly new to Forest House. However, the acolytes she had entered Penthe House with four months ago now looked to her for guidance. The story about Red Robin grew and she was much admired by many for her boldness and bravery. There were some who did not care for her behavior, however, and felt that she had done Robin a disservice. These, of course, were the same ones that placed themselves in the path of Red Robin every chance they could.

What Robin himself thought of all of it no one seemed to know. He had not been seen for several days before the Path Walking Ceremonies.

Mariel and Tasa took meals together and often met in the evenings to talk quietly into the night. One evening Tasa thought to ask Mariel why she didn't mind the treatment that she had given to Robin.

"I love to see the old fool get knocked down! He's pompous and thinks that he is a gift to all women everywhere. Love 'em and leave 'em is his way. He needs to get the stuff knocked out of him more often! Make him appreciate a good partner, it will. Not some fluffy little girl, but someone strong that'll make him do his best. His problem is he's good and he knows it. Handsome too and he knows that. Been that way his whole life, he has." Mariel tossed a rock into the darkness. It hit something with a dull thud.

"You've known him his whole life?" Tasa asked with a bit of surprise. She hadn't considered that Mariel thought that much about Red Robin and the strength of her opinion was startling.

"Known him? We grew up together. He's my cousin." Mariel launched another rock along the same arc. It crashed through leaf and branch and, this time, there was no thud.

7

Of the Blood of the Dragons

"THE CHILD, SHE HAS A WAY WITH FLAME AND FIRE. 'Tis my belief she carries the blood of the dragons within her veins, and with great strength too, as the old ways once were." Hearth Mother Bae stood clad in the red robes of her order in front of a fire at the center of a circular white room, the flames providing the only light in the room. Seated shadows of five other women quivered low upon the curved walls. A hole at the top of the dome released wood smoke while revealing starlight.

The elderly Woman in Red continued, "She also had a way with the changeling. This fair concerned me in the beginning. I first felt she may be one of the eastern beast men. Now that we know they are all male, well, I am quite relieved."

"Why?" Someone in the shadows posed the question.

"I like her. I mean, I like all of the girls in their own way, but there is something about this one that is more…" Hearth Mother allowed the lack of words to carry the thought.

Forge Mother raised her hammer, the representation of her order at Penthe House. Hearth Mother raised and lowered the edge of the red cloak about her shoulders, symbolically yielding the floor. Forge Mother stood, casting a large shadow against the wall.

"I like her too." A low murmur of surprise passed between the others. With some difficulty they all politely quelled their astonishment. Forge Mother did not openly like anyone of her order. She respected their abilities. She admired their skill. She appreciated their work ethic. She was well pleased with their adherence to rules, or she recommended them for certain paths due to her strong and logical assessments of their character. Never did she express an emotion or a sentiment to or about her girls.

Forge Mother cast a squinted eye around the group in a mild challenge. "'Tis true. This one, there is a different way about her. I agree with Hearth Mother. She does have a way with the flame. Some of the girls are good. They make fine forge fires and can keep a constant temperature for cooking or for light in the winter. This girl's way with fuel and flame is something more than the others. Tasa..." Forge Mother shook her head and rubbed her jaw. "Her fires seem to be alive."

The voice from the shadows asked, "Do you share the thought that she is of the blood of dragons?"

Forge Mother stood in contemplative stillness for a long time. Her yellow robes were clean, but in the leaping light of the fire looked like they were smoking. Finally, she raised and lowered the hammer and took her seat in silence. No answer, and this was not unusual for the giantess. The group joined that silence for a few moments more.

The Woman in White raised a leather-bound book, her chosen symbol and, when no one else requested time for contemplation or an opportunity to express their feelings or thoughts, stood and spoke. "I know this one from a long time, before she was born in fact. We all know her mother and her aunt. I suspect I know her father." This last she spoke with a faint air of resignation. "We probably all know her father." Except for Forge Mother, the group chuckled.

"It is true, then, she is of the blood of the dragons, but that is no more than what many of us can claim. This does not explain her ways. She is, as you have said, more than the other girls, but does not exhibit a desire to lead. Nor does she follow. Maybe for Forge Mother, but then water follows the stony river course and wears away the rock. You will agree that she takes your direction well, Forge Mother?"

Forge Mother raised the hammer but did not rise. "Aye. She does so, but often goes beyond direction. Never breaks the rule, only uses the rule in a way that I did not expect it could be used. Never for mischief, mind." She lowered the hammer.

"Does the House of the Violet Door have an observation?" The Woman in White stepped out of the circle center as the Woman in Violet raised a feather.

Rising out of the shadows, the Woman in Violet stood as she spoke. "I have met this one. When the ship arrived that carried Tasa to our shores, she was injured and brought to the healing house. We happened to be in attendance there. We were there in response to the arrival of refugees from the continent, those desperate women and their children who arrived earlier in the month and were still being placed, though not yet transported. That intense autumn storm had brought us all to a halt.

"The members of the crew and passengers of Tasa's vessel were in very bad shape. You recall many ships were harried by the great storm. The Mali was considered lost by many. Most on board thought themselves to be dead. Even the captain admitted as much. All except the master of the ship and the girl, Tasa. In speaking with them, I felt they did not have the fear of death or dying the others felt. Amir, we all know, and this is to be expected from such an ancient one as he. But this girl...deep within her I sense she carries the same spirit as Amir, that sense of unending. She was unsettled, greatly so, but far from frightened.

"As others here have already said, I liked her right away. She was quiet in a way that many of the girls that arrive on our shores are not. She looked about and assisted when she saw the need. One evening we found her bed empty. The night had turned cold. She had gone to find the blanket closet, raised the fire's heat, and was warming extra blankets for the others' comfort. Mind you, her arm was still slung, and her leg splinted. The bruises upon her body were still fresh and bright. Her head still ached, according to her own report. Yet that report came only after she was asked. Never did she complain about her own injuries.

"The adepts first sought to counsel her and return her to the bed. I redirected them, entered the hall and worked with her directly. I did not seek to lead, only asked what she was doing. She handed me the blanket she was warming and asked if I would take it to one of the refugees while she started another one warming. We acted in silence for a time, until I finally distributed to all in need. Then I gathered her in a freshly warmed blanket as well. She responded to my arms and allowed me to carry her back to her bed.

"We spoke for a few moments. Never once did I hear a complaint. She did voice concern for her mother, and the master and the captain of the ship as well. She does not seem to know Amir from any place other than her voyage and perhaps an earlier visit to the island. We must be cautious with this situation. Kila may have some reason for keeping the child's lineage secret. I am certain Karia will be aware. She is powerful in her intuition. And she is once again close to Amir through their son Kamir."

The Woman in White raised her book. The Woman in Violet nodded acknowledgement. The Woman in White remained seated and asked, "Then you are of the belief that Tasa is Amir's child? Though we all suspect this is true, you speak with a level of certainty."

Without hesitation the Woman in Violet replied, "Seeing them together, especially their eyes, I feel confident in my interpretation. Yet, I have said this to no one outside of this room or until this very moment. The split between Kila and Ikara was strong. The split between Karia and Amir was timely. Kila taking passage away from Albion on the swift craft Mali allows for other events to be timely as well. The timeline fits. Tasa is of an age that spans Kila's absence from Penthe House. Amir's return to Albion and the subsequent mending of his rift with Karia allows for Kamir's appearance to be equally timely. As you said, 'We all know her father.'"

The Woman in Violet allowed a faint smile, then continued. "There is more to Tasa. I feel strongly that she is incomplete somehow. I also sense that she herself is unaware of the special nature of her existence, whatever that may be. I, too, like her. However, it is important to not let our affection cloud our judgment here. We cannot let our feelings interfere with her path. We cannot place expectations upon her.

"We are in critical times. We at Wisdom House are doing what we can to shield the green and pleasant islands of Albion. Amir and Karia returned with much of Tethys' power those decades ago. We are still learning how to use that power to Gaia's greater good. We all sense our limitations. The question returns to us: How do we follow Penthe's charter, our mission as given to us by Brigid herself, and yet isolate the islands of Albion? We reach out, freely in the past, but now we do not reach so far or so easily to just anyone.

"The refugees tell of harrowing days on the continent. That men would turn on their families is something we have difficulty conceiving as reality, yet we have seen the wounds, heard the stories. These women did not bring their children to Penthe for learning, for a path. They came for succor and protection. That is not why we exist.

"What do we have that resists violence? We are not a fighting force. We are not Battlecrafters. If the beast men come, what do we do? We cannot welcome such ones. But are they not still worthy of respect in some ways? Or are they? What becomes of the changeling? What of his mother? Would that she was alive, and the child had been the one to…" The Woman in Violet paused and pressed her lips together tightly, refusing to follow through on her own thought.

The gathering of women remained silent until the Woman in Violet continued. "These are the choices thrust upon us now. We have too long been able to accept the peace of the times. Distance protected us. Now we are faced with difficult decisions, and we have failed to prepare ourselves by refusing to explore the possibilities.

"Tasa's mother Kila was not incorrect in her assessment of Penthe House's purpose. We are to be open to all. The New Men, those who are mortal and short lived, should have the opportunity to serve Gaia in the same ways as those who are of the blood of the dragons.

"Kila's sister Ikara sought to create an exclusive, elite domain, only those strong in the blood of the dragons, out of the Penthe House ideals. Yet was she wrong? Did she have a sight beyond her times? Are we now pursuing such a path, albeit reluctantly?

"We must ever be aware of the tendency to judgment. We see the results of members of Penthe House taking strong opinions as pure fact. We became divided. That rift we are yet healing. As the Woman in White, Ikara actively opposed her sister Kila. Yet, who was wrong?

"Kila was unsupported by the House of White. Thus, Kila left us to seek fulfillment elsewhere. It appears she has achieved much in a short time. Is she now facing the same realities that we are? Is the nature of the human male also bestial where she now resides? We may consult with Master Amir regarding this matter.

"Kila, in my vision, is still our sister, still a valued member of Penthe House. We may seek to comfort and protect her if she is in need. Though

Kila, by her own sight, is never in need." With that statement the others smiled, all save Forge Mother, though she did slightly nod.

The Woman in Violet, the Mother of Wisdom House, continued her perspective. "Kila left with Amir in calmer days. Now her daughter arrives in fierce winds and waves. Just as Kila is, or was, unlike those calm seas, Tasa appears to carry none of the fierceness which heralded her arrival. She is quiet and still. At least for now. There is a sense of destiny about her, yet again, I have the strong sense she is incomplete in some manner. Perhaps the separation of child and mother is the cause for feeling, but I believe it is more than that.

"I would return Tasa's mother here if she will have us again. Kila is a valuable being. She has done us this favor of allowing her only child to continue her growth in Albion." The Woman in Violet stood quietly with her eyes closed for a moment. "Ikara, our former Woman in White, is doing well. Ending her tenure and passing from the status of Keeper of the Words was not an easy passage. She went to Kila and sought reconciliation. That did not go as well as she wished. From the perspective of those who know them, it went as well as we all might expect of the sisters. That rift has always been wide.

"The important thing is that Tasa is here now and safe within the shores of Albion. It is a step to reconciliation and may help us bring a resolution in regard to the state of the world and our place in it.

"Some in the Wisdom House have seen visions. A young woman, they say, astride a dragon. They fly. They are still. The description matches closely with Tasa. And yet, where be dragons?" With those words the Woman in Violet again settled into the shadows.

In unison the Woman in Blue and the Woman in Green raised their respective emblems. Each carried a short staff, carved with symbols of tides and moon phases and other useful information that was too complex to carry in one's head. Each staff was the color of the house represented, a deep blue for Beach House and bright green for Forest House.

The Woman in White spoke. "And our other sisters each have something to say. Hopefully it will be a unifying thought, if not necessarily in unison." The women laughed, and the blue staff was lowered to allow for Forest Mother to speak first.

The Woman in Green stood up easily, tall and lean. She shook her thick red hair and allowed it to tumble across the cloak of green about her shoulders. "I would begin by thanking Mother Stone for allowing Tasa to precede her time from Forge House to Forest House. I know that this was irregular. My reason for the request is that, in her visit to us, with your kind delivery of the excellent blades and tools for the forestry work, young Tasa met up with a few of the others and seemed to spark some friendships."

Forge Mother had given the Woman in Green her full attention at the mention of tools and had a contented look about her face from the use of the term "excellent."

"It is my understanding that, while she is friendly, no true friendships had yet been formed. However, in one short visit it seems she created a small bond with at least two others." Forest Mother continued. "One budding friendship in particular came to my attention, that of Mariel."

Now Forge Mother opened both eyes wide and said, "Mariel! No! She, fummmm, she is too…no! Mariel. Irregular. Tasa is…" As if realizing that she was speaking out of turn, the woman raised her hammer up and down three times and, choosing to not speak, finally clamping her mouth tight, set the symbol in her lap and crossed her arms. Forge Mother's face tightened and everything: mouth, lips, even her nose, seemed to turn red and close, all except one eye which stayed open at a squint. The flames of the fire moved away from her.

"Ah," Forest Mother said. "An opinion then, Forge Mother? I accept your concern and offer my apologies if I have allowed a step you may not have desired. My niece," she glanced at the Woman in Blue and smiled, "that is, our niece, Mariel, is of concern to me and I may have acted hastily in that regard. She sought Tasa out. They became friendly right away.

"Mariel has since become regular in attendance at meals for the few weeks that Tasa has been at Forest House. She helps Tasa in many ways. I assure you that Tasa remains diligent about her duties, all of them, and continually seeks to serve others as well. She is quiet and private and not prone to speak without first being addressed. Please let my words alleviate any concerns you may have for the fine discipline and keen edge you honed with Tasa. She is the better for her time with you, Mother Stone. I only wish Mariel to gain some direction as well. In a sense, your training is continuing on into Mariel through Tasa. For this I am grateful."

Forge Mother looked away and made a noise that sounded like, "fum," or "fee" and seemed to express some level of approval, but she did not raise the hammer. The Woman in Green cast a glance at her sister, the Woman in Blue, and gave her a fast wink and even faster grin. Beach Mother kept a straight face, though there was a gleam in her eye.

"All of this being as it is, Tasa also rebuffed Red Robin." This statement caused a quiet stir as well. Forge Mother's face relaxed and something akin to a smile passed her lips. It did not linger long, and no one noticed it. The Woman in Green arched her eyebrows, sighed, and gave a little shake of her head. "I admit, I take some pleasure in this occurrence. My son needs to be taken down a branch or two. I, too, like Tasa. There is something…more to the girl. I confess that I am unable to capture this quality of hers in words."

The Woman in Green nodded now to the Woman in Blue and returned to her place in the circle. Beach Mother formally raised her staff and stood still. "Already this one is having an effect on all of Penthe House. She is known for this rebuff all the way to Beach House. Young Bria brought the tale with her. Many did not believe it at first, but once the story filtered through from other sources, Bria gained a heightened status with some of the older girls. Her friendship with Tasa and the letters they exchange are a known source of gossip, though Bria never breaks a trust.

"I would like, at this time, to be assured we will speak of the rest of the girls before the night is concluded. There are many others to be concerned about. We seem to be much on the subject of Tasa. She and I have yet to meet. Although your worthy company is in agreement on her likeability, I will hold my own counsel until such time as she comes under my care. She has much to live up to."

The Woman in White spoke with a smile. "You have our assurances, Mother Marion. This one is a special case for us, but you are, as usual, wise in your restraint, though I believe that the incoming tide of recommendation will prove too much for even you to resist. How often does Mother Stone give such lofty approval?" If Forge Mother caught the smiles and twinkles in their eyes she did not let on. She only pulled a pipe from a pouch and sparked a tiny flame in the bowl. The Woman in White continued. "Do you have a further observation?"

The Woman in Blue nodded. "I do. Bria is our friend in this matter. She is open with me and communicates regularly with Tasa. Partially for this quality I have arranged for Bria be a part of my inner circle. She willingly shares much, and I will know if she is omitting or holding anything back. Bria is also accepted by Mariel at the present time. Any concerns of mischief that Mother Stone may have will be exposed and quelled before things go too far. Bria would not allow it to go far. She is too...regular. It does sound like Tasa is more level-headed than most of the other girls.

"Although I choose to reserve my conclusions until I have personal experience with Tasa, I know you all well and trust each one deeply. I will agree that, based on anecdotal evidence, Tasa is truly of the blood of the dragons in the manner of the old ways. I am interested in observing this element of 'more' of which you each speak. Yet I caution all present not to set her apart, not to set new precedents that place her above or away from the others. Penthe is about acceptance and community. We do not ourselves hold these places of leadership indefinitely.

"Tasa's aunt Ikara herself felt the weight of this leadership and now seeks atonement for her rigid ways. Too much favor in any one being's direction tempts a belief that they are better than others. Tasa may be somehow 'more' in some ways, but she is still a girl amongst girls and women. Allow her that commonality. Let her seek her own path, take her own journey, find her own home."

With that the Woman in Blue lowered her staff and took her seat.

The Woman in White rose again. "We are in agreement then? We will observe Tasa's progress closely, yet we will allow her the space to develop her own ways, just as the other acolytes enjoy. Tasa's early precession from Forge to Forest House was an anomaly and not the setting of a new rule. She is worthy of this small consideration and this action benefits Penthe House and also Gaia. Signify agreement with the raising of your totem."

All did just so.

8
Little Men in the Forest

THE IDEA THAT PENTHE HOUSE WAS A PLACE OF EDUCATION for only girls and women seemed to be one that was ignored by Forest House. It wasn't that a lot of men and boys were around, but the simple fact that any were there at all was a surprise to Tasa. Not an unpleasant one, just a surprise.

Much had been made of it by her peers on her home island of Solaine. Tasa was coming to the realization that there they emulated Penthe House in structure, though not quite so formally. Many boys, sons of the women taking refuge or children of travelers, lived on the rocky isle. There were more young girls and so the boys tended to band together, but all played with one another, sharing pleasant days in the sun and in the sheltered coves of the clear blue sea.

Tasa believed the stories of Penthe House being a cloistered group of females all dwelling in isolation. It was mostly true in the first two houses that she served in...well, with the exception of the young male babies and toddlers in Hearth House, anyway. Forest House curried many exceptions.

The biggest exception seemed to be the tribe of the Greensmen, but following close on were the Oakmen. One warm afternoon, Mother Meg asked Tasa to deliver a message to a particular part of the Forest House lands. Tasa followed a winding trail until she arrived at a massive circular clearing. In the center stood a great, ancient oak tree. Approaching this tree, she came upon three short males dressed in browns and wearing hats made of oak leaves.

Tasa stood quietly watching them. To the side, in a clearing, they were planting a small sapling. Once it was in the ground all three moved in a slow rhythm around the thin, tiny tree. It looked a little comical to Tasa, at first anyway. Then she thought that she saw the tree shiver a little. She squinted and stared hard. Had the tree gotten taller just then? Were there more branches than before, and longer? And thicker and there were definitely more green buds…no, leaves! And suddenly the sapling was a small tree!

The Oakmen stopped moving and looked at the growth approvingly, congratulating each other and smiling and joking. They pulled out long pipes and passed a pouch around, sharing. Together they turned and walked right towards Tasa.

"You have something for us?" The speaker's voice was high and strong. Tasa nodded and handed over a piece of willow bark that Forest Mother had written on in charcoal. The writing was odd and consisted of vertical lines with slanted lines branching off or intersecting. She had been told to wait for a reply.

"She's a quiet one," said the second Oakman.

"And tall," said the third.

"Good trunk," said the second.

"Nice foliage," said the third, looking at her hair.

The first Oakman showed the bark around and they all nodded in agreement. A couple of swift lines were made below Forest Mother's message, and they handed it back to Tasa.

"She wants to ask," number three said. They all stepped back and stood in a line facing her, waiting.

Tasa looked at the tree and then at the trio. "How…?" She didn't really know what to ask.

"We ask Gaia to help." She wasn't sure which one answered her, and she lost her chance to ask any more questions as they gathered up their spades and sacks and walked off into the woods, vanishing from her sight almost immediately.

It was a strange encounter and when Tasa turned around to find Mariel sitting on a low branch within a hand's breadth of her she let out a little yelp.

"It's something you'll learn if you become a forester. It is woodcraft and not easy. It makes you feel small. It also makes you feel connected." Mariel's tone was strange and distant, peaceful. "Come on. I shouldn't do this, but I think you'll do alright." She took Tasa by the hand and they walked over to the new tree.

Mariel stood slightly behind Tasa's right shoulder and spoke in a slow rhythm. "Now, don't try to think about it. Just look at the tree and look at the leaves and look at the branches and look at the lines of the leaves and the pattern of the bark. Now, just breathe and wait a bit. That's it; look at the light around the tree…" Tasa began to notice what looked like a green glow all around the new leaves. Mariel continued, "Gentle, just breathe and look at the shapes of the tree, the trunk, and the buds, and just breathe…"

Tasa imagined that she could hear the tree breathing. That's ridiculous, she thought, and the light began to fail.

She again let Mariel's voice and words permeate her mind, "…easy, just breathe, don't think, and notice how the ground feels at the place where your feet touch the earth…"

Suddenly Tasa felt a power, something flowing beneath her, and movement, like she could feel the earth spinning. Without thinking, she let her arms float out from her sides and felt the green light touch her hands and face. She felt strength rise from the ground up her legs and into her spine and she smiled deep inside of herself as her body relaxed and her lungs loosened, and air flowed all through her form and she felt wonderful and connected and…small. It was as if she could see herself against the massive planet that she dwelt upon and the planet tiny in the sky of the universe. And in the end, she was fine with it all and felt right and peaceful.

Her eyes opened slowly. The tree was taller than before. The sky was twilight, the afternoon had passed into evening. Mariel was sitting some distance away as Tasa regained a sense of awareness. She was still standing, arms loosely stretched to her sides, feet slightly apart, and knees soft and slightly bent. Her head was tilted to catch the fading rays of the sun. She turned and walked to Mariel.

"Don't you feel small?" Mariel said brightly. "Happens to us all!"

9
Dragons and Dreams

THAT NIGHT TASA DREAMED. Just before falling into sleep, she heard the once familiar voice in her head say, "Again I sense your presence. I will soon be at your side." Up to that moment in her days at Penthe House she thought the voice lost. In her own mind she felt that perhaps it was only her own mind all along. Perhaps the storm forced her to be less of a dreamer than she once was, back on that solitary island. Did she really hear another being all her young life? Was the voice merely a daydream, the wish of a child for a friend? Or was it an intuition, some sort of subtle recall from dimly heard stories or books skimmed as a child?

The tales told by the men who visited her island from the sea were shared and, she knew in her heart, embellished, but she loved to hear them all the same. The world, it seemed, was quite a big place, and diverse. Magical beings from ages past, remnants of ancient civilizations, books themselves held power if only one could learn their language, men of great height called giants, men of smaller stature called dwarves, and some who were between them in size called elves, men who changed appearance or their very nature becoming creatures of the wood or sea, beings who lived in a separate reality, hidden and found only through secret paths and, of course, always there were legends of the dragons. These were saved until last, until late in the night, and told in quiet reverence. Mostly.

There were some tales told in fear: of anger and dragonfire and a day of great ruin. Some spoke of the blood dragon, and this tale always began with a fearful tremor in the teller's voice. These ones, the speakers of fear, were often hushed by the mothers of attending children before the story could properly begin.

On her island home, the tales of the dragons were kept at a distance from the youth. Only on occasion would Kila allow such talk. Solstices and equinox and some full moons, but always her mother would say to the teller of tales, "Is this telling to benefit yourself or Gaia?" and she would not await a reply. Always she instructed, "Speak of these stories in the deep quiet of the night."

In the later night the younger children would be asleep, their breath a gentle music to the quiet tales of majestic flight and deep wisdom shared with a fortunate few still awake and in attendance. "The beginning of men," they would say, and talk would turn to the giants and the first four, the immortal children of the Illuminators. Tasa may have seemed to be asleep in her mother's arms, but only her eyes and slow breath were signaling slumber. Her mind was deep and enjoyed such quiet. When the stories were being told she felt a reserve of energy rise. The voice within her said, "We will listen through your ears if you allow." Peace and stillness would wash across her form, but sleep was as distant as the age of the dragons itself. Tasa thrilled to those words and tales.

She would ask her mother in the morning, "What about the dragons? Where are they now?" And in reply her mother would say, "Not here, not now, if they ever were. The ancient ones are stories, and we live life now, Tasa. There is planting and growing and harvesting. We work, and Gaia gives us the fruits of our labor. There is no magic in this, only life. Life is magic enough for us. Life is enough for you just now. Time for magic later, if at all."

But Tasa knew in her heart that this was not entirely true. The voice in her head would say, "Life is magic." And it meant something completely different.

∗∗∗∗∗∗∗∗∗∗∗∗

Now she dreamt. She could see her small hut at Forest House, not from the ground, but as if she were in a tall tree and looked down upon the acolyte circle. She looked out over the forest and saw the giant oak tree where earlier the Oakmen performed their magic with the sapling. The great, ancient oak glowed deep green in the night.

The stars in the night sky above were bright lights that pointed to paths and places for those that knew their language. Those like Master Amir and Captain Troylis. Amir's face now came to her sight. She looked deep into his eyes, and he turned his face skyward. It seemed that she now saw how he did, and certain stars became connected by lines of pulsing silver light. She witnessed the night through Amir's eyes and felt a deep learning available.

Before she could seize upon that knowledge, Amir faded into the dark. The last she saw was his bright smile and light deep within his eyes. The lines faded from the sky. She cast her gaze earthward and there, traveling out from the roots of ancient oak, were lines of pulsing green light. She felt herself float high above the planet and watched the lines travel on to the north and off to the west. A faint pulse went east, and to the immediate south a channel of choppy water lay between Albion and the continent.

The lines to the north passed beyond her vision over the curve of the earth. Amir told her of the curve, but the storm prevented her from witnessing such a thing. Amir told her one day she would see such a thing and know her true size. Now she felt small indeed. Smaller even than in the forest.

The lines westward passed into the ports of Albion and on into the ocean off the coast. In her dream she saw the swift craft Mali, fresh and clean, whole once again, setting off to sea and following one of those bright green lines as it turned a deeper blue. Above her the sky glowed with green curtains of sliding light.

"Dragonfire," said the voice in her head. "Look upward and show me the path to where you are." And Tasa looked up again at the stars. No line appeared, and she felt sad. The voice was her friend and she wanted him to return to her.

"Look upward and close your eyes." And Tasa did just so. The line of light, golden and glowing, appeared just above her. It was beautiful, and she longed to reach for it. She held back. Even in her dreams, Tasa was cautious.

The glowing light sang a pure note and Tasa thought, "I can at least sing along." She pitched her voice soft and exhaled a sound that wavered until it matched the tone coming from the golden light. Her body rose, and the light passed through her torso at the level of her heart.

In this moment of light, she knew there were truths of the world that were left unspoken. Belief in magic faded in many, but lack of belief did not still reality. She knew that stories came from somewhere and if they were not to be completely believed there could still be a strong truth within the tale.

In her vision, she opened her eyes. In her dream, she heard the voice in her head say, "I will be with you soon."

In the morning she awoke and looked in the mirror. The light she witnessed in Amir's eyes, she now saw within her own.

10

A Song in the Night

"My time aboard the Mali left me less than desirous for the life of the sea. It is with some trepidation that I approach my time at Beach House, knowing well that it is also called Sea House. My uncertainty of what lies ahead is no indication of fear on my part, I believe. I will faithfully perform whatever task is set before me here at Penthe House and willingly learn all that I can. It is just that I have no desire to experience the ocean in the form of a storm ever again."

Tasa wrote often to Bria and Bria to her. The two became closer despite a physical distance. This led Tasa to reflect that the map of Penthe House was drawn evenly as an example only. The reality of locations and geographies was quite irregular. The land that Penthe House occupied was large and stretched from the southern center of the Albion Isles to the western shore. In her dream she saw reality. Her own island was hardly the size of the Penthe House area, and she was aware that there was a much larger land surrounding them and that the sea was larger still.

She recalled a map from her library on the island of Solaine. Hand drawn lines and circles were filled with irregular shaped markings. Much of the map was in blue, marking the waters of Gaia. Prior to her departure, she studied the map thinking she would then know where she was at all times. Her rough passage across the sea and ocean left that illusion far away. Her travels by foot about southern Albion allowed a new reality to grow. On occasion she also allowed that she might yet have that illusion shattered.

It was the time of turning again. The three days before the full moon began that day. All the acolytes would be shifting from one of the five houses to the next. Once again, Tasa was being made an exception. Mother Meg tearfully called Tasa to her office. Together they stepped into the inner chambers where Forest Mother held her most private meetings.

"It is my weakness that I love you all and with all my heart. It is in all ways a sadness to me when we must part and parting from you, Tasa, is more difficult than many of my acolytes. It is my desire that you one day return to Forest House and stay as an adept, a forester. You bring much to me in your peaceful manner, and you are a strength to me when I am less than pleased." Tasa smiled at that, recalling Bria's warning to her of the need for Mother Meg being kept happy. The Woman in Green took a slow, deep breath. "I am sending you on to Beach House now." Her voice caught, and she looked at Tasa through welling tears.

"Dear Bria precedes you and has set a course for you that will be favorable. I have sent ahead to Mother Marion a full account of your skills and potentials, and she is eager to greet you. When you arrive, you are to go straight to her, and she is not 'Mother Marion' to you lest she grants that privilege. She is Sea Mother or Beach Mother always.

"When you meet with her you are to show her the scarf from Captain Troylis. This is important. Answer all of her questions directly and without hesitation. Feel free to express your thoughts to her on this occasion." Mother Meg thought a moment and added, "Only on this occasion. Unless you are specifically asked. And then be cautious." She sighed and waved a slender hand in a vague dismissive gesture. "Use your own good sense, Tasa. You will do alright." Tasa smiled at the words that Mariel often said to her.

Mother Meg observed Tasa's smile, wiped at her eyes and said, "Look at me! What a mess! And you sit so calmly, listening to my words." Tasa may have looked calm, but inside her heart was breaking. The two months she spent at Forest House were the first time she felt truly happy since she left the island of her birth. Forest House swiftly became home to her and in the short two cycles of the moon she had never been happier, nor could she imagine more happiness to be had. The smile fled her face. She leapt from her seat and flung herself into Mother Meg's arms, openly weeping and sobbing her dismay. The two women held each other for a time until they cried themselves out.

"We entered laughing and now we part in tears." The Lady in Green smiled as she and Tasa held each other at arm's length. "It must be poetic somehow. Perhaps you can ask Robin along the way. He is a poet, and you will have time for idle conversation. He is also good at idle conversation."

It took a moment for the words to sink in, then Tasa said, "Robin? Your son?"

"Yes. I wanted you to arrive safely, and he well knows the way. He is a good companion, and you will enjoy his company."

Bewilderment settled over Tasa. It was never a thing that she had thought to bring up to Mother Meg. She assumed that since everyone else seemed to know about the incident with Red Robin that Forest Mother also knew what occurred between them. Now she and Red Robin were to be companions on the path to the House of the Blue Door? Perhaps he had forgotten about her effrontery. Perhaps he had forgotten about her entirely. Perhaps, like the world, she was much smaller than she imagined. Perhaps the incident between her and Robin only seemed larger because Mariel liked to tease.

"Yes, that is a problem!" Mariel would say later with a delighted smile on her face. "You'll be all alone with him for four days and four nights!" She laughed merrily at Tasa's horrified look. "If he gets on your nerves, just remember the punch you gave me and let him have one like it, only harder. You like me, and that really hurt! You'll probably break his arm."

"Perhaps he does not even recall me. Perhaps it was something that we have made large in our talking. Why would he remember me at all? He is so well known, and he is such a well-traveled person, and he has many girls to pick from, and they all fight to be picked by him and he, he, he is such a…he can go…"

"He well remembers you, Tasa." Mariel stared at her friend. Tasa saw that she was not teasing. Suddenly, in comparison, going back to sea did not seem so frightful.

✳✳✳✳✳✳✳✳✳✳✳✳

Contrary to Mother Meg's prediction of idle conversation, they made the journey mostly in silence. Robin spoke only when necessary and was polite and helpful at all times. The midsummer weather stayed pleasant, and they made good time. He was not angry or cold. In fact, he seemed quite pleased to be able to walk in silence. After she got past an initial nervousness, it occurred to Tasa that, as a bard, he rarely got the chance to be quiet.

She watched him as he walked. He was long and moved easily. Every now and then he would take a fancy little step as if he was dancing or a skip or a hop just like the little boys did at Hearth House. His hands wound grasses and vines as they walked, and he attached them to various parts of his backpack.

Once, he pulled his harp from its case and began strumming softly, inventing a tune as they walked. If there were words, he did not sing them. Tasa found herself humming the tune in her head. It was one of the most beautiful songs she had ever heard.

A strange thing happened late that same night. Tasa lay awake and she knew that Robin had fallen asleep by the depth of his breathing. She watched the stars cycle across the sky and felt the need to hum the tune out loud, though softly enough so as not to wake the bard. As she matched the notes to her breath, the wind seemed to shift. A shadow, large and long, passed between her and the light of the stars. Somewhere nearby she heard a soft rustling and it seemed as if something or someone joined her in the humming of Robin's tune. The feeling was a vibration and came from the earth. She thought at first that she might need to be alarmed, but the presence was one of strength and power, not force, and not to be feared. It was a presence that seemed familiar to her. They hummed together for a time until Tasa fell into sleep. In her dreams she was flying.

****

Tasa the acolyte and Robin the bard made better time than Mariel predicted and early on the third day the Beach House compound came into view. When they arrived at Beach House, Bria ran out to greet her friend. They embraced and hugged and laughed and compared each other to the last time they had seen themselves together. Bria was a deeper color, warmed by the sun, and wore the shorter tunic of the summer months. Her long brown hair was lighter and streaked with summer lights.

"Tasa! You look so beautiful! You look like you grew up or something!" Bria jumped excitedly around. Tasa bent at the waist, ducked low and laughed.

"It is true, my Lady. You have grown up in many ways." Robin spoke directly to Tasa. Bria stopped bouncing and took a stance beside her friend. Robin looked at them both and said, "May I now present myself to you both?" His voice was melodious and pure. Something shifted in Tasa's chest. She forced herself to stand straight. She looked him in the eyes. His green eyes.

"Yes, my good sir and guide. Please present yourself." Later on, she would feel a little silly at the courtly way she spoke, but it was the only way her heart would let her speak at that moment.

"I am called Red Robin, ladies, though my name is always Robin Green. Some call me Robin of the Green and others Robin of the Wood. It would please me if you would call me simply Robin, your servant." He spoke to both of them, but his eyes were on Tasa. His green eyes.

"Well, *servant* Robin…" Tasa wondered where she got the boldness to tease him, "it will be my pleasure to call you *Sir* Robin if you would accept the title, for you have done me great service and I honor your efforts. My companion and friend is called Bria. As you served me, I would ask that you treat her likewise. I am Tasa."

"She is Tasa of the Quiet Night," Bria said impulsively. Later she would claim that it just came to her that a title was appropriate for Tasa and the only thing she could think of was what Mariel always called her.

"Tasa of the Quiet Night." Robin looked at her with a quiet smile. "It is a song that is waiting to be sung, fair one. Would you permit me to be the one to sing it?"

Tasa could feel her face flush. Bria spoke for her. "If the song serves her as well as you have, then the quiet one will be well pleased, Sir Robin."

He took his leave then with a promise to see her again before long. Tasa sank to the ground after he was out of sight. She let out a long, thin, keening sound, like a scream stretched to its limits. Her eyes were wide, and Bria lay next to her laughing out loud and saying, "Wait 'til Mariel hears about this!"

11

Temple in a Storm

THE MOTHER OF BEACH HOUSE, the Woman in Blue, was not present that morning, so Bria took Tasa to find lodging in the acolyte hut. All the other acolytes were preparing to travel to Life House, the House of Five Doors, to participate in the Path Walking Ceremonies. Bria was no exception, but she had been charged not to leave until Tasa had been delivered faithfully to Beach Mother's offices. Tasa did not know if she would be asked to attend the ceremonies at all.

The girls found themselves relatively free of duties and so Bria showed Tasa all around. The actual structure called Beach House was just that: a large, long, and low house overlooking the beach. Large stones painted blue, but well weathered from the ocean winds, made up the walls. Wooden frames held windows and large shutters were attached by stout iron hinges Tasa recognized from the Forge House workshop. Three sides were completely stone, but the landward side was a mix of wooden walls and enclosed patios. Slate tiles covered the whole building with the seaward side of the roof taking over three quarters of the top at a specific angle. Just past the off-centered line of the roof, a sheltered lookout sat in the approximate middle of the building.

Beach House was set on a wide, flat area atop a high hill with rocky cliffs tumbling all around and down to the water. Around it were smaller, but similar buildings assigned different purposes, but common to each of the Penthe House communities. Stairs and ramps led from the houses down to a wide bay that held a sheltered dock. At rest were two larger sailing vessels and many smaller skiffs and assorted little craft. From the top of the short cliff where Beach House actually sat, they observed desultory activity centered mostly on one of the larger vessels.

Bria pointed at it and said, "That's one of the Dagda's ships. He is a great person from the past. It is said that he walked with the dragons." Tasa looked at her friend, wondering if she believed what she said or if it was just a story being passed along. Bria looked back, her brown eyes bright in the summer sun. "You may hear a lot of things here and I think that there are many here that believe them. I don't know if I do or not, but many fantastic people come through the harbor, and I think it is a much bigger world than we can know." Her voice held a note of wonder as she looked out to sea. "I may try to travel, to see what I can see…"

Tasa had seen that look before. It was not as intense in Bria, but it was the same far-away vision that Master Amir held. She looked into Bria's eyes and now saw that same spark. Deep within her own eyes she felt a quickening of sight. The world wavered for a moment then: colors felt brighter, the land and sea took on a glow, the same glow she recalled from the Oakmen's sapling, the same glow she lately felt in her dreaming. She and Bria leaned close and gazed out to sea, their arms wrapped about each other's shoulders.

A short time later they watched a sleek craft round the rocky head at the northern end of the bay. The sail was taut, and the prow cut sharply through the high ocean waves. As the ship made the protected harbor they lost the wind and the sail drooped. The vessel slowed in the calmer waters. A bit of activity on board and sails were trimmed to catch the slight breezes blowing ashore and once again the prow cut through the smaller waves of the bay.

The two friends watched as the craft pulled neatly to the dock and four people disembarked. Bria said, "That is Sea Mother, but it will be hours before they get everything settled and back to land work." Her voice brightened. "Let's go to the Wisdom House!"

Tasa was a little confused. Although she paid close attention to the maps, she knew to ask questions about distances. The maps were not the reality, only guides. Everyone said that Wisdom House was north and back east a ways, three or maybe four days travel on foot from Beach House. They could not possibly make it that far in a few hours.

Bria jumped up and took off running at a light pace. Tasa could only follow diligently and in silence, trusting Bria's lead. The girls scurried and scrambled along a high path above the shoreline, winding between rocky outcrops and near stony cliffside edges. Soon Tasa became enamored of the wind-wound trees and sea-sculpted rocks along the way. However, the pace set by Bria left her little time for reflection.

A raven flew near Bria and the slight girl scurried along an uphill path and through some short, twisting pines. They soon came into a clearing. A round building sat atop a rocky plateau. From where they stood, the Beach House bay was no longer visible. To the west and south, all that was in view was the top of the stony cliff dropping into the heaving ocean, the shoreline being out of sight and far below. Clouds swept across the sky, the wind pressing against them, pushing away from the cliff's edge and back inland.

The round, domed building was encircled by a tall, columned terrace. High arches opened at what Tasa believed to be the points of the compass. Inside, Tasa could see a figure moving near a central brazier. She could not see the flames but saw the waves of heat rising.

Outside a gust of wind blew and Tasa shivered a little. Clouds were building off the ocean and the sea breeze caused the temperature to cool rapidly. Far out and down she witnessed the wind blow foam off the caps of the white waves below. The sea turned a metallic grey. Tasa felt uneasy and stepped up off the ground onto a wide marble stair. The raven landed on Bria's shoulder, cawed a complaint to the gathering clouds, and flew to the east.

"Storm coming," Bria said. "They told us so last night at evening meal. I wish I paid more attention in the weather class." Bria took Tasa's hand, pulling her towards the building. "Come on, it will blow over quick, I think. We can stay here with Karia. She's a priestess."

Turning their backs to the coming storm they ran up the stairs. Once inside, the structure seemed bigger than it appeared from outside, not unlike the tree dwellings at Forest House.

The wind picked up and drops of rain flew just as they entered. Warmth from the brazier filled the room and the wind seemed to stop just outside the portals. The walls were colored a deep blue and faded into violet at the top of the dome. Although it was still daylight, pinpoints of light, like stars at night, glowed gently above.

Karia walked over to Bria, smiling broadly. Her face was wide, and she was tall. Very tall. Her robes were the pale violet color of an adept in Wisdom House. They flowed loosely down from her waist and stopped above her ankles. She wore sandals that laced up her long legs above the hem of her robes. A "v" neck and open back showed off a fair amount of ivory-colored skin, pale as if the sun never touched her. Her long arms looked strong and were bare up to her broad shoulders. Pale blond hair flowed straight down from her head and was collected loosely into a long thick strand falling down to her waist. Her eyes were ice blue. She placed her large hands on Bria's shoulders and pulled her close to kiss her on the forehead. Karia had to bend down to do so.

"Hello, Bria!" Her voice was cool and even, but friendly. "Is this your Forest House friend?"

Bria stepped back as Karia turned to face Tasa. Bria said, "Karia, this is Tasa. Tasa, this is Karia." Tasa caught Bria's polite tone and resolved to match her. Bria continued, "Karia is the Wisdom House Priestess here at Beach House. She has been helping me prepare for my Path Walk to Wisdom House Center." Suddenly Bria lost her formal tone and, hugging Karia, finished with, "And is one of my best friends here." Bria smiled at them both.

Tasa had read Bria's letters telling of Karia, but she had not mentioned the connection to Wisdom House. She also did not mention Karia's lofty height. "I am pleased to meet you, Karia. Bria mentions you often in her letters to me," Tasa said.

Karia looked Tasa deep in the eyes and said, "But not that I am a priestess?" She smiled at her own words. "It is what I prefer. Some feel that they must be careful of what they think or say around the adepts of Wisdom House, as if we are always to sit in some judgment of the inner life of others' minds."

The House of the Violet Door was tasked with quelling disputes and overseeing agreements between the houses and individuals. They served as a balancing force for practical matters. They also assisted others to gain internal balance between heart and brain. Amongst the acolytes passing through their first season at Wisdom House, tales were told of mystical moments where it appeared that the adepts knew what they were thinking and feeling without them ever saying a word. Many found the adepts unsettling at first. Most

Wisdom House adepts kept to themselves. This lent to the aura of mystery about the path of the Violet Door.

Tasa's only direct encounters with members of Wisdom House occurred during her recuperation time at the House of Healing after the sea voyage. A woman appeared at her bedside late one evening. Pulling a cloak from over her head, long, straight, night-black hair fell about her white face. It felt familiar to Tasa, not unlike when she was near Amir. The woman smiled in a way that made Tasa feel calm.

"I am told you have disturbing dreams." Tasa recalled the dark-haired woman's voice lilted slightly, an accent that she had not yet encountered. "From your experiences, it is easy to understand why." She laid her hand on Tasa's. It felt cool at first, then a pleasant warmth grew within Tasa's bruised arm. "They say that you do not speak about the journey unless others speak about it first. Here I am speaking of the passage first to you now. Would you tell me of your feelings, Tasa?"

And Tasa did. Not against her will, but she surprised herself with how many words she did say about the matter. The Woman in Violet did little to coerce or coax the words, only sat still and quiet, listening and holding Tasa's hand. At one point, Tasa began to weep in her gentle, almost silent way. Then the dark-haired Woman in Violet placed her hand upon Tasa's chest, covering her heart. She slid her other hand behind Tasa's head and cradled her lightly. Tasa cried a few moments more and slipped into a deep and restful sleep.

In the morning she awoke feeling lighter at heart. Many of her bruises seemed faded or nearly gone. Walking was easier. Her head no longer rang with the violent sounds of the storm. Her heart no longer felt the strange constant fear it had learned during the voyage. On her bed, next to her pillow, lay a little note. It read, "You did your best. You acted well even in fearsome times. You are a strong being and you have been tested. All your life now, you will know that whatever arises, you can face life with strength and skill. You are a being of balance and power."

Tasa carried the note through much of her life. She reflected on those words often. She did not then feel like such a person of balance and certainly not one of power. At times, late in the night, if she awoke feeling the fear of the storm, she imagined the Woman in Violet's hand upon her heart. She recalled the words of the note. Then she did not fear.

Tasa listened to other acolytes talk of Wisdom House adepts with trepidation and knew that they were mistaken. From her bedside, the black-haired adept of Wisdom House seemed diminutive in size. Now Tasa looked upon Karia. She felt some trepidation that she might experience a sore neck after conversing with her at length. Karia's next words broke her reverie.

"It is my path to help others achieve balance, to find their own true power," she said, and Tasa wondered anew if Wisdom House adepts could read thoughts. "I wish only to serve and assist others in their personal path. I want to be thought of as a friend, despite the vows I've taken. From what Bria has told me of you and your letters, it seems that we share a great love for the forest and groves. I have many places of beauty to show you while you are here." Karia looked at Tasa from her great height. Tasa felt very small.

****

Outside, the storm broke loose, and they could hear the wind rise and howl. Rain slanted hard across the portico and steps, but neither wind nor water entered into the temple. "It is an old art that we use. It is from the lost days of Tethys' Islands." Karia spoke quietly and her voice seemed to move around the room. "Much that you may learn from Wisdom House is from those days. There is much that is still lost to us.

"You sailed here with Master Amir, did you not?" Tasa was startled by the question. How did Karia know that? Before she could reply Karia said, "I traveled with him many years ago searching for remnants and peoples from those ancient days. We journeyed far, and I ended back here."

Tasa did not know what to say and so said nothing. Many of the words Karia used were puzzling. Tasa had become aware of the larger nature of Gaia herself, but now Karia spoke about things long past. They had just met and Tasa was feeling uncertain of her own place in the tapestry of life.

Karia had been speaking quietly in that faraway manner that Tasa was observing in those drawn to the sea. Now she spoke brightly and energetically and again seemed to fill the room. "I am sorry! Where are my manners? Let me get you something for your thirst."

Karia led the way to a spiral stairway that wound downward below the main temple area. As they arrived in the lower level Tasa saw there were chambers and rooms opening up from a larger central room, circular like the upper temple, but with a high flat ceiling, and walls painted with idyllic scenes of nature. Tall buildings with high spires were distant and beyond the horizon in the pictures. Low, columned buildings lay in the middle distance.

The landscape shifted as Tasa turned in place. Mountains and valleys and veldts and rivers all were represented in a realistic manner right down to the floor, which was painted like water, a central sea surrounded by land. The hallways that ran off from the central room were similarly painted and the illusion was often that you were walking down a river or stream into a different landscape. One large chamber seemed to be a cave that was carved into the side of a cliff. The chamber sparkled with crystals set into alcoves in the walls.

Karia led the way down a gentle mountain stream and into a room with tables and benches shaped and formed like rocks. Or maybe they were really rocks shaped into tables and benches. It was very unique.

Karia set tall glasses of cool juices in front of the girls. Tasa drank readily and deeply. When she set the glass down, it was still full.

"Shouldn't you be getting ready to travel to Life House, Bria?" Karia asked.

"Mother Marion asked me to stay with Tasa until she returned. I'm not certain what I will be doing after that. I'm glad I got the opportunity to see you once more before I leave. You will take care of Tasa for me, won't you?"

"Of course. It was my intention all along," Karia said.

Tasa was not aware that she needed to be taken care of but felt appreciative of the fact that she had people around that cared about her. It seemed like a good idea to Tasa to get Karia talking. "Are you here all the time?" Tasa asked.

Karia smiled and nodded at Tasa. "This is my assignment, yes. Penthe House decided that Beach House needed a personal temple, as it was so much farther away from Wisdom House than the other houses. I came to Wisdom House after being an adept for the House of the Blue Door, Beach House that is, for many years. That is how I came to be a shipmate aboard the Mali and travel with Amir and Captain Troylis."

Tasa was liking Karia much better now that she was sharing her story and decided that she would share part of hers if asked.

As if she read her mind Karia asked, "Tell me about life aboard the Mali when you came here. Did you enjoy your time with Captain Troylis and Amir?" There was something about the way Karia said Master Amir's name that made Tasa believe they were closer than just shipmates.

"Well, there is not much to tell, really," Tasa began. "We ran into very rough weather right away and I did not see the crew much during the voyage. Captain Troylis asked me to help in the lookout bubble and I said yes. I didn't really see anyone until after we made land." Karia stared wide-eyed at Tasa. "The Mali seemed like a good ship, but I really don't know much about such things."

"It was you?" Karia was staring hard at Tasa. "Bria did not tell me her friend was the brave person that saved the Mali." Tasa was confused. Saved the Mali? She just spotted land. Bria also looked confused. She knew nothing of the matter at all. Tasa rarely mentioned her travels to the Albion Isles, or anything really about her home or life before Penthe House. Karia went on. "You don't know, do you? You don't know how close you all came to being lost at sea?"

Tasa felt strange in the pit of her stomach, as if she were back in the pitching prow of the storm-tossed swift craft. "Tasa, the voyage you took that brought you here, was it just this past autumn?" Tasa nodded.

"You didn't arrive on the Mali's spring voyage?" Tasa shook her head no.

"My dear, the Mali was long in the shipyard at Leist finishing repairs! That storm was the worst in memory and history and blew up to the surprise of everyone. No master or captain would have dared the passage had they known or suspected the severity."

Tasa wanted to speak but did not know what to say. A Woman in Violet had brought her some measure of peace about the journey, but now another adept of the Violet Path was removing her balance. "It was a storm, yes, but I have no experience with such things. To me it was just a storm. I just helped where I could." Tasa felt tears welling in her eyes but did not know why.

Karia looked at her from across the stone table, her own pale blue eyes held the beginnings of tears. She took a slow breath and continued, "Amir and Troylis were being counted as lost when you were spotted by the watchers in Lyonesse. The Mali had been blown off course and came in from the north and west instead of the south. When Lands' End heard of your whereabouts, they tried to put out a rescue craft. Amir signaled them away." A single tear escaped her eye. "Later we learned that a young passenger volunteered to stand lookout and spotted land. Amir was able then to calibrate the swift crystals and found a dragon line to pull you all to Ivis Bay."

Karia looked at Tasa with her mouth open. She huffed a bit, closed her lips, and said, "Only Amir could minimize such a..." Her voice caught, and she paused for a slow breath again.

Through pursed lips she continued, "You stabilized at Ivis Bay as the storm died out, but Troylis said another day at sea could have seen the end of you all. They said that if you had not spotted land, they were of a mind to turn northward again, thinking all the while that they had been blown south and far to the east. If they had done that you would have sailed into ice and certain death. They tell me, they tell everyone, that *you* saved the Mali with your sharp eyes."

Tasa was breathing hard, her eyes wide. She had no idea what to say and felt the room spinning all around. She closed her eyes in an effort to regain some balance. Blackness, as black as the wings of Bria's raven friend, spun into her mind.

When she opened her eyes, her head was in Bria's lap and Karia was washing her face with a cool, wet cloth. "I am sorry, dear." Karia looked truly stricken. "I did not know the tale would impact you this way. I can be too direct and thoughtless. Please forgive me."

Tasa blinked her eyes and took Karia's hand and said, "So, not all sea travel is that rough?"

12
Rite of Passage

WHEN BEACH MOTHER HEARD THE STORY, and heard also Tasa's question, she laughed. The summer storm that kept Bria and Tasa at Karia's temple home had blown out quickly, as was the way of summer storms in Albion in those days. Tasa still felt dazed, and Karia and Bria assisted her back to Beach House. "Forgive me for laughing, Tasa," said Beach Mother, "and be assured it is not at your expense. Your bravery is a growing legend. This adds to it by quite a measure."

"I did not mean to be brave, only helpful, Mother. I did as Captain Troylis asked, that is all. I only did what must be done." Tasa still felt a little weak, and a young woman dressed in acolyte robes brought a tray of steaming cocoa laced with a strong black tea from the eastern lands of the earth. It was very hot, but the smell alone seemed to give her some strength. Tasa clutched the thick mug of brew in both hands and let the aroma fill her head.

"Forest Mother said that you received a particular gift from Troylis. Is it possible for me to see it?" Beach Mother spoke quietly, and her request was gracious. Tasa recalled Mother Meg's words of parting and had placed the scarf in her leather satchel that she received from Mariel. Everything seemed so far away suddenly and Tasa was aware of her youth and inexperience. She gently and reverently pulled the scarf from within her bag.

It had not seemed like much before this: a token, a pretty gift that might be given to a young girl. Now she looked closely at the colors. In equal measure the yellow of Forge House and the green of Forest House lay in the threads. Along two sides and parallel to each other were bars of the soft white of the House of Five Doors.

"It is the scarf of the Order of the Southern Gate, Tasa." Beach Mother spoke with stillness in her voice. "It is not given lightly. You have been acknowledged as having done a great service for the Southern Gate. In a way, you are considered to be a member of that Order. Master Amir spoke of you highly, but indirectly. He insisted that you remain anonymous until you had charted your own path here in the Albion Isles. Master Amir did not even indicate that you were an acolyte. His wisdom is well taken. We have gotten to know you for who you are and not what you have done. He is very sly, that one." She cast a half smile in Karia's direction. "His heart is very private."

Beach Mother went to a large cabinet near a tall, wide window. From within she pulled a scroll, bound with leather and sealed with three wax stamps. Beach Mother was tall, though not nearly as tall as Karia. Her arms were long, and she now reached out to Tasa, handing the scroll to her.

"Master Amir came to me yesterday. He handed this to me and told me that someone would arrive soon that was to receive the message within. He did not tell me anything beyond that. My own curiosity bade me to look at the seals, but not within. The first seal is Captain Troylis'. I know it well and often receive missives and orders from beyond these shores sealed and identified by it." She held it near her face and inhaled. "It smells of honey.

"The second is Master Amir's personal seal, not the one he uses for the business of the Mali. I well recognize it for there is one here that often receives letters from beyond these shores that are for her eyes only. Master Amir will often press his two fingers into the wax. It is his wave of friendship as he takes his leave of those close to him. You will notice that there is the print of two fingers on the second seal.

"The third took me by surprise and I must confess that my curiosity is quite high at the sight of it. Master Nicholaus, Dagda or Father to the Order of the Southern Gate, has also included his personal seal. You will see that it carries the shape of the globe of Gaia held protected within the claw of a dragon. I have received messages from Grandmaster Nicholaus many times in the past, always with his official seal of a dragon-winged water vessel. I know of his personal seal only by legend and tales passed down.

"I believe that this is meant for you, Tasa. If you open it and find that I am clearly wrong, please return it swiftly, but I do not believe that I am mistaken. I rarely am in matters of import."

Tasa took the scroll and looked at each seal in turn. When she came to the third seal, she felt a thrill of familiarity. She had seen this image before, and recently, but the memory was loose, and she could not quite place it.

"Quite right, then, for you to wait to open such a document in private." Beach Mother sighed her impatience and set her face in resolve not to pry into this matter further. "A very wise course.

"Karia, perhaps you and Bria would see Tasa to the library and a silent study room. Make sure she remains undisturbed and remain close to counsel her if she needs." Beach Mother's tone was officious and direct: orders given, not suggestions.

****

Tasa soon found herself alone in a room paneled with weathered woods. A chair straight and firm, but comfortable and with curving, carved arms sat before a simple table. The final rays of the day's sunlight slanted into the room from a skylight. A lantern on the table sat waiting to be of service should the darkness gather before she was finished. Karia left the room with assurances that Bria would be just outside the large wooden door. Karia needed to bend down to get through and Tasa knew she would walk hunched in the hallways.

The seals parted from the parchment with some working of the flat blade Beach Mother provided Tasa. She was careful to preserve them intact.

The scroll was long and written in three hands. The first addressed Tasa directly and spoke with great gratitude "for services rendered." It gave directions to any mariner "to give free and grateful passage to the woman bearing this document to anywhere she may choose to travel along your chosen course with reasonable detour, knowing that by this action you will have the debt of Captain Troylis and the crew of the swift craft Mali. Ensure her safe passage on land as well as sea, for she saved us all and we owe her our lives."

The second was from Master Amir and followed in similar fashion at first. He then gave personal advice to her and offered his service to her at any time in the future as needed. It also concluded with a decree of safe passage, free for her for a lifetime and to extend to her heirs at two generations.

Master Amir recommended to the reader of the decree that they protect Tasa "with their very lives, for she has done the same for members of the Order of the Southern Gate." A separate line recommended her to one at Penthe House called Karia and gave the message to Karia that "every consideration be extended for the bearer's comfort within reason and the bounds of the Order of Penthe House."

Tasa was quite stunned by all of this, for in her own mind what she did was little. The tale she was being told was seemingly epic in proportion and she felt disconnected from it, as if it had been someone else all along. She felt smaller than the person everyone was talking about.

She sat looking out the tall window of the private room in the large, low, stone walled library. Every building in the Beach House complex that Tasa had been in so far seemed to invite the outside in and the view of the sea was often uninterrupted.

Karia had shown her around the library and then excused herself. Through that tall window Tasa watched Karia walk across a wide swath of short grass. A fountain danced in the center of a field of green where a tall boy was playing.

Tasa told Karia that she would "be alright" and smiled at her own echo of Mariel's assurances. Now, as she pondered the words that she had just read, Tasa casually noted Karia as she returned. Accompanying the priestess was the tall, curly-haired boy. They disappeared from Tasa's view as they entered the library building. A shake of her head and she returned to the remaining words of the scroll.

It was necessary to allow the first sections to roll up into the spiral of themselves. As the third section became visible, Tasa saw that it was written, partly, in the same sticklike figures that Forest Mother used in communications with the Oakmen and some of the Greensmen tribe.

She stared awhile at the lines and strokes hoping to recognize a pattern or perhaps a single letter or meaning. Mother Meg had not taught her this way of writing, though she explained it a little. "Each character corresponds to a particular tree and in this way the meaning of each word becomes deeper and linked strongly to growth and Gaia. It was," Forest Mother had said, "the oldest of writing from a time when writing was new." Now, only a few used it, as more worked their words in more complex and sometimes easier ways.

Mother Meg liked it because there were so many layers of meanings and it was a challenge, then, to create and craft a message that was both direct and also poetic.

Tasa could only stare at the words. Her head was heavy with many thoughts, and she felt like crying. She took a long, slow breath and let her tired eyes droop a bit. Her gaze still on the scroll, her sight became unfocused. She thought she might look like Master Amir at that moment, seeing things far away that were not visible to others.

Tasa relaxed. Something shifted on the table. The lines on the scroll shimmered and wobbled in her hooded vision. She thought she saw them move a little, waver perhaps or shift places, like a wind had come and rustled the branches of a tree. She felt an odd wave pass over her sight, and it appeared that the parchment glowed a little and came apart in smaller and smaller pieces. Or rather, that it became translucent, and she saw many things through the parchment that were not there if she looked without it. It was a difficult thing to comprehend at first. Tasa suddenly lost the urge to understand the individual words. Great thoughts, it seemed, were rising from the page and pouring directly into her eyes and brain. Great feelings were pouring directly into her heart.

Pictures and vistas opened up before her and she felt a thrill to see so many things. History passed with images of great waters and waves pouring and cascading over high mountain peaks while watercraft fought the currents and sought to rescue stranded beings. Flights of dragons soared above lands of wonder weaving amidst tall spires. Great voyages and sojourns and heroic quests all ran together and the spirit of them all poured across her consciousness without ever stopping for her to examine closely. It was a great circle, whirling in ever-changing play and cause and at the center one large figure stood smiling and laughing. His eyes twinkled, and she found herself accepting his mirth, as if it were a gift given directly to her. She recognized him from…somewhere.

She woke with a start. Had she dropped into a nap and fallen asleep? The light in the room was different, the day becoming twilight. She was unaware of the time. A feeling of confusion surrounded her as if she had been far away in time and space and pulled back to the present moment without warning.

The scroll wrapped itself up on the table in front of her when she awoke. She had been leaning on the table with her head upon crossed arms. Her long, dark black hair lay spread all around the tabletop. It flowed back across her shoulders as she rose from her place of rest. She had the image of deep blue waves at night as she observed the movement of her own hair streaming towards her off of the scroll and table in undulating waves.

Tasa found herself smiling without knowing the reason why.

The sun was lower on the horizon, and she watched it sparkle on the summer waves of the western sea. Standing slowly, she stretched and went to the door of her study room. Opening it, she saw Karia was sitting nearby with the boy Tasa observed earlier. They were each engaged in a volume of their own choosing.

As the door opened quietly, Karia looked up and smiled. Tasa indicated that she should enter the private study, then walked back to the table. She unrolled the scroll to the place where Karia was mentioned and then a little further, allowing the priestess to read the entire passage from Amir.

"It is what I would have done away," she laughed. "Amir is very private and could have given me this instruction himself. He wrote this for your benefit more than mine, but I am glad to see his words and my name written in his hand." A look grew in Karia's eyes, one of distance, and her smile softened as she gently touched the letters on the parchment.

"I have someone I wish you to meet." Karia stood and turned toward the boy outside the room. He seemed to sense her and turned his own eyes to meet Karia's. Smiling, he entered the room. He seemed to be a few years younger than Tasa. Tall and a bit thin, he moved with the restrained gait of boys waiting for a game to begin. His hair was light blonde like Karia's but was tightly curled. His eyes had the same tone of blue but were deeper in color. Tasa thought she had seen those eyes somewhere before.

"Tasa, this is Kamir. He is my son." Suddenly all the pieces fell into place for Tasa, and she recognized the eyes of Master Amir in the face of his son.

13

A Return to the Sea

"BEACH MOTHER, I DON'T KNOW HOW TO FEEL," Tasa began. "These great men have given me a gift that is heavy. I only did what I was asked to do, and I do not feel that I deserve this scroll and the importance of the words and images. They honor me overmuch!"

Beach Mother sat with her forefinger and thumb framing her cheek and chin. She gazed at Tasa for a moment before speaking. "I know these men. They are not given to expressions of great emotion..." she paused a moment pondering, "or even subtle ones. They are men who know the paths of the seas. They live by the tide and its turning. They know every star by name and can tell where they are on this world by the location of a single point of light in the sky.

"This scroll, this Right of Passage, is a true expression and I am certain you must have done a deed that matches the honor." Beach Mother was firm and direct. Tasa had shared the contents with her, and she carefully scanned the document, her eyes growing wider with each curve of the scroll's unfurling. They were alone within her inner rooms, and it was late in the evening.

A young acolyte brought food and drink: fish and potatoes with some greens that Tasa could not identify, and hot, dark tea with thick cream and some dry, sweet biscuits that Beach Mother dipped in her drink. Tasa followed her example after unsuccessfully trying to bite into the hard substance. The dipping softened it and made it palatable. The combined flavors made it very tasty and Tasa helped to clear the plate.

"It seems that you are a remarkable person." Beach Mother looked at Tasa as if she did not quite see what was remarkable about her. "You have this scroll as the highest commendation from three men that I respect and admire very much. You have this letter of commendation from Mother Meg." Tasa glanced up just then at the familiarity in her tone of voice. "Yes, yes, I know all about the informality of my sister's house."

Sister? There was so much Tasa did not know about people. The thought never occurred to her to ask anyone about their own family relations. Mother Meg and Beach Mother are sisters? Tasa tried to keep a straight face. "She will no doubt have told you that I have my informal ways as well. My decision is to leave the formality in our relationship, Tasa. I believe it will serve you better.

"You also have been given a rather glowing recommendation from Forge Mother. That may be the most impressive one of all for she is not free with her praise and indeed is most critical of the first-year girls. Did she also grant you some personal name to use?" Tasa shook her head. "No? I doubt that she has one." Beach Mother laughed abruptly at her own joke. "Hmmm. I am losing Bria but gaining you, and frankly, dear, with the level of expectation building, I am not certain that you can live up to it all.

"Who are you planning on telling about this scroll?" Beach Mother looked very deeply into Tasa's eyes.

"Tell?" Tasa spoke the word like a gasp of breath. She was planning on never telling anyone and now she said so to Beach Mother. The tall woman in blue ran her long fingers over the scroll, gently lifting it and handing it to Tasa. She held it until Tasa took it in her hands.

"This…is a thing of great value. Tomorrow I will get you a wrap for it that will protect and disguise it and also the scarf. It will be wise for you to keep this private. It is not something that is a secret, you understand, for secrets can be sought out and revealed. If it is something private, then you are simply not speaking to anyone about it and you are tacitly requesting that they respect your inner life if such a thing be discovered.

"Bria can be trusted with things private and, as she was in the room when you received the scroll, it is best to have her informed rather than curious. She is a valuable ally to you. I hope you realize this.

"You were expected by some to take her place at my side. That expectation was not mine. I have chosen to let you experience Beach House from a slightly less prestigious position. As I said before, I think it will be to your benefit to become a little more common in your first turn around the House of Five Doors. It does not serve one well to become too elevated too soon." Beach Mother looked Tasa up and down and added, "Or at all.

"Bria has told me of your trepidations about returning to sea. She did not reveal this lightly or freely, only to my ears. After becoming aware of your experience, I sympathize and so will not order you to do so as was my initial inclination. However, I would be pleased if you were to willingly take a position with the Harbor Order. It will require you to become familiar with boating and sailing, but only within the bay. It is rarely rough there and you may have a chance to regain your sea legs.

"If you say no, I will understand and give a different assignment: the library perhaps, or better still, the kitchen. You are good with fires and can stoke the early morning cooking stoves. We can always use assistance with the morning laundry, and you have some skills in that from what they tell of you from Hearth House." Beach Mother looked at Tasa waiting for a reply.

Tasa, for her part, was considering the options offered. For her first four lunar cycles at Penthe House she had been more or less kept inside of buildings and she was happy about that for it was winter and the weather was cold. Now, she had been at Forest House all through the shift from spring into summer, spending much of the time outside. On her island home she spent much of her life in fresh air and sunshine. Here in Albion, the summer season was bright, and the days were full with heat and light. Beach Mother was offering the sea and being outside, or, respecting her fears, offering her an opportunity to stay away from the water, but to wake up way too early and be inside buildings all day. Tasa was sure she was being guided by the choices offered, and possibly tested as well.

"I think," Tasa said, "that I will regain my sea legs."

Beach Mother smiled.

14

Things Being Relative

SCUDDING ABOUT THE BAY IN SMALL SAILBOATS, hauling nets of fish from out in the channel, scraping and painting hulls, rowing tiny skiffs, and always getting wet from spray or actually falling overboard, the summer passed by for Tasa with much more enjoyment than she believed she could ever again gain from the sea. In a certain way, it was more like being at home than any of the other houses of Penthe.

On her island home she would often visit near the port. Strolling the dockside, watching the vessels come and go, Tasa became well known by some of the regular sailors and they often brought gifts to her. Catching their mooring ropes when they arrived, she sometimes lent a young hand to unloading. She delighted in seeing the various animals that some of the ships carried as mascots. And always she listened to their stories.

Beach House offered Tasa many similar experiences. It also required more from her. Lessons in navigation, weather observation, ship building, sail mending, inventory, logs and records of all kinds, swimming and diving, catching fish in many ways, all challenged and excited Tasa beyond what she dreamed. Days off were spent with Karia and on many occasions Bria, who travelled back and forth from the main center of Wisdom House to the temple Karia maintained. This, Tasa knew, was orchestrated by Karia and Beach Mother for her benefit. Tasa did not mind in the least.

Little Bria was a delight to Tasa and, as Beach Mother said, a quiet and private ally. There was much that she and Tasa found to share by way of secret concerns and fears. In each other they found the opportunity to express their darker thoughts and bring some commonality of experience to one another. Bria especially assisted Tasa as she sought to navigate her way around the sometimes stern Woman in Blue.

"She must be that way, Tasa. Life at sea is tricky and as you know, sometimes dangerous. If a knot is tied loosely, a sail could shift unexpectedly and throw a sailor off the ship. It is not easy to regain your craft once you are in the water."

Tasa smiled when she listened to Bria defend Beach Mother. It always seemed there was a lesson to be taught woven into the explanation of why Mother Blue behaved in so strict a fashion and Bria repeated these lessons well. Tasa felt Bria would become a fine teacher as she grew.

Bria's size was a puzzle at times. Often, she appeared to be of average height, perhaps slightly smaller than the other girls, and Tasa first thought that Bria must be quite young. But when the girls were alone together Bria could appear quite small. When walking in wood or along the shore, she seemed possessed of great knowledge of the trees and quite able to scamper about in the high branches. Not unlike Mariel, Tasa noted.

Bria was definitely not a child, as was Tasa's initial impression when they met at Forest House. Bria spoke of her experiences at Hearth House as if many years had gone by in her life. As devoted as she was to Beach Mother, Tasa found that Bria felt a deep loyalty to Hearth Mother Bae and an adept named Malee.

"In a way, they are my parents, Tasa," Bria told her one day while walking toward Karia's temple. "I am a foundling. This is not something I often share. Karia knows. Mother Marion, I mean, Beach Mother knows too. I would still be at Hearth House if they had not encouraged me to take my path through the Houses of Penthe. Being away from Hearth House is difficult. Even though I am a second-year acolyte, I just never have gotten used to being out in the open. I cannot imagine how you and some of the others manage, being so far away from your homes."

"This is starting to feel like home in a way," Tasa said. "It is easier when I can talk with you and Mariel about things. I have so many questions, but I am not comfortable asking things that I think might be private."

"Now you are talking like Beach Mother!" Bria laughed. She stood up and folded her little hands in front of her chest, mimicking the Woman in Blue. Frowning slightly and pressing her lips tight she said, "Private is not secret. But private things are also not to be spoken about. No talking about things allowed. And no talking in weather class! Or anywhere else. And do not talk to me or about me. Or anything. No talking!" She finished with a striking hand-to-the-sky motion.

Tasa laughed then and said, "Does she give everyone the speech about privacy and secrecy?"

"Most everyone, I think," said Bria. "She is not really that bad, I know, but I heard the speech quite a bit. It makes me think Mother Marion has some secrets of her own."

"We all have secrets, I guess," Tasa said. "Sometimes I think I have a secret and don't even know what it is! I have a secret I keep from myself!"

They laughed together, and Bria said, "I don't think you have so many secrets, Tasa. Nor I, but we are private people. Mother Marion will get to like you when she learns more about you. She mostly only knows what other people say and she doesn't like to let anyone else make up her mind for her. I think when she comes back from the monthly meetings with the other Mothers of Penthe House, they must talk about you. Mother Marion asks me about you then.

"I don't say anything I think you do not want me to say, Tasa, or I try not to, only sometimes when Beach Mother asks, I must trust her because she gets me to say a lot."

Tasa wondered then at what anyone would have to say about her. She was just a girl. Not very remarkable at all when she looked in the mirror. She said, "I think you probably don't say anything I wouldn't say, Bria. I would tell Beach Mother anything she wanted to know. Mother Meg told me that was the best thing to do so I follow that course. So, yes, I agree. You and I are private. So is Mariel and so is Mother Marion…I mean, Beach Mother. It is fine that we talk to each other and maybe even about each other, but only to other people who are private as well. Thank you for telling me, but really, do they not have more important things to talk about at the full moon meetings?"

"Next time I'm eavesdropping I'll find out!" Bria said. Tasa noticed she wasn't laughing.

In addition to Bria becoming a close companion, Tasa and Kamir also became more familiar and grew to like each other during her two months at

Beach House. Karia would often grow quiet when they were together and never left them alone for long.

Kamir would talk about his father and Tasa listened. Kamir liked being at sea and expressed his wishes to be in the Order of the Southern Gate. But he also expressed a desire to be a hunter, a forester, a bard, and a worker in the forge. It was times like these that Tasa saw him more as young than a young man. He did not often appear tall to her, but occasionally when they wandered off from the temple area or Karia was distracted, Kamir seemed to be more than a few inches taller than Tasa. And when she looked at Karia without the priestess knowing it, Karia herself seemed far taller than she appeared when they walked together or sat for a meal.

Always there seemed to be something just a little different about certain people here at Penthe House, thought Tasa, and always the differences were just out of the corner of her eye and never something she could focus upon.

****

Tasa's time at Beach House came to a conclusion. One day, Beach Mother called her into the office as she passed by with manifests from one of the small local skiffs. "Tasa, leave those upon my desk please. I will have Akken file those for you." She turned to a dark-haired woman and nodded, saying, "Please, Akken? Thank you." Beach Mother walked from her desk and opened a wide, windowed door. Stepping out she called to Tasa, "Come along, my dear."

Tasa briefly smiled at the familiarity, then adjusted her face to look serious. Beach Mother did not look back and Tasa stepped long steps to catch up. They walked in silence for a while, descending a lengthy wooden stairway to the bay. Inside a boathouse, Beach Mother began loosening the mooring ropes. Tasa assisted and Beach Mother sat in a comfortable seat to the center of the craft. "Will you take us out, Tasa? Out of the bay and then northward along the coast please."

Many times in practice and lessons Tasa had done just so. Now it was only she and Sea Mother. A wave of nervousness broke across her belly. Without a word she did just as she was asked. First the oars, then the sail, and always a hand on the tiller to assist in tacking to and fro. The turn from the bay onto the sea was a little wobbly, the trimming of the sail not quite smooth, but the day was peaceful and calm, and the little craft handled well. Neither of them got too wet.

The coast was beautiful in the late morning sun. Sea Mother faced forward, away from Tasa. Few words passed between them until sometime after noon. "In a short time, there will be a little inlet," Sea Mother said. "We will stop there for a midday meal. If I know you, and I believe I do, you will not have eaten a proper breakfast yet." It was almost true. Tasa always carried a little pouch of nuts and dried fish and meat, a trick she learned from Mariel. The two girls often found themselves far away from the mealtime gatherings where they were expected.

Well, where Tasa was expected. Bria too, but never Mariel. Mother Meg gave Tasa a pass most often, but Beach Mother was not so lenient. However, the habit was set and Tasa followed her own patterns. She had been sneaking bits of food all the while she charted their course up the coast and it seemed like Sea Mother, facing away from Tasa, was not aware of her doing so.

The sun was past zenith. Currents and a gusting wind challenged her skills. Sea Mother made no comment and Tasa brought the craft closer to shore. Spotting the inlet, Tasa leaned into the tiller and let loose the rope holding the sail taut. The small craft glided obediently around a little rocky head and skimmed across quiet water to a sheltered beach.

Diminutive and dark-haired, a woman stood still, just at the edge of the water, just beyond the gently breaking waves. A cloak of deep purple hung from her shoulders. Her hair flowed from beneath the raised hood and her face lay in shadow, despite the brightness of the day.

Sea Mother rose from her seat as the craft slid towards land. Her balance was perfect as the boat pressed against the gravelly shore. Stepping easily from deck to earth, Sea Mother bowed slightly before the woman.

"May I present my acolyte Tasa?"

The small woman nodded and smiled at them both. She clasped her hands in front of her form in the manner of Wisdom House adepts. Beneath the cloak showed a dark violet robe, short and belted at the waist with a white sash. Loose pants rippled in the slight breeze. The same breeze blew back her thick hair giving a glimpse of her features, yet the hood kept her eyes in shadow. Tasa felt she knew this cloaked woman but could not immediately place her.

"I understand you are now known as Tasa of the Quiet Nights?" the woman asked. Tasa nodded yes. The woman did not identify herself nor did Sea Mother offer an introduction. "Walk with me," said the woman dressed in violet, and with a slight motion of her cloaked head beckoned Tasa to follow. There was no sense of arrogance in the command, but acquiescence on Tasa's part was understood. Though puzzled, Tasa felt that Beach Mother set the tone for this meeting by her slight bow. If this was a person Beach Mother respected, then Tasa would do no less. Together they wandered a slight distance away from Beach Mother.

"Are you happy at Penthe House?" the woman in deep purple asked.

It was a question that occurred in various ways during discussions with the Mothers and more often the older adepts, but Tasa felt there was a deeper thought being sought than simple yes or no. She allowed her response time to grow from her heart, and then said, "There are many things that I am happy about. Penthe is a fine place, beautiful and lush, though I am not overly fond of the winter season. There are things about my home that I miss."

"Your mother?"

"Yes, deeply, but she has taught me the changeable nature of life. Since the Mali has again begun passage to the Ringing Sea, I write to her and she to me, though I feel her words are reserved. It is not the same as when we were together."

"It is distance and your own changes that may give her pause to address you in the old manner," said the woman in deep violet. "She is wise and remembered well by many."

"You know my mother?" Tasa looked at the woman, seeking to see her face beneath the hood.

"I do." The woman dressed in violet answered without hesitation. "She served well as Forest Mother and also for a short while as Beach Mother. I hear she is well suited for her chosen task upon her new island home. I hear report that she is well appreciated by those she administers to, and they make fine progress in the ways of Gaia's wisdom. These reports please me."

Tasa remained quiet, for these words brought confirmation of something she suspected. As a child she had been curious enough to look into trunks and closets. She remembered the green and blue robes she found. Those robes were now explained. She also recalled finding a white robe.

They approached some fallen trees, artfully stacked in varying levels. The woman chose a spot and took a seat, leaning back against the largest of logs. She swept her arm at the pile of old trees, indicating for Tasa to join her. Tasa took a place in a nook, lower in level than the diminutive woman's seat. Their eyes were equal in height and Tasa now saw the woman's face clearly in the sun. She felt the memory of the woman flow into her consciousness. Once before at Penthe House did they meet, during Tasa's first days upon the Albion Isle, during her convalescence? Or...before? The memory was just out of reach.

"Do you know why you are here?" the purple-clad woman asked.

Tasa looked back down the shore. Beach Mother was gathering driftwood and piling it in a stack. "I believe that I am being tested in my skills."

The woman laughed. "You are! But I did not mean just today. Do you know why you are *here*?" Tasa turned and looked at her, studying her face. There was friendliness there, but seriousness as well. A slight smile, a remnant from her laughter, faded slowly. Tasa knew that smile and also that laugh. She seemed much like...again the memory slipped sideways and away.

Tasa understood that the question itself was a test. "I am at Penthe House in Albion because there are more things that I might learn here than within my mother's own Penthe House upon our island. I am here because the world is a larger place than I can know if I only remain in my home. I am here because I was invited by the women from Penthe House in Albion who visited my mother. Mother presented me to them, and I made the choice to say yes." Tasa paused, considering. Had she covered everything? "I am here to learn the wisdom of Gaia and how to live my life in accord with such wisdom."

"And what is the guiding principle that we use in this regard?"

"We ask, 'Is this action I am about to take for the benefit of Gaia?' After asking, we act accordingly."

"And is your presence at Penthe House..." the woman paused just long enough for Tasa to notice the space, "...Albion, for the benefit of Gaia?"

Tasa had no answer at hand. She sat still for a moment and then said, "It is not a question I have ever considered. In the vastness of the world, even in the large area that is Penthe House Albion I do not suppose I am all that important. There are many here who act and perform important tasks. There are many with greater skills than I. You ask if my presence at Penthe House is a benefit, but you may well ask is my existence on the earth to the benefit of Gaia. That I do not know. I may yet perform some task or learn some wisdom that will be of great benefit. I believe Penthe House prepares me for such an eventuality. I see life is more random than I once might have thought." She thought again of the white robe which she had discovered in her mother's trunk. "I might become prepared, yet have no opportunity to serve, or another person may also be prepared and act swifter than I.

"If I must give an answer to your question, then I would say I am prepared and preparing to be of benefit to Gaia should the opportunity arise. Until then I will do no harm to her or the earth itself and I will train those I meet in these ways by my example."

The woman dressed in deep purple looked at Tasa for several long moments. Smiling again, she nodded back towards Beach Mother. "Come. Let us see what is for evening meal." And with that she stood and walked back towards the little boat. The craft lay tilted to one side, the water having receded away from the hull.

****

The tide had gone out while they spoke. Now the sun was lowering in the western sky. The evening would turn chill despite the warmth of the late summer day. There was wood gathered, but the fire was not laid. Beach Mother walked from the shallows carrying three fair sized fish she had speared.

"Tasa, would you kindly prepare the fire and our meal?" Beach Mother said. Though posed as a question, there was the tone of command in her words. Already Tasa had been visually choosing the right pieces of wood for the base of the fire and mentally separating the rest into phases should the flames and embers need to last them through the night. It would be tricky, but she thought it possible.

Without a word she prepared the fire. The women watched her while they spoke of random things. Tasa listened without seeming to listen. She felt like they were giving answers to questions she could not hear. Or perhaps instructions to someone she could not see.

"The woods are deep here. Silence is easy in a place like this."

"One can see outward from inside the forest and yet never be seen."

"Shelter can be obtained easily. In a short while a home of comfort can be constructed."

"There is much life within the shadows."

"It is close to Penthe House proper. It is a short path to travel if one should feel it necessary."

"Albion is a safe haven and has been so for many generations."

"It is a place of learning. One can learn in safety here."

"The world changes but, for now, we continue safe."

"Protection from real danger may be necessary, but subtlety is needed. Adding fear to fear is not a path we wish to follow."

Tasa built the wood into two cones, one larger with the smaller one inside the first. Kindling and leaves went into the base at the center, and she took some dried moss from one of her pouches. Not so many pouches as Mariel, but Tasa learned the wisdom of small leather carryalls from her friend. Once Tasa began doing so, others in Forest House had begun to follow this practice.

A stone scraped against another and sparking created fire in the moss. The bloom of light rose steadily and soon the late afternoon air was warmed by the cheery, dancing flames. The cove, sheltered by high cliffs to the north and south, was backed by a wooded area that rose upwards into a forest. They faced west and watched the setting sun grow larger at the horizon.

Tasa cooked the fish Beach Mother speared and added little dried berries and herbs to the flesh. The woman in deep purple added some fruits she carried in a satchel, and they buried some tubers under small stones near the base of the fire. After the little voyage and the walk along the beach Tasa did not, at first, realize just how hungry she was. Rocks smoothed and flattened by the sea made platters for the food and soon the trio had cleaned every bit from the stones.

The woman in deep purple walked off a ways, returning with some drinking skins she pulled from a cache just inside the forest edge. Each skin was full with liquid. Giving one each to Beach Mother and Tasa, she then took a swallow from hers. Tasa followed suit, but only after Beach Mother also drank. The fluid was thicker than water and tasted of mint and fennel, or perhaps anise. A slight bite from fermentation made it refreshing and soothing. It tasted familiar, like a potion her mother would concoct for some of the women on her island in the Ringing Sea.

"You are near to moving from Beach House to Wisdom House, Tasa," Beach Mother began without preamble. "You have done well. More than that. You are every bit the exceptional person I was told about. But an exceptional person is not above the mores of the society they exist within. You are still a young girl in many ways, though more a young woman in shape and nature. Do you feel the changes upon you?"

"Yes, Beach Mother." Tasa paused to consider the appropriate words. "I feel more…complete in some ways, more confident, but I do not feel sure of myself at all times. Penthe House is a different experience for me and much has occurred here that I do not feel I fully understand."

"Hmmm. 'Beach Mother' you say. Let us for this night allow you to speak my name. I hear it seldom enough and, if I recall correctly, never from your lips. I am Mother Marion to you for the rest of our journey. Agreed?" Tasa nodded in affirmation, her eyes wide. "You say there are things you do not understand, yet you do not appear distressed by this state. Are you holding back in any way that might affect your progress? From my perception you engage fully in every activity assigned you."

"I am not distressed, Beach Mother…Marion. Only that there are things I have not seen revealed. I am not in a hurry for them to become so, only, well, there are differing ways here and I do choose to fit in when I can. For me it is better to be quiet and observe. I do not wish to offend or overstep my boundaries. You say I am exceptional, but I do not know what that means. I only do what I am told."

Mother Marion gave a sly smile. "It seems you have an inner compass that guides you well, Tasa. You often do more than what you are told, but always in the spirit of the direction given. You exceed where others merely fulfill. What do you think of the others you have met here in Albion?"

"I have not met anyone I disliked, Beach...Mother Marion. There are things about each person that are unique. Some of the girls tell tales...things that are puzzling."

The woman in deep purple leaned forward. "What kind of tales, Tasa?"

"Words that sometimes carry fear, but more often hold awe. The older girls will not long let the younger ones speak of scary moments, but they themselves will tell words of...legendary beings. They speak as if the stories are more than tales."

"What are the topics of these tales?" The woman seemed to be smiling deep within, though the smile did not reach her face. "Are these things that concern you? Things you do not understand?"

Again, Tasa paused, then, "They speak of giants and dragons..." She wanted to address the woman but had no title for her. She settled upon one of her own choosing. "Noble Mother, the girls speak of giants, dragons, and elves. They tell of battles and healings and why Penthe House is called so and of Brigid and her dragon and a burning man who fought but did not slay a dragon and how she was a healer and he came for healing and her dragon helped that one and she taught others her ways and then called Penthe House such after her dragon and we are not here for healing so much as for learning Gaia's ways and others structured Penthe House and why we travel the five houses and why there is a central house and a Woman in White over all the houses and of Dagda Nicholaus as if he is a giant, but I have only ever known humans and everyone seems to be human here on Albion, though some are rather large and others do certain actions that seem like the magicks of old and some are rather small, and there are some other differences that are subtle and I cannot put a name to them and I do not care about that so much only it is puzzling and I do not feel exceptional in the midst of all these other people who are so much more accomplished than I and certainly not in comparison to the legends and stories and no one ever speaks of it as if it is true today though they do not ever say that giants and elves went away only that sometimes they say dragons have gone away but others say that there are still dragons and sometimes I think about a dragon..." Tasa stopped. She was babbling, and she knew it. Ducking her head, she sipped at the skin of liquid and ran the fluid around her tongue before swallowing.

"Noble Mother." The woman in deep purple spoke the title slowly and thoughtfully. "I accept that gift, Tasa, but for the rest of your journey with Mother Marion, would you also do me the honor of calling me by my name? I am Ikara."

The world seemed to glow a little for Tasa. She looked out to sea as the sun made its last light above the horizon. A subtle green glow came as it settled out to sea for the night. The woman in deep purple leaned close and Tasa felt safe. This surprised her, for she did not realize that she felt fear. Uncertainty perhaps. "Yes, Mother Ikara," Tasa said.

The women dressed in violet spoke. "Only Ikara, my dear Tasa. It would be unseemly for you to call me 'mother' given our history." Tasa looked deeply in the woman's eyes and again felt the surge of familiarity. What history did they share?

Ikara continued speaking. "Marion, you told me she is a quiet one. It seems we now have a deep well with all the words bubbling up." This time the smile did again reach her face and Tasa was left with a vision of her own mother. "Tasa, I will not tell you what is truth. You will learn this yourself and yours will be a different truth than mine. I will say that legends exist for many reasons. My truth is that the legends are not to be feared. Indeed, very little is to be feared in this world, though we must be respectful of the power inherent in Gaia's natural ways.

"Presently you will know more of the world and in years to come even more than you might imagine. I see, for you, that the future is not always a safe place. I also see that through your actions the world becomes a safer place for many.

"You keep your curiosity in check. There is no harm in this. Yet, I encourage you to begin to ask more questions about your immediate world. Take note of all that you are being shown. Allow your perceptions to be tested in conversation with others. As you move into Wisdom House, there will be great opportunity to reach out to trusted associates. Learn from what they say and also from what they do not speak.

"I will not tell you your truth. I will say that you are an exceptional person. My reasons for saying so differ from Mother Marion's. After this night you may not feel so incomplete. After this night another will feel better for your presence."

Night deepened, and stars appeared. The sun, having set some hours ago, no longer brightened the skies. Light was growing in the east as the waxing moon rose.

Ikara continued, "No matter the depth of dark, there is always light. Even if it is shielded from our eyes, it remains present, and we only have to wait a little until it once again appears. Be it moon or sun, not even clouds prevent all their gift of light from casting shadows. I have been through dark times, the darkness being in my heart.

"Tell me, Tasa, do you see? When you look at people, do you see?"

This was a very puzzling question. Tasa now had to ponder just what Ikara meant by the word "see" for certainly she knew that Tasa possessed eyesight and could see people and objects just fine. "Do you mean, do I observe beyond the mere presence of what a thing is, a person's body or the shape of a tree or the pattern of its bark?" Tasa responded with a question and Ikara remained silent. "I have seen, in dreams sometimes but also in life, the green glow that emanates from a tree freshly planted and tended by the Oakmen. I have seen a light in the eyes of some, a kind of shining from within: Mariel often, Mother Meg at times, Karia in her quiet moments." She turned to Beach Mother and said, "Once with you, Mother Marion, when I brought a message and you thought no one was near and you stood upon the shore gazing out to sea."

"Any others, dear?" Mother Marion asked.

"My own mother, sometimes, but only in happy times. There were certain men who came to our island, and they often would smile at me when I questioned them about the world. I would see the shine in their eyes at that time." She thought a while.

"Others, Tasa? Do not be shy about this," Ikara said.

"Master Amir. Only it was different with him."

"How so?" Ikara leaned close.

"It felt that I was recognizing or knowing something, but I do not know what." Tasa sighed. "This is the kind of thing I mean when I say that I am incomplete in some ways. But I still choose to wait and maybe the knowledge will come in some fashion. I do not want to be a bother or offend. Perhaps it is simply that I do not know what questions to ask."

The trio was silent for a moment. Tasa saw the flames were still high. She did not recall anyone adding wood to the fire and now that she looked, the pile of fresh fuel did not seem to have diminished at all. Out to sea the tide continued to rise as the moon also rose behind them. A vast stretch of the ocean now gleamed darkly beneath pale white lunar light.

"Is it ever in your nature to offend? Have you ever given offense and been rebuked for your words, Tasa?" Ikara asked.

"I would sometimes ask mother questions, questions about the very things we are talking of tonight: giants and elves and dragons, mostly dragons. She was never cross with me, but also never seemed to answer me directly. I feel that maybe I was inconvenient to her at those times. It may be that there were other important matters, and she did not have the time for such things. She was often busy with the work of the island."

Mother Marion laughed and it startled Tasa. Beach Mother rarely laughed, and this seemed derisive. "So Kila learns that there is more to running several houses than to running just one?"

Ikara spoke. "She works hard. She does well. She is well respected by her students and well loved by her sisters on the island." Tasa noted that Ikara was speaking directly to Beach Mother and the tone was one of discipline and correction. "Kila made a choice based on the Question. She does well for Gaia where she is, and she has brought Tasa to the world."

"Yes," Mother Marion began. "Yet she has not had time for Tasa's questions? She has not seen fit to bring the Words of the World to her? She wished to be the Keeper of Words, but that does not mean she keeps them to herself."

"It is why I brought her child to our shores, Marion. It is much for a mother to love her child and allow her to leave. It is much to judge the child's development from a distance or after a mere two month's cycle. Her choice was not to withhold the words, Marion. Only to allow for a different setting. There is more here than you know."

"Yes, Ikara, but..."

"There is more here than you know." Ikara's sharp words cut across Marion's voice. "You criticize one sister, but in your words you judge me. You and I have not yet seen revealed the full weight of the Words of the World, nor have any upon this island save those closest to Brigid. I devote myself to her in penitence, but I am ever aware of my past authority. I am also aware of my past transgression. Kila is sent such learning and does not yet respond. She is deemed ready by Brigid. You are not now and may never be prepared for those words. Your silence now will teach you much." Beach Mother fell silent then and cast her eyes downward.

Tasa, eyes wide at the rebuke given to Mother Marion, felt confused by the words and a little fear at Ikara's presence. She seemed ever so much larger in stature and now appeared to loom higher above her. Tasa felt very small just then and determined to become very still and quiet. There was much about this that brought to mind her own mother in her sterner moments.

Her heart was pounding, accelerated by Ikara's powerful words. The thought that someone would speak to one of the House Mothers in such a way never once occurred to Tasa. Did the Mothers also have someone above them? It appeared so. Ikara's words made little sense to Tasa. What she did sense was that there once existed a powerful conflict and it involved her own mother.

A thought, a whisper, a voice appeared in Tasa's mind. "I am near." Tasa's heart slowed. "I am here now." The voice came again. Tasa was tempted to look around but restrained herself out of fear. "I am silent in the woods. I cannot yet be seen." Calm flowed around her head and shoulders. "There will be a place of strength and safety. There will be shelter if you need such." She felt strength flow into her limbs and chest. She looked at Ikara. The woman in deep purple seemed smaller again. She did not seem to have heard the voice. Neither did Beach Mother.

"Tasa, are you alright?" Ikara asked. "We all receive lessons, Tasa. Beach Mother as well. Sometimes we teach ourselves our own lessons. Such is what your mother is doing. Do not fear lessons, Tasa. Fear not receiving them."

Ikara sighed when Tasa did not speak in response. "Best that we allow ourselves sleep. Your journey was not as long as some, yet you still must be weary from your exertions." With that she wrapped a cloak about her shoulders and leaned back onto the sand.

Tasa looked at Mother Marion. The Woman in Blue did not meet Tasa's glance, only unrolled her own cloak and likewise lay back to sleep beneath the night sky.

Tasa followed their example but did not feel that she would easily find sleep. There was no longer any sense of fear, but her world had shifted. She turned her head to the edge of the woods. The light of the fire cast long shadows and left the woods impenetrable to her sight.

On a whim she relaxed her eyes slightly, like Mariel had shown her that day in the oak forest. She recalled Mariel's words to her mind and now sought the same feeling. It may have been sleep finding her, it may have been her imagination, but Tasa saw that there was light emanating from certain trees. She stole a glance toward Ikara's sleeping form. The glow was very strong and differed in color than the wood.

"There is much life in the shadows." The voice returned. "I am in the shadows by my own choosing. No life in the shadows may threaten you here and now."

Tasa thought. "Are you a dragon? Are you the one I have known? Do others hear you? Are there other dragons near?"

"I remain close to Penthe. Also to my mentor. They ask for patience on my part. It is a swift flight to you if I feel it necessary. The safety of the Albion Isles is not guaranteed. It is safer now that I am here. I wish you strength."

Tasa continued looking to the woods. One area grew brighter in her vision, but she could not bring clarity to the sight. "I cannot see you. When can I see you?"

"My presence is one of protection. The sight of me may cause fear in others. Adding fear to fear is not a path I wish to follow."

"Am I dreaming?"

"I remain in the shadows, but you will see me before long. Fear not. Be strong."

With those words sleep came upon her.

15

To Wonder at the Truth of Things

THE GIFT OF THE SCROLL FADED FROM PROMINENCE in Tasa's thoughts after a while, though at times in deep night she would awake and ponder the mysterious images that arose from Dagda Nicholaus' section of the communication. After consulting with Beach Mother, only Bria and Mariel and, of course, Mother Meg were informed of the scroll's existence and were, by turns, excited, sarcastic, and enthusiastic for Tasa. One other was informed, but later, at the turning of the year.

Tasa kept the scroll wrapped tight within a leather cylinder given her by Beach Mother. The scarf that Captain Troylis gave her was rolled within the scroll. These lay at the bottom of her leather satchel from Mariel and atop them was a variety of writing implements that she had collected or crafted for herself.

Tasa often drew maps based on the vague images she could recall from Dagda Nicholaus' words or what passed for words. When she tried to focus, her work was scratchy and seemed incomplete. If she allowed her mind to drift slightly the work became art, though she could not always place the finished images within the maps of the world she herself had seen.

And always there were the thoughts of dragons. So often in her life these thoughts came to her and deep in her heart she believed that they were real. Yet, no one else seemed to want to speak of them.

Early on she would ask her mother, and later Parla and Caraphino. Her questions often were diverted, or an answer was promised "when she was older" but that mythical time never arrived.

Back on Solaine, Tasa would speak to certain ones: fishermen, sailors, or the captains of sea craft who took an interest in her. These men would bring gifts of books and maps and Tasa always appreciated the items received, but there was more to the men. They also would bring tales of lands far away and creatures strange and exotic. They would speak of ancient civilizations and peoples who no longer could be found.

And there would sometimes be a subtle reference to dragons. As the years went on, as people declined to speak to her about the ancient stories of dragons, young Tasa ceased asking.

Days would come when, while pouring over a new book or map, a short passage or small illustration would catch her eye. Secretly Tasa compiled a list of these references and one day she planned to copy them all together in a new book. As a child she called it *Tasa's Book of the Dragons*. Leaving Solaine for Albion meant leaving the books and maps behind.

After the night on the beach with Mother Marion and Ikara, Tasa began to write her own heart's impressions and thoughts about dragons. The next morning Ikara was gone before they woke. Mother Marion and Tasa sailed back to Beach House and no more was said of the day. Tasa tried to convince herself the vision in the night was all a dream. She did not succeed. She did, however, remain quiet about the matter and resolved to open her senses wider.

She did not simply believe in the existence of dragons. She believed her dragon was near.

****

Mother Marion, that is, Beach Mother, Tasa reminded herself, made certain that Tasa was prepared to travel the path from the House of the Blue Door with the rest of the girls. Tasa was not to be an exception. There was to be no deviation, no wandering. All left together, all would arrive together, and to that end the Woman in Blue assigned three Beach House adepts to walk with the acolytes, first to the House of the White Door where they would receive their Wisdom House robes, then on to the House of the Violet Door itself.

Tasa did not mind this in the least, though some of the older acolytes chafed at the idea of needing to be "shepherded like children" by the adepts.

These girls, Tasa mused, were the exact ones that did need watching, for they were the most likely to wander. Especially as it was rumored that Red Robin may be near.

Tasa did wish for a glimpse of Mariel and felt certain that her friend was nearby, only hidden from everyone else's sight. Yet there was no appearance and Tasa found herself at Wisdom House proper within the three-day full moon period of change.

The House of the Violet Door was definitely not what she expected, if she had expected anything. The focus of instruction was not readily apparent. There was talk of the way of plants or of animals, how they flourish in some climates or perish in others, how they breed in some months and not in others, how one eats another and in turn decomposes to fertilize the ground, creating a cycle of life. But then there was more. There were ideas discussed about who a person really was: Did they possess a purpose, or was life random?

Mornings began early, but not in the way of Forge House. Not abruptly, with the clanging of a bell, but gently.

Some clear water and a mix of a few grains were served. Everyone met in large groups throughout the temple area. There they performed slow and steady movements. To Tasa it was almost like dancing, only extremely slowly. Some of the adepts held long poles in their hands and swung them about gracefully. Some held wide fans, while others had spheres of stone that rolled from one side of their hand to another, seemingly defying gravity.

None of the acolytes used anything but their own physical form. Tasa quickly grew very skilled in the poses and steps. A type of level was achieved and as you gained abilities you were moved around within your group. This made it easy to advance as you always were practicing with ones just slightly more experienced than you.

After morning movement, everyone sat to a fine light breakfast of cereals and honey and tea and juice. The first-year acolytes then went on to laundry or housekeeping or cooking or mending, if they were skilled, or fire tending or any of a myriad of tasks required for daily life to continue. At mid-morning they gathered for a period of silence and meditation with everyone being called by a gentle chiming that echoed about the temple area.

All things were scheduled, but nothing ever felt forced to Tasa. Even early mornings came easy for her at Wisdom House. Rather than stop for a meal at noon, everyone continued on until about two bells after the high sun for a meal of vegetables and rice with fish or the occasional bit of game meat. Mostly the fare was meatless, but there was no strict taboo regarding this. Many chose to not eat their food with meat added in and seemed none the worse for it if they structured their diet correctly. After the meal a general break was called, and you could pretty much do what you wanted. Many took naps in the heat of the late summer days, some swam in the pools, others read books or wrote letters, some just sat sipping a cool ferment or clear juice and talked together in quiet tones.

A gentle chime called everyone back to tasks and then later in the evening, before they all went their separate ways, there was more movement. This was decidedly different from the morning, however. These movements were swift and decisive with some dramatic bursts of noise as they all expelled breath and made loose fists, swinging arms in circular motions, or launching kicks into empty air. Tasa was surprised at how much she enjoyed this activity. Afterwards, everyone felt energized and went off to separate projects or classes until long after darkness.

Tasa was heavily involved in classes, of course, but found time to join a group that was giving dramatic presentations of some of the famous tales of old. Mostly they would be of Athene or Pandora or Brigid. Sometimes they would be of the dragons.

Tasa participated in a poetic recital of a great sea voyage, "The Forgotten Lands of Amir." The subject was a sea journey to locate lost wisdoms and peoples who once lived with the Ancient Dragon Tethys. It surprised her to discover that some of the older girls, adepts, believed this to be about *her* Amir. Surely, she thought, it must be that her Amir, Master Amir, was named in honor of the legend. The story seemed to speak of events that happened so long ago, it was impossible for the man she knew to be the same being. The adepts heading the production just smiled and said that many things were different than people sometimes believed. Tasa kept quiet and watched and learned. She recalled Karia said that she once was on a journey with Master Amir herself.

Instructors at Wisdom House raised questions and did not always provide answers. Tasa continued to wonder at the truth of things. It seemed that she may know little of her world, less even than she might have believed. A determination grew in her heart. It would be good to know the world, but she would begin not with great journeys. She felt she must learn more, first of herself and then of the place in which she dwelt. She realized that she had been learning about the world and letting it shape her view of herself. Perhaps it would be better to learn about herself first and shape her world around her.

She also must know more of those she called friends. There was much about them of which Tasa was unaware. She must begin to pay closer attention. When she first could, she would ask Karia about this poem. She would then decide to believe or not.

In those two months at Wisdom House, the voice in the night came to her, rare and faint, speaking vague assurances.

In the two months Tasa spent at Wisdom House, the House of the Violet Door, she did not see or hear of Ikara.

In those same two months, she saw Mariel not at all.

16
Speaking of Changes

THE WARM SCENT OF THAT PLEASANT SUMMER lingered into early autumn as Tasa entered the last phase of her first year. Like every other acolyte, this was spent at the figurative center of the Order of Penthe, the Life House. Here, she was asked a great many questions by a great many women all dressed in white robes, mostly with silver sashes or sometimes a sash the color of a particular house. All the acolytes wore robes of white with black sashes. In between the sessions of questions, the acolytes were given tasks to do, different all the time and often conflicting. It was at times very confusing. Tasa set her mind only on doing the last thing she was told.

One morning she arose early to continue her practice of the movements learned at Wisdom House when one of the older girls spotted her in the grove near her bunk house. With a wave of her hand, she indicated that Tasa should follow her and they walked off to an open glade near a quiet little pool where about two dozen others were already engaged in the gentle form. That night, the same girl found Tasa after evening meal and silently waved her to follow. They returned to the pool and here they began the practice of the faster form, only silently.

No one spoke. No one discussed the session. Unlike Wisdom House, it did not begin or conclude with any marking of time. One girl or another would start to sway, and others would join in as they arrived. The movements shifted and altered from one moment to the next. Sometimes they would be following one girl and then another would seem to be leading. Never was instruction given and not all followed perfectly. The session sped up as the sunlight faded and the stars appeared. A few small torches stuck in the ground provided flickering light.

Tasa kept up the best she could. At times she struggled with new or complex positions and motions. A few times one or another of the silent women around her would pause in their own routine and step nearer. They would look at her and begin to move in specific way. Tasa would then follow, slowly at first but gaining speed. In a way she did not readily discern she would suddenly be in motion with the group. People drifted away as the night progressed. Tasa stayed quite late one evening and saw no sign that the group completely dissolved. From then on, she took her leave when she felt the call to bed. During the day she rarely saw any of the girls or women from the night before and no one ever talked about the practice.

Tasa did not know if this was a secret or somehow disapproved of by the Keeper of the Words, the Mother of the House of Five Doors, but she found it thrilling to move in harmony with the others and in silence. It brought to mind her moments with the oak sapling, Mariel guiding her thoughts, and the sense of power she felt flowing all around her. The memory surprised her as she realized that Mariel often moved in these same ways, stepping lightly forward and silently moving branches from her path in the same circular motions.

Mariel was rarely in attendance at Life House. She rarely was found by Tasa anywhere except Forest House and, on occasion, at Beach House. Once, along a wooded path, while transporting a sheaf of messages from Life House to Hearth House, Mariel appeared quietly at Tasa's side. Despite the time apart, they fell into comfortable conversation. They walked close together, laughed easily, and spent a pleasant mealtime in the cool winds of autumn with Hearth House Mother and some of the newer acolytes.

A little boy, a toddler barely, grinned laughing when he saw Tasa. He came to sit upon her lap. He cooed and made little grunts and puffs, playing with her long, braided hair, and clutching her white robe tightly. She laughed with him and hummed little tunes. One of them was the tune she recalled from Red Robin and the nights he escorted her to Beach House. The little boy eventually fell asleep in her arms.

Mariel watched the process from across the room while she played with some of the older children. Tasa held him loosely and let him drift. She smiled a little. Her eyes roved about the child's face. Mariel sensed that Tasa was searching for something.

Tasa looked up just then and caught Mariel gazing at her. Their eyes met and held. Tasa felt energy flowing through her to Mariel and back once again. She witnessed the glow of green light and in Mariel's eyes she saw the shine, bright and powerful. The little boy awoke with a start.

Tasa tried to turn her gaze from Mariel and found it difficult to do so. The child seemed prepared to cry. An intake of breath about to become a wail was drawn. Tasa took a calming breath. Time slowed for her. She drew that same light that passed between her and Mariel down toward the little boy's face. She imagined it seeping into his eyes and ears, coating his face and entering every pore. The wail stilled in his lungs. He looked afraid at first. Mariel came to sit next to them. The child looked at both of the girls. Fear altered and shifted across his face. He blinked and little tears rolled from both eyes. Mariel wiped them away with a fingertip. He sighed and took a long breath. Within his eyes, Tasa saw the shine growing. Soft and pale at first, she imagined a flame and mentally cast a quiet breath toward the light. It grew and steadied. The boy relaxed his body and returned to sleep.

✳✳✳✳✳✳✳✳✳✳✳✳

"She held the child for just a short time," said Hearth Mother. "Though it has been nearly a year, he seemed to remember her from her time at Hearth House and went directly to her. She did not hesitate to embrace the changeling and indeed seemed happy to see him. At least as happy as I have ever noted her to become.

"Tasa still is very quiet and rarely seems to display any emotion outward. But this child made her smile. Mariel joined them, and the two girls kept silent, but I must say the impression that I received was that they were communicating in some manner."

The Woman in White did not move her form, but her eyes narrowed. "Hearth Mother, do you ever note Tasa and Mariel as companions? What I wonder is this: Does Tasa, or Mariel for that matter, smile when they are together?"

"Mariel is not as observable, Mother White. She does not easily enter doors. Though we have always been kind to her at Hearth House, I believe she was not always treated well by the other girls when she first arrived after her mother's passing. I feared the same fate for the changeling, in some fashion. Tasa's presence increases the possibility of my seeing Mariel but does not guarantee such a thing.

"If you wish to know if they are happy in one another's company, I must say that it is my distinct impression that they are well pleased and most comfortable with each other. It is a strange match in its way, but not one to which I see any clear objection."

The Woman in White relaxed her eyes and said, "Well, there are those who would object to Mariel on the grounds that she is 'irregular,' but I hardly find that argument compelling in this case. As long as Tasa is not remiss in her duties or is being tempted to such a path.

"Mariel remains an unknown for us, but she does find acceptance in Beach House as well as with…Mother Meg." The Woman in White smiled and glanced at Forest House Mother. "She finds her home in the realms of Forest House most often and it is there that Tasa also, I believe, felt the most comfortable.

"We were of a mind to remand Tasa to Hearth House as an adept path following her second year. She would be an excellent source of calm and centering for incoming girls. Now I believe we will reconsider her path. Thank you for this report, Mother Bae. Does anyone have anything to add?"

A larger hand raised a large hammer and Forge Mother spoke. "Tasa is stronger material than she first appears. She is flexible but retains her strength despite bending. I do object to Mariel's behavior and lack of structure. You may find humor in this if you wish, but it is my way and I know we do not all share the same patterns. That being said, I will say that I support the pairing of Tasa with such a one as Mariel. Tasa is firm in ways that are not obvious. She will potentially bring some measure of regularity to Mariel. It can only serve that child well." She lowered the hammer and turned as the Woman in Blue raised her staff.

"Mother Bae, did the child…" Beach Mother paused to find the right words, "the one you call the changeling, does he still change after Tasa's visit? Does he still…shift under the moon light?"

Mother Bea pondered her answer, then said, "It is a puzzle to me that he changed in the first place, but now that you ask, no. He seems to be calmer in the night. The girls who tend the youngling sleepers no longer whisper in complaint of the boy. Where once he stayed apart from the other children in the day, he now engages. Only with one or two at a time, but that is different than before when he would sit still in darkened corners or beneath tables.

"Perhaps the trauma of the loss of his mother is healing. This can occur swiftly when children are young, though they often retain some measure of the pain of absence. But this child was more than mourning his mother. He was unlike any I have known, and I have served in Hearth House most of my days. You may recall that I am one who arrived as an orphan.

"The girls would speak, sometimes in fearful tones, of the boy changing into a beast. The world is wide. This may be a thing that is possible, though I have not witnessed such a shifting, even in this child. I now feel remiss in not choosing to observe him more closely in the night, but, in my aged life, the night is a difficult thing for me to exist in. I sleep early and wake the same. I can find one of the adepts and learn more from them if they have actually observed this supposed change."

The Woman in White smiled again at the Woman in Red. "Hearth Mother, dear Mother Bae, you have served Penthe House well since long before I was even an acolyte. You are most respected and your love for the girls keeps you in your place. We will, you and I, spend some time discussing your adepts and perhaps make some arrangements to relieve you of some of the more burdensome tasks of Hearth House. Do not despair that you have somehow fallen short in your duties with this boy child. It is a world of variance now. None of us knows for certain what to expect. We must, in fact, address this very topic and soon. For now, let us continue our course. Forge Mother, will you offer us your monthly report? We trust all is regular at Forge House."

17
Tracking Mariel

THIRTEEN LUNAR MONTHS MADE UP THE CYCLE OF THE YEAR that Penthe House adhered to as a timetable. Two months spent in each of the six houses and one month that they called the void. Tasa was approaching her void month and there was much to look forward to from her perspective. These last two houses that she attended, Wisdom House and now Life House, were places where she came to find much of her own inner self. But, at the House of the Violet Door, she found that something was missing.

That something was Mariel. The friends and companions she met and attended classes with were fine and she was fond of a few, but none delighted her or made Tasa laugh the way that Mariel did. In their times together that previous year they had grown very close, but Tasa now realized she really knew very little about Mariel. She also wondered what exactly it was about herself that made Mariel such a close companion. Then she thought: what if Mariel does not really share my feelings? What if Mariel has other friends that she does things with, and I don't even know who they are? What if Mariel does not miss me the way that I miss her?

These thoughts began to interrupt Tasa's days and nights. At Wisdom House, Mother Mii and the adepts encouraged solitude and quiet moments. Tasa did not recall seeing Mariel at all those entire two months. It was not that she did not notice, only that the practices being taught kept her mind active and focused elsewhere.

Mariel did show up as Tasa walked her path from Wisdom House to Life House, but again, slipped off before they arrived at the White House. Tasa wore the white robes of Life House and Mariel still wore greens, browns, and leathers.

Tasa did not give this much thought at the time. Now, less than one month into her days at Life House a subtle shift seemed to have occurred in her daily routine. She had been asked by the Woman in White, Mother Theacaris herself, to deliver a packet of papers to Mother Bae at Hearth House. This excused her from regular duties and classes.

Much of the time spent at Life House was a kind of test. Questions were asked of the girls, and it seemed to Tasa that the adepts were seeking to discover how many connections the acolytes could or would make between the five disciplines they experienced during their year. For Tasa this seemed easy and a little bit silly. She never actually considered the houses to be separate entities, only aspects of the whole of Penthe House. The adepts gave her subtle praise in this perception. For Tasa, this was simply the way she had been taught by her mother on Solaine.

The other girls continued to be called to one or another class, given some task, or scheduled to train with this or that adept, but Tasa suddenly found herself walking alone and to nearby places within the Life House area and then, after a week, she was sent farther afield. First, she traveled to Mother Bae's, and it was here that Tasa and Mariel began to regularly meet one another once again.

Life was pleasant for Tasa once more and, for her part, Mariel always seemed to be willing and able to find Tasa when she embarked on these little errands. Soon the messages and deliveries that Tasa carried for Life House were also directed to Forest House. Mother Meg was delighted by this and expressed herself openly.

Mother Theacaris spoke with Tasa nearly each day, but only in the morning or evening. Tasa, it seemed, was no longer on the same vague schedule as the other girls. "Only be mindful of what you see," said Mother White, "and also of what you do not see."

In these words, Tasa began to open her eyes to everything. It was not just the path through the forests, but why did the path take the course it did? It was not simply the fact that Forge House was some distance from Hearth House; it was the fact that a small hill separated the two, giving a kind of protection against the constant sound that emanated from Forge Mother's mighty fires and workshops. It was not that Tasa wore the robes of white with a black sash; it was that every acolyte did so. It was that everyone in Penthe House wore a specific color and sash of some type. It was that there was a regularity to the way things were run that existed all throughout the community. It was that Mariel arrived and departed without any sign of affiliation at all. Ever.

Even Red Robin wore the colors of his Order. Even Captain Troylis wore the colors of his Order. Even Master Amir. As Tasa thought about the fleeting glimpse she had gotten of Dagda Nicholaus, even that great personage wore the colors of his Order. Only Mariel did not.

Tasa wondered how she could have gone so long without taking note of Mariel's lack of affiliation. The girl wore brown leathers with bits of green, but nothing that truly corresponded with the colors of Forest House. Mariel wore no sash, despite having a multitude of straps and belts about her waist and shoulders. The tunic on her body hugged Mariel with a pleasing patchwork of the leathers of deer and rabbit accented by bits of fur and feathers and laced with strips of braided grasses and cloth that held a variety of pouches. Each pouch having a specific purpose known only to the wearer, Mariel constantly was plucking flowers and leaves and bark, stuffing each in its own place.

Tasa first noticed the lack of acolyte or adept colors while she trailed Mariel in one of their "training sessions." That is what Mariel called them for she was determined that Tasa learn the art of woodcraft and the ways of the creatures of the forest.

"Forest House will teach the facts. I will teach the reality," Mariel told Tasa one afternoon not long after the incident with the Oakmen. "You will learn to track best by tracking the best…me." Tasa smiled when Mariel spoke that way.

She often heard her friend chide Red Robin about being full of himself, yet she displayed much the same quality at times. Tasa thought of Bria's words regarding Mariel's self-proclaimed skills. Bria had said that Mariel was good, but she, Bria, often spotted her. Tasa wondered if Mariel was just letting Bria spot her or if maybe she was not so sneaky a creature as she wanted others to believe.

Tasa now looked about the forest, seeking a shape out of place. Mariel was here somewhere. She had her in sight for a long time now, and then, gone! Tasa held quite still, senses quiet, expanding. Mariel had done it again. While Tasa was woolgathering, her thoughts drifting to questions without available answers, Mariel vanished from view.

Tasa let her eyes unfocus, her ears relax, her nose open and flare, and held her hands open, palms forward. Mariel was near. Tasa allowed her senses to widen. The forest took on the same glow she first witnessed with the Oakmen's sapling. One tree in particular seemed bright and, despite its size, quite fresh and new. This place seemed familiar, but…

"If you were deer, you would be my dinner." Mariel's voice was in her ear and Tasa fought not to jump in fright. "Concentration is key, Tasa." Mariel swung down off of a branch just next to where Tasa had stopped. How had she done that? Tasa thought furiously. She had seen Mariel slip through the low shrubs at the far side of the clearing and then she stopped for just seconds. Surely Mariel could not have gotten back here so swiftly even had she run across the clear space?

"Yum yum!" Mariel squeezed Tasa's bicep. "Very tasty!" Tasa stood still, taking the abuse with good grace. There was a question she needed answered.

"Race me," Tasa said.

"What?"

"Race me to the other side of the clearing, past the tree in the center and to the other edge." Tasa was fast. Her long limbs responded well to motion. She was slim and light and regularly won races with others at Penthe House. She usually beat Mariel in a flat out run, though she had never formally challenged her.

Mariel rarely let a challenge go by. "You are on!" she laughed, and Tasa knew to start right then. Mariel rarely waited to get something started. The girls bolted from the woods and scampered across the green glade like rabbits breaking cover. Tasa's legs stretched out and she leapt small growths and roots smoothly. Mariel was close behind, her shorter form pumping fast. But she was behind almost from the start and finished two lengths back.

Tasa hit the edge of the glade and rather than stop she merely slowed to a trot. Mariel followed, and the girls dashed about side by side for a bit before returning to the glade. Laughing, they sat together beneath the larger central tree, the one Tasa saw glowing.

"You are a swift giantess of a girl! I will never keep up with those long legs of yours, Tasa." Mariel breathed hard, but more from laughing than exertion. Tasa could not recall ever seeing Mariel breathless from activity.

"I am no giantess," Tasa said. "Maybe Karia." And here she ceased laughing. She reached for Mariel's hand and Mariel reached back. "There are many things strange here at Penthe House, things I once read about in books. I did not think them to be false but knowing they might be real is somehow hard to accept." Tasa's breath slowed, and her voice steadied. "How did you get behind me so fast? How did you get from one side to another and climb that tree and...scare me?"

Mariel laughed again, quieter than before. She raised Tasa's hand to her own cheek. "I cheated." Tasa wanted to pull her hand away when she heard the admission, but she liked the closeness of her friend and did not want to lose this moment. Sensing the subtle movement, Mariel held Tasa's hand tighter. She said, "You don't recognize this place yet. You see it, but you are not looking with your true sight, Tasa."

Mariel went still and quiet. Tasa let her awareness expand again. She did recognize the place but could not recall clearly. She cast her eyes about and from where she now sat, her back against the tree, a memory came forward. There, just beyond the line of the wood she remembered Mariel sitting patiently waiting while Tasa observed something...something...the tree! It was the Oakman's tree! It was huge and in less than a year! Less than two seasons! Tasa was about to ask the how of it all, but instead took a deep breath and relaxed against the welcoming trunk.

"You were really good today, Tasa. I tried a lot of my best tricks and you just kept following me. I came here thinking that you just might get disoriented enough for me to get away. It worked. This place is filled with green magic, and you are still not steady in its ways. You wobbled. I could have been long gone and you would still be standing in the slow time." Mariel looked down quickly and back up to face Tasa. "Only I didn't really want to get away."

They sat in companionable silence for a while. Cool winds blew dry leaves from thinning branches. The sun's rays slanted, and dusk was nearly upon them when Mariel spoke again. "Days are short. Samhain will be here before we know it. The year is moving fast, Tasa. It is my best year in a long time. You are my best year, Tasa."

For her part, Tasa had wanted to ask Mariel about her colors, her status, her affiliation, her purpose, the why of her existence at Penthe House, and any other of a myriad of things. Mariel's words washed all those questions from her head. Her heart swelled, and she reached for Mariel with both arms. The girls held each other in the Oakmen's glade, securing their friendship.

****

Days passed and Tasa wondered if it was easy to track Mariel when they were formally training because Mariel secretly wanted Tasa to succeed.

There came to them the Samhain days and a quiet festival of lanterns and gourds. There would be a Samhain circle at Life House. Theacaris, the Woman in White, made it clear that Tasa was expected to join in the ritual. The Woman in Violet, Mother Mii, would lead them in a deep meditation of the earth and the cycle of planting and harvesting, birth and death.

"Will you be there?" Tasa asked Mariel.

"No. That is just for acolytes and adepts of certain houses. Besides, I have to be somewhere else that night. A message I have to deliver." Mariel looked sideways away from Tasa as she spoke and Tasa knew she was not being completely truthful. It was an odd experience, for Mariel above all was a plain-speaking being. She did not have time for word play or games. Now Mariel let the truth slip away.

Inwardly Tasa determined that there should be no secrets between them and that whatever was taking her friend away on this important evening was something she should know about. She struggled with the thought that Mariel should have her own life and her own secrets. After all, Tasa did not share everything about herself. She did answer any question Mariel might have though, if she was asked directly.

On the day of Samhain Tasa tracked Mariel. I will, she thought to herself, only track her as far as I can before I need to turn back to get to the circle on time; Mother White would not take kindly to my missing my first Samhain circle.

Mariel went about her business for the morning, joining Tasa for breakfast, but as Tasa's duties appeared to call her away, Mariel wandered off into the wood. Tasa had no true duties that day. She had planned for this moment and accomplished all that would be asked of her the day before. Her mock errands were designed to create an illusion that Mariel was free to wander, as she often did while Tasa performed tasks.

Tasa let a few breaths pass after she saw Mariel slip past the tree line off to the north. She stepped easily to the edge of the path, not quite looking into the wood. She let her senses expand. Her awareness grew, and she listened to the small sounds of the forest. In a matter of heartbeats, she caught the sound of branches moving counter to the motion caused by the autumn winds. There she turned and slid between trees and into the shade of the forest. A leaf wiggled, and she walked that way. Further ahead a twig lay farther away from the tree it had fallen from and she pointed her feet in that direction. A fallen branch had specks of dirt on the top. A wide oak leaf lay pressed into soft moist earth. Two trees too close together and she walked around them. Seeing an open area, she glided to the edge and let her ears note the breeze sighing through the upper branches. A sound like wind came from too low in the wood and she let her eyes follow that breath. In this way Tasa let the forest close around her and she trailed the leather-clad girl.

Twice she caught sight of Mariel, barely a glimpse, and both moments she paused, imagining light passing through her, her arms balanced and floating like branches. Mariel did not turn, only adjusted belts and straps, placing flowers and bark in various pouches. She walked on and Tasa, after a few breaths, stepped back onto the path Mariel created.

She knew Mariel well and sensed the need for water. She listened and smelled, and this led her to the skinny stream of water flowing from a rock and sinking back into the ground a few paces later. Mariel knelt on one knee, ready to spring away, cupped her hands four or five times as was her way, and drank of the water. She then wet her left hand and wiped the left side of her face, keeping the right eye open. Repeating the process on the right, she then took three more handfuls of water. Tasa imagined Mariel would fill a bladder with the fresh water and followed exactly the same pattern.

Mariel was heading north in an almost straight line, as straight as one could in an irregular forest with no distinct well-worn path at least. Tasa allowed herself to wonder where Mariel was heading. There was no one from Penthe House this far to the north. Wisdom House had a temple quite far northward, two weeks walking and with some boating between, but Tasa did not imagine Mariel was going there. And suddenly Tasa wondered where here was. In her eagerness to track Mariel, she now realized that she had been caught by the shortening days. The sun was quite low on the horizon. Shadows deepened, and the wood grew dark. A small panic grew in her heart. She did not know how far she was from Life House and the Samhain circle. She sensed she could not return in time even if she knew the way well.

Except for the moving Mariel, Tasa had no fixed point. She paused and centered herself with a slow breath. Mariel. She must not lose her now. She widened her hearing. The forest would provide few visual cues for her eyes after dark. There, just ahead, was the subtle snap of a dry twig. Beyond that the brush of a leaf against something that was not another leaf. Tasa moved quicker, but still with a hunter's gait.

She could, if need be, create a camp, stay warm with a fire and sleep in the wood until daylight. She could find her way back south given time and, once in the vicinity, Tasa felt confident that she could locate Penthe House. She would walk directly up to the Woman in White and admit what she had done. She would take whatever discipline came her way, for her foolishness would certainly have consequences.

Why could she not have simply trusted in Mariel and let her have her night away? Why did Tasa think that she could invade Mariel's private life in such a way? Perhaps she should stop now. Make that camp and return in the morning. She would admit her actions to Mariel as well. She would apologize and seek her forgiveness the way they taught at Wisdom House.

Off to her left came a low moaning sound. Weird and unfamiliar, it faded and went lower to become a growl. Thoughts of camp fled Tasa's mind, and she renewed her efforts at tracking Mariel. A moment of stillness rewarded her with the sound of a cough far ahead. Tasa moved that way.

Fear of the unknown heightened her senses. She made good time locating Mariel. A sliver of early starlight grazed Mariel's form as she passed between two tall trees. Tasa kept close to her. One ear forward and one ear back, making certain she herself was not being tracked.

****

The journey came to a conclusion suddenly. Tasa noted a bright glow flickering through trees and leaves. She saw the shadow of Mariel emerge from the woods into a clearing. Tasa slowed and crept to the edge of the forest. She saw two cloaked figures turn and greet Mariel. They were vaguely familiar, but the bonfire was behind them, and their hooded faces were indistinguishable in the shadow they cast. Just past the bonfire a large pair of tall stones stood side by side. On one was a carving of squares and triangles, on the other circles and spirals.

The two figures stood on either side of Mariel, close but not touching. The three began to sway and chant. The two figures wore long robes with deep hoods. Tasa had the impression that they were women but coming from the dark of the wood into the bright firelight left her eyes unadjusted.

A mist rose, gathering around the standing stones. The night sky remained clear. Stars cast silvery beams toward the earth. Tasa began to sway with the trio's rhythmic pattern of sound and motion.

The bonfire burned away the dry kindling and settled to a lower flame. Coals glowed at the base. Shadows settled into firmer lines. A song came from far away. Tasa looked about for another person, for this was a new voice. She saw no one.

The clearing around the stones became more and more misty. The silvery glow of the stars seemed to gather between the carved stones. The mist pushed away from the center as if someone had opened a door and wind pushed leaves about the floor.

Tasa saw a new being emerge from between the standing stones. A very tall, very thin man dressed all in gray. As the light of the fire caught his features, she felt that even his skin must be a grayish nature. He bowed low and the two robed figures bowed back. Mariel remained standing, facing the misty portal between the monoliths.

A second figure appeared behind the gray man but did not emerge. Mariel started to step forward, but the robed figures reached out and held her still. The gray man stretched out one long arm. His long hand held open, waiting. The two robed figures stepped forward in front of Mariel. They lowered their hoods and Tasa gasped. Mother Meg and Beach Mother were now clearly recognizable in the steady light of the bright stars and bonfire. They leaned toward one another and kissed each other on their cheeks. Mother Meg again raised her hood and took the hand of the gray man. He turned, guiding her between the stones.

Tasa watched as Mother Meg vanished into the mist. The shadowy figure that was once beyond the light now emerged. A woman, shorter than Beach Mother and Mother Meg, came from the misty portal between the stones and into the light of the fires. Mariel leapt across the low blaze and threw her arms around the woman. The woman hugged her in return.

Beach Mother stood silent, eyes intent on the portal. Her gaze was locked upon the spot where Mother Meg had entered. Mariel and the new woman talked and laughed and cried. Mariel became animated and lively and danced about and showed the woman her pouches and the little woodland treasures she carried. She came to the larger pouches and from these pulled flowers of all varieties. The woman smiled wide and said, "Thank you, Mariel! You remembered all of them!"

"Of course I remembered, Mother!" Tasa heard the words quite clearly and watched as Mariel's mother held the flowers to her face, inhaling the fragrance deeply.

So intent was Tasa on the tableau that she failed to note the approach of another being off to the east. Her first thought was that an enormous stag had wandered into the area. As it approached the firelight, she saw that it was, in fact, a man wearing stag horns on his head. Mariel and her mother laughed and threw themselves into his massive arms. He gathered the women to him and lifted them off the misty ground.

His laughter was deep and fine and filled the woods. Tasa felt that the trees laughed along with the man and felt a deep joy in her own heart. Owls hooted from branches about the clearing. Deer passed into and out of the firelight. Wild cats and foxes consorted, pausing to watch the fire-lighting beings, with glowing eyes of gold and green. The night felt timeless and Tasa stayed quiet and still just inside the forest, watching and listening to the happy family noises.

But time does not cease, and the darkening of the night sky bade them pay attention to the coming dawn. The woman who emerged from between the standing stone portal suddenly clutched at her abdomen.

"Mother!" Mariel cried a gentle alarm and steadied her.

"Kelle!" said the horned man. He too reached for her and together they held the woman. Tasa saw that her gown was bloody just below her rib cage. She started to move forward to assist. The voice in her head said, "This is not a thing you can help. Be still now and learn."

The mist reappeared between the stones, as did the gray man. A figure stood behind him and Tasa knew the silhouette belonged to Mother Meg.

The woman, the one called Kelle, the one Mariel called mother, gripped them and said, "Thank you for always remembering me in love. I will wait for you to enter the Gates of Annwn when it is your time of passing. I must tell you now that Gwynn is waiting for me, and I will no longer make this journey back to Albion. I am needed for other things beyond the mists." Mariel began to cry and Tasa again sought to move to her friend, pausing as the voice in her head whispered, "Observe, Tasa. Learn and prepare."

"Tears, then, for a while, daughter, for you are precious to me first in my life and then beyond. You also, my mate, for I have seen your tears in the night. Go now, both of you and be alive. No longer are you tied to me but through love and memory." Kelle looked up into the horned man's eyes. She stroked his beard and pulled at twigs and leaves she found stuck there. "The hunt is good. My wound took me, but my, what a wild hunt!"

Her form slumped, and the gray man moved in, scooping her away from Mariel and the horned man. He walked between the stones and paused a moment to set Kelle on her feet. She spoke to him, the words indiscernible from Tasa's distance. He nodded, and she turned back to the world and her family. Her gown was clean again, free of blood, and she smiled and held her hand aloft. Mother Meg stood beside her, and they spoke quietly. An embrace, brief but deep, and Kelle walked into the mists. Mother Meg walked out and together with Mother Marion they embraced the weeping Mariel and her father.

In the silence of dawn sound carried clear and soft. Tasa listened to their words.

"My gratitude, dear sisters," the horned man said.

"Dear brother, what love we have for you, we also have for Kelle, and always for your child," Meg spoke, stroking Mariel's hair.

"She is no burden then?" he said. "She is always welcome in the northern lands." And here he cupped Mariel's face in his large hand. One rugged finger, scarred and rough, brushed away some of Mariel's tears. She smiled at him and reached upward to hug him about the neck.

Beach Mother replied, "She is no burden. She is one of us and welcome everywhere she travels at Penthe House."

"I love you, Father," Mariel said, "but I have responsibilities at Penthe House. I have friends who need me." Mariel gained control of her emotions, wiping away the remaining tears.

"What of me? What if I need you?" The horned man smiled as he spoke. "Your friend seems well trained in woodcraft. Can she learn more?"

"She can, and she will. She does well. She can track me and that is not something just anyone can do!"

"Can I meet her someday?"

"She's right over there." Mariel pointed directly at Tasa. "Tasa, come on out and meet my Da."

It was dizzying and took Tasa a few extra moments to realize they were talking about her. Had Mariel known all along she was there?

Tasa emerged from the deep shadows of the forest edge. Mariel rushed to her friend and embraced her with fierce strength. "I am sooo happy you are here!" Mariel whispered in Tasa's ear. "How did you find me? You are really good, Tasa!" Mariel pulled Tasa to the horned man and also to Mother's Meg and Marion. They seemed a bit shocked and a bit more disapproving.

"Father, this is Tasa." Tasa looked upward at the man, only then realizing his true stature. Not as tall as Karia, but taller than anyone else she had met in her life.

Mother Meg stepped in before Tasa could respond. "Tasa, this is Dagda Hernunn, the Green Man." The girl pondered this. If Mother Meg was the Woman in Green was there another Penthe-style community elsewhere made up of men? Forest Mother continued, "He is our brother by blood. Mariel is our niece by Kelle and Hernunn's handfasting. You, my child, are far from your expected place." She frowned while speaking that last sentence.

Tasa heard the counsel and knew again that there were consequences approaching, but her mind could not stay upon that thought. She was trying to come up with a greeting, some sort of protocol or symbolic action appropriate to introduce herself to Mariel's father. Instead, the Green Man asked her, "Are you my daughter's true friend?"

"Yes," Tasa replied instantly. "Our friendship has deep roots, and we grow well together." The Green Man smiled down at her in the gray morning light. Mist gathered about the fading fire, dampening the remaining fuel. Smoke rose into the sky.

"You speak well. She speaks well of you." Tasa wondered when exactly Mariel spoke with her father and what exactly was said. Hernunn placed his large hands on the tops of both of their heads. Tasa felt a strong pulse of energy pass from his hand through her and into the earth. "Hmmm. A child of the dragons, I see," Hernunn said as he let his hand fall away from her.

Tasa looked at Mariel who said, "Dragons?" They looked back at Hernunn, but he was gone. Not a leaf or branch stirred or quivered to mark his passing.

"Better than me," Mariel said in quiet wonder.

18

An Agreement of Dragons

EVEN DEEP FORESTS HAVE WARM GLADES where sunlight can gleam off a dragon's scales. One, a deep white, not bright, but pure with no other colors, lay stretched fully, forelegs far forward and tail straight and still. It was he that spoke to the smaller, younger dragon.

"We are quiet now for reasons that you do not perceive. You are young and that is a strength. Yet the more time spent alive grants increasing perspective. In youth this is a lack, but not a permanent one. You can listen and learn. You do not have to agree with all you hear. Only listen first so that you understand what it is you disagree with.

"We, of the Dragon Council, tell you to be still and yet I know that you hear this not as a protection but as a restriction. Hear now why I ask you to remain still."

The black dragon looked about, deep eyes sparkling in the noon sun. He sat upright, glancing left then right and then again. His tail curled and unfurled in irregular spurts of energy. Black wings spread and fluttered, the sunlight giving them a ruddy glow as it shone through the skin twixt slender, recently mended bones that gave anchor to the leathery membrane. The white dragon spoke again. He explained, and the young dragon felt there must be much to explain in the world, for the white dragon did it so often.

"There is a motion in the world today. It is a mingling of those who came before and those who now arise. Let us say the First Men, those giants and elven, are in motion to mingle their strengths with the New Men, Gaia's humans. We, that is, you and I, but certainly the dragons, generally speaking, we are not in the same motion. Gaia has asked that we remain quiet and still and allow the humans, all kinds, to learn themselves and trust themselves and no longer seek the dragons' help in their days."

"Did we help them so much in the past?" the black dragon questioned. The scales along his form held a silvery sheen. "Did we help them often and now they do not miss our assistance?"

The white dragon said, "We did in our way. We were not often direct in our assistance. It was not always such a life that we were so physically bound to the earth. Once we were free to feel, and also to project those feelings. In such a life we maintained a balance of vitality for Gaia."

"Yet you tell me, and I see with my own vision that Gaia is in a state of imbalance now. Does she no longer request our assistance? Are we not still her stewards? Do we not still ask the same question they ask in Albion, 'Is this action for the benefit of Gaia?' When we ask, is the answer not obvious? We must now act in the humans' behalf, for their survival!" The black dragon's eyes flashed with silvery flecks as he spoke.

The white dragon lay still, pondering how his student knew what they spoke in the human communities of Albion. Or anywhere else for that matter. "Let us imagine that we do act. And what do they lose when we act in their behalf? Their opportunity to growth and maturity through testing. You fear that without your direct intervention they will become lost, either their lives or their freedom. I say that the length of living gives perspective on the matter. You are young. I am not so old as one might think. Yet I do see the longer view. Not only of the world of the humans, but also of the dragons, specifically you. Soon you will choose to take action and then you will receive the lesson of consequence. In the interest of you gaining growth and maturity through testing I will no longer prevent this from occurring."

The black dragon pawed at the forest floor. Bowing his head towards the white dragon he said, "I will not let my egg-bond sister fall to the imbalance. She is near to me again. I feel her presence. I feel more complete, more balanced within myself, and wish to enhance this feeling. In her passage from our home island to Albion she was near lost to me. You were there with me in the lands of Amen. You saw my weakening. You witnessed my grief. I will no longer allow that weakness to afflict me, nor will I allow her to continue to exist in a reduced state of mind. She is more than what she perceives, and I am also. Together we will be more." He stood taller yet remained upon the ground.

The white dragon stood up and sat near the black dragon, assuming the same posture, though taller by a head. "I see your choices ahead. I will remain your mentor. In this matter, I will not follow the will of the Dragon Council and seek to place restraint upon you any longer. Note that they tell you how to behave. Note also that I politely ask for behavior and do not tell."

Torin went still and considered the white dragon's words. For two more days he sat with Wollston, the white dragon, and they posed questions to one another. In time he took flight from the forest along the north coast of Albion. Sails of wings caught winds. He layered his flight through the lowering clouds and near to the sea. With his mind, his heart, and his thoughts, he reached out to her, his egg-bonded sister. "I am here," he said. "I am near."

****

In his reaching out, the dragon Torin learned much. The child, Tasa, was accepting and grateful once again for his presence. She felt complete, as did he, when they were together. Yet, were they together? She did not see him clearly or even fully sense his reality. He saw through her eyes then, though she was untrained in this communication. He saw through her, and she was unable to see through him. This would be rectified, thought Torin, but he saw how small, how fragile the mind of humanity was. They accepted too much of what was told them. They did not fully open to the energy of Gaia. Even those who were of the blood of the dragons grew dim in their senses.

Torin explored Tasa's memory and experience. There were bright lights there. A giant…no, two! And a dragon! Deep within the earth and slumbering in service to Gaia. And the girl did not know? Or rather she did not see, for the magic of these beings asked to be overlooked. They desired to appear ordinary in the sight of the humans, Gaia's New Men. It was a puzzle.

The lights Torin saw were many in the land and also upon the seas. Some glowed bright, some were indistinct and faded, diluted, as if in deep fog. Tasa herself grew brighter as Torin reached out through her to her world. She cared deeply for some, but not many. She did care about many, but not deeply.

He remained at sea for some days. In deference to his mentor, Torin cycled to and fro in the morning fogs and the evening mists, high in the daylight clouds and low in the starlit night. Wollston had impressed upon him the need for caution. Torin did not fully understand such a need but chose to allow this to be his action until he felt otherwise compelled. His deep desire was to reveal himself fully to Tasa. Life would be a joyous thing when he did, but for now, he understood she faced limits. If only they had been allowed to play together as babes. The thought gave him a sense of injustice committed and opportunity lost. It made him angry again at the council of dragons.

If only. This way of thinking set him apart from the dragons. He could look back in time and feel regret for paths not followed. Most dragons, if not all, rarely looked to the past and when they did, they saw only what occurred and wasted no time imagining what might have been.

Tasa should be stronger, thought Torin. She should know more. When they came together, life would be better.

His days went to weeks. Torin returned now and again to his mentor who waited patiently and unmoving in the north, near a small bay along the coast. At times women in violet robes moved about him. When near, he remained quiet, practicing stone silence. Some few of the violet-robed women were aware of Wollston's presence. Torin often heard them speak together.

In deference to his mentor, he remained apart. Torin would lie quiet in the forest overlooking the bay and listen to them in the near distance. He learned to sense those that were strong in their lineage, strong with the blood of the dragons. These were the ones who tended to them. They had granted Torin healing. They tended him after the passing of the storm. He existed in slow time then, in stasis like many dragons. Gaia gave him strength. He dreamt deep. In his dreams, he sensed truths.

Torin's desire was to be connected to the humans who carried the blood of the dragons, but he did not want these ones in violet robes to be his first contacts. He wanted Tasa. And she was not yet strong enough. He witnessed this reality now.

The women came from the place of wisdom gathering, what they called the House of the Violet Door. They spoke to Wollston of the days of the world. They spoke of the short-lived humans who came directly from Gaia. They questioned, and the white dragon patiently explained and instructed and told them tales of the ages past.

"The dragons came from the stars," Wollston said. "The giants came from the dragons. The elves came from the giants. The dwarves are giants who live beneath the earth. The humans came from Gaia's own life, her ever-evolving desire to witness diversity and variety."

"Where did Gaia come from?" they asked. And his mentor replied that some things were unknown. Gaia had been here when the dragons arrived from the stars, he said. She was immature and unaware, but the dragons tended her and made their home with her. Now Gaia stabilized and thrived. The dragons lay in stasis by her request.

Gaia's humans grew in number. Some of them reverted back to the animalistic ways. These ones now threatened Albion. The dragons did not act on behalf of the ones who are in reality their children. Torin flew the seas with new thoughts. Those ones, the beast men, would not arrive on Albion's shores. That was his choice.

****

There came a day. Boats approached and Torin sensed they carried life that was strong with a dragon's energy. Yet this was not like the dragons he knew. It was not a quiet energy of peace and stillness, but a jagged force, erratic and driving, desperate and rapacious. He sensed too that this was a different way, not dragon energy within the humans, but rather engulfing them. It was not their own, but something that clung to them, forcing its way into their frail systems. Torin had seen sickness before, in some humans, yes, but more often in animals. They weakened or went mad with pain. Sometimes they perished from the invasive parasites that thrived by killing their hosts. Torin saw these boats approaching and saw the infection the men aboard carried to the shores of Albion.

He flew near. He kept to the sea and flew just above the waves. He kept apart from the other vessels at sea but stayed near the boats of the bestial men. In this way he witnessed the first boat wreck itself upon the rocky shore and the inhabitants begin to clamber upward in a bid to harm those upon the cliff tops.

Torin witnessed the death of those beast men by the hands of the other humans. He felt the reluctance in the hearts of the other humans, a reluctance to slay another. He did not sense the same emotion within the beast men. They sought death for others at all costs, including their own lives.

While their boat crashed and dashed against the rocky shore Torin heard, in shock, the cries of children below deck as they perished in the shipwreck. What manner of human allowed such a thing to happen? For the beast men left the ship purposefully, knowing that their children were trapped below.

"Should I have saved the children?" Torin wondered. And he felt regret. If only...

A second craft sailed further up the coast. Torin sank beneath the waves, swimming in pursuit. Water was not his element, but he held no true fear. Only Tasa's memories gave him pause about being on the sea.

A port, a place of gathering and dwelling, a trading place, now lay in front of the beast men's craft and they steered their way straight to the land. Torin, looking with dragon eyes, could see the strength of the beings onshore. There were many who were strong with the blood of the dragons. Yet they did not see the approaching beast men as a threat.

Torin sent thoughts forward, seeking ones who might hear. What should he say this is? Danger? Peril? He did not always have a human word. He sent the thought of *awareness*. He felt a stirring in some, then it spread.

The beast men gathered arrows and set flame to them. Firing now at passing ships, aiming for piles of rope or sails being raised, they sought to set alight and burn the vessels on the water. They were successful, and Torin saw the crew of one flaming ship dive for safety into the sea. Others battled the blazes as best they might. Still the beast men's craft sailed into the crowded port. They were howling now and no longer carried the appearance of human, though they stood upon two legs. They carried weapons in what once were their hands. Hairy paws gripped battered blades and axes. Torin saw the sense of bloodlust and knew he could not allow these inhuman beasts to accomplish their mission.

"Human does not kill dragon. Dragon does not kill human." The words came into his consciousness with Wollston's voice, his mentor projecting communication. It was an old lesson and Torin never understood the need for such words. Why would anyone kill another sentient being? He did not understand what was happening. Only that it must end.

With a sweep of a wing Torin rose and poured seawater upon the deck of the ship aflame. Men aboard did not see him clearly as the water swept the flames away.

Another ship received the same succor as Torin heaved beneath the keel of the vessel, allowing it to splash heavily back to sea. The bow dipped, and water flowed across the decks, extinguishing the deadly blaze that had been growing.

He swam below men and women who had gone overboard. They found themselves gathered to an unknown sea creature who carried them to a larger craft for rescue. None could tell for certain what had occurred for it went so swiftly past. Dolphins? No, a whale! And yet what whale came so near the shore? What manner of sea dweller rescued people?

And then the boat of the beast men was ahead of him. They turned and saw Torin nearing. Howling, they fired arrows at him and hurled stones and rough spears. Jagged blades swung about their heads. Several dove into the sea to attack the black dragon, hacking at him with crude axes and pitted knives.

Torin dove quickly, his twisting mass causing a strong vortex to form, and the beast men were pulled deep. Torin no longer thought of them as beast men. They were merely beasts, unreasoning and savage, like the wild boar of the woods or the sharks of the sea. He twisted his body and dove further until he sensed them no longer.

In the dim light of the deep sea he turned, looking upward. He moved back towards the light of the sun. A shadow grew larger upon the surface. Detail of wooden planks, bowed in the shape of a hull, grew in his eyes. Just before he collided with the vessel of beasts, he again twisted and broke the waves just to the side of the ship.

Startled, they ceased their howling, grabbing for support as their boat rocked steeply to one side. Sea water poured heavily over the lowered side. The boat swamped and floundered.

They still were far enough to sea that those ashore could not fully witness what was occurring. They saw splashing and great upheavals at sea.

What was there? A whale? A massive sea creature unknown to them all? Many stood along the dock in readiness, makeshift weapons visible. Just beneath the waves Torin spread his wings.

Those on the shore saw the boat capsize. They heard the angry howling turn to desperate growls and then to panicked screams. No boat was near enough to attempt rescue. All had been warned off when they witnessed the fiery arrows flying.

Torin dove, twisting one more time. In the vortex the beasts followed him down until they were beasts no more. Their pursuit of death was complete.

After swimming some distance to sea and off to the north, Torin emerged and slid from water to the air. His young wings beat strong and carried his body into the sky. From three wounds across his shoulder, dragon blood dripped.

The Women in Violet were waiting when he landed in the glade. They treated his wounds with poultices and dressings. They did so without a word. Wollston stood near and observed in rare silence. To his student he offered no rebuke, presented no approval.

Torin allowed the women to care for him and when they were through, he turned to his mentor and said, "You and I eat for sustenance the lower orders of life. We do not waste such creatures, nor cause them undue pain or fear. You have said there is an agreement. 'Humans do not slay dragons. Dragons do not kill humans.' If this is a truth, then it is also true that humans do not *try* to slay dragons." Torin looked at his wounds and then back to Wollston. "I listen to your lessons well. This day, it remains that dragons do not kill humans. Shall I find us a boar to consume?"

19

Different in a Different Way

THE DAY PAST SAMHAIN WAS A QUIET JOURNEY for Tasa, Mariel, and the sisters, Meg and Marion. Little was said about the night, for all were tired. Tasa thought to question things, seek an explanation, but instead was content to walk hand in hand with Mariel along a wide and straight path through the woods, leading back to the House of Five Doors. Beach Mother and Forest Mother also walked close to one another, though at times they walked on either side of the girls, arms around their shoulders in affectionate and companionable silence.

When they arrived at Life House, consequences for Tasa's absence were postponed by stories of events at sea. The House Mothers and the elder adepts sought to quell gossip, but the tale already existed, and some even sang a song that carried elements of the story within. Tasa heard the tune and knew it was one of Robin's.

The Mother in White finally called all to a gathering and bade them silent. She stood in the center of the circle within the building of Life House proper. As Keeper of the Words, she often addressed only the other Mothers and some of the senior adepts. Information floated down from her and into the individual houses through the attendees. A rare time, then, when all are gathered for a reason other than a Sabbat. The autumnal décor of the Samhain celebration still in place reminded Tasa that she had not actually been here for the original gathering last evening. They arrived tired from lack of sleep and long travel by foot. Sleep, it seemed, was still a distance away.

The Woman in White said, "We have much to say that is of import, but we have little by way of true knowledge. Many of you may be aware of a disturbance in the world beyond our lands. There are those who do not seek to promote a peaceful existence in life. These ones apparently seek to disrupt the co-existence we all share with Gaia." A low murmuring rose. The Woman in White called for renewed quiet. "The reason for this is not a thing that I nor anyone I know can fathom. We hear that members of the Kingdom of Kane are seeking to quell violence. In legend, the giants often answer violence with more violence. We know King Kane and he is a being of great wisdom. He is also a being of great power. In mine own eyes I believe he will seek to put an end to this reported imbalance. If force is needed, he will supply such as is necessary."

Tasa thought about Kane. For so much of her life she felt that he might just be a story in a book, but now that Mother White was describing his actions as a reality Tasa was again forced into reconsidering her life's knowledge. This was happening at an ever-increasing rate. Mariel sat beside Tasa and they looked at one another. There was no fear in Mother White's voice, but this was a far different topic than the two girls could recall from other addresses given at Penthe House.

Mother White gathered herself and stood straight, smoothing her robe as she began. "On the day of Samhain, two boats approached Lyonesse. Many of you know, it is not a port and sits high on a rocky promontory. One boat seemed to purposely head onto the shore. Naturally it broke apart as the ocean tossed the vessel against the rocks. The…" she paused in her delivery, her face pressing into furrows and a frown, "the *men* who survived the shipwreck began to crawl, that is, to climb the cliffs upwards to Lyonesse. Ropes were lowered to assist them." A tremor in her voice revealed strong emotion. Tasa was not certain if it was fear or anger. "The survivors were pulled up to safety. They then…attacked the good people who sought to save them. They were repelled back down the cliffs. The guard forced them off the wall and into the sea. The attackers plummeted to their deaths, but not before they seriously injured those who were on lookout.

"The second craft sailed on. It was moving towards the Port of Leist. Warning was sent, and the docks were staffed with defenders. Arrows were fired from the craft as it approached the town. Many innocent people were struck at random." Mother White clutched her hands together, knuckles white to match her robes. There was no mistaking her emotion at that moment.

Angry tears slid from flashing eyes. "These…men, these attackers, could see that an armed force awaited them. They…they lit their ship on fire and steered it straight at a dock filled with other ships." She paused long and took several deep breaths. Regaining composure, she said, "What occurred next is mysterious. Observers say that just before they reached the dock the seas rose up around their craft. Water flowed in to the burning vessel from all sides. The ship went down. None survived. All of what is being told to you is truth. We have this part of the story from many witnesses, reliable and true.

"Some are saying that a sea beast destroyed the ship to protect Albion. Some are saying the survivors of the wreck were purposely pulled down into the water. Others have said that they witnessed these men on the craft as hairy beasts. These are stories without proof.

"There is truth in the world and wonder. We do enjoy the bard's embellishments, but here is a lesson now to all of you. Do not succumb to tales designed to frighten you. There are no reliable witnesses to any such 'sea beast.' No one can truly claim to have seen any of these attackers sink to their doom by any means other than their own folly.

"We do not have any motive for their behavior. We do not, at present, see any reason to alter our routines here at Penthe House. We teach you all to be alert and aware in your daily lives. We only tell you to continue this path of awareness. It will serve you well. We ask one more thing: Be prepared in your life. Think ahead. Live for the day but prepare for tomorrow. You observe the ants. They prepare for winter all summer long.

"It is rare that we issue an edict or give strict rulings. We offer this stern advice and will encourage you in days to come to follow our next words. Spreading stories with no basis in fact and for no purpose other than to create fear or terror is not a quality we look for in a Penthe House acolyte or adept. Following that path may be a reason for you to depart from your path at Penthe House."

Mother White concluded by stepping out of the circle. Forge Mother stepped in and gave clipped orders to those of the Yellow Path. They lined up and filed out neatly. Sea Mother stepped into the circle next and gathered her acolytes with a wave of her hand. Together they flowed out of the blue door.

Mother Meg planted herself just inside the circle, faced the scattered members of Forest House and said, "We will all leave together. Gather in the shade just inside the wood. I will join you all in a moment."

Hearth House Mother already had her acolytes near. The adepts, having stayed at their posts with the children, would receive this news from her own mouth. Tasa knew that she would speak verbatim. Hearth House delighted in the telling of tales to the younglings and insisted on a bard's accuracy. They all moved together, like chicks with a hen, through the red door. Many stopped and looked out the door before proceeding. Tasa could hear Mother Bae clicking and cooing soothing sounds. "It's alright girls. Step lively, Prisca. We mustn't get lost, Annaly. This way, Dasza. Home awaits. Cakes for all of us this night. Spot, spot! Walk right now." And the sound of her voice faded as the red door closed.

It seemed as if Mothers Marion and Meg had completely forgotten about Mariel and Tasa. Tasa knew a postponement was not a reprieve and consequences were still impending. In the emptying room, Mariel turned to Tasa and said, "Wait until I find Robin!"

****

The consequences Tasa expected from her absence at the Samhain circle never materialized. Life at Life House went on and Mariel remained close, even quietly taking some meals in the communal hall. At the end of Tasa's first lunar year at Penthe House, Theacaris, the Keeper of Words, met her on a path through the main garden. They walked and talked, and Mother White asked few questions, only pointing out the way things were and the different ways that things grew. Some plants, she said, grew well in any conditions and this, then, was how she saw Tasa.

"The people that are invited to the Albion Isles are special people. Not better, mind you, just different in a different way. They are…more in some ways than the majority of humans on Gaia at this point in time. We look long and constantly to find these ones and it is a true pleasure when one such as you is discovered." The Woman in White did not really look in Tasa's direction while she spoke, only continued walking. Tasa followed obediently.

She only vaguely realized the meaning of what the Keeper of Words was talking about.

"In the years to come you will learn many things about yourself, surprising things, though I expect you to take them in stride. It is your way. I have a vision of things; it is a way that I would like the future to look. In my visions I find that it is not probable that we succeed, at least not for many, many…periods of time.

"There is a time coming when we will be challenged by those we most wish to assist. The world will change and not for the betterment of Gaia, I fear. Do you know the question that guides our every decision, dear Tasa?" The Woman in White now turned to look directly at Tasa. Her eyes were deep pools of violet that now swirled in front of Tasa's own clear blue eyes.

Without hesitation Tasa responded, "Will this action be to the benefit of Gaia?" The Woman in White smiled and touched Tasa between her eyes with two fingers. A tingle ran through Tasa's head and shot down her spine. A warm feeling grew in her abdomen, and she felt very light.

"You may have dreams, dear, dreams and visions that you do not understand. Do not fear them and when they seem particularly real speak of them to a representative of Wisdom House or the Mother of the house you are attending. Yes, I see Mother 'Meg' comes to your mind." The Woman in White spoke the word "Meg" like she was poking fun and slightly disapproving. "In the years to come you will learn to trust these dreams and others will come to trust you. Powerful friends are gathering around you now. You are becoming a part of a larger group on a specific path. In this way you will serve Gaia by your actions, and she will be well pleased. This I know.

"In three days' time you and all acolytes will enter the period of time we call the void. You are free to attend to personal matters until the next full moon. Some will use this to pursue fun and enjoyment. We expect that you will fill this void with purpose. You are being excused from a second cycle of all five houses, Tasa. We are making an exception in your case for we feel that this will be to the greater good of Penthe, Gaia, and also yourself. We do not make exceptions lightly, only we have been recommended by…one who is wiser than we. Gather your belongings in three days and proceed to Forge House for I sense you have a gift for the Mother of Stone. Then, Tasa, your path will be on to Forest House as a trial. That is your choice, is it not?"

20
Smile on a Stone

SO IT CAME TO PASS that Tasa departed Life House and entered the void period. Tasa went straight to see Forge Mother. Walking up the cobbled path and entering the regularly spaced and sized houses and workshops was an odd experience for her. After the way Forest House branched out in many directions, and working with the constant waves of water at Beach House, and gaining the flowing movements during her time at Wisdom House, coming back to such strict regularity was a little jarring.

She knew better than to just walk in randomly to any workshop, so she sought out the receiving room and there was processed by one of the adepts just like any other job. In time Forge Mother emerged, standing large in the frame of the huge door. Sweat ran down her work clothes and off of her face and she was flushed and bronzed from fresh flames. A wet cloth in her huge hand washed away soot and ash from her neck and arms. She closed one eye and regarded Tasa with no other expression on her face. She seemed to come to a decision and gave a short-clipped signal to the girl and strode out the door without checking to see if she was being followed.

Tasa, of course, did follow and they marched to the home of Forge Mother. Once inside, Forge Mother washed and changed clothing and said nothing at all until she sat down on a large, hard-looking chair. Standing patiently and quietly just inside the door Tasa realized that there was only the one chair in the room.

Forge Mother looked at her from the chair and said, "Irregular." Her hands were on her knees, and she once again squinted at Tasa and spoke again. "I do not do irregular. I have told you that. You are irregular, and you bring irregular things where you go, but I do not think you would come to see me without some purpose. So, what is it that you want from me?"

Silently Tasa reached into her pouch, the one that Mariel had given her, and pulled the scroll of passage from within. It was now housed in a firm cylindrical casing, the kind she had seen maps and charts kept in at the harbor and the library at Beach House. Opening the case carefully she extracted the scroll and showed the seals to Forge Mother. A sudden intake of breath came from the woman at the sight of the last seal. She looked sharply at Tasa. The girl had stepped quite close to Forge Mother and now took the scroll and opened it to Nicholaus' section and the stick letters. Handing it to Forge Mother, she then stepped into the shadows while the Woman in Yellow read in silence.

When she finished, Forge Mother had tears streaming down her face. She turned to Tasa and smiled. It was a mildly disconcerting moment. To the girl's chagrin, Forge Mother rose and walked over to her and, placing her mighty arms around her, picked her up and hugged her very tightly. Tasa had been hugged before, and recently, by her friends and even some of the adepts that worked closely with her. She had never been hugged like this before. The breath whooshed out of her, and her eyes popped opened. She tried to get her arms out of the grasp of Forge Mother's mighty thews and only succeeded in releasing her left arm. Pressed tightly against the strong woman, she could only return the hug halfway. Surprised and pleased and slightly alarmed, Tasa hung in the grip of the surprising hug, her feet high off the ground.

Her head was pressed tightly against the big woman's chest, and so she could only hear out of one ear. Forge Mother was repeating her name over and over. "Tasa, Tasa, my dear, dear Tasa!" Finally, just when Tasa thought she might never breathe a full breath again, Forge Mother let her slip down to the floor. Staggering a little as she regained a full flow of blood into her lower extremities, Tasa stepped back a bit until she could loosen her neck and look up at this stranger. She never expected anything, but if she had, she could NEVER have expected this outpouring of emotion. Forge Mother was absolutely beaming, a huge smile on her face.

Another tale was added to the story of Tasa at that point, for the acolytes and adepts at Forge House knew only that Tasa arrived and departed and left the Woman in Yellow smiling for months after that. Forge Mother even laughed. Twice! The adepts that had spent years and sometimes decades within Forge House never even heard of this being a possibility. Much speculation occurred over this event and in truth no one, not even Tasa, knew what the message said that meant so much to Mother Stone. The Mother of Forge House insisted afterwards that Tasa call her Mother Stone, and not just in private.

In all her time at Penthe House and for all of her life, Tasa would recall this moment with a sense of pride, for she brought happiness to someone that seemed to rarely feel happiness.

When Tasa had looked at the personal seal of Grandmaster Nicholaus, she eventually recalled the symbol from the cover of the book in the picture above Mother Stone's desk and remembered also Forge Mother's glance given the painting when the beautiful stone was replaced in the drawer. Tasa trusted her own heart and the reward had been the happiness of another person. In later years when she chanced to meet the man in the picture, she related the tale to him, and he beamed in much the same way that Mother Stone had on that day.

21
Good Together

THE FIRST YEAR AT PENTHE HOUSE WAS ONE OF HARD WORK as acolytes were trained and acclimated to the ways and patterns of their new home. The Mothers of each house made certain, however, that their acolytes had ample time to themselves, partly to build relationships and partly so that they had time to process all that they were learning. For many, this was their first experience outside their birth country, and many were very young when they arrived. For others, those who were orphaned for various reasons, it was a time to gain trust and emotional bonding. Above all, the experience of the first year was to be positive and the Mothers and adepts were trained to watch for signs of stress in the newlings.

It was the second year that was supposed to be the hardest. There was no more adapting, and all of the members of the Order of Penthe House were expected to work diligently in classes and also in practice. Studies were often linked to tasks and results were demanded. The process of becoming acclimated was finished; it was time to learn a craft. Becoming an adept and attaching to a specific house was not expected of everyone. Many chose to follow the acolyte path throughout their days and in this way always served between two houses.

On rare occasions, young acolytes who showed particular promise in certain paths were offered trial positions within the house of their choice. They would take on the title of apprentice, but they were still considered to be acolytes. Adepts must complete at least two years of general training before attaching themselves to a single house, it was true, but many showed signs of natural ability within one or another house quite early. It was the way of

Penthe House to encourage ones to grow in their area of strength. It was the goal of many to serve one house or another as an adept. Still, the acolyte's path was always between two houses.

After completing her first year, Tasa, having been offered and chosen Forest House apprenticeship as her trial position, hastened to return to Mother Meg. The warm greeting left no doubt in Tasa's mind that the House of the Green Door was home for her, at least for the present year.

Her introduction to the Green Man at Samhain and her close friendship with Mariel left her with a clear desire to achieve an affinity for the Path of the Green Door. Her focus as an apprentice would be on the study of the ways of the woods.

She must also serve as acolyte for Beach House. This no longer concerned her as she trusted and enjoyed Mother Marion. The Beach Mother's ways were cool and measured and Tasa felt she too possessed such a way in her own life. She delighted in Mother Meg's engaging talk and energetic approach to life but did not share such a path within her. The balance between the two sisters was comforting to Tasa.

Her visits to Beach House would continue her education and experience with the sea, but her primary attention would be upon the House of the Green Door. Mother Meg began to entrust her with the carrying of packages and messages back and forth and Tasa grew to know the distance and paths between the houses well. Mariel accompanied her often in these errands.

The Mothers of each house, though they favored her personally, did not go easier on her for it. Tasa suspected that Mother Stone and Mother Marion both kept a hand in her discipline. Inwardly this pleased her. The thought that two powerful people were concerned with her individual development was comforting and she determined to do her best.

Bria had actually been in attendance at Penthe House one year longer than Tasa. Now in her third year, by tradition, Bria also was offered the opportunity of a trial position and chose to apprentice with Beach House. In this way she also served Wisdom House, but had things much easier than Tasa, for Wisdom House assigned her to assist in Karia's temple. It was true that Bria still made many trips to Wisdom House proper, but the urgency that Tasa sometimes faced seemed to be missing from Bria's experiences. Bria never traveled alone and always was offered the use of carts and horse.

Tasa's assignments often were more in the nature of speed, and she took to running from house to house with messages and small packages. It became a game to find the shortest distances or make the journeys in the shortest times. Mariel joined her often at first but learned that sometimes Tasa just went faster without her.

In her early days returning to Forest House, Tasa quickly became Mother Meg's first choice for any assignments that needed delivery or pickup from anywhere in Penthe House. Albion was a vaster place than Tasa would know in those days. That it was an island, she knew, but a far different sort of island than her home in the Ringing Sea.

For her part she stayed within the southern and western lands of Albion, which is the locale of Penthe House, though no strict borders existed. In the days leading into winter, she learned a great deal about the trails and paths that wound through forests and over hills. As winter set its heavy blanket of snow across those same forests and hills, Tasa's duties were kept closer to Forest House proper.

In the course of days, winter always turned to spring and Tasa and Mariel emerged from beneath the snowy white world happy and refreshed. The small acolyte hut in which Tasa dwelt on her initial arrival at Forest House became their winter home. Bria shared the little cabin on a few occasions when she ran errands to Forest House for Karia.

For the most part, there was little travel accomplished in those cold days. There was plenty to be done within the scope of Forest House proper. Seeds were planted and tended, leaks were discovered and mended. Shoes and boots were strengthened and repaired. Utensils were carved and polished. Woods were crafted into shapes for future use. Some of these shapes were not recognizable, but others took on familiar patterns. Curving arms for harps and hollow bodies for dulcimers, lutes, or viols were tended by adepts who had practiced long. Each time Tasa wandered past the workshop and witnessed the care and perfection being wrought, she wondered a little at the whereabouts of Red Robin.

"That old fool?" Mariel said. "He got a journeyman to take him about the islands somewhere south. He is no doubt singing to all the little, laughing lasses and thinking all the while he is important."

"He really is very good, Mariel. He will make a fine bard." Tasa chided her friend. "When he is seasoned, anyway."

"A good dose of salt in his eye for seasoning. You're not still sweet on him, are you?" The cat-like whiskers now stood straight out from Mariel's face.

"I am NOT and never have been 'sweet on him' Mariel, thank you very much. He is much too bold and besides, as you say, he has too much of an eye for the little laughing lasses." Tasa made a face and flitted about the room as she said the words.

Mariel laughed aloud. "Ah, you would be good for him, Tasa." She sighed. "You are good for me."

"We are good together, Mariel." They went quiet for a moment, then Tasa said, "I am sorry about your mother, Mariel. We have never talked about that night. I always want to ask about it, but I never want to pry. Does it hurt you to think about her?"

"I was so happy that you were there at the standing stones that night. I really was surprised that you tracked me. I had no idea you were there until right at the end. You did good. Not as good as me, but…"

"You are not answering the question, Mariel. I miss my mother often, but I know I will see her again. Or at least I know I can. She writes me notes and I write her as well. It is different for you. I don't really understand what happened that night. I heard the words and saw what I saw, but…like so many things here it was all very strange, and I do not know how to think of it now.

"All I know is that I care about you. I think you must be very sad, Mariel, deep inside. You hide from others and that is fine, but you cannot hide from me. I see you. And you see me. I followed you because I don't want there to be any secrets between us. We can have our private things, things we know about each other but respect and stay quiet about, but no secrets, alright?"

"Alright." Mariel spoke quietly. "Alright, Tasa. I do see you. Only, you're right. I do hide and I'm good at it, so it is hard to not hide, even from you. I hid from you while you went to Wisdom House. I was…afraid of what you would learn there, of how they see things and know things about people without being told. I was afraid they would change you, Tasa. I was afraid you would not come back to me. I liked you right away and I don't know why and that scares me sometimes. You are not normal, Tasa." They laughed at that.

Mariel went on. "You know what I mean. You are not like anyone else. And neither am I. I mean, everyone is different, but some are farther apart than others. You and I, we're distant from most. My Da', he's distant too, but sometimes he comes around to check on me here. He misses mother and so do I. We could see her for a while, but now, he tells me that she has gone deeper into Summerland. He says she is happy there, but not happy without us. She is waiting for our arrival someday and I think that I will see Summerland again before I get too old." Mariel paused. "Listen to me babbling like a brook." Tears were in her eyes. "I want to be with you, Tasa. I am comfortable with you, but it is more than that. I am scared to lose you, like I lost my mother. Nothing is permanent, I know, but I would not like to be without you, Tasa."

The two embraced and held each other for a time. Soft tears came and went. Tasa said, "I haven't felt the depth of loss you have, Mariel, but I do have absences in my life. I do not know my father. Mother is often aloof and busy with business on the island. When we met, I felt that some part of me was found. I still feel that something is missing, but every day we are together I feel more complete. You are right. We are different than most in a lot of ways. We see each other. I see…" Tasa did not have words for her thought.

"I see into people, in their eyes. Sometimes it is more than just the eyes. Some have a kind of glow to them, a shine. You have it. Mother Meg and Mother Marion too. Most of the Mothers, and a lot of the adepts. But I don't know what that is or what it means. I do not see it in myself except when we are together. You and I, we glow together. I don't know if we always will, but this is good right now. So, let's be together for right now and happy and no secrets, okay?"

22

A Simple Song

THE SONG WAS SIMPLE. Tasa hummed it a while without thought. She whistled a section and caught herself. Being in the woods was not a place for undue noise. Birds may tweet, sing, and whistle, but her lessons in woodcraft taught that she ought to remain quiet in these moments.

Walking from Forge House and Hearth House, she had been still within herself and contemplated the beauty of the upcoming summer. It was by no means wrong to sing a bit or even whistle, but Tasa enjoyed the spaces of silence, away from the oft-times chattery nature of her fellow Penthe House acolytes.

She did not recall where she learned this simple song. There was a basic rhythm. There seemed to be words that spoke of a young girl's heart and the affection a boy felt for her. He wanted to win her love, but she did not notice him. Tasa evidently knew the words, or some of them at least, but could not recall having first heard a bard sing the words to that tuneful melody.

Tasa cast her mind back to Hearth House and then further to Forge House. She was intent on delivering the messages to Mother Stone and then Mother Bae. She noted that Mother Bae was assisted now by adept Proticia. It was Proticia who accepted the note and framed a reply, though Mother Bae signed the missive before it was sealed.

Traveling back to Forest House, Tasa sang the simple song and wondered where it came from. She entered the realm of deep green woods and mighty oaks. There was a special scent to the air here and Tasa loved returning to this quiet glade. Despite the nature of the girls to giggle and speak together rapidly, there was a subdued nature to the noises here that did not exist in the other houses, save Wisdom House. Even there, the youngest among the girls were prone to find gathering spaces where gossip and laughter was freely exchanged and enjoyed. These were not spaces Tasa frequented.

She sang the simple song softly and should anyone have been near, they may not even have noted the sounds. Yet, the song seemed to fill the glade in front of Forest House proper.

"Oh no." Mariel's voice fell about Tasa's shoulders. "Not you too!" Mariel herself now tumbled from the branches above, landing next to her friend.

"What?" Tasa asked.

"You are singing that…that…ooohh! It is maddening!" Mariel held her hands to her ears.

"You know this song?" Tasa asked, paying no attention to the blocked hearing.

"Of course I know it! EVERYONE knows it, and EVERYONE loves it, and EVERYONE is singing it all the time! Even you are singing this stupid song!"

"I don't even know where I learned it! Why are you mad about a song?"

"I'm not mad. EVERYONE else is mad! INSANE! HE did this. It is like a disease that spreads fast and infects everyone before they even know there is a sickness." Mariel's whiskers bristled and twitched.

Tasa grabbed Mariel's arms and pressed them to her side. "What are you talking about?"

"Do you even know that you are singing this song?"

Tasa pondered a moment. She realized she had been singing quite mindlessly. Now that she gave the song some thought it was really rather silly. Why on earth would she even be singing such a tune? "I guess that I didn't even know I was singing it. The song just sort of appeared in my head. It is not very good, is it? The words are pretty…well…stupid now that I think about them. I don't really even want to sing this song again. But it is in my head." Tasa rubbed at her scalp.

Mariel continued her rant. "It is HIS fault! He infected everyone with this dumb song and made them all stupid. I rescued you. I won't let you sing this song anymore! If you do, I'll just disappear. You will never get to see me again. You will be lost without me!"

Tasa smiled at that. Mariel's drama amused her, and she knew that the threat was hollow. She gripped Mariel's shoulders and turned them both face to face. "*Who* did this? What are you talking about? If you are saving me I must know from whom."

Mariel pressed her lips tightly and narrowed her brown eyes to mere slits. "Red. Robin." Despite there being no "s" in his name Mariel still managed to make the words come out in a hiss. "He wrote this song just to torment me. All these silly girls are so in love with him. They think if they sing his song he will notice them and fall in love with them too. Buffoon! Buff. Fooon." She stretched the word.

Across the glade the door in the massive tree that served as Forest House proper swung open wide with a thump as it bumped against the trunk. This was irregular, Tasa thought. One of the first things taught the acolytes was to be quiet and subtle in entering and exiting rooms and dwellings. Seek not to disturb or distract. Seek to blend and bend with the forest. Doors opened slowly and rarely wide in Penthe House. Especially in the House of the Green Door. Who could wish to cause such a commotion or draw attention to…

"Ho! HO!" Red Robin did not shout the syllables, but they carried out, and some distance nevertheless. Tasa and Mariel watched mutely as the glade seemed to fill with giggling girls of all ages.

"Where did they all come from?" Tasa wondered aloud.

"Like autumn leaves in a wind storm. They just sort of get blown his way," Mariel said in a state of annoyed wonder. "What is wrong with them?"

They were still within the shadows of the wood and now sought to slip deeper into the shade. Red Robin was laughing loud and telling jokes. He draped his arms around one girl's shoulder then another, slipping through them with ease and subtly forming a circle around himself. The girls allowed themselves to be shaped. From over his shoulder he unslung his harp. Tasa noticed it was not in its protective traveling case.

With a few small movements of the tips of his fingers, Robin caused the girls to settle down. He sang a few lines, not too fast, not too slow, and made some humorous remarks that set them all laughing together.

From the shelter of a leafy bush Tasa and Mariel watched as the bard manipulated the girls. To Tasa's amazement and Mariel's horror some of the adepts and even some of the older women of the Green Door now arrived and stood at the edge of the circle. Smiles covered every face that Tasa could see.

Red Robin, smiling as the laughter died down, began again. This time the song was decidedly sad. Notes and words of lament and languish flowed from him and washed over the group. He was good, Tasa thought, but she knew now was not the time to mention this to Mariel.

Instead she said, "I need to get these messages to Mother Meg."

"And that old fool is in your way. He did this on purpose. He knew you were coming. He set himself in front of the door, so you would see him." Mariel spat the words.

"Why would he do such a thing? He is just visiting his mother. He came out the door and everyone saw him. He really is quite..." Tasa had almost said that Robin was quite good, but Mariel shot her a look of disapproval, "...popular," Tasa finished. "He doesn't even remember me, Mariel. It's been a year and he's been on some journey. Why would you even think that he would plot something so stupid? I'm not even expected back until tomorrow."

Mariel sighed. "You poor fool," she said. Tasa punched her.

"I am not a poor fool!"

"You don't even know. The song is about you."

Tasa went cold. She caught her breath high in her throat and swallowed hard. Her heart seemed to be in the way. It also seemed to be stopped. She felt the world waver in her eyes and felt Mariel's hands grab her arms.

"Hey!" Mariel said with alarm. "Hey, Tasa. Don't faint on me! You're not a fool. I take that back. I'm sorry!"

Tasa tried to gather her strength to punch Mariel again. She swung and missed. "What do you mean, the song is about me? He can't do that! He doesn't say my name or anything. How would you even know that? You made it up. Say you made it up."

Mariel kept quiet for a moment until Tasa gathered her wits and stood on her own. "He told me," Mariel said simply.

Tasa looked again at Robin in the circle of girls. The sad song ended, and he began a lighter tale, more of a poem spoken with gentle notes spaced at certain intervals for accent. A journey of some sort, a night spent beneath stars, a silent companion. Then, without a break, the bard started singing another tune and Tasa recognized it immediately as the one he sang in the night on their way to Beach House so long ago.

"Tasa, he asks about you. He couldn't stop asking me about you once he learned we are friends. He is stupid about you." Mariel's eyes glittered a little and Tasa didn't know if she was crying or if the sunlight just filtered through the trees at the right angles.

The song ended. Tasa thought she could sense a breeze from all the sighs released by all the girls gathered around Red Robin. Certainly, his curly locks were moved about by such a wind, she thought. She took a deep breath herself. "I have to get these messages to Mother Meg. And I do not want to be bothered by Sir Robin. Not at all."

Mariel grinned. "You mean 'we' have to get your messages to Aunt Meg! And I know just the way to do it. You ready to practice some arboreal movements?" She looked upward into the nearest tree.

"No time like the present," Tasa said.

Mariel leapt into a tree, a lower branch than she might have if Tasa was not following. Tasa took a calming breath and let her eyes soften. Lines of green appeared, and she stepped into one that pulsed from the ground to the branch. Together the girls slid upward to the fresh, verdant spring leaves and supple branches of the canopy. It was a winding path and Tasa did well, silent, though not so swift. Around the glade and above the activity they wound their way towards the higher reaches of the tree of Forest House proper. At one point there was a gap.

"We'll have to jump," Mariel said, "but I don't want to make any noise that can be heard."

Tasa looked at the gap and looked down. The height was dizzying. Far below she could make out Red Robin's red jerkin. All along they could hear him perform. Despite being annoyed, Tasa found herself enjoying the music. She looked again at the gap and said, "Too far, Mariel. I can't do that."

"Nonsense. With those long legs of yours, you could step across. Now get ready." With that, Mariel raised herself to a crouching position, pulling on Tasa's arm to follow. Reluctantly Tasa also took the position.

Just then, Robin began singing. It was a simple song. Catchy and bright. Well paced and silly with words about a boy who loved a girl who didn't know he existed. Or at least acted that way. And then Tasa heard the words of the chorus. "The Girl of the Quiet Nights" he sang, and she knew Mariel was not lying.

The girls around Robin all shouted in excitement and began singing along. Without waiting for Mariel, Tasa took the leap, landing well along the supple branch on the far side. No need for caution about noise. The glade was sufficiently noisy with Robin's silly song. A great thundering storm could be approaching, and none would hear.

Mariel followed, eyes wide. "That was an amazing leap! I've been going easy on you, but no more!" With that she sped through the upper canopy and descended to the great trunk of Forest House. High above the glade Mariel opened a slight door, invisible to any who did not know its existence. Together the girls slipped through and tumbled down a little air shaft, smooth and curving, emptying out in a hallway near some stairs.

They scampered down the stairs and found Mother Meg's office. The door stood open, as it often was. Mariel jumped into the office and said, "Look who I found wandering lost in the woods, Forest Mother!"

Mother Meg stood and laughed. The girls looked fairly disheveled from the travel through the trees. Tasa's hair in particular was tangled and threaded with twigs and leaves and even a small acorn cluster.

"So you found Tasa? She was lost and in need of rescue?"

Grinning, Tasa said, "Yes, Forest Mother. I needed to be rescued. Mariel is my salvation today." The girls were trying to stand straight, like Forge House girls did when addressing Mother Stone or Beach House girls when being inspected by Beach Mother. Tasa crossed her eyes, cocked her head to one side and whistled a few notes from Robin's simple song and together they laughed. The laughter gained energy and the girls doubled over.

Mother Meg, never missing a chance for a good laughing spell joined in, saying, "So you were calling for help by whistling that tune?"

They all laughed for some minutes. Mother Meg, wiping her eyes, walked to a table and poured some lemoned water for the three of them. A plate of pastries sat upon her desk, and she offered them around. Tasa and Mariel gratefully accepted, and the message pouch was opened and delivered.

"Oh, dear Tasa. My world is better with you in it. Don't you agree, Mariel?"

"Yes, I do," Mariel said, putting her arms about Tasa.

23
A Crew Begins to Form

A LONG, THIN STREAM OF WATER ORIGINATED NEAR FOREST HOUSE and grew to a lazy river that flowed indirectly west towards Beach House and the sea. In their explorations, Mariel and Tasa discovered a rough dock. Tied to it with nearly rotted cord was a small, rough sailboat equipped with two sets of rough oars. Or perhaps it was a rowboat with a crude sail. In either case, Tasa now found the opportunity to practice her boating skills in her travels as she took the water way back and forth, rather than walk the four and sometimes six days, depending on the weather and whether or not they were in a hurry. The boat shortened the journey to a day and a half or even a day in the right conditions and if she got an early start.

Despite the praise that she received from the master mariners and her work within the area of Beach House Bay, Tasa still felt some trepidation about putting to sea. A peaceful, well-mannered river, however, was more like fun. Mariel would often join her, and they would safely imagine an adventure as they floated downstream. It was harder on the return trips as they rowed against the current, but all in all it was more pleasure than working the laundry or kitchens.

Occasionally a breeze would be blowing in her direction and Tasa took the chance to practice with the tattered sail on her little craft, tacking to and fro on the wider sections of the river as she learned the secrets of wind on the water. The rowing served to keep her fit and strong and, after several months, her shoulders and body were well toned and her back well muscled.

The girls began this practice in the late winter, thanks to an early thaw. Not having to travel through snow on foot was the incentive for Mariel to be aboard in the first place. Being with Tasa vanquished most any other concerns she may have felt regarding water travel. Together they repaired the little craft the best they could and with Beach House as their destination, also started ferrying goods from Forge House as well as messages to and fro from Life House and occasionally Hearth House.

In her fourth month of apprenticeship at Forest House, on a beautiful spring morning as the girls prepared to depart from Beach House, they were hailed by Karia.

"Kamir has been accepted by the Greensmen for a special project," Karia said. "He needs to be based near Forest House. They will be choosing trees to assist in ship building on the Isle of the Order of the Southern Gate. Would you be able to transport him there? I would feel so much better if he were in your care than if I just release him into the wild to find his own way."

Tasa quickly agreed, but not before Mariel said, "Don't worry, Karia. I'll keep him in line for you." And she smacked her left fist into her right hand.

"Well," Karia said laughing, "better he arrives bruised than not at all."

"I'll get him there safe for you, Karia," Tasa said, taking a playful swing at Mariel, "and undamaged." She enjoyed the idea that Kamir was going to be under her command if only for the short trip upriver. What she really enjoyed was the trust that Karia placed upon her. Taking small shipments and messages was an important task, but it was one that anyone could do. Somehow taking on a passenger felt more...adult.

Karia went off to find Kamir and send him along to the little docking area. He returned with her, excited and eager. "This is going to be fun, Tasa! I can show you how to sail your boat! Da takes me out whenever he is in port and I know a lot about sailing. Even a dinky little bucket like this."

Mariel's eyes narrowed, and she pressed her lips together. "We've been doing pretty well without you so far. You just make sure you don't fall overboard. Leave the sailing to me and Captain Tasa." It was the first time she used the term and Tasa liked it.

Kamir noticed Mariel's fists curling and looked at Tasa. "Uh...oh...um...so, yeah. Sorry, Tasa. I just meant..."

"*Captain* Tasa, green boy." Mariel leaned in close, her whiskers curving outward. "And I'm First Mate. Got it?"

"Yes ma'am...uh, Mariel, that is. Yes, I got it, Captain Tasa and the rest..."

"Stow yer gear, green boy," Mariel said, and quickly turned away so that Kamir wouldn't see her smiling. For her part Tasa wanted to laugh but held it in for later.

Despite the few years difference in their age, elder Tasa and younger Kamir became good friends during her first year at Penthe House. Traveling between Forest House and Beach House gave them time together and was strengthening their bond. Tasa often visited Karia's temple, spending the night before she traveled back to Forest House, if Beach Mother didn't have any other tasks for her.

As an only child, Tasa now had the experience of someone she considered a younger sibling. That is what Karia had taken to calling them, little brother and big sister. Tasa enjoyed the feeling of being a big sister. She clapped Kamir on the shoulder and said, "Come on, little brother. You can watch us and if you have any suggestions, you just let me know. But you respect the crew, passenger boy, or I'll let Mariel toss you overboard." She smiled and gave him a hug, pulling him toward the little boat.

The trio of young river boaters was nearly all of the way back to Forest House when the bottom of the boat started filling with water. "Don't worry. We're used to it," Tasa said.

"Bail," Mariel said as she handed him a little wooden bucket.

"So..." Tasa said, steering the boat a little closer to the shore, "tell us about this Greensman thing of yours. I thought you wanted to go to sea with Master Amir?"

"I do," Kamir said, looking at the leaky bucket, "but Da says I have a lot to learn about building boats and ships and stuff before I can be a sailor." Kamir scooped water for a bit, then realized he would have to pick up the pace. Mariel joined him.

"You do have a lot to learn, Kamir," Mariel said. "How to walk, how to feed yourself, how to stand and..." Kamir launched a bucketful of water over the side, but much of it splashed on Mariel.

"Sorry, Mariel. The wind must have blown it back." Kamir didn't smile as he said it and Mariel looked up at the trees to see if the branches were moving. They were still, and she was wet.

Before a fight could begin Tasa intervened by asking, "So you are going to cut down some trees and build a ship? I thought this was only supposed to be five or six days long. That is what your mom said. Can you build a ship in that time?"

"Yeah, can you build a ship in that amount of time?" Mariel asked. "Because we're busy and your mother asked us to look after you. We can't be spending all our time making sure you don't stand on the wrong side of a falling tree, green boy."

"Ma also said that it might be ten days or maybe twelve because you never know what might happen when the Greens are involved." Kamir didn't exactly ignore Mariel. "Anyway, it is going to be a big thing I guess. The Order of the Western Grove has a lot of trees ready to fall and I probably will only get to carry stuff, but Dagda Nicholaus will be there, Ma says, and that will be something. So, it's kind of a big thing for me, but maybe not to you."

"Maybe they'll invite you to stay and help build the ship," Tasa said, trying to change the tone. Kamir could get glum, and Mariel wasn't helping. "Maybe you can learn how to patch a hole in a little bucket like this one." The water was still coming in, but Mariel and Kamir were keeping up with it. Tasa too had noted that the breeze had vanished. The ragged sail hung limp from the splintery mast. She sighed and said, "Guess we'll have to man the oars, crew."

They arrived at the boathouse just as the boat started to swamp. Jumping to the rickety dock, Mariel hauled on some ropes and Kamir jumped out to help. Together they managed to pull the poor craft enough out of the water to drain.

"I guess we'll have to patch it again," Tasa said. Her shoulders slumped. In a flash her eyes brightened, and she stood straight. "You can help, Kamir, but we'll do it when you are finished with your apprenticeship."

She knew it wasn't really an apprenticeship, but Kamir brightened at the word. "You mean it, Tasa? I mean, Captain Tasa. Can I help fix the boat?"

"It is wet and dirty work," Tasa warned.

"That's part of the fun!" Kamir said, and Mariel gave him a strange look.

"You help us fix this boat and I'll make you second mate," Tasa said and watched Mariel roll her eyes.

"Yes sir...uh, ma'am, um, Captain!" Kamir threw her a salute.

****

As it turned out, almost two weeks passed before the girls saw Kamir once again. They heard about the progress from various visitors that passed through the forests surrounding Forest House proper.

Red Robin was in the area and little songs made their way back to the girls through the other acolytes, ditties about felling great trees to create great ships for great journeys and everyone knew the chorus about the sailor leaving his lady love. Eventually all the little pieces became one song, and everyone was singing or humming it by the end of the project. Almost everyone. Mariel couldn't help rolling her eyes every time they heard the chorus. In all, the time was exciting and the mood of Forest House buoyant.

At one point, Tasa even met up with the three Oakmen from so long ago. They recalled her as well and greeted Tasa like a long-lost friend.

"Not such a sapling," said one.

"Still good foliage," said another.

"Laying down strong roots," said the third.

"Very good limbs on this one," said the first.

"She is coming along nicely, Mariel," said the second.

"Yes," the third beamed at Mariel, "very good woodcraft on this one." He patted Tasa's arms.

They asked Tasa to show them her green magic. It was intimidating, but she did her best. Together the five of them raised a seed into a sapling with Tasa bringing the young tree out of the ground by herself. It was thrilling work. The Oakmen slipped off into the wood after that and Tasa and Mariel returned to Mother Meg with the tale.

Between Forest House and Beach House, Mother Meg and Beach Mother had been keeping the girls quite occupied for a few months with messages and shipments. It was now odd to be in attendance for so long without traveling. Mother Meg found other things for Tasa to do. "After all, you are a forester first and Mariel is an excellent teacher for you," Mother Meg said as she assigned them some weeding, trimming, and gathering of herbs. The days went past and were pleasant.

****

In their hut late one evening, with the candles blown out and sleep approaching, Mariel and Tasa spoke of the days ahead and Tasa's travels. Mother Meg needed several packages and messages delivered and Tasa was supposed to depart for Beach House the next day. Mariel decided to join her.

"It will be an adventure," Tasa said in the deepening night. "We'll be away for at least four days, maybe more if Beach Mother isn't there to respond right away." Beach Mother became Sea Mother when she went away on short jaunts over the sea. Tasa's journeys sometimes stretched into six or seven days.

"We can visit Karia. Maybe Bria will be there," Mariel said. "I like her a lot. I like that she takes care of the animals of the woods. She is one of us, I think."

Tasa was unsure who the 'us' was that Mariel was referring to, but the words seemed right. "So, there are three of 'us' then?"

"Well, Karia is kind of one of us," Mariel said as she lay back on the bed. "I guess that kind of makes Kamir one of us too. But he's a boy and probably won't stay long on Albion if he gets accepted to one of the Orders. Unless he doesn't want to go. Maybe he'll just stay and…" Mariel yawned. "Oh, I don't know, and I don't care, really. Are we leaving early?" she asked.

Tasa did not want to leave early. She wanted to sleep in, but the boat needed patching and that lengthened the day. Starting early was necessary if they wanted to get to the best camping spot. Reluctantly Tasa said, "Early it is, but you'll have to wake me."

Mariel had already rolled over. "Early then," she mumbled. "Wake me."

As Mariel slipped into slumber, Tasa rose from their bed and stepped out into the late spring night. Stars glittered above, and she climbed a familiar tree.

From deep in the woods, not too distant, she heard a lone voice singing. It was the song Robin wrote when they traveled together. It sounded like magic. Tasa smiled.

****

Tasa managed to rise just before the sun broke the horizon behind the verdant forest walls. As it turned out, Kamir's duties with the Greensmen had concluded and it was now time to return to his home near Beach House. He met Tasa as she gathered Mother Meg's letters and together they went to the rough little dock.

"Remember, you promised to help us fix the boat. It's either that or you have to walk all the way home," Tasa said as they approached the little pool they privately called Boat House of Penthe House. She glanced about confused. Had she gotten distracted and become lost? It would not be the first time. She and Mariel often managed to wander off aimlessly, but she had Kamir with her. She couldn't let him see her lost.

There was no escaping the fact that there was something wrong. This should be the right place. Boat House should be right...over there, Tasa thought. No, she knew this was the right place. There was the willow, there was the oak, there was the alder, but...

The dock and her little craft seemed to have vanished! Theft did not enter her mind; it was so uncommon in a society where everyone worked for the good of the community and lived so closely together. It was just unnecessary to steal anything. If you needed something, all you had to do was ask.

So where, then, would her boat have gone? And where would a dock get to? As they approached the place where she tied up her boat she suddenly realized that there *was* a structure of sorts near where her dock had been. As they got closer, she noticed Kamir trying hard to stifle a smile. Tasa looked him in the eyes, narrowed hers, and the lad laughed out loud.

"What have you done?" she asked in mock severity. Kamir laughed more and pointed at her and then at the water. She looked back and saw that the little spring that fed the stream was now a small pool. Almost invisible on the shore, a little house opened on to the water. She was amazed. She had been looking right at it and was unable to see it.

"Green magic!" Kamir said with excitement in his voice. "Isn't it wonderful? Look inside!"

Tasa peered through a portal that was open on the side. There was her boat, polished and clean, with some obvious improvements in the hull. "I hope you don't mind." Kamir's voice was suddenly dubious. "I know it was a liberty, but we had that leak on the way in and the mast was so shaky and some of the wood was rotting, and I just asked if they could help me patch it up for you. One thing led to another and…"

Tasa smiled out of the corner of her mouth and shook her head. As Karia always said, that was the way of it with the Greensmen, one thing usually led to another. It was the way with Red Robin's songs as well. She shook her head as the thought of the bard rose unbidden into her mind.

Tasa looked inside the boat's shelter and saw beautiful lattice work of branches and leaves and thatch, and it looked like they used living trees as the corners of the walls and there were stones piled neatly along both sides of the boat, making a smooth walk for getting into and out of and…really, it was quite wonderful.

Kamir stood silent, doubt filling his young mind. Perhaps Tasa hadn't wanted anyone to touch her boat. Now the older girl was turning slowly towards him, and he felt like he may get a punch. It had happened before when he snuck up on her and scared her. He wore the bruise for a week before it faded. He didn't really want another.

Tasa walked up to her "little" brother. He was actually a bit taller than she, but now he bent backwards. He didn't actually step back. Kamir didn't want to appear to be scared. He was in danger of losing his balance as Tasa stood on her tip toes and leaned her face close to him. She gave him a swift kiss on the cheek.

Kamir really did not know how to react to that. It was a peculiar thing that boys all around the world did not like the idea of kissing girls for most of their early years. Somewhere along the way, it stopped being a bad idea and turned into something mystical. This was that moment for Kamir. He blushed furiously, started to wipe it away, stopped, touched his cheek where her lips had landed, blushed harder as he noticed her smiling and watching him, tried to look away, but all he could do was notice how pretty she was and how wonderful her eyes were and suddenly she kissed his other cheek and laughed and punched him hard in the shoulder. It was the most wonderful punch that Kamir could ever imagine, and he fell backwards laughing.

Much time was spent dancing and jumping about as he showed her all the little touches and bragged about his small contributions. This was the reason, then, for the extra days of his trial apprenticeship.

The pool was the product of a little dredging and some stone barriers to stop the flow of water the opposite direction. It cleaned up a little swampy area and gave Tasa a small pond for maneuvering in and out of the boat house. It was even designed to look like a miniature version of Beach House (that had been Kamir's idea). It was tall enough for her, but not for anyone much taller (that had been his idea too). The seats in the boat were shaped so that they weren't flat anymore but curved and so more comfortable to sit in and there were places for their feet to press against when rowing (that also was his idea) and the sail was stronger and the ropes were rerun to make it easier and he would show her exactly how to use them on the trip back and then they realized that it was getting late in the morning and it would be a near thing for them to make the midway camp, let alone the whole journey.

At that moment, Mariel dropped out of the trees nearby and walked casually up to the duo. She hauled off and punched Kamir's other shoulder and said, "I saw Tasa punch you, so I figured you shouldn't get off too easy. What did you do?" Before Kamir could respond or even protest the unfairness of it all, Mariel swiped at her whiskers and said, "Where to, Captain?"

"Beach House by way of my new Boat House!" Tasa waved her arms proudly at the new structure. "Kamir did this!"

"And she punched you for this?" Mariel asked in wonder. "I would never cross her if I were you!" She hauled her arm back as if to toss another blow his way. Kamir jumped backwards and, smirking, Mariel put her fist away. "So…boat's all patched already? Good job, Second Mate. We gotta get going, Captain! Light's getting away. Good thing we're going west." And with that the girls gathered their packs and Kamir's and stowed all the gear on board. Kamir jumped to the new ropes and with a few practiced moves the crew got the sailing vessel under way.

Kamir was a good sailor, having been raised near the sea and often going with his father on shorter journeys throughout the near isles of Albion and the Green Isle. He was also a good teacher and soon Tasa had the hang of the new ropes and the new mast, and she learned many new techniques that made things so much simpler. She wondered why she hadn't thought of asking Kamir for lessons before.

Even Mariel joined in for the occasional see, try, and do lessons that the boy taught, but mostly she sat in the front, the prow, Kamir corrected, and kept watch. Sometimes she kept watch with her eyes closed and her head forward on her chest. Daytime often brought catnaps for her enjoyment.

****

Night arrived as they floated to the makeshift dock at midway camp. A meal of some fruits and dried meats and they quickly fell asleep. The sky was just turning rosy with dawn when they awoke, or rather, when Mariel woke Tasa. They washed up a little in the stream and boarded the small boat to dry in the rising sun. It is the way of good friends that what might seem crowded to some is plenty of room for them. Mariel and Kamir were soon trading pokes and playful slaps.

The morning breeze began to pick up and Tasa threatened to give them fish cleaning duty if they didn't hoist the sail and do things to the keel and jib and other words that Kamir used that she really did not understand yet and all in all gave her best impression of a strict sea captain, even though she had no experience in strictness or sea captaincy.

The sail went up and Mariel began laughing. Tasa had never publicly named her boat. In truth it didn't officially belong to her. That she was the only one that used it and that everyone called it "Tasa's Boat" didn't make her any more comfortable about claiming ownership. Unbeknownst to her, Mariel had privately let it be known to any and all that it was, in fact, Tasa's property and if anyone had a different idea they needed to talk to Mariel. No one ever challenged Mariel on the subject.

Despite not officially naming her boat, Tasa and Mariel secretly called it, "Sir Robin." The only other person in on the private joke was Bria and all were sworn not to tell anyone.

Tasa had conversed with Red Robin on a few occasions since their first official meeting and he was always very attentive to her when they were together. A difference of age was something to be considered, but Tasa was well aware of propriety and Forest Mother was adept at making certain her son was also aware. Red Robin appeared much older than he was. He had traveled quite extensively throughout his youth, and this laid an air of maturity about him that he did not always display in private. Mariel, too, kept him honest. She was free with her punches when Tasa was involved.

The sail unfurled and there at the bottom corner was a picture of a bird. A robin. Colored red. The same bright red that now rushed up Tasa's neck and into her scalp. Mariel laughed even harder as Kamir looked around, lost as to what was so funny and eager for it to not be about himself. He suddenly noticed the insignia.

"I don't remember that being there." His innocence was true, but that didn't stop Mariel from laughing more and taking a swipe at him. Kamir had gotten good at avoiding her blows and now swung the boom about in the gentle wind, tipping the boat rather more steeply than Mariel was ready for. She entered the water with little grace.

Kamir expertly swung the boat around and let Mariel grab a trailing rope. He tacked back around, giving her just barely not enough time to pull herself aboard. The wind caught the sail and Mariel was dragged downstream awhile before successfully pulling her soggy self onboard. The sail was between her and Kamir and that was just the way he wanted it.

"So, what's so funny," he glanced at Tasa and noted her lips pressed tightly together in a definitely unamused way, "or not, about a picture of a …red…robin…" It dawned on him then and he too was unamused. He had heard the rumors and they hadn't really meant anything to him. Until now. Now he had an emotional stake in all this, and Kamir got a chance to have his first crush and his first bout with jealousy all in the same couple of days.

"Tasa, I swear that wasn't there when we…" He lost his words as he looked at her. She looked angry.

"I know, Kamir." Tasa exhaled and so did he. "It doesn't change how I feel about your gift and the wonderful work you did with the Greensmen on my behalf." Kamir felt a warmth in his chest, and he blushed. Mariel noticed and filed the information away for later.

"It wasn't there when we set sail yesterday either," Mariel said. "Robin is a tricky one. I smell a bard's magic."

Tasa sat quietly for awhile and the crew kept silent as well. Suddenly, she pulled a sharp knife from its sheath on her belt. A deft swipe of the blade and the offending picture was gone. She reached into her travel pouch slung around her shoulder and pulled out a little flat piece of folded leather. She opened it up and pulled a heavy needle and some thick thread from inside and swiftly hemmed up the loose and trailing ends. In no time it was as if the sail had always been that way and no trace of any picture remained. What exactly happened to the piece of cloth with the red robin upon it, neither sharp-eyed Mariel nor Kamir could say as they later compared notes privately.

"Not a word to anyone!" The command came from Captain Tasa and the crew nodded in obedience. "I mean it!"

Mariel secretly couldn't wait to tell Bria.

And Karia, but that was all.

Maybe Mother Meg.

24
Changing Course

REPAIRS ON THE MALI WERE FINALIZED by the summer of Tasa's first year. The storm damage had been extensive. The Mali tested her worth in the waters surrounding the Albion Isles and then took her regular passage to the Ringing Sea for the first time since the great storm.

A backlog of letters reached Tasa from her mother, Parla, and Caraphino shortly after the swift craft returned from its first long range run. She excitedly followed every word in chronological order, learning of births and passings and growths and harvests and travels and arrivals and visitors and all the things that people place in words in their own style to distant ones that they hold in their hearts.

During Tasa's second winter in Albion, which marked the beginning of her apprenticeship at Forest House, her heart was warmed by words from her homeland, delivered by the once again faithful ship and crew of the Mali. It was wonderful that regular communication had been established. Previously Tasa had kept diligent in her letters to her mother and a few others, though she knew they were not being sent. She never thought to ponder why letters never arrived borne by any other ship.

The Mali took many short runs during the repair period, testing new masts, sails, or rudders. Master Amir, piloting a smaller craft, often visited Kamir while the Mali was in dry dock.

Tasa, despite being friends with Kamir, and often in attendance at Beach House, had seen little of Master Amir or any of the crew in all this time. Embarrassed by the honors they had bestowed upon her, she was of mixed feelings as to what she would say to any or all. So she did what many young people do when confronted by a situation that they do not know how to handle. She kept out of sight.

With the guidance of Forest Mother and input from Beach Mother she had early on written her gratitude to the captain and the master of the Mali, extending her appreciation to all the crew for their bravery and service. She was generous with her praise and hoped to reflect some of the honor she had received back towards the crew. She failed.

The entire crew had written her in return and reinforced the opinions given by Captain Troylis and Master Amir. It seemed they all credited her with changing their course to safety and away from danger and death. She simply did not know how to feel about this situation.

With the Mali repaired and back at sea, the odds that Tasa would run into Master Amir or any of the crew lessened considerably. This was fine with her, for the most part, though she often thought about the strong and quiet swift craft master. She wondered of his story, where he began, where he traveled, and mostly why he chose to live apart from the son he loved. There was much that fascinated Tasa about the man and she felt not a little silly at her trepidation at being in Master Amir's presence.

****

Warm spring turned to hot summer. Tasa and Mariel explored their little world of waterways and riverside forests with the help of their own freshly repaired vessel. The small spring and pool they called their home port was merely a tributary that led to a larger river system. On occasion Bria accompanied them, laughing and speaking with the otters that lived and played in the waters.

The main river wandered slowly and grew into a larger flow arriving at the greater port of Leist. They rarely wandered that far, preferring the smaller passages. Their primary course was always to Beach House, however, and the river grew rocky and shallow as it approached the cliff-side bay. A dock was rebuilt just for them, and it was a gentle walk from there to Beach House proper. Beach Mother insisted they handle their own manifests and papers as part of their training.

Kamir, too, was a frequent crew member, much to his delight, and Mariel came to accept his presence with good grace and fun. If Captain Tasa liked him, so would she. Besides, the first mate could boss around the second mate.

On a bright summer day, the Sir Robin pulled into the little dock near to the path to Beach House. Kamir stood up and tossed a line to someone waiting ashore. The sun was in their eyes just then and they could not clearly see who was assisting their landing. The craft was quickly tied up and, as the crew jumped to the dock followed by their captain, they all stopped short in front of the man who had secured the line. Master Amir stood tall in the noon sun, smiling at them all.

Kamir came alive and shouted, "Da!" as he leapt into his father's strong arms, nearly knocking Amir down in his enthusiasm.

"Great oceans and heaving waves! You have gotten to be big for a sea pup!" Amir was laughing and the two hugged each other tightly and swung each other around. "Oh ho, lad, who is the master of this worthy vessel?" Amir was smiling and looking deeply into Tasa's eyes. She felt color rising in her face and wanted to hide, but she found her strength and stood her ground.

"Da, it is Captain Tasa! You remember her, don't you?" Kamir was trying to wrestle his father and failing pleasantly.

Amir stood strong and said, "Of course I remember her, my stalwart lookout and worthy crew member." With a wave of his arm he settled Kamir down and reached out a large, strong, brown hand to Tasa. "So, it's 'Captain' now?" he said with a touch of a smile.

Blushing furiously, Tasa said, "No sir, Master Amir. Not really. It is just a game that we play while we travel." Tasa was red-faced, but never looked away from Master Amir. She wanted to look at him. She wanted to look in his eyes. She wanted to see what he saw.

"Captaincy is no game, Tasa. Never." Amir's voice was low and steady and rolled across her consciousness like a wave. "Do you have the respect of your crew? Do they follow your orders?"

"Yes, Father." Kamir spoke up on Tasa's behalf. "We follow our captain, and she definitely has our respect." He rubbed his shoulder where, from his point of view, he had been unfairly punched by Tasa for some imaginary infraction. How was he to know she would lose her balance so easily when he simply leaned heavily against the rudder? He smiled at the memory.

"And you?" Amir leaned sideways to look at Mariel, who had retreated to the deck of the Sir Robin, ostensibly to gather gear.

Mariel, rarely cowed by anyone, now stood at attention and replied, "Yes, sir. She's the best captain I know of. Best I've served with in all my days."

Tasa wished she would shut up and promised her a punch later when she wasn't expecting it. The best captain? Not in front of Master Amir!

"That is strong praise, Captain Tasa." Amir stroked his jaw thoughtfully and returned his gaze to Tasa. "Recall what I told you when we parted on the dock after our first voyage together?" Tasa remembered the sound of the wind and the waves and the way the light was and the touch of his hand on her arm and exactly what he had said. She nodded her head yes and did not say a word.

Amir laughed a little. "Still the quiet one, I see. Let us walk awhile and perhaps you will learn something. Perhaps you will learn something of your own truth."

25
A Time for Truths

WALK THEY DID. Tasa felt the strength of this man and pondered his appearance at the dockside. Had he been waiting? Did he know they were arriving? How could that be? They were just given their cargo last evening. That morning a fine east wind brought them swiftly down the waterways to the Beach House landing. Yet here was Master Amir, and he most definitely seemed to be awaiting her approach.

A short few steps took them away from the Sir Robin and the crew. That same morning breeze had become a warm afternoon wind that gusted about, tossing Master Amir's thick and curled hair. Tasa kept her own tresses pulled back and braided. The wind ruffled the sailor's loose tunic. Tasa's own green jerkin was close to her form and only moved as she did.

"It is a time for truths, Tasa. You do not mind if I simply call you Tasa, do you? Or do you prefer Captain?"

"No, Master Amir. Just Tasa is fine." She wanted to explain again that the title of captain was one of play and she did not mean to disrespect the office it represented, but the words did not rise easily in her mind.

"Then I would count it as an honor if you would simply call me Amir. There may be other titles…" his voice trailed off. Tasa glanced up at him and again witnessed the gaze that seemed to be seeing beyond what was present at the moment.

"You and I," he began again, "we have shared something that few people can or ever do. It is a trial of sorts. It is a purification. When our lives are on the line our true selves come to the fore. Not all beings perform as selflessly as you did. I want you to understand that, even though you feel you did just what was in front of you, just what you must do. As we said, it was more, far more than what others offered. This does not make them wrong. They did not carry the strength that you do.

"Some at Penthe House question the decision Captain Troylis made when he granted you the scarf. They feel that it conferred upon you too great an honor. I disagree. Their reasons are based on keeping your personality from becoming too full with itself, to prevent you from believing you are too important and deserve special treatment.

"I know you also feel in a similar manner, that the honor is too great. Your reasons are humility. My disagreement remains, but I understand your reasons. I also release you from them. You are important, Tasa. More than you are allowed to believe here in this place. Already you have respect and privilege. You are, by the reports I hear, given special regard by some who rarely do anything irregular in the ways of Penthe House. That is not your goal, I believe. Am I correct in my assessment?"

All of these words made Tasa's heart quiver. What did someone like Master Amir know of her life at Penthe House? Why would he have taken such an interest so as to gain reports of her activity? And why would he be allowed access to Forge Mother's thoughts? That, thought Tasa, was truly irregular of her!

Tasa gathered her thoughts and said, "My goal, Master Amir, is not to rock the boat. I am here to learn what I can and eventually I imagine that I will return to Solaine and my mother. Perhaps she will journey here one day with you, and we can return together." Master Amir turned then and looked at Tasa with a quizzical expression. His deep blue eyes focused on her face, and she felt as if he was looking into her heart.

Tasa then recalled the words and tones of the conversation she overheard between her mother, the woman dressed in white, and Master Amir all those years ago. She was so much younger then, sitting in the tree branch in the dark, eavesdropping on adults. Their words and meanings were still a mystery in so many ways.

The meeting outside the door between her mother and this man, the one she now knew in a very different context, left Tasa with the impression that they carried a long history together. But it could not have been so important, she had reasoned back then and in the intervening years, for her mother rarely mentioned Master Amir, save the brief references to his rare visits to Solaine and, of course, when Tasa was to depart from Solaine.

Yet…Tasa knew in her heart that they did know each other and well. Is this what she really wanted? For her mother and Master Amir to travel together and she to accompany them both? It was a new and peculiar thought, yet something about it felt right.

Amir was laughing quietly. "Rock the boat," he said. "You are funny, Tasa." He put his hand on her shoulder and they stopped walking. Looking at each other they began to smile together. She found herself grinning wide and felt happy. Amir continued, "You are special, Tasa. Not better than anyone, but you have a truth that is larger by far than most people.

"Soon you will learn a great deal of that truth. It may hurt you in some ways. I believe you will find that storms come in many forms. My truth and your truth, they intersect. And not just at the great storm we survived together.

"You will have questions in the very near future. I will answer all your questions, Tasa, and without reservation. I will tell you things straight and true and not leave anything hidden. It is a lesson that I learned long ago. I believe you are worthy of such honesty, but it is not always an easy path to ask for the plain truth and receive it."

Despite the odd words and strange turn of the topic, Tasa still smiled, though not as strong as before. She said, "Master Amir, I am unsure of the deeper meaning of your words. I do appreciate the offer. I do have questions and I wish to ask them, but they pile up and become a jumble in my head. There are so many. I do not know where to begin."

"Let us start at this point. Please, call me Amir."

Tasa again smiled wide and took a deep breath. "Yes Master…yes, Amir." She looked in his eyes as she spoke his name and saw tears. In no way she could then explain, she too felt tears well within her own eyes.

"Amir," she said again and sobbed. The tears flowed freely for both of them then and they held each other in a tight embrace. For a time she cried and felt him also releasing his emotions.

Finally, her breath returned to normal and, though the tears still came, she spoke. "Amir, I was so scared, and you just kept at the wheel. You just stayed calm, and I wanted to be like you, so I pushed my fear away. But I was afraid. Terribly afraid, and then when we made land I dreamt of the fear."

He held her gently by the shoulders and looked her in the eyes. "Tasa, we were all scared. I was scared. Scared that I might die, yes. But more. My responsibility was to gain you and the others safe passage. My great fear was that I would fail. You prevented me from failing, Tasa. You may wonder at my attention to your life. There is a deeper truth that you will soon learn in that regard. It must begin in a different way than mine own words. But know this: I am indebted to you for your actions. Being who you are, I also am deeply proud of you.

"I say I will answer you direct. I wish to speak of greater things now and I endeavor to be just as direct, but the truths I tell you now may be a winding path.

"There are two things that form us in life," he said as they continued to walk away from Beach House landing. "One is learning, and the other is experience. When combined together these things become wisdom and I believe that you will become quite wise in your days."

They had walked a good distance, and no one was in sight. The conversation shifted since they had shared their fear and tears. As before, Tasa could sense Amir's power as they moved away from her boat at the little dock on the river down towards the end of the stream.

The river narrowed and emptied in a thin waterfall down the cliff and on into a shallow delta and then to the bay. Beyond the edge of the bay, past a curving arm of sheltering stones, the vast ocean lay waiting for the fresh water to join. Tasa thought about the gentle spring back near Forest House, the one that fed the pool around Boat House where it all started.

Amir said, "When we picked you up at Solaine, I had the chance to speak with the head librarian of your island, the man called Caraphino. He said the library was started by you." Tasa was startled at that for she had not really started a library so much as collected books. Her mother dedicated the building to house the volumes, but that was more to keep the books out of the house. Caraphino had started organizing things into a library.

Amir continued, "He also said that you were very well read. Far beyond others your age. That, then, is the knowledge part of your forming. Do you know why you were invited to Penthe House?" Tasa shook her head no. "Has no one explained it to you? Have you never thought to wonder?"

There were some who had given vague explanations to her over the years, but Tasa thought that Amir might give her different information, more facts perhaps, or a reasoned opinion. She was quiet a moment and then replied, "I have wondered. I just thought to wait and see if I could learn for myself the reasons for my being here."

Amir chuckled at that. "We all would like to know the reasons for our being here." Tasa knew he was speaking of a greater meaning than she had purposed for her words.

They had descended the cliff by means of a set of stairs, ladders really, and stood on a beach of smooth pebbles. Close by, the waterfall made soft sounds as the tumbling river misted in the ocean breezes. Amir gathered a few of the beach stones in his large hands. He rolled them over and examined them while he spoke. His tone became one similar to a lecturer, not unlike one of the adepts giving the girls a lesson.

****

"There is more to the history of our world than men talk about freely. There are two types of human on the planet. The first, what we call the First Men, were born of the energy of the dragons. They came to be in a way that is often called magic.

"The second type of human, what we call the New Men, were born of a long, natural process through the actions of Gaia herself. They are her true children in many ways. Truer than the First Men, some would say. These New Men are imbued with a similar type of vitality as the First Men, a consciousness and the ability to know that there is a past and also a future. This is different from the animals from which they descend. The New Men might not have this gift were it not granted to them by certain stewards of Gaia.

"Like the First Men, the New Men are self-aware. They know that they are mortal. They know they do not live as long as the First Men do, nor are they capable of doing what the First Men are able to accomplish. The New

Men are weaker in many ways. They know this, and it causes them fear. This does not mean that the First Men are better, only different."

Tasa looked sideways at Amir. New Men? First Men? She thought about Amir's words when he said, "what we call the First Men" and she wondered who he meant by the term "we." There was much that she did not understand here. Amir looked quite serious. So she kept quiet and listened.

"This sense of fear brings with it a feeling of inadequacy. The New Men compensate for this sense of inadequacy by cultivating a desire for power or control. They act in ways that are not conducive to Gaia's well-being nor for maintaining a peaceful community. They do not want to be ruled by the First Men. In truth, it is not and has never been the intention of the First Men to rule, well most of them anyway.

"Most of the First Men can envision a time when the New Men will join us as stewards of Gaia. It has always been the intention of the First Men to assist the New Men and raise them up, help them to find their own strengths and abilities. At this moment in history, there is...resistance to this idea, in both groups."

Amir grew quiet and lowered his head for a moment. "My own father was one who opposed this. It is ironic then that he had as a partner one of the First Men, my mother. Like yourself, I am of each group."

Tasa's mind whirled. What did Amir know of her parents? How could he make such a statement? And what of this tale of New Men or First Men? The words were unsettling and Tasa did not understand why. Master Amir, a man she respected and admired, a person she trusted, who promised to give her truth and in a direct manner, now spoke in riddles. He said he was to tell her the why of her presence at Penthe House. What did any of this have to do with her?

Amir turned to look at Tasa, took several long breaths and continued. "There is a gathering now, of those like us, who carry the blood of the dragons, and of the First Men, those who can claim to be born of the dragons. It is clear to some that the New Men will have difficulty adjusting to us completely. So we become private about ourselves. It is clear that they will fear us, for we have ways of seeing and acting that they cannot reach.

"Should any of the New Men desire to associate with us they will benefit and there is evidence that this will give them a strength beyond their days. My own crew is one that is mixed in this way and the New Men are well strengthened by their presence aboard the Mali and in my company.

"The First Men are long lived, Tasa. Some say that King Kane is the first of the First Men and I cannot dispute this. He is a giant; I can tell you that for a certainty. I have met him face to face.

"You will be long lived as well. How you live your life and with whom will determine the length. Choose to live amongst the New Men and you will live long according to their standards, but not according to the standards of, say, the denizens of Penthe House. It is our desire, my desire, that you live long with us."

Tasa heard his words and although she did not comprehend fully, she also knew that with the word "us" often came the word "them." And there it was, the concept of a separation of peoples. In her time at Penthe House, acceptance and equality were some of the primary lessons the acolytes were taught.

"It is a difficult thing for us," Amir spoke again, still looking at Tasa. "We do not desire to live apart from the rest of the world, but the New Men are numerous and often fail to see that their actions do not benefit Gaia. Above all, we seek to remain as stewards for the benefit of Gaia and this motivates our decision and our actions in this regard."

At that moment a cynical side of Tasa revealed itself and stepped forward into her consciousness. These words and phrases, "us" and "them," "we" and "they," and now "for the benefit of Gaia," bothered her. It sounded like a most noble excuse for this action, this gathering and separation. Yet, she could see no other way if what was being said was truth. Was it her truth, she wondered? Up to this point she trusted Amir and believed their truths ran together. These words and ideas confused her.

Amir continued, "I have been to many places. Far away and some not so far and I will tell you this planet…this is a beautiful world and worth our devotion. It is not a safe world, however, and nothing we can do will make it so. We can only increase our abilities, Tasa, hone our skills to the point where we respond to the planet and life naturally and are not taken unaware.

"It is why we put you into the lookout position during the storm. I suspected you had the sight, the ability to see far and away beyond the reach of light. No one amongst the crew had this. You were our best hope at the time."

Tasa remembered then, looking all around the storm-tossed sea and wishing and willing land to appear. She remembered the shift, the feeling that she was looking with different eyes and the sudden appearance of the coast seemingly very close. It had stayed close for a long time as she spoke through the communication tube to Captain Troylis.

When they finally approached land, it did not look like the land she had seen, but she did not care. At that point there was no wrong land to be on. Anything that was not constantly rising and falling would do.

Tasa remained quiet and looked out across the bay. Amir stood still, looking at Tasa for a moment longer before allowing his gaze to join hers.

"These words must seem strange to you. My timing in saying them to you may be faulty. I have little experience in the matter of teaching and guiding young ones. I choose this time because I fear you may soon be beyond my words, my…influence.

"I do not ask you to believe anything," he said. "This is the knowledge part of what forms you. You now must have your own experiences to learn your truth. Gain skills, Tasa, and accept the helm of your life. Others already align to your star, and you already lead them. Ask your questions to me and I will give you my honest perception, my truth, but you must always follow what your own true eyes see.

"I must delay this no longer. Tasa, there is a letter from your mother waiting for you. I believe that in it much will be said that can clarify your life and grant you insight to those around you. Remember what I have said this day after you read her words."

26
Letter from Home

DEAREST TASA,

In the too few years we shared together, I sought to bring balanced vision to your young life. In the two long years you have been absent from my life, I realize the balance you brought to me. I write now to offer an explanation, though you have not asked for such a thing.

I am better at speaking words straight. It is a reason I am no longer welcomed at Penthe House. There are circular ways to speech that are more pleasing, and I have never been attuned to that way of communication. So here is the story, plain and direct. I do not apologize for my errors, only acknowledge them. I tell you what is true from my perception. Others may not share the tale in the same way.

My sister, your Aunt Ikara is, or once was, the Woman in White. In those days I served Penthe House as the Woman in Blue. It is there I met your father, but I will speak more of him later.

There is much in the world that is changed since the days of the giants and dragons. When Penthe House was created, wise Brigid, the giantess, and her companion, Penthe, the Ancient Dragon, were present and active. Once this was a tale told to all. These days it is something hidden, as if we should be ashamed of our origins. These days Brigid is relegated to the status of myth. It is not so. She is real.

In the face of a changing world it is Brigid's wisdom that we sought to follow, but the world is altered to such an extent that we did not see a clear path to apply such ancient wisdom.

Once, Penthe House was welcoming to all beings. In your day there is no clear distinction between the giants, the elves, the dwarves, and the humans. This is not by design or discussion so much as simply the way things have evolved. Many people are parts of all of these races, as are you, though some are more of the early beings than others.

I say "others", and these have always been the humans. Purely of the earth and raised by Gaia from her animals, nevertheless they are far from her true energy. Being short sighted and short lived, they are more akin to the beasts of the fields and veldts.

Yet the giants, especially the one known as Kane, always felt they held potential and strong purpose in Gaia's way. These humans have not always proven this to be true. The giants, the elves, and the dwarves all speak of themselves as carrying the blood of the dragons. You carry such a thing, dear daughter. You, my daughter, are much less of the human race and far more of the elves.

I see this letter is less straight than I might have wished, but it is a necessary thing to establish these facts before I speak of my opinions. They were strong opinions, Tasa, and I feel now they were too strong. I am alienated from my community and friends for my principles. I would say that is a fine thing in many cases. Now I question the actions I have taken. Distance has granted me perspective. Distance in time and space certainly, but also distance from you, the one who taught me love.

Ikara saw the world changing. She saw the pure humans, the New Men, that arrived, and she felt they must be limited in their ability to enter Albion. Penthe House, she argued, was a place of training and not of sheltering. Acolytes were to become adepts and then proceed into the world to disseminate the knowledge and wisdom they gained. They were to be stewards of Gaia for life. In addition, they were to continue to gain knowledge and, when possible, make pilgrimage back to Penthe House to share the varying ways of the world, increasing Penthe House's knowledge. In this fashion, Gaia's wisdom was to be spread and cultured.

Those humans that were arriving on our shores were seeking this wisdom less and less. They came to Penthe House bruised, battered, and often torn. Women with their children arrived frightened and in pain. As Beach Mother, I was the one who first granted them landfall, I and my adepts. We witnessed them firsthand along with the adepts of the House of the Violet Door. Together we sought to give them safe haven and healing from their fear. We turned no one away.

The rest of Penthe House did not see them in this raw state. They saw them only after we had tended their wounds, cleaned, warmed, and fed. There was unspoken disbelief in our stories. The tales of their experiences were too foreign, too unbelievable. As I have said, I am strong in my opinions and stated my case boldly at the monthly meetings.

Ikara, who was responsible for the balance of all five houses of Penthe House, had difficulty reconciling these women, who brought little of use to our shores and had shown no previous interest in the ways of the House of Five Doors. To Ikara, and I confess I now see her point clearly, the human refugees were a growing strain upon our resources, not just in Penthe House lands, but Albion itself.

I see her point because I now have firsthand knowledge of this migration of wounded women and children arriving here on tiny Solaine in greater numbers than we can accommodate. Ikara saw the future. At the time I was privy to the quantity of our stores of provision. I witnessed the fishing boats return with full nets. Such was the present that I felt we had enough, and abundance to share. Ikara looked into the future and saw the limits and impending lack. I see this fate now, here in our home island, dear Tasa.

The world is changed. There seems to be a new presence on the continent. Your father warned me of them and pled a case for us both, you and I, to return to Penthe House in Albion. Your father pled his case and I allowed pride to respond to his request.

Daughter, when you are older you may understand the difficulty pride puts upon relationships of the heart. I loved your father once and you are a product of that love. Time tempered that love for both of us.

We knew that he must be at sea. I knew there was another that he must return to, a woman fair and strong who I once called friend. I would still think of her in that manner, and I believe she of me. Much passed that is not reconciled and my pride, mine and only mine, has prevented such reconciliation.

When your aunt, my sister, Ikara arrived upon our golden shores some years ago, she sought to strengthen the case your father presented. I only allowed my pride to weaken the logic they spoke. Yet in my heart I felt the right thing for you was to be present at Penthe House. Time passed. Your father, patient and kind, continued to reach out to my heart. Your passage was arranged.

You were prepared the best I knew how and still my pride prevented me from giving you all that you needed to know. When I learned of the terrible trial of your journey, I wept at the possibility of having lost you without declaration of my true love and the truth of your life. And still the power of pride kept this letter from you for nearly two years.

I am ashamed for many things. I am not ashamed of you. The reports of your progress are glowing, and I rejoice at the woman you are becoming. Would that the world turns safely enough for us to once again be in each other's arms.

My responsibilities to the women of this island, your once upon a time home, are deep and I cannot easily resist their needs. The same thing that drove my sister from my love now keeps me a willing captive here in the Ringing Sea.

There is more about your home, here on Solaine. Men have arrived and taken residence here. These ones are less of the humans and more of the giants and elven races, though some humans join them and are accepted as equals. These men come in response to other lands seeking succor and protection. They use our beautiful island as base to prepare for battle.

I am at a loss as to how I feel about this turn. Once I would have felt they needed to be expelled. They bring imbalance with their weapons and training. Yet they only seek to prevent a greater imbalance from occurring and growing. I see no easy way to bring balance without their presence.

You know I always sought this as a haven for women and a place of peaceful learnings. My vision was for Penthe House to continue to grow in the world and we would be the first community to carry the principles afar. Now I see the violence being delivered upon mothers and children. My peaceful nature is frayed and breaking. What manner of beasts accomplish such terror on the ones they once pledged love?

This then is what the new beings are called, "the beast men." I now see the wisdom in the creation of borders. I see the wisdom in closing the borders once they are created. Yet, what of Penthe House's first principles? They slip away from me as does my quarrel and anger with Ikara. I wish my daughter and friends to be safe. I wish for the borders of Albion to be tightened.

Is it time to add battle craft to Penthe House's curriculum? The thought saddens me, yet I would cast a white stone in favor of such a course. I now train daily with a sword and knife and sling.

This missive is far from the straight tale I thought to tell, yet it is closer to my heart and truth than the straight tale may have achieved. No doubt there are questions raised by my words. I pause in the writing to reread and sometimes the tears cause days to pass before I resume my writing. From my window, the one that overlooks the vineyard, you will recall, I see the ship that will carry this parchment to Albion arriving at dock. The worthy vessel will not linger more than a day so I must make my points quickly.

You are Tasa, a carrier of the blood of the dragons. It seems that you are more than that, for there is a society of those who know of the existence of the dragons directly. They are called Disciples of the White Dragon and claim a lineage to the Illuminators. They convinced me to prepare your birth cradle in a cavern near the ocean.

What I was not aware of was the cavern also held the egg of a dragon. Only since you have been absent from my world have they revealed this to me. This being, this dragon, has since hatched. They tell me that your birth energy gave the dragon a sense of life and reason for breaking from its egg. They call this "sparking" and it often occurs that the dragon will then communicate with the one who has been its partner in the process.

You often spoke of dragons when you were an infant. I dismissed your words. Your gathering of books and scrolls began with charts that carried illustrations of dragons. I do not know what you recall of your early days. The tales of the Illuminators drew you often in your first years. As you grew, your interests responded accordingly, and you became voracious in your studies and collection of knowledge written.

In your private times, you often spoke to someone when I saw no one else present. I believed that you were a solitary child with imagined companions. It is not such an uncommon thing. But you were never a common child.

Now I believe that there is more to you than I could believe. The men and women who follow the White Dragon now tell me that the dragon sparked by you is missing from the gatherings of other dragons. I do not know what to do with this knowledge. There are tales that accompany those of the beast men, tales that speak of dragons gone mad. Fire drakes who, like the beast men, seek only the destruction of life.

In your days I did not approach the question of the great beings of old nor did I welcome your curiosity. You asked, and I was oblique in my responses. It was somehow for your protection, or so I told myself. Many of the humans, the New Men, do not believe in the existence of such ones and to make claim to be descendant from them often creates separation and dissent. I sought to protect you from any useless animosity from other children.

In time I would have been forthcoming. Your departure for Penthe House in Albion, I felt, would shield you from the need to know these things. There is magic in the lands of Albion and the denizens there practice shifting people's vision. What you see is what they wish you to see. Reality is deeper, and mere humans are not comfortable with what is true.

How foolish I then was to send you to a place where the energy of the dragons is a daily thing and expect you to remain shadowed from your own true nature. It is known amongst all those who serve as Mothers in Penthe House that Brigid still walks that land, and her dragon sister remains near. Albion is a haven for those of the blood of the dragon and I expected what? That you would stay ignorant as a child? I now feel that my protection was more negligent than effective. You are growing now, and I am absent from that precious closeness. Yet I choose not to fail in my instructions to you for the benefit of your life.

This letter must suffice in your instruction to lineage. It is a pale lesson, and I will expound deeper at a later time. For now, trust when I say that you are descended from giants and elves, as well as some minor human concerns. The giant and human nature comes from your father. Myself, I am of elfin and human nature, though the human strain is weak and distant. Barring accident or violence, you will live long.

My sister Ikara will receive a letter in this packet as well. If she has not already identified herself to you as your aunt, she now has my permission. It was unfair of me to prevent you from her attention. It was unfair of me to make a demand of silence upon her as well. A demand that I now see kept her from your love. Though I suspect that she will have been discreet and indirect, she has likely already guided you through the efforts of others.

A third person will receive a letter from me. I desire you to be associated with her for she is wise and caring beyond other's abilities, though she is also known for her great capacity to verbal irritation when Gaia's ways do not progress her way. This one is Karia of the House of the Violet Door. Unless things have changed greatly, she can be found dwelling near Beach House in a temple overlooking the sea. She positioned herself there to see when ships arrived. Partly this was to know when damaged vessels carrying injured crew and passengers required her assistance. More, I believe, she watched for the return of her lover, the man who is also your father.

It is among my regrets that I will not say to your face the identity of this fine being. He took me from Albion when we both were in need of solace. Karia had taken a pledge to remain in attendance at Albion. Together they had traveled great journeys and her choice was a difficult thing for him to comprehend. Acceptance was not an easy state for him to attain.

I was in strong disagreement with Ikara and the Mothers of Forest, Forge, and Hearth House. In truth, Karia was my only supporter in Wisdom House, and she was not the Mother of the Violet Door. That lofty one sought a neutrality that I also objected to. Theacaris, who was then Mother of the Violet Door, was kind to me and, in my anger, I was not able to return the favor.

I am humbled at my own pride, for I did not welcome either Ikara or Theacaris when they accompanied your father to our island. Tasa, they came to gather the both of us, but instead altered their path when I resisted them. They took my child from me, and I was angered and defeated by the enormity of the argument. Only, you were willing to follow your path to Penthe House. Thus, I came to realize the decision was not mine to make, but yours.

Return to me one day, Tasa. Amir will arrange passage for his daughter without question. He is a good man. Fine and strong and it will be a blessing for you to know his ways. Know that I did not take him from Karia, only that we traveled away from Albion and came together on the journey. I sent him back to her life and dream of happiness for them both.

Stay safe, dear daughter. Learn about life. Discover the old ways. They are powerful, and you are connected in a manner that I once believed was lost. Seek Gaia's will. In a changing world her wisdom will sustain you.

I weep as I write these final words. You may see the tears that stain the fabric.

I love you, dear daughter, more than I can say. You taught me how to love the day you were born. I desire only what is best for you in this world. I love you, Tasa, and hope that you find love.

Tasa sat stunned as the missive came to a conclusion. She did not know how to think about all of these words. Her thoughts piled one atop another. Only her heart knew how to respond. Tasa allowed her own tears to stain the fabric in unity with her mother's love.

27
A Quiet Edge

AT FOREST HOUSE DURING HER SECOND YEAR, Tasa was able to develop a sort of temporary permanence. She began by filling the shelves in her hut, the one that she inherited from Bria when she first arrived, with some collected volumes. She also acquired a writing kit of quills and parchments and some inks and cutting tools for trimming brushes and the charcoal sticks that were sometimes used in the illuminating of her maps and letters. A smooth, oval-shaped piece of wood that fit in her lap completed her rudimentary desk. Mother Meg attempted to gain what she termed "a proper desk" for Tasa's use, but Tasa insisted that it was unnecessary. She liked to go off to different spots and write and draw. A permanent desk would hold her back, she felt.

One day she awoke to find a small package outside her door. It was a smooth leather satchel that was just large enough to fit all her implements and then a few more things. Straps held it firmly and comfortably across her back or could be adjusted to sling across just one shoulder and hang upon her hip. It was beautiful and Tasa loved it instantly. Several pockets on the outside opened to various sizes and as she examined her present she noted that in one pocket, just under the flap, was a small picture carved into the rough leather of the interior and colored red, a picture of a robin in flight. She recognized the leather and the style then from the sheath that held Red Robin's harps and other stringed instruments. She smiled to herself and let her heart feel Robin's presence within. It was a good gift.

From that day on she had her kit bag with her or at least very near almost everywhere she went. It actually sealed up quite tightly and when oiled regularly was fairly water resistant. Inside, she kept her most treasured possessions including the scroll of passage from the master mariners.

****

In late summer Tasa received a second package, this one delivered by a tall woman with long hair so blonde it appeared white and dressed in an orange robe, not dissimilar from the Forge House robes worn there by the adepts. Yet the color was completely different from Forge House's deep yellow. On that day, Mother Meg had called Tasa to the office, excusing her from Forest House duties for six days at the request of the Mother of Forge House.

The orange-robed adept led Tasa to a dark clearing in the deep forest some distance from everything. She carried a large leather sack across her back and when they arrived set this to one side of the clearing.

Pulling the sack open, the woman, silent and unsmiling, presented Tasa with a long, tightly wrapped package of thick, fine cloth. Protected within the fine cloth, a slender sword lay in a magnificently crafted sheath. Tasa had never before owned a weapon. She had a knife, of course, and a staff that she sometimes carried when walking a distance. She knew that some were skilled in the use of these items as weapons, but never really considered them as such. Now she was confronted with an item that could not be thought of any other way.

A short letter from Mother Stone accompanied the sword.

To Tasa, Apprentice of Forest House

Dearest Tasa,

It may seem odd that you are receiving this sword from me. I do this by way of a vision given me through the flames of my forge. Understand first that I have crafted it myself in my personal forge. It is created especially with you in mind. In the mastering of the metals I used the highest quality of fire available to me, a fire like none that can be created by human hand, only obtained by those who are friends of the dragons. I am such a one and count it as a blessing.

Young Tasa, you are such a surprise, for when I sought my draconian friend she said that she knew of you from the one called Torin. You are quiet indeed and did not mention such a thing to myself, or anyone as far as I have been able to ascertain. In these times it is perhaps the best way to be, and I am aware of the fact that I did not mention to you my own draconian association. This explains your natural ability with flame.

Please accept this gift from me as well as the lessons that accompany it. The blade itself is of dragon scale and will speak to you if you are discerning enough to hear. I believe you are. I also believe that with this sword you will shape the future.

The lessons are a forge fire. They will purify and temper you. You will be honed to fine edge and made worthy of this gift.

With deep appreciation and affection,
Mother Stone

Tasa was given precious little time to ponder Mother Stone's strange letter. Dragons? Again, she was being told that she carried an association with dragons. And now she held a sword that Mother Stone claimed to be forged through the elements of dragon fire and dragon scales. And who was Torin? She spoke the name aloud, "Torin." The sound felt right and proper. The world felt more complete, the air clearer.

The woman pulled off her orange robes, revealing a leather tunic that formed tightly to her torso. Gauntlets were strapped tight upon her forearms from wrist to elbow. Leather boots rose past her knees. At her belt hung a sheathed sword. She drew the weapon and said, "Begin."

Tasa learned nothing about her at all, not even her name, only that she was relentless in her teaching, and tireless. In six days Tasa had never been so fatigued. They never left the clearing, pausing only for water and food and occasionally sleep.

Tasa came to think of the woman as "Blade" for that is about all she would say except "Again" and "Begin" and "Arise" and combinations of those terms. "Blade" meant that Tasa was to draw her weapon. Failure to do so resulted in a sharp, flat whack on the shoulder or rump delivered by the adept's own weapon until Tasa complied. She became very fast at unsheathing her sword.

"Again" followed any movement that was first demonstrated in silence, then tried and then "Again." And again and again and again until Tasa had the motion down and then she would be given something new to see, try, and perform. Again and again and again and so went her days and nights for they would work well into the black of the sunless forest. Only occasionally would Blade light or allow a fire in the night, only if there was a move that she wanted Tasa to observe and then, after she had accomplished it, the light would be doused, and the call would come, "Again!" Blade spoke her few words with an odd accent that Tasa could not recall hearing before.

They would sleep for short spurts wrapped in long, hooded cloaks that Blade pulled from her leather sack. In the midst of dream or deep sleep Tasa would hear Blade shout, "Arise! Blade! Begin!" and off they would go. Much of the movement that Tasa learned at Wisdom House came into play with her lessons, only much faster. And with an opponent, one who did everything she could to interrupt Tasa's familiar patterns.

Mother Stone said the sword would speak to her and at times Tasa felt the sense of that, for she quickly learned the weight and balance and how best to shift her own muscles to bring the weapon into the positions Blade seemed to require. The sword began to feel like a part of her arm, then a part of her whole form. The intensity of the training drove out all other thoughts.

On the fifth day the instruction seemed to have ended. No more direction was offered. No more movements demonstrated. Instead, the day became one long battle. Blade drove attacks and lunges at Tasa constantly. They did not formally pause for sustenance but snuck a bite of apple or swallow of water during lulls in the attacks.

Her senses heightened, Tasa strove to keep her eyes upon Blade at all times. Blade did not respond the same way. The warrior adept strolled about the glade, often seeming to ignore Tasa completely. In those moments, Tasa would wander behind or slip to the forest edge. Blade would fly at her, knowing exactly where she was, exploiting whatever weakness of stance Tasa displayed at that moment.

The sun set, and the shadows deepened. Blade allowed a fire in the center of the clearing, and they fought in the depth of night, flickering shadows of ringing steel. When the fire burned itself out, Tasa watched Blade recover her cloak and roll up next to the embers. Tasa stood a long while waiting for the inevitable attack, but none came. She leaned against a tree at the edge of the clearing, just beyond the faded glow of the dying embers. In this way morning light found her.

Blade arose. She shouted "Again" and sprang at Tasa in a totally unexpected motion. Nothing like this was presented to her before. Tasa responded the best she could. A flurry of edges and sparking metals and Tasa became indignant at the trick. This was not "Again," this was "Different."

"Not fair!" she shouted at Blade, who promptly circled her sword several times around Tasa's and then flipped Tasa's sword off into the brush some distance away.

"Blade!" she shouted and lunged in Tasa's direction. Tasa ducked and jumped in the direction she had last seen her gift from Mother Stone. It felt wrong to be without it in her hand.

Blade sprang in front of her and shouted, "Blade!" and smacked Tasa hard in the upper arm. Tasa dodged left and right and feinted backwards and tried to leap out of the way and into range of her own sword. Her sword. Crafted by her friend. For her. For Tasa. All the while she heard the relentless shout, "Blade!" and watched the leather-clad woman do everything she could to prevent Tasa from retrieving her weapon.

During one roll and leap away, Tasa's mind cleared. It wasn't something she did consciously, she just ran out of tricks to try, things to think, and emotions to feel. She was exhausted, in pain, and frustrated. She wanted to get out of this relentless attack. As she landed in a crouch, the world became still. She heard the intake of breath of her opponent as she prepared to shout. Tasa shouted first.

"Blade!" A rustle and a flash and without thinking, Tasa stretched her arm out to her side, palm facing front. Time slowed. The forest glowed green. Her sword rose from its place in the brush around the clearing, flying into Tasa's waiting hand. Spinning about, Tasa met Blade's charge with a cool ferocity and skill.

Her sword whispered to her. *Left, cycle around, slip left, drop, now rise!* Tasa left thought behind and whirled, following lines of green and blue. When their swords met, arcing flashes of reds and yellows flared in Tasa's vision, like the sparks flying from hot metal hammered in the forge of Mother Stone. The ground revealed itself in patterns of flowing green energy. Tasa followed that flow and soon was driving Blade backwards. Through the ground itself she felt the movement of her opponent's footsteps. Strength surged into her, washing away the weariness of the previous day of training.

They battled until the sun set and into the evening. Tasa was sensing her teacher's every move. The sound and guidance of her weapon's voice came clear and deep within her mind. She was drawing strength and balance and energy from Gaia herself. And Gaia gave it all freely.

Somewhere in the night the glow faded. The blows against her sword diminished. She reached and sought the energy of her opponent and found only trees and stone, grass and leaves. She knew that she was alone.

Exhausted by the battle, the girl settled into the branches of a wide oak, her back against the tree, sword resting in her grasp. Cloak gathered about her against the chill of the night, she first rested lightly. Sometime in the night a voice arrived in her consciousness and said, "I am watching. You are safe." Tasa fell into a deep, dreamless sleep.

****

Upon awakening, Tasa snapped to alertness. Dropping from the tree she assumed a defensive stance. She was swift in her movements and silent. The forest remained still save the natural noise of distant birds and gathering squirrels. Circling slow and steady, her sword at the ready, Tasa opened all her senses the way she had been taught. She did not detect the presence of Blade or any other being greater than the creatures of the wood.

A faint trail came into her perception, a vague, nearly invisible passage Blade made through the forest away from their glade. Mariel taught Tasa well and the imperceptible signs came into her view. Unsure of whether she was still in training, Tasa moved cautiously. She walked a parallel track, keeping to the long morning shadows of trees and crouching low through brush and shrub.

After some travel an opening appeared in the forest. Tasa circled it warily and crept closer. There was no track away from the new, smaller glade that Blade had led her to. Spiraling inward, Tasa found no trace of the woman warrior.

Arriving at the center she scanned the ground and found evidence that something larger had lain sheltered beneath a bushy, short tree near a large stone. The pattern came into her mind, and she recalled two other stones as she approached the glade. They appeared more obvious once she looked for their presence and realized that she was in the midst of a circle of standing stones.

The pack that lay beneath the tree was gone but left a long impression in the dirt, longer than either she or Blade were tall and just wider than Blade's shoulders. No other evidence of the warrior remained. The sky above brightened with the rising sun and Tasa noted leaves freshly loosened from the treetops. Blade was gone, as if vanishing straight into the skies.

28

The Changing of the World

THE ATTACK CAME WITHOUT ANY ADVANCE WARNING. The world would come to know this way and it was unfortunate for all. The reality was that fierce beings of great force began attacking randomly and whether it was fair or not mattered little.

A general feeling of unease descended over Penthe House during a period of two days prior. The day of the attack everyone was inexplicably on edge. Two boats had gone out into the bay to assist what seemed to be a fishing boat of unknown origin having difficulty making way and achieving the dock. Three men were in the small, seemingly distressed boat. At least they appeared to be men when first seen from shore. Some on the dock quietly called to mind the Samhain day attack of a year past.

Beach Mother left her tasks for the day and walked down to the broad stairway that led to the dock area below. She signaled to her assistants and spoke in low tones. They sped away with startled expressions.

It was getting on to winter and the sea was whipping up lines of froth off the wave tops. The temperature had not yet changed, but a certain coolness was present in the air. Sea Mother was wrapped in her long cloak, and no one thought anything of it.

The feeling of unease intensified as the small fishing craft was towed to a spot on the dock and tied up tightly. The three men disembarked their craft and boldly strode past the inspectors and pushed aside the receivers and began to mount the steps. Slowly at first and then quicker, they were strong and seemed to leap slightly rather than step upwards.

A small band of women were gathering and approaching Beach Mother, who now stood very still in the center of the landing at the top of the stairs.

****

This was the scene as Tasa remembered it later on in her letters. She had arrived at Beach House two days previously. Mother Meg sent her and Mariel along with two other young women from Forest House. There was no specific errand or assignment given, just a vague "stay there for a week or so and see if you can be useful." Mother Meg did not look well as she sent the group on to the sea and Tasa expressed her concern before they left.

"I am alright, Tasa. Will you make sure that Mariel has her staff, the stout one. And be certain that A'Tienne and Kianna have their bows and full quivers. You always bring your sword, do you not?" Tasa felt the unease then and nodded affirmatively. She did indeed always take her sword with her on her travels, but this was the first time Mother Meg inquired about it. As she gathered her crew, she wondered what it was that Mother Meg foresaw.

It had become a point of honor with the acolytes and adepts of both Forest and Beach House to gain a position on one of Tasa's river journeys. A'Tienne and Kianna were familiar with the routine of Tasa the Forest House apprentice becoming Captain Tasa. A'Tienne, a gifted hunter, had taken to transporting large game using Tasa's sturdy river vessel. Always Kianna accompanied her partner A'Tienne and in this way Mariel had begun to call them "crew members," a rare title to be bestowed. While they were on a journey, everyone understood that Tasa was in the lead. Dutifully they went to fetch their arrows and bows at Captain Tasa's command.

A'Tienne brought along her long bow, newly acquired from a lad she knew in the Order of the Western Grove. She blushed as she admitted it was a gift of intention. During the voyage down the river the crew spoke about whether this young man knew about A'Tienne's current relationship with Kianna and considered him as an alternate match for another girl attending Forge House, and they spent long stretches of conversation debating the pros and cons of a boy from the emerald lands of Albion. The conversation was scattered and random and underscored by a certain nervousness. They could not shake the oddness of their orders and the strange specific inclusion of weapons in the direction from Forest Mother.

Their arrival was met with reserved enthusiasm from Beach Mother. She allowed them a certain freedom and again the crew felt the strangeness of things, for Beach Mother always had a specific project and no one was allowed idleness at Beach House if she could help it. There was always something to be cleaned at the very least.

Tasa decided that they should split up into pairs and meet twice a day to check in and compare notes. Something was up; they all knew it, but what? In this they agreed that no one seemed to know, though all were affected.

Mariel and Kianna went to hunt and helped supply the larder of Beach House with some fine venison and wild hare as well as some wild birds. They found a grove with some mushrooms that they gathered. The staff in the kitchen was excited to see the mushrooms. They were a great delicacy and had been scarce of late. For a short period of time the tension seemed to lift as word spread that a treat was to be had in the next few days. Soon the cloud descended again.

Tasa and A'Tienne kept together, walking the coast up and back looking for anything unusual. It was they that spotted the fishing boat in distress. Using a mirror, Tasa signaled to the harbor, and they watched from afar as the harbor crew set out to assist and rescue. Without a word, A'Tienne turned and set off back to Beach House at a swift pace. Tasa quickly followed.

"Stop where you are! Come no further!" Beach Mother's voice was commanding and Tasa and A'Tienne stopped automatically before realizing that she was not speaking to them. A low snarl came from below their line of sight and suddenly a figure like a man was springing upward at Beach Mother.

A whirling motion and her cloak spun outward and up above her head, wrapping tightly about the flying figure. A short staff appeared in her hands and a second figure was met with the blunt end pressed swiftly and sharply against his left eye. He spun and fell back down the steps with a savage howl.

Tasa did not think. Her sword was in her hand, and she was rushing to aid Beach Mother. From the side of the steps a screaming rose and a weird figure followed, leaping straight at Tasa. She whirled in the same fashion as Beach Mother had and let the sword spin across the beast's chest.

She saw clearly now that they were not men, but some form of animal that walked like a man. Blood sprayed from his wound, but he was undeterred and landed near Tasa. She feinted backwards and drove the tip of her sword at him. The beast rose up again and leapt high over her head. She nicked his ankle deeply and he landed roughly and with a yelp of pain.

He did not stop moving and leapt at Tasa with great force, catching her about the waist. She felt the jump and realized that they were going over the cliff. It was a great distance to the bottom and, though it was not a direct drop, it was very steep.

The last thing she saw as they went past the edge was Karia running toward her and A'Tienne losing an arrow that connected with the first beast's throat. He had Beach Mother by the neck and she appeared to be very limp and then nothing had Tasa's attention except the feeling of falling. The beast was going to carry them to their deaths.

Her sword was too long to wield easily at these close quarters. That this creature must be destroyed was foremost in her mind despite the danger that she knew she was facing.

Tasa knew that she would likely die in this fall. She did not want her death to be without meaning. She sought a way to ensure that the beast failed to survive as well. It would not live to harm her friends.

A jarring motion almost tore her free from his grasp as they fell hard against an outcropping. The beast landed on its feet and crouched in an attempt to regain momentum and leap downward again. The outcropping was fragile, however, and started to crumble beneath them.

Tasa was still thrown across his shoulder, but now her sword arm had come free of his grasp. She scraped the edge of her sword across the beast's broad back, and he released her with a howl of pain.

They were temporarily still as the dirt and stones around them seemed to stabilize for a moment. Tasa now lay on her back, stunned by the rapidity of the events and ferocity of the attack. She was looking upward at the edge of the cliff and realized that they were only about a quarter of the way down.

Karia appeared, flying over the top and descending silently and with a ferocious look in her eyes. Her robes spread out and she looked like a winged woman falling upon them from the heavens. In her hand was a massive hammer.

The beast's face was suddenly above Tasa's. Spittle fell on her cheeks as he growled and bared his teeth. Tasa had seen wolves and dogs do this just before they tried to bite. She shoved the pommel of her weapon into his open mouth and pushed it hard down his throat.

If the beast thought she would be easy prey it now had time for second thoughts. Tasa was not certain the creature could think at all.

He reared back, seeking to escape the choking sword handle. The ground shifted, and the beast lost balance. Rising from her prone position Tasa whipped her blade in a series of curving arcs. Deep cuts opened at his throat and belly. He screamed a terrible sound, as if he burned.

Claws clenched as he again reached for Tasa. Sharp nails and teeth scraped and snapped at her face and neck.

Once again, he was too close for her to effectively wield her sword. Once again, she drew the blade across his back. This time she acted from a point of strength and balance. The dragon-forged sword bit deep, cutting clear through ribs and spine. The beast writhed in dying agony. Tasa fought to throw him off of her.

Karia landed then and the man-shaped beast died with a whimper at the blow of her hammer. The force of her swing hurled him from atop Tasa and out and away from the side of the steep cliff. The body landed with a grotesque thud, crumpled and broken and very dead, at the base atop some boulders near a short stretch of sandy beach.

The outcrop was steadily sliding away from beneath the two and Karia scooped Tasa up in her arms and scrabbled sideways, gripping some scrubby vines that were growing tenaciously along the side of the cliff. They hung there panting and silent for a few moments.

Above, they could hear shouting and commotion and dimly Tasa's brain registered the fact that ropes were being gathered and secured and help was on the way. She let her arms wind around Karia's neck and hugged her tightly.

Tasa thought of her last glimpse of Beach Mother and asked, "Did they kill her? Did the…what were they, Karia? They were not men. Beach Mother, is she…?"

"Shh, quiet one, we will know soon enough. Let us first get ourselves to safety. You fought magnificently, and I am so proud of you." Karia's voice was gentle and her tone soothing.

"I only wanted to help Beach Mother. I only wanted her safe." Tasa's voice shook and her breath seemed to come shorter and harder just then.

Hands and other voices reached for her and ropes were secured to them. Gently they were hauled to the top of the cliff and there Tasa's crew gathered around her protectively, A'Tienne and Kianna standing looking outward while Mariel cradled her friend's head in her lap, wiping away blood and sweat from her face.

"Rest, now. Rest," everyone kept saying, but Tasa would not rest and kept asking about Beach Mother, struggling to rise to get to her until Karia returned and said, "She is gravely injured. I must tend to her, Tasa, and I need you to be strong enough now to let others tend to you. Your injuries are also serious, but not in the way of Beach Mother. Please Tasa, lie back and rest while we tend to you all." With that, Tasa calmed down and lay back.

She glanced to her side and saw a man with A'Tienne's arrow sticking out of his neck. He was dead. The bestial nature now fled, leaving only the remains of the human.

A woman dressed in white held a cup to Tasa's lips just then and she drank the liquid. The taste was slightly bitter, but she recognized the flavor and drank it down, knowing it would alleviate the pain that she was starting to feel in her body. In moments she was asleep.

****

In normal days Penthe House was quiet and well ordered. It was not without its moments of insanity, and, on occasion, things could get a little out of control. Usually, those times were met with laughter and the mess was cleared up and a stern lecture was meted out to those deemed responsible, and any who may have been involved, by the attending adept or even the House Mother. Lessons would be learned and reinforced, and things would return to normal until the next bit of humanness occurred.

Nothing would ever be the same after the attack. Beach Mother carried a scar across her face for the rest of her life. The Women in White could have lessened the mark or even removed it for her, but she refused. "Let it be a mark of the lesson of preparedness," she declared, and ever after wore it without comment or complaint.

A tradition arose. On the anniversary of the attack some would gather privately in the evening and retell the tale over a bonfire. At the end of the evening as the fire went cold and darkness fell, those in attendance would draw a line of soot across their faces in the exact pattern and location of Beach Mother's scar. They would do this in secret at first, but as the gatherings grew, some took to wearing the mark until it wore off. Beach Mother never commented on the practice.

Red Robin wrote a ballad. He called it "The Quiet Edge of the Sea" for Tasa had taken to calling her sword "Quiet Edge." Red Robin became very serious after the attack and visited Tasa every chance he could. She always smiled as she heard him arrive, plucking a tune so that she would know he was on his way.

Many took to carrying staffs and knives and bows and arrows. A brisk business was done by Forge House in the crafting of swords similar to Tasa's. None was the equal of Quiet Edge, however, and only a few realized at first that the vanquishing of the beast was due in part to the power bequeathed the weapon by the materials used in its creation.

Still, any weapon rather than none became the wisdom of the day. Much training was given in the use of these items and with great reluctance the leaders of Penthe House established regular drills and orders for varying contingencies.

In this way, quiet and order returned to Penthe House. In this way, a peace that was not peace came to be.

29
Reasons to Believe

WHILE SHE LAY RECOVERING FROM THE ATTACK of the beast men, Tasa recalled Amir's words to her the day that he greeted her at the Beach House dock, before he handed her the stunning letter from her mother. Before all of Tasa's reality changed.

When Amir had spoken, Tasa's world expanded. Her reality shifted, and innocence was lost. It is ever this way when childhood is given its first true look at the realities of life. Tasa first thought to deny the things presented.

At that point in time, Tasa did not yet know of the existence of her mother's letter. She had not yet learned the strange revelations about her heritage. She was not yet angered and confused by truths withheld. After reading the letter, the sense of love for her mother remained, but something now shadowed that love. A sense of betrayal.

In the weeks that followed her mother's startling claims and Amir's curious and mystifying conversation, Tasa would find herself retreating from everyone, unwilling to speak about anything, for it seemed that all she knew, or thought she knew, was simply untrue.

In any other circumstance, it would have been natural for Tasa to seek out Karia for counsel, or Beach Mother, or Mother Meg. But, if her own mother's words were true, they also knew of a past that was kept hidden from her.

Before Tasa found the strength to confront any of them in anger, Blade had appeared. In a way, the rough discipline had been a fine distraction from her tumbled thoughts. After the training, she and Mariel were kept busy until the day Mother Meg requested they attend to Beach House and carry their weapons.

Until that very moment, Tasa had been able to submerge all her anger, all the deep emotions, and postpone dealing with the confusion. Here now, in the House of Healing, she lay quiet and still, with only her own thoughts and emotions. Here they tended to her physical wounds and Tasa was left to face her inner pain. Here now she also knew, for a certainty, that the world was unsafe. Her problems and emotional confusion was quite small in comparison.

There would come a time of reckoning, hopefully a time to feel her betrayal shift back into love. For now, each day was a gift. She willingly drank the potions and sleeping draughts offered by the Women in White. Enough trouble had descended upon them all, she thought. Time now for peace and healing.

****

Tasa slept in her bed in the white rooms of healing at Beach House. Her physical injuries were serious, but were really only deep bruises, bites, cuts, and rough scrapes. She was resting and trying to be obedient in the aftermath of the attack three days ago. Now the sun had set, and she was restless.

Quietly rising from her bed, she found her long robe in the closet. Feeling just a little silly, she strapped on her sword belt and pulled it around to her back, so it would not be noticeable. Barefoot, she glided silently out her door and down the hall. Candles were placed in reflective alcoves at regular spaces, casting warm, soft light in the hallway. Tasa glanced in several rooms but could see nothing. There was no way that she could tell who might be within.

One of the Life House adepts appeared at the end of the hall and Tasa expected her to scold and guide her back to her own bed. Instead the white-robed adept said quietly, "This way, Tasa," and stepped down a side hall. It occurred to Tasa that the adept seemed to have been expecting her. The side hall was short and held only one door. The white-robed women pushed it open silently. Inside Beach Mother lay still and quiet.

A small lamp burned near her bed and Tasa noted that the oil must be one of the fragrant healing oils used by the Women in White, for the room smelled of lemons and oranges, lavender and frankincense. Beach Mother had her face bandaged on the left side. Her left arm was also bandaged and was held tightly against a straight board. A chair was next to the bed, wide and comfortable. Tasa turned to the adept, dressed all in white. The woman held one finger up to her lips and made a nearly inaudible "Shhh," then walked away. Tasa entered the room.

In the morning there was a flurry of activity as Karia and Kamir arrived to find Tasa missing from her room. The night attendant quickly calmed everyone down, but not before Kamir had excitedly run outside and alerted Mariel and A'Tienne and Bria and Kianna who were standing guard at all four corners of the building. The confusion passed swiftly though not the concern, until Karia was shown Tasa, asleep in the chair next to Beach Mother, her sword resting tightly in her hands.

****

"Good morning, Mother Marion." Tasa placed a hot cup of tea on the table on her right-hand side. Beach Mother was still having difficulty with her left arm though she was showing improvement at last. It had been three lunar cycles since the attack and her face was free of the white swaths of cloth that kept her injury protected. Few had seen her since then, but word spread of the scarring.

Many of the daily tasks had to be delegated during her convalescence, but such was the way of the House of Five Doors that there was always someone trained to take over in the absence of anyone. In this way no single one became vital to the continuance of the realm of Penthe House. That did not stop ones from being devoted to certain others.

Mother Meg had been the first to arrive after the attack. In quick succession Forge Mother arrived with a band of armed adepts, even though they had the furthest to travel, then a group from Wisdom House arrived, also armed. None of the other House Mothers came lest all the leaders be found in one spot and put into danger all at once.

All houses sent delegates, and all arrived with alacrity. It seemed that the House Mothers sent them almost as soon as the event had happened. The acolytes wondered at this, while the older adepts instructed them to be patient, as all would be explained in time.

Tasa's crew let no one in to see her save the Women in White, the Life House adepts who were skilled in the healing arts. That is, until Forge Mother arrived. She later complimented them on their loyalty and determination, and they all agreed that this must pass for an apology for the bruises suffered when Forge Mother swept them all away from Tasa's door.

Armed Forge House adepts appeared at every house and in a short time the Realm of the Order of Penthe was secured against any possible further attack. None came.

Life slowly returned to a more relaxed pace. Mother Meg granted "Captain" Tasa a leave from Forest House, as well as her crew. They were to be considered a special contingent in service to Beach House. They were also strictly charged to continue their studies and Karia guaranteed that reality to Mother Meg's satisfaction. Rather than take rooms at a distance, Tasa's crew set up a camp close to the White House of Healing where Beach Mother convalesced.

They all learned much about the healing arts those days from the adepts in white and the women were grateful instructors to the young acolytes. Mariel used her green magic to good effect in the planting and growing of specific herbs the White House of Healing required.

Tasa had finally become Beach Mother's personal attendant and rarely left her side in those first critical months. "Thank you, Tasa," Mother Marion said as Tasa poured a steaming cup of tea with just a hint of orange and honey. "How are your studies going today?" It was an old routine and Tasa just smiled. Her studies suffered terribly at first, until Mother Marion asked her to read aloud while she was confined to bed rest.

Tasa was a good reader but had never found cause to use her voice much. It was a struggle at first and she was embarrassed by her clumsiness. Soon though, she was able to read for long periods of time. Sometimes, when she thought Beach Mother had fallen asleep, Tasa would grow quiet. Always Mother Marion's voice would say, "Continue if you please." In this way, Tasa's lessons became whatever it was that she was reading aloud.

They grew close in those days and Tasa learned much about Penthe House. She asked many questions of Mother Marion, about dragons and the First Men and the New Men, and many things about humanity and life and Gaia, and always Mother Marion spoke evenly and told Tasa just what she asked and always she would conclude by saying, "That of course is how I understand things. You may have a different truth. Now I grow weary. May I have my nighttime tea?" Tasa would then pour out a smooth, soft, herbal tea and add a little sweet cream. Mother Marion would drink it with her eyes closed and fall asleep.

****

In the days that followed the attack, wreckage from several craft washed ashore. The ships appeared to be of a style used in the rivers and canals of the continent across the channel. No bodies appeared, as was often typical in the case of shipwreck. The craft did not seem to have suffered from being dashed against stone. Rather they were rent and splintered as if some large hand had torn them asunder. Talk grew of the sea serpent that had destroyed the beast men's vessels late last year during the Samhain season.

No one sought to quell such talk any longer. Events had passed from what everyone once thought of as normal. What could they believe in any longer?

Tasa thought of her letter from home, a single parchment rolled tight and kept in her satchel along with the right of passage. Each bore words that challenged her and altered her life beyond what she once believed was normal. Amir spoke of her truth and his truth and honesty. Was it even possible to believe in anything?

Tasa would stand beneath the stars and the night sky and wonder at what was true and what she should believe in. One night she awoke to the sound of a voice inside her heart saying, "I believe in you."

30

Tea in a Temple with a Dragon

TASA SAT QUIETLY NEAR THE FRONT ARCH of Karia's Beach House Temple. Outside, winter slashed wildly at the sea and trees. Sharp sleet plunged sideways, slicing long icy paths through the air, sliding on the harsh breezes as they flew in from the west. A thin sheet of ice built up along the outer porch that circled the temple. A keening sound came from above as the icy air slipped and slid through the vents at the top of the dome. The interior was warm and dry and Tasa could feel the soft heat from the central brazier.

This art of keeping the wind away with no visible barrier was one of the ancient magicks that were yet out of reach of her mind. She appreciated it on this day. The storm had intensified as she made her way to visit Karia and Kamir. She had gotten soaked by the first wash of rains, and they soon turned to sleet, making the climb treacherous.

By the time she attained her goal there was nothing dry on or about her person, except the interior of the pouch that she had received from Mariel and the satchel that she received from Red Robin. There was more magic, she knew. Sometimes she felt small when she realized how little she knew and how much skill her friends possessed.

Tasa had come to see Karia with the intent of gaining a clear truth about her life. The Wisdom House Priestess was mentioned specifically in two powerful and unsettling documents, both having been written directly to Tasa.

Of late, Tasa saw things on Albion quite differently than when she first arrived. It was as if she had been blinded to certain details of people's appearance. How had she not noticed the soft fur on Bria's face? Or the pointed tips of the ears on Mother Meg and her sister Marion? And not just them, but on many of the women and girls.

Thoughts and words, once confusing and mystifying, now led her to conclusions that swept logic away.

And then there was talk of dragons.

She could have asked Amir. He had offered. But he was away at sea.

So Karia became her next choice. Tasa was determined to gain the truth about things today. Deep inside she felt this would most certainly happen.

****

When she arrived at the temple, the portals allowed her within and immediately kept the weather out. Had she been a stranger, she knew the portals would have allowed entry, but only just so far. Into the warmth, but not with free access to the temple. Not until they were invited. Not since the day of the beast men.

Karia said she was sad about this. Once the temples of Wisdom House were open to everyone and always. Once they were shelters to all wayfarers and welcomed even the most humble traveler. Now they were another building to be defended. To this end, all trees and bushes had been cleared back and away from the walls and now all of the temples stood in the open, separate from the growth of the earth.

Tasa had entered and found that she was alone. Karia and Kamir were absent. Walking quickly and slipping more than a little down the stairs, Tasa made her way to the bath. She slid out of her cold, wet clothes and let them fall sodden to the marble floors. Soon a shower of warm water cascaded over her body, heated by the brazier and central cook fires and circulated through piping laid beneath the upper temple floor. She was below in the living quarters and had set water on the stove for tea before she went to the stone shower. A small pool swirled gently around her calves as water fell from a ledge above her. The room was designed to look like a grotto and the light was soft and blue and shone upwards through the pool and from behind the rocks that made up the ledge. She leaned against the smooth stone wall now and felt the warmth from the rocks against her back. When her body had returned to a more human temperature she stepped out of the pool and wrapped a thick robe about. It was the color of Wisdom House, a deep violet with striations of indigo barely visible throughout.

A borrowed pair of Kamir's thick boots helped her feet remain warm as she prepared a large pot of well-honeyed tea. She added a dash of pepper to her mug as she poured out and smelled the mix of fragrances before taking a sip. On impulse she gathered three more large cups of tea and added water to the oversized teapot, filling it back to the top. She placed them all on a tray and carried it with her upstairs. Some areas of the floor were warmer than others and she set the tray on one of these places. A thick cushion was nearby, and she set herself down to watch the storm.

Rather than blow itself out, it seemed to intensify. Tasa wondered if somehow the wind and the water were after her. Just outside the western arches of the temple, a large black rock that she never before noticed now spoke to her.

"It is only that the weather is changing. Gaia herself is changing. She has done so before. You must not take it personally." Tasa smiled at the voice.

"Is that what you believe? What if that is not what I believe? Can my truth be true and yours also, even though they are not in agreement?" Tasa watched her rock closely and saw the eye open slightly. The mouth also stretched in what she interpreted as a smile.

"Who says they are not in agreement? Perhaps Gaia is changing her weather just to get you! That may make sense to you, but it does not to me. I believe that Gaia likes you." A head formed, and the rock took on the shape of a dragon. Tasa felt no surprise. She felt that very little could surprise her anymore, just some things were more unexpected than others.

"The simplest solution is usually closest to the correct one, I know." Tasa repeated the words she learned from her short time at Forge House.

"But not always the correct one, Tasa. Some things are unimaginably fantastic to our perceptions and the easiest answer that we can conceive of is limited to what we know. We know so little." The dragon's voice was wistful.

"Like your name? We have never been properly introduced," Tasa scolded with a smile on her face.

"Shall I wait until you and Bria are together, like The Robin had to?" Tasa was surprised. How did the dragon know that?

"No, I will accept an introduction now." She kept her voice low and steady, another skill she learned in her time at Penthe House.

"I am called Torin." The dragon spoke softly. Tasa wondered how she could hear him above the wind and from this distance. "I was present at your birth, and I am in your thoughts when you wish me to be. That is not how I know about the bard. I have been watching over you for some time now. I am sorry I was not there when you were attacked. There were other…matters that commanded my attention."

Tasa did not follow that line of thought despite the questions it raised. She did file it away in her thoughts for later. Did the dragon know that she had done that? "Are you not affected by the weather?" she asked.

"Less than many," he replied. "Though I miss the sun of our island. Don't you?"

Perhaps he already knew the answer to that question too. Tasa had much to ponder about this being. She looked around the wide circular area inside. "Perhaps you would like to come in by the fire? Do you drink tea?"

"It is not something that I have ever been offered. I would like to try this if you would allow it." Torin turned and now sat looking openly at Tasa. He did not look so big, as she might have thought a dragon should look. "I am young and have yet to achieve my full length. I am told my father and mother are both moderately sized and I should think that I will not grow much beyond them, if at all. You are certain that it will be approved by the priestess when she returns? I should not wish to cross so great a warrior as she."

Karia a great warrior? What did Torin know of the priestess' past? Torin raised many questions in Tasa's head. "Please enter. I will take the responsibility for your presence." With that Torin entered the temple. As he walked forward, he shook slightly just at the portal and attempted to remove as much of the water from his form as possible.

"I do not wish to bring the storm waters with me. Will you allow me to remove the moisture in my own way? It will heat up the interior just a bit." Tasa's curiosity was high and getting higher all the time. She nodded yes to Torin's request.

His wings arced outward slightly, and he ducked his narrow head. Torin's tail stretched backwards and out of the building, and he inhaled deeply of the air above the brazier. Flames from the coals flared up and burned brightly, swirling into his nostrils. Torin's body started to glow, and the room became slightly brighter. Steam rose from the dragon.

Torin pulled his wings closer and closer into his body and slowly pulled his tail into the temple. The water that had pooled beneath him also steamed from the floor. Humidity and heat rose within the walls. Tasa loosened her robe. Torin exhaled carefully back into the brazier. For months to come the fire burned without additional fuel and it would be years before the stewards of the temple needed to tend the fire completely.

Tasa poured some tea into the largest of the three mugs she brought from the kitchen below. She paused slightly as she wondered what it had been that made her bring three mugs in addition to her own. Torin sat down facing the same direction that Tasa had been facing, outward with a view of the wind-lashed ocean. He reached for the cup on the floor next to her and picked it up in his fore claw. An opposable finger like a human thumb allowed him to hold the mug steady. Being close and next to him, Tasa realized that he was not so small as she might have thought at first. The room seemed to expand to accommodate the dragon.

He raised the tea to his mouth and a long slender tongue slipped between many sharp teeth and lapped the hot fluid. "It tastes slightly different than yours smells," he observed.

"I pepper mine," Tasa said. "Not everyone appreciates that. I only pepper my cup." There was something a little surreal about all of this and Tasa wondered if perhaps she had fallen asleep and was dreaming.

"I should like to try it with pepper the next time. It is delicious as it is, however." Torin lapped a little more. "I can only hear you when you direct your thoughts towards me. Or when you speak out loud of course. Sometimes you do think very loudly, and I often hear those thoughts as well, but I do try to respect your privacy." They sat in silence for awhile watching while the wind bent the trees, and the rain soaked the earth. The ocean waves looked frightening even from far above.

"I tried to get to you." Torin was very quiet, his voice almost a whisper. "I was still in the lands of the Ringing Sea. The Order had asked me to stay. I was receiving instruction and lessons. They assured me you would be alright. I heard your fear and tried to find you in the storm. Had you been trained to hear me as well...I have some issues with how you have been...educated, trained…I am not here with the approval of the council. You should know that."

Tasa did not know what council he was talking about. She thought about it for a while. She decided she did not care for the council's approval.

There was something about sitting here with Torin that seemed familiar and comfortable. She recalled Forge Mother's words, *"Little Tasa, you are such a surprise, for when I sought my draconian friend she said that she knew of you from the one called Torin."* There was much Tasa did not know about herself it seemed.

"If it is my decision, Torin, I would like you to remain with me. I believe there is much you can teach me. I do not know how your presence will be accepted at Penthe House, however." Tasa reached out and laid her hand on the dragon's arm. It was a gesture of friendship and it seemed right.

"It seems we share a belief again." Torin spoke and there was laughter in his voice. "We must be subtle, for the presence of a dragon is not always viewed as welcome in the world these days." He became serious again. "I believe you know how to remain private about things. I believe I will stay, for there is much that you can also teach me. Our first test will begin now, however."

At that moment Karia and Kamir stumbled into the temple, dripping and gasping. They held large empty cloth bags in their hands, the bags they used when they emptied their traps of small game.

"Olorin's staff and Berggeist's beard!" Tasa had heard Karia in high temper before and always enjoyed the curses she came up with. She had yet to gather the courage to use any of them herself. It was a game that she and Bria played, counting the different legendary beings that Karia incorporated into her vocabulary when she was angered. It was not often that Karia showed anyone this side of herself and most that knew her from her role as Wisdom House Priestess would not have thought such a thing possible from this calm and peaceful personage.

Now Karia threw down her capture bags and pushed her long, wet hair from her face. Kamir wisely stayed out of his mother's way during these moments and now stood well back from the scene. He had raised his eyes and taken in the visitors that awaited them.

"Ainu's truth! No game and the worst weather of the year and wet, wet, WET! Tiamat's tablets! The animals are out there right now laughing at us, Kamir! They were smart enough to stay out of the traps and to stay sheltered, warm and dry! Are we smart? Anguta's arm we...are...the...least..." Karia finally realized the presence of others and lost all her momentum as she raised her eyes to take in the dragon that was calmly sitting with Tasa.

"I made some tea. Would you care to join us?" Tasa smiled.

****

Torin helped warm the tea and offered to do the same for both Karia and Kamir. They politely declined the privilege, not certain just how they would fare being warmed by a dragon. They did accept the offer of hot tea.

Torin held the kettle in both of his front hands for a moment and when Tasa poured out, the brew was steaming. After that Torin returned to the brazier. Without seeming to do anything except stare at the flames, the coals grew bright, and the temperature of the interior rose a few degrees. Tasa excused herself and darted down the stairs to gather some dry clothes for Karia and Kamir.

She stumbled slightly as she ran back upstairs, tripping on Karia's robe. No matter how much she lifted she still couldn't seem to get all of it wrapped in her arms. By the time she got back, Kamir's natural boyness had overcome any discomfort at the appearance of a dragon in his home. He stood next to Torin, looking up and dripping.

"Yes," Torin was saying to him, "I believe that I am a real dragon." Tasa could not believe that Kamir would ask such a boneheaded question and gave him a half-hearted punch as she went past. She tossed his robe at him and smiled when he missed the catch.

"Ow! What was that for? I only meant, you know, was I dreaming or something!" Kamir rubbed his shoulder for effect more than pain. He had taken much more serious blows from her. Now it was just a matter of indignity.

"And you expected a dragon in your dreams to say what?" Tasa was enjoying the whole scene immensely. Karia stood still where she had stopped, looking at Torin with something between suspicion and disbelief. She had not regained her ability to speak. Tasa fussed with Karia's cloak clasp and pulled wet over-clothes away from the priestess' form. She had to reach high to pull anything from Karia's shoulders.

Over her own shoulder Tasa had a large towel which she now tried to implement in drying Karia's long hair. She was able to reach about halfway up. The priestess took the towel absently and finally turned to look at Tasa.

"I hope you don't mind my inviting him in; he's a friend from home." Tasa was close to laughing at Karia. Taking the towel away from the acolyte was a way for Karia to try and regain her proper standing and a semblance of composure and control. It was hopeless at this point, but she was determined.

"So…you have a friend from home, and it is a dragon." Karia tried to look away and turn her eyes to Tasa.

"He," Tasa replied. "He is a dragon. His name is Torin. He is quite funny, when you get to know him."

"Funny. Yes, hmmm, and what brings Torin here to see you?" Karia was almost straining to not look Torin's way. Her neck muscles were bunching beneath her pale skin.

"You can talk to him if you want," Tasa teased. "He won't bite."

"Bite. Yes, hmmm, er, hello, uh, Torin is it?" Karia was striving now for nonchalance. Torin nodded "yes" in the manner of a human. He seemed to do many things in the manner of a human. "Well, um, what, that is, why have you traveled all this way to visit Tasa?"

The dragon lapped more tea, revealing his long row of teeth. "Well, in her letters she spoke of the lovely weather and I wanted to see it for myself."

It took Karia a moment to realize that she was being teased by both friend and dragon. She had to process the thoughts one by one. A dragon. Drinking tea. From a cup. Her cup. Here at the temple of the Wisdom House. With Tasa. Her friend. And his friend. And she wrote the dragon letters. The dragon could read. Lovely weather…

Just then the wind screamed outside, and sleet pelted the roof. "Weather," she spoke aloud, and the spell was broken. Karia regained her composure as Tasa laughed loudly in her direction.

"Yes, well, all and good to make fun at the expense of your host. I don't suppose you've brought any fresh meat with you? I hope dragons like beans and rice, perhaps a little barley for dinner. That's all we have to share." Karia had a little bit of a disapproving look about her, but Tasa could tell that she was just put out at being surprised.

"I am sorry if my presence surprised you, Giantess." Torin spoke low and offered to pour more tea for Karia. She declined, but Kamir held his empty cup out. Tasa looked sharply at Torin, had he heard her thoughts? And what did he call Karia?

"It is not so common as it once was to see members of the dragoncy," Karia said, walking towards Torin. "At least you didn't make a mess. The last dragon I associated with was less than tidy. What really brings you around, Torin?"

"My reason really is Tasa. She is one of the descendants, you know." Torin spoke while glancing at Tasa.

"Yes, I know. Nicholaus told me. He said I was to help her make her way here, see to it that she learned well. Mother too. He did not mention draconian assistance was available." Tasa looked back and forth at Karia and Torin as they talked about her and many things that she was unaware of. Nicholaus? Mother? There was always a certain strangeness to her experiences at Penthe House. What was this about a giantess? Again, what she had once believed she felt now would be challenged and altered. Inwardly she prepared for a new truth to appear. After all, it was why she had come to Karia.

"My assistance is not necessarily official. You should know that before you have any further conversation with your parents. I came because Tasa is a friend to this dragon whether she understands it or not. I came because I have heard of too many close calls during her stay here. I came because it is so boring on that island with all those men running about. I can hardly go anywhere or do anything without being seen. Mostly they do not see me. They cannot see what they do not believe in anyway." A low sigh rumbled from his chest and Kamir's hair blew about.

"Hey!" Kamir patted his head. It was steaming.

"My apologies, youngling!" Torin was appalled at his clumsiness.

"Hey!" Kamir was offended. "I'm not a youngling! I took the apprentice oaths for the Order of the Southern Gate!" He looked over at Tasa, saw the surprise in her eyes and lost some of his bluster. "I'm sorry. I was going to tell you when I saw you."

Tasa smiled at him. This was good news. It meant that Kamir was getting serious about things.

"My apologies, then, to a future journeyman of the Southern Gate! You will do well, I am certain. I know of your father and he is of the finest of humans. Though he does not yet know me, I have had occasion to count him as a friend. May I count you as a friend also?" Torin spoke directly at Kamir, whose wet hair was now dry in the front. It stuck straight up and looked quite silly.

Torin knew about Amir? There was definitely going to be a clarification session later, thought Tasa.

Karia brushed Kamir's hair back in place and he tried to dodge her motherly ministrations. "Well," she said, "I am hungry and bid you welcome, Torin of the Isles of the Ringing Sea. You are a surprise, but no more so than our friend of the Quiet Nights over there." Karia dipped her head towards Tasa. "I apologize for such meager fare, but there are plenty of the grains to go around if you wish to join us. I am going to prepare our dinner now and assume that everyone will be spending the night." The wind threw more sleet against the building, as if to emphasize the folly of travel on a night like this.

Tasa walked over to Torin. "Will you stay? Please."

"Of course, my friend. There are many questions in your heart and I have many answers to share." Torin lowered his head and was now face to face with her. Now he lowered his voice as well, glancing at the retreating forms of Karia and Kamir as they descended to the lower levels. "I hope you didn't leave a mess." Tasa thought of her wet clothes still lying on the floor, quickly excused herself, and ran after the others.

****

Things went quickly in the lower living quarters as Karia and Tasa got water boiling and spices simmering, and wet clothes were hung near warm walls to dry and beverages of thick cocoa and tea were prepared. There was not much time to converse except regarding the tasks at hand. They were walking back upstairs carrying large trays of food and drink when Tasa said, "So, you're a giantess then."

"Honestly, Tasa. Didn't you even wonder?" Karia laughed a little.

"I did not know that giants were actually real."

"But you have a dragon for a friend?" Karia stopped suddenly and looked back at her. "Just how well do you know Torin anyway?" Just then they smelled something wonderful coming from above. Quickly climbing up the last few circular steps they looked at Torin and saw he was roasting some fish, some very large, delicious-looking fish, over the center brazier.

"I hope this is proper use of the central flame, Priestess." Karia responded by digging in and happily enjoying every bite of the gift.

31
A Dragon's Eye View

LATER IN THE EVENING, AFTER THEIR REPAST WAS COMPLETE, Kamir, exhausted by the day's futile and icy efforts, as well as the excitement of a real dragon in his home, fell into a deep sleep. Karia hoisted her son to carry him to bed and bid Tasa and Torin goodnight. Outside, an early snow had begun to fall, and the wind lessened a little. A few days' supply of fresh fish from the wild ocean lay just outside the northern portal. The interior floor was spotless.

Despite being sleepy, Tasa struggled to frame her questions in some logical order. Torin spoke first. He was speaking in a way that she now understood he had been using with her for a long time. "You must not be concerned with the order of your questing. It is not from your head that the questions arise, but your heart."

Tasa was seated on a pile of cushions and Torin now encircled and lay next to her. Together they faced the outside and the falling snow. The light from the brazier dimmed a little, but Tasa felt warm inside the circle of the dragon. She had begun to think of Torin as "her" dragon. His voice was warm inside her mind. "Sleep now," he said, "and I will help you to see things clearly." She adjusted the cushions and leaned them up against his shoulder.

"This okay?" she muttered quietly.

"Fine, Tasa, just fine. Sleep now and I will be with you." Torin's voice led her down a long path. It was well lit, though she did not see the source of the light. It was also smooth, though not hard, and they traveled together easily. The path started with soft images, vague and distant, but as they moved along things became clearer.

The image that was the clearest was of dragons, many of them, and much larger than Torin. Following was the image of giants, male and female, and they all were laughing and speaking and walking freely with the dragons. "This is the way things once were." Torin's voice was felt throughout her entire being. "They are the First Men and have been here longer than you may imagine."

Tasa found herself upon his back, astride his shoulders, though she did not recall climbing up. They were in flight and the world turned below. Animals of all kinds roamed in great herds and prides and packs. The earth was green and glowed with vitality.

Suddenly a great fire swept the plains, melting mountains and boiling seas away. Far below she saw dragon turn against dragon and their breath was like fire and terribly they scorched each other and all the area surrounding them. All life was being wiped away, vaporized, and Tasa heard herself cry out to stop.

"It is a past event and we cannot undo what has been done." Torin's voice flowed around her, but she was distraught by the vision and not easily comforted by mere words.

Gaia turned, and the fires spread, burning randomly in different spots all about the globe. Rains fell and still the dragon fires would not be extinguished. The earth quaked and the waters churned. Far below an island continent shook and then shattered. A beautiful dragon flew to and fro pulling people from crevasses and sudden lakes and pools as many islands formed from the splintering one. Boats and ships tried to put to sea and were hurled back upon the broken shores.

"We must help." Tasa's distress spoke.

"It is not something we can affect. It is past." And they flew further across the surface of Gaia and a land of vast forests and large animals roaming free. There were few dragons and no humans, giants or otherwise. It was beautiful and untouched by the fires. They turned south and flew across long rivers and massive bays until they came to more land. And vast stretches of pristine forests and colorful birds and many creatures that Tasa had not seen nor heard tell. The air was pungent and smelled of growth and life. Yet the earth still shook.

They flew southward now past the tip of land, and she saw in the distance another lush land and a beautiful dragon flying over it. Below, life seemed strange, and the creatures looked not unlike dragons. They lacked something, and it was not a thing that Tasa thought she could see with her eyes. The land seemed to be changing and the creatures were in distress. The dragon that flew above looked sadly and helplessly upon his world.

They flew past the bottom of Gaia and now saw the fires flaring above the horizon. They were quite high above the earth, and she could see the circle of the planet clearly. Far below, waters were bursting forth and ice was melting from the tops of mighty mountains. Clouds grew and soon the earth was hidden from sight.

Torin circled down and through thick mists of rain and lightning. Below the clouds, giants gathered themselves and others together in vast boats or sealed themselves within mountains behind massive doors and gates as waves of water rushed through valleys and ravines, washing away villages and towns and cities and animals and trees and anything that was in the path of the surging flow. Tasa was stunned at the magnitude of destruction. Her heart went numb.

All around the land three of the First Men, giants all, struggled and sailed and risked their lives to rescue people from hill tops and then mountain tops and then from whatever floated that survivors could cling to. Many failed to find succor and the three grimly continued past bodies floating in the currents.

"They are the first of the First Men, born of the energy of the Ancient Dragons themselves. They are brothers." Torin's voice was a vibration that she felt...elsewhere. She dimly wondered where they were actually and recalled the warmth of the temple and the peace of Penthe House.

Torin's voice again called to her being saying, "Tasa, the answers to your questions are within our journey," and she looked back to see the world, and the waters receding. The shape of the land became familiar now, looking more and more like the maps she had studied at Beach House. They flew lower and saw that many types of humans walked the planet now. Giants and dwarves and elves and what she had always thought of as humans.

"They are the New Men, raised by Gaia herself." They were numerous and at times animalistic in their actions. They fought with each other and left behind their waste and in general did not seem to be aware of Gaia at all. The First Men sought to guide the New Men but seemed to abandon the effort. Still, some of the New Men sought out and sat in the halls of learning of the First Men and they were welcomed.

"How am I seeing this, Torin? How am I knowing these things?"

Torin replied, "You must continue to listen with your heart, for these are matters best comprehended there and not within your brain." Tasa slowly let her thoughts fade back to the sound of Torin's being.

Children were born of the unions between the First Men and the New Men. Communities of these people grew in the high mountains first and then in the deep forests and the islands, distant from the New Men who gathered behind walls and armed themselves against one another.

The three brothers worked and traveled to bring many groups together and sometimes they were successful. Often, they were not. The dragons themselves seemed to vanish from the earth. "Not vanished," Torin said, "but returned to places of power and centers of energy, connected by lines of force that guide people today." Torin's voice resonated within her mind and she smiled, knowing what these lines were from her lessons about the swift craft of Master Amir.

The New Men continued on their way, disregarding the First Men and even attacking them in their homes. Any who consorted with the First Men were hunted and persecuted for their association. Young dragons were born, and they too were hunted by the New Men in fear and hate. Even among the New Men there had been diversity, but now they sought to destroy any who were not like themselves. The First Men gathered ancient energies to themselves. They cast light about their forms, shifting their appearance until the New Men saw no differences.

Torin flew Tasa all about the globe. Vast sheets of water covered the continents in the north and finally all the dragon fires were extinguished. The waters receded, slowly at first and then more rapidly as the earth began to cool and ice formed at the poles.

Tasa was saddened when they flew over the land at the bottom of the earth. The abundance of life had vanished, and one lone dragon sat at the base of the planet, still and covered in ice, snow building up all around him.

The islands that were birthed from the larger continent now eroded away by the storms of the largest ocean. The civilization that once flourished was now sinking completely and the beautiful dragon spread her wings and covered the remnants of her main land and sank beneath the waves with it and the survivors. Ships traveled to and fro seeking to save what was left of their once beautiful life. Eventually, they simply sailed away as the spires of their culture sank into the sea.

A vast island continent nearby, once lush and green, now turned stark and hot. The First Men there adapted to the earth, singing along with Gaia and feeling her power in their feet as they walked about.

Torin and Tasa soared above the Ringing Sea, the middle sea where Tasa had been born. She could see now how small it was and felt small herself as she witnessed history in this way.

"What happened to the three brothers?" she asked, and Torin said it was "a tale for another time." She saw in her mind's eye a burnt and shattered form being tended by a Woman in White, dark-skinned and beautiful. The woman turned and looked straight into Tasa's eyes. She liked those eyes and felt drawn to this one. There was power there, strength and balance that Tasa could feel. In the woman's eyes Tasa could see the light, that same shine she now observed so readily in others, only here it was stronger. She leaned forward as the woman reached out a strong hand to her. The image of the woman passed as Torin's voice called to Tasa. She was falling through clouds, and he circled beneath her and gently caught her on his back.

"It is the first woman," he said, "the one now known as Brigid, but she has been many women. You should stay with me during this journey. It would not do for you to get lost at this point." And Tasa wondered how she could get lost if they were dreaming. For surely this was a dream; she had fallen asleep and now these things came to her mind in images, imagination.

"It is a dreaming of a sort and there are those that say we are in the Dreamtime. It is a place that you can go if you choose, and I will always try to find you here. You must think of me if you do, for I will hear you then clearly."

Tasa was lying on Torin's back with her arms around his long and slender neck. She wanted to shut her eyes for just a moment but was not certain how to do that. "Perhaps my eyes are already closed, but what do I do if I don't want to see something?"

"Do not believe in it, then it will not exist for you," Torin spoke again.

"But will it still exist?" Tasa asked.

"Only if enough people believe in something does it continue to be real," Torin replied.

"That makes no sense," Tasa said to herself, "or does it?"

"It does if you believe it does," Torin said. "Look now."

The New Men and the First Men had looked different for a long time. Now it seemed that there were no First Men around. "I will let you see through my eyes." Certain ones then took on a glow as if they had a bright light within them, an aura. "It is the creative fire. It is what the Ancient Dragon Prometheous gave to the First Men long ago."

"I see that light sometimes," Tasa said. "In people's eyes."

"It is the way of things that some see the fire in others. Not always in the same way. You now see through my eyes, and I see things as a glow. Should I witness events through your eyes I should see as you do."

They circled close to an island, Tasa's island home, she recognized. Torin spiraled about and she saw the women all around. Few glowed in the way that Torin saw those of the blood of the dragons. "They are New Men, humans mostly, but they seek peace from others who attempt to dominate the weak. Your mother offers them shelter on Solaine. They sense her strength and hunger for the same."

Near the narrow center of the island, to the northern side amidst lush green grass with grazing sheep and groves of olive trees, a small hill rose up. They flew into a cave and surely it must be massive for Torin's wings did not touch the sides! Now she saw that there were others within, and the cave was not massive at all, and she and Torin must be very small. "How is this possible, Torin?"

"Do not think on it, merely observe."

She saw a woman lying on a wide bed and near her were two more women, both in white robes. In their arms they held a baby, newly born and freshly cleansed of the birth process. The Women in White handed the child gently to its mother and Tasa recognized that woman as her own mother.

"What is this now, Torin? My mother is giving birth? I will have a brother or a sister?"

"Pay attention now, Tasa, and look further to the back of the cavern." The walls were smooth, as if polished, and the floor also. A lantern burned clean flame and gave light to the birthing scene. At the rear of the cave, where the light did not readily reach and lacked strength to dispel shadows, she saw a small, dark rock. It was odd because there were no other rocks or boulders within the cavern. The small rock opened one eye slightly and watched the baby being handed to its mother. Tasa recognized that eye.

"It is you!" she spoke excitedly.

"And it is also you," he replied.

The Women in White had the glow about them. Tasa's mother also, but the baby was brighter than them all. "You are a descendant of the first of the First Men, Tasa. In the way of lines of birth, yes, but also in a way that I cannot describe. Your energy is purer, stronger somehow. It happens still, and it can happen to any who are of the First Men in lineage. It is something the New Men lack, and it is why they are short lived. We believe they can be like the First Men if they choose and if they believe, but they believe so little."

The walls of the cave dissolved, and they were above the island again. It was night time and the villages were lit with lamps. People walked about in the darkness and Tasa could see that they too had the aura, but it was faint, weak.

"There are some even now that are learning, watching and walking with the first ones and gaining knowledge and growing. Some are looking for such ones, those that burn bright with Promethean light."

Below, a man walked through the night and he had the light, brighter than most. Tasa recognized him. It was Caraphino. "A New Man he is," said Torin, "but with an understanding, more than most, and he has walked with dragons."

Darkness closed in as the night deepened and the lamps went out. A single point of light was visible moving across the island, returning to the library and the repository of knowledge. Tasa watched until she could no longer see the light.

32

Tasa's Journey

THEACARIS, THE WOMAN IN WHITE, STOOD IN THE CENTER of the circular room. Sunlight meandered through heavy clouds and gave the central vent of the domed ceiling a gray glow. No candles were yet lit, and the meeting room of the House of Five Doors was full with shadows.

Before speaking, the leader of Penthe House smoothed her white robes as was her habit. Taking a deep breath, Theacaris said, "There is much about the world now that I wish were different. My words to you this day are difficult, and I expect that you may disagree with much of my assessment and direction. I myself am in a state of disagreement with the decisions I lean towards. Yet I see no other path for Penthe House at this time. We must close our doors to any who are not of the blood of the dragons."

If Theacaris thought there would be murmuring or swift disagreement at her words she found herself mistaken. None of the seven other women made a noise. She went on, her white robe hanging still and straight from her shoulders, her silver hair tied back. "The attack on Beach House, the battle there, and the wounds inflicted upon our friends, all these things have passed to the bards. They make legends and poems of those involved. We have recovered as best we could from such a thing. Mother Marion, you are doing well?"

The Woman in Blue nodded but did not rise. She met everyone's eye as she gazed about the darkened room. "I am well. My scars will remain by my choice and as a lesson. The stories will be told and while I live they will stay accurate to the facts. I am no heroine in this matter. I am also no victim. None involved are heroines nor are they to be pitied. We did what we must have done to protect our lives and those of the others. All should take as a lesson that they too should do what must be done. All must be in state of awareness."

Beach Mother spoke in her steady fashion, her words measured and precise. "The import of the matter of the attack is passed, save that we now face larger choices. I regret that I must agree with Mother White.

"A filter must now exist between Penthe House and the world of the rapidly spreading humans. Gaia's children they may be. We are the first and we exist to serve her. What the wisdom is in the existence of those beings I confess I am unable to fathom. I do ken the wisdom of our own survival. From my private conversations with you all, I know we are in agreement on this course, though some are more troubled than others."

Mother Stone raised her hammer and Beach Mother nodded, granting the floor to her. Forge Mother stood tall, casting large shadows in the dark room. She said, "My reservations are not so much that we construct a barrier. The nature of such a thing is limiting and I will say that I do not care for limits. That may surprise some of you, knowing that I do build walls and fences. These are more for organization, rather than restrictions. I like things to be…" she paused and twitched a smile.

The smile fell away, and the giantess continued. "I also want us to do this from a place of strength and not of fear. I will not hide from these beast men. I can tell you here in this room that already a movement is under way by the giants to resolve this issue. The difficulty is that the issue also involves dragons." This comment received attention. A low murmur spread and faded as Forge Mother added, "Our immediate issue here at Penthe House also involves a dragon it seems."

Theacaris, who had remained standing, stepped into the dull glow of light from the hazy sun. She sighed before speaking, less an exhalation of breath than an effort to allow the words to be released. "I only have learned of this dragon in our lands just prior to this meeting. I must say that this comes as a great surprise to me.

"We long suspected there was something quite different about one of our flock. That some in this room knew about this dragon for some time and did not come to us all with the knowledge is troubling to me. It feels like mistrust, though I can see from a different perspective where it also might feel like privacy from another view. It is now a critical factor in our decision."

From the deepest of the shadows a woman emerged. Taller than the rest and dark-skinned, she wore leather and metal. Her voice rang clear and vibrant. Her tone was low, though all heard her words distinctly. "It is not mistrust, dear daughter. You know of the existence of dragons, you all do. You also know it is Gaia's wisdom that the dragons remain in shadows and stasis for the time. It is not a thing I fully understand.

"I tell you true; I walk with a dragon and yet do not pretend to understand their ways. I am the daughter of a dragon and yet do not see what they see. When dealing with the Dragon Council it is often difficult to comprehend their purpose. We of the blood of the dragons often find that this complicates our lives and we have no choice but to carry on. The dragons' worldview is as different from ours as we from these beast men. Our lives and the decision we make this day is made more complex by the fact that the beast men appear to also be linked to a dragon.

"We, Penthe and I, did not tell you of the existence of this youngling for it is the will of the Dragon Council to bring him back to the dragon lands. He is resistant to such a thing because of his bond to a young girl. She has faced much danger and he found himself restrained by the will of the council. He will not leave her. In this he now has two draconian allies."

"Tasa?" Mother Meg spoke without requesting her turn. "We are talking about Tasa?"

"Yes. She is not just of the blood of the dragons, like all of us here; she is also bonded to this youngling dragon. In this way she is like myself. It is not an easy course and I have taken a personal interest in this matter. My own dragon sister, Penthe, is in communication with the youngling called Torin. We seek to guide them. Matters are overtaking our plans, however. Where once we felt we had time, now actions must be accelerated. There are difficult decisions to be made on many levels."

Theacaris tilted her head slightly and the woman in leather nodded, allowing her to speak. "Brigid is kind to be here to counsel us this day. I ask that we all remain in love during our discussion, and I believe that Forge Mother makes a fine point. We do not want to act from fear. Bravery may come at a cost, but as Beach Mother said, we should all be prepared to do what we must."

Theacaris spread her hands and looked about the domed room saying, "Our agreement is not yet sealed, but I believe we are all of one mind, that Albion must be secured. There are magicks for this and Karia is constructing them now. She instructs the adepts at Wisdom House in this way, but we see clearly that this will be a weak wall at best. If there were a smaller area we may make things stronger. I am not of a mind to shrink Penthe House."

"Hear, hear," said Mother Stone.

"There is more to our decision," Theacaris said. "There are those in the world beyond Albion's shores who are strong in the blood of the dragons. We feel that they should be gathered together while this threat exists in the world.

"The tales we hear from the journeymen and travelers make me go cold inside. Our few experiences are frightening enough. Things are far worse elsewhere. To this end we are considering sending emissaries out to invite those most like us to return to Albion.

"It is our intention to offer to train them in the ways of Penthe House as much as they might choose to participate. It is also our belief that the more energy of the blood of the dragons we can gather, the stronger our…defenses might become." Mother White was reluctant to speak in terms of defense, for the counterpart to such a concept was offense.

She looked down, swept her robes with her hands and continued. "There are other places that the First Men might gather. Kane's Kingdom is one such place and we hear that it is a stronghold already. Mother Stone gives report that it is there that we have a strong support against the rising tide of the beast men. We will send an emissary there soon. It is my thought that we send one of our own from within this room. Mother Stone is my choice for this should she accept the position.

"The first emissary from Albion is en route as I speak. Ikara travels from Wisdom House in the north highlands to the port of Leist where she will sail with a journeyman handpicked by Dagda Nicholaus himself. Ikara goes to the island of Solaine to seek her sister, Kila, and discover the true nature and strength of Kila's home.

"There is reason to believe that there is a strong community of draconic power already in place there. It is where the dragon Torin and Kila's child

Tasa were born together. If this proves to be a stronghold as well, then we will seek to lend support, under Kila's guidance and leadership, to the furthering of her plans." Theacaris paused, frowned, and again smoothed her robes before saying, "This is contingent upon Kila agreeing. We are unsure of the welcome Ikara will receive, but she was insistent on taking the journey. It is my thought that we also send Tasa. Kila's daughter may be a tempering influence to her mother. She would be accompanied by her dragon companion and thus we feel there would be a high level of safety in such a mission."

Brigid, strong and tall, stepped forward again. She did not ask for the floor. The Woman in White yielded nonetheless. "There is a different way for Tasa. The world between here and Kane is different than what we know in Albion. Mother Stone would be an irregularity in such a place. Though she might also have the protection of a dragon, her size and demeanor will not blend well with folk that are more used to human style communication and life. The magic we use to disguise our true appearance is weak between here and Kane's Kingdom.

"Tasa is clever and quiet. She already is part of a trusted crew. Torin knows silence and he knows stealth. He has existed on this island of Albion and indeed within the very environs of Penthe House for near two years without our knowledge. I see a twofold path for them. Tasa sees those with the shine of dragon light within their eyes. She can discern those who may wish to return to Albion and attend to Penthe House.

"I must warn you. Do not prepare for a great number to flow to our lands. There is complacency in the world. Many of the women are bound to their men and know no other path for themselves or their children. Even those of the blood of the dragon may be unable to see a different way for themselves.

"Tasa will be able to gain confidence and speak from the point of view of the children. In addition, the presence of Torin at my brother's kingdom will lend her an air of authority with him that I fear neither I nor kind Nicholaus possesses."

The Woman in Green abruptly stood up and said, "Now wait! Are you proposing that Tasa, our young Tasa, venture into the heart of the world to face the beast men alone? That she and Mariel and their friends might somehow succeed where Mother Stone or I could not? Mother Brigid, with all my deepest respect, I cannot allow such a course to be considered. There must be another path. This cannot be Tasa's path. Are we not all in agreement?"

A heavy silence followed.

"She is a skilled fighter. Her weapons are keen and fine," said Mother Stone, her face still and hard.

"She is good with children and coped well with the changeling," said Mother Bae, as she let tears flow from her aged eyes.

"Her inner strength is deep. Her balance unmatched in many twice her age," said Mother Mii of Wisdom House, body still, eyes gazing into the distance.

"She is battle tested. She is independent and self-reliant. She is resourceful. She already is a leader of her small band of companions," said Mother Marion, her lips pressed thin.

Mother Meg looked about the room, astonishment racing across her face. "No. This cannot be the only way. I will go. You and I will go, sister. We can build a crew of able women and..." Her voice trailed off as she saw the reality of a choice already made. "She is only a young girl." She let herself join Mother Bae in tears.

The Woman in White spoke. "It is a place where we must be brave, Mother Meg. Trust me when I say that I do not enjoy this choice either. We have some time to consider alternate possibilities, but the sooner we act the better. Mother Brigid gives us the solution we fear, but the one we must act upon. We, in this room, are all needed here in Albion to lead and guide."

With a sigh Theacaris turned to Brigid and asked, "Can you also travel with Tasa, good Brigid? You and Penthe could be in the shadows as you are here in Albion."

"It is not the same there as here, Theacaris," Brigid replied. "The humans have dwelt in the continent for many generations. They travel and grow. They have multiplied to a state where there is little space for a dragon the size of Penthe to hide. As for me, I too am not the right choice, for the same reasons as Mother Stone."

Brigid turned to the others. "The magicks needed to create the barrier around Albion can be accessed swifter if there is a dragon of great power near. Penthe serves Gaia and she is awake, not lying in stasis. She senses other dragons who do exist in stasis by Gaia's will. The lines of power between them will assist Karia and her adepts to create the membrane that will filter danger away from Albion. It is Tasa who must take this journey."

Theacaris brushed her eyes and slid her hands down her white robe. She tightened the belt of gold and took a calming breath. "The time has come. The discussion must be concluded. There are two items we must decide upon. Let us now vote regarding the first matter, though I believe we all will speak with one mind. All those in agreement with the cordoning off of Albion?"

The answers came back subdued, but all in the affirmative. "So mote it be," said the Woman in White. "As Keeper of the Words, I will scribe this in the book of our days. Let the future understand our difficult choice.

"Now we will have one remaining decision before we continue with our monthly planning. All those in agreement with sending Tasa…" Marta Bae slowly stood. Her aide, the adept Proticia, rose and assisted the Woman in Red.

Mother Bae began speaking when she saw Theacaris nod in her direction. "I have been Mother to the children of Penthe House for a great length of time. I have cared for them and kept them safe and warm for longer than many in the land of Albion have been alive." Her voice wavered slightly. She laughed a little and continued. "I am alive by the grace of our dear Brigid and gracious Penthe. In all my days, I have never been a voice of dissent.

"Today, I must make a choice. It is one that is long in coming and you, my dear sisters, have been kind in allowing me to take my time in reaching this point. Proticia is more than my adept at Hearth House. She acts in the capacity of Mother of the House of the Red Door already. She is skilled. She is wise. She is loving. She possesses the strength to make the decision which, I fear, I cannot make regarding sending this child into danger. We will prepare to close our once open doors and I can see the need for such an action. My heart cannot clearly see the reason we would send dear children to danger."

Mother Bae turned and took Proticia's hands. Her voice grew strong. "Do you vow to make the best choices you can on behalf of those too young to choose for themselves? Do you vow to shelter and feed those who are too young to feed and clothe themselves? Do you vow to be a mother to strangers who are absent parents, a sister to women in tribulation, a leader of the young in the ways of compassion and charity?"

Proticia gazed into Mother Bae's eyes and said, "I do so swear."

"I ask you now: Will you accept the position as Mother of Hearth House?"

"If it be the will of the circle of Mothers of Penthe House, I accept the honor and duty of Mother of Hearth House."

A chorus of "Aye!" and "So mote it be!" rose from the others in the room. They gathered about the two women and wept tears of joy at the passage and growth witnessed. When some time passed, Mother Theacaris gestured for everyone to become quiet once again.

"We have one more decision still. I laud Mother Bae's strength and wisdom in this matter. In spirit I believe we all agree with her sentiment. Yet we must act with our brains and thoughts now, for our hearts may betray the course that is the best, not only for ourselves and community but also the world away from our haven.

"We still need agreement in this matter of Tasa's journey. We must remind ourselves that Tasa herself will need to be in agreement to this proposal, so our decision today is not a final one.

"All in agreement with sending Tasa and her companions to seek out those who possess the blood of the dragons and direct them to Penthe House, please speak 'Aye' now."

The first to speak was Mother Stone, strong and firm. "Aye. The right tool for the right job."

Next was Mother Proticia. "In the interest of the safety of all the children we harbor and nurture, Aye."

Mother Mii added, "Her strength will carry her through a time of testing. Her balance will guide her companions. Aye."

Mother Marion reached for her sister and they held hands. "In the certain knowledge that we give this endeavor the greatest chance of success by this action, Aye."

Mother Meg wept openly. "I cannot find the will to speak against you, my sisters. My heart says loudly, 'No!' But the wisdom combined is also strong. My logic says, Aye, and yet weeps."

"So mote it be," said Theacaris. "As the Keeper of the Words I will enter our decision into the book of our days. May the future understand the difficulty of our choice. May the tears that will fall from mine eyes as I record these thoughts give stained evidence of our regret at the course thrust upon us."

Brigid spoke, "I will take the words and choice to Tasa myself. In presenting the matter to her, I will refrain from speaking of this meeting. We should allow her to consider the matter without the pressure of our reluctant opinion. She will need to consider the course and her companions. She will need to consult with Torin. She will face many tests before she makes her way home. The decision whether to accept this task will be her first. I will guide her where I am able."

33

To Be Bound to Dragons

SHELTERED BY WIND-TWISTED PINES and wind-scoured boulders, Tasa felt the light of the pale winter sun. Earlier she had removed her long, hooded cloak in the warmth of her efficient little fire. The cloak now cushioned her as she sat, legs crossed, and eyes partially closed. The evening encroached upon the day. Soon the light would subside and Tasa would be alone in the last light of the sun. Cold winds ruffled her green tunic and dark hair.

The waves of the ocean drove steadily into the shore in a constant effort to reshape the coastline, a never ending creative expression of Gaia herself. Clouds scudded across the horizon and as far out to sea as her vision allowed. Night approached, and the air passed from cool to cold. She fed the small fire. Smoke rose in a thin, slow spiral, the scent of burning wood adding to the fragrance of the seaside forest.

Tasa knew that a woman, a giantess she sensed, approached. She stood near and silent, just a few spans away. Tasa's sword and shield were within reach, but she did not. There was nothing to fear from this one.

"Please feel free to approach if you wish." Tasa's voice was low and even. It floated from her mouth with an exhalation and joined the wind. "The earth is large and there is room for us all."

"I am pleased to meet you, Tasa of the Quiet Nights." Brigid's voice was commanding even if it was soft. The wind pulled her words around the small area of the forest where they both were. "We seem to have met before, though I do not know how."

"It was in a dream. I was with a dragon. You were tending a man. He was burnt badly. You looked up and saw me. I fell from the dragon then."

Tasa had not turned around. She recognized the woman in a way that she could not describe, a sense of her presence perhaps.

"Yes, with Torin you were. He was not yet alive when that event occurred." Brigid's voice was accented in a strange way, soft and beautiful, but with a feeling of distance and sights never to be seen again. "He is with you now, isn't he?" Tasa nodded. Brigid continued, "I was once with a dragon in a similar way. Closer we were, and I still miss his presence.

"You are unique in this way. A dragon bond with a human is rare in these days."

"Is that what I am?" Tasa asked. "A human? It seems that I am not. Different. More in ways. It seems that we are not human the way others are human."

"This disturbs you?"

"No. It puzzles me. There is much in legend that appears to be truth. We should be taught such truth. We, the acolytes and adepts of Penthe House, should know more of this, of ourselves. Instead, it is knowledge hidden. That seems like a lie. Lies do not breed trust."

"You do not trust?"

"I do trust. But I now reserve my trust for those who are proven to me worthy. There are reasons for the stillness of such knowledge, I imagine. I do not know what they could be."

"You are a human. In shape and design and appearance you are human, as am I."

Tasa turned and looked at the woman for the first time. Very tall, taller than Karia or Mother Stone, and dark, her skin colored like rich earth or the shell of the chestnut. She wore leather and metal. At her side hung a sheath with a large hilt exposed. The sword might be taller than Bria, thought Tasa. Pouches hung from belts that crisscrossed her torso. They were more orderly and much neater than Mariel's scattered gatherings. Brigid's hair was pulled back, but the volume of it formed a vast, dark halo about her face. The last beaming rays of the sun shone into the shaded forest edge and Tasa saw Brigid's large brown eyes gleam. A small smile gave the woman an aura of peace, despite the weapon at her side.

"It appears there is great variety to humanity," Tasa said. "Please, sit if you will. The sunset will be beautiful tonight. The clouds have been full and white all day. The moon will rise soon after. We will see her light behind us." Tasa stopped. She did not want to talk about the simple knowing of moonrise or cloud light.

"You are here for the night?" Brigid asked.

"I needed some time alone. Some time to ponder. Is that what humans do? Is that what dragon-bonded human girls do?"

Brigid laughed. "They do what they choose to do. They get less of an argument from people if the dragon is present. Would you like to be left alone? You did invite me to sit down."

"I believe I would enjoy a conversation with Mother Brigid, founder of Penthe House and legendary being who also walks with a dragon." Tasa heard the cynicism in her voice and softened it. "Perhaps she will help me know what the world actually is like and what my place in it will be."

Brigid stepped near the edge of the forest and began to divest herself of blades and bags. She swung a long cloak from her shoulders and spread it out upon the ground. It covered a fair amount of territory. She lowered her body, scissoring her legs as she came to rest near Tasa. The fire sputtered a little in the wind. At once the two women reached out hands and the blaze steadied.

"So we can both do that," Tasa said very matter of factly. "When I was younger I just always took it for granted that everyone could. I thought everyone must have a voice in their head too."

"They do. Or rather, they can if they listen close enough and allow themselves to hear clearly. It is not a dragon's voice though. Not most of the time. It may be Gaia sometimes, but mostly it is just something inherent in each person. It is guidance, a way of navigating and doing the right thing. It separates us from the animals. It is Gaia's gift, her gift by way of the Illuminators. We are her stewards. That is what I know from my association with dragons. It may be true.

"You are human, Tasa, but you are also more. That is not to say that you are better, but I confess, I wish some humans were less like the humans they are and more like the humans you and I represent. It is not a path of thought I willingly pursue. It is good to know who you are, to have confidence in yourself. It is not often beneficial to believe you are superior to others."

Tasa thought about asking who the Illuminators were but passed the thought as a distraction. Brigid seemed of a mind to talk about more personal things. Hidden histories could wait. "I do not feel special. I only feel different. I know what I know, but I do not require others to share my truths. They have truths of their own." Tasa added little branches to the fire and fresh smoke rose. She passed her hands through the smoke and pulled them to her face, inhaling the scent.

"Being different is often enough to be asked to accomplish different tasks. It is why you were asked to give vision to the captain aboard the Mali. Master Amir knew you might have the sight," Brigid said.

"He knew that I was like him. He knew I was his daughter." Tasa snapped the words, but they did not carry any real anger. "Did I not have the right to know who he was to me? I now know my mother requested a silence on the matter and he honored this privacy. Still, I feel that it was a silence that held me back. We may have died on that voyage. And what would I have lost for knowing that my father commanded the ship and crew? What would I have lost for knowing of Torin before my arrival at Penthe House? Did your parents keep you in a secret world? Does your dragon disappear from you? Is your dragon with you physically or are you left to wonder if perhaps you are not quite normal?" Tasa puffed out a breath and the fire flared bright. She threw her hands into the air and asked, "What is normal?"

Brigid smiled wider and said, "Look at me. Do you think I am someone who knows what normal is?"

Tasa smiled at that and asked, "Are you a giant then? A giant with a dragon? Where are the giants and dragons today? Where are the dragons and why do they want Torin to be hidden? What is wrong with this world?"

"I am a giant," Brigid said, "and one of the first. My first sight was of my dragon mate. It was different for my brothers. I may not be able to explain the actions of the dragons, but I am used to them being different than what a human might expect.

"In these present days, Torin is at risk if he exposes himself to the...humans who do not carry the blood of the dragons within their veins. You see them, but not all do, even those who are of the blood of the dragons. You see them as beings with a certain light within their eyes. I see them as beings with a kind of shine to their skin. Some see them but are trained to disbelieve their own sight, so they become blind to the truths of the world.

Thus we: dragons, giants, and such other folk become mystical beings to the world. It is not so, not truly. We are the most normal beings upon the planet.

"The world is not wrong, only unbalanced. When we act in a balanced way the world stabilizes just a bit. It is just that so many are acting for themselves only and so we, the beings of the world, find that we react out of fear. This is dangerous. Not only for the dragons. There are others in danger as well."

"Those of the blood of the dragons?" Tasa asked.

"Yes, but still others. Even the ones we now call human, those who are not of the mystical energy. There is danger in the earth."

Tasa looked out over the last rays of the sun fanning from behind a distant cloud across the sea. The water twinkled as daylight passed below the horizon. Above, the sky cleared, and stars appeared. The night wind sighed through trees and the world shifted from light to darkness. Yet it is all so beautiful, she thought. "The earth is not safe, I know, but it can be a place of great beauty and we are safe here. On my island I was safe with my mother. It is hard to understand the danger from where I sit this night, though I well recall the attack on Beach House. What can we do to make others safe? What can we do to stay safe here in our home?"

"It cannot always be safe, Tasa. But danger can be diverted and faced down. The problem is knowing when to face it and when to allow it to pass by. Just as we do not want another being to disturb our home, we must be cautious not to threaten someone else's home. It is like the bees and their honey. Act with respect, provide them a safe place to hover and fly, flowers to attend and open sky, and they will do what they have always been doing from before I was alive. But, to gain their honey, you must be cautious and understand they will sting you if they can. They are not evil. They are not bad or wrong. They are just bees. And if they feel threatened, they sting."

"And we sting those that attack us as well?" Tasa asked. "We did not seek to take anything from the beast men. They came to us and attacked without cause, did they not? Or is there something we are not being told?"

"They, too, are of the blood of the dragons, after a fashion." The giantess took several slow breaths before continuing. "There is, was, one dragon who was different from the others. I do not know why. He was a being of fierce nature, a killing beast, yet also intelligent, reasoning. His reasons for his actions were not understood by the council of the dragons. He argued with them. He caused anger and resentment to grow between the other dragons. He started a war amongst the stewards of Gaia. Dragon killed dragon on that day. Dragon also killed human, or tried. My dragon died saving me." Brigid allowed tears to roll from her eyes. Her voice wavered as she said, "Would that I may have perished with him and thus be spared the pain of my heart. Yet," she touched her lips and her voice steadied, "I find I am useful to the beings of earth. I seek purpose. I look for paths of service. It is not an easy way.

"Those called beast men are not so inclined. They threaten life with no reason. It is for that reason that we are closing off Penthe House and, to the best of our abilities, Albion herself. Yet we want to serve the world still. We desire others to arrive still, just as you came to us, and train and grow. The invitation now must be more..." Brigid sighed and closed her eyes, "more specific. We are no longer open to any and all. Not for the foreseeable days ahead."

She opened her eyes and Tasa again looked at her face, dark in the shadows and hidden. Yet her eyes glowed and Tasa knew that others did not see what she saw. "Only those with the shine of dragon light in their eyes?"

"Yes, Tasa. And for this we need you. You have sight that is beyond others. You have not been blinded by belief. It will help you see who should be told of Albion and who should be left alone."

"Left alone? To die at the hands of the beast men? How do we allow that to happen?"

"It is the question that led to your mother taking her leave of Albion. It is the question that separated her from her sister. It is the question that caused her to keep knowledge from you about who you truly are. In a way, it is the question that caused you to exist. I have no clear answer. I only know that this is the action that most benefits Gaia at this time. And my answer is colored with the perception that I believe those with the blood of the dragons are superior and need to survive. I am not certain my perception will be the truth of history."

****

Moonlight filtered through the tops of the surrounding pine trees, casting pale silver light into the needles and creating sharp, jagged shadows on the surrounding rocks. Clouds pushed out to sea and left the sky above quiet and clear. Tasa added more branches and once again smoke rose as leaves burned away in hot, crackling blazes. Light flared and faded in those moments. When it had passed, the shadows seemed deeper.

"Yet you go on," Tasa said into the night. "You do what you do."

"I do the best I can for who is with me at the moment."

"And is this the best you can do for me at the moment? Ask me to…what are you asking me to do, anyway?" Tasa left the edge in her voice this time.

"Across the sea, there are some who would benefit from life at Penthe House, or at least in Albion. There are many who are descendant from giants and elves but, like yourself, are also from human lineage. Once, we expected that we would all mingle and at some future time the world would achieve a balance. We expected that the world would exist in a harmony, where all beings would seek the will of Gaia and her benefit. This is an interrupted dream. We may one day return to this dream. I hold it close to my thoughts. But now we need to bring those who already possess the blood of the dragons to safety. The beast men are not inclined favorably to their lives. They, too, have a form of the sight you possess.

"We are asking you…" Brigid stopped herself, pressed her lips together and took a breath. "I am asking you to travel the continent and seek those with the shine. Direct them to Albion by any means."

"What makes you think that I am the person to do this? Because Torin will protect me?"

"No. Torin must be cautious. The Dragon Council would prefer he not travel with you at all, but I know the ways of dragons enough to see that he will ignore this admonition. Already Torin feels he has been apart from you too often when danger was present. Yet I would wish that he remain hidden from most eyes. I will counsel him in such a way, and I trust Penthe herself will also offer such wisdom to him.

"There is anger at dragons in the east, past my brother Kane's lands. I do not fully comprehend the fear, but believe it has to do with the one called Tepes, the dragon I spoke of before. He was chained, imprisoned, and left trapped a long time ago. In your vision, you saw me tending my brother Nordu's wounds from that day.

"I ask that you travel with your friends, that you lead them across the land and through the forests. Find those that you believe will be of benefit to Albion and Penthe House."

"Not just the benefit of Gaia?" Tasa asked, and the cynicism was again in her voice.

"We are making a difficult decision, Tasa, and in my heart I hope it is not a permanent one. I have seen a vision myself. You travel. Albion thrives. Those of the blood of the dragons are safe. My vision is not always clear in this regard.

"I do know that you take this journey with the full support of the current Mothers of Penthe House. They are not enthusiastic about this effort, but they are in agreement."

"Because I travel and tell only certain people that they are allowed to come to this land, those of the blood of the dragons are made safe." There was no question in Tasa's statement, only acceptance. "I need to ponder this idea. I need some time to think about this. I need to speak to Torin and Mariel and...others. You say the Mothers of the Five Houses know of this plan? Have you all been talking about this with me in mind? All knowing before I am even aware?"

"You are talked about often, dear Tasa. We see you as special even if you do not see this within yourself. Yet, I think you do see your own nature and seek to suppress it in the pursuit of a life like others have. But you do not truly fit with many of the other girls, do you? You have never truly fit with other children."

Tasa nodded slowly. "On my island home, I was more at peace with my books and maps. It seemed always that I was older than everyone else, or that I knew more about the world. But I am not. It is the connection with the dragons through Torin that made me feel this way, is it not?"

"That is much of it, but you are still who you are. Your mind, your personality, these are things affected by your bond, but they are not who you are at the core of your life force. Myself, I once sat still for many years, just seeking my own voice, my own words and thoughts, my own feelings.

"There is much that you have learned in a short time. You are quiet and in this stillness there is a knowing, a growing wisdom. It helps to the understanding of what you have been shown in vision. But, as I have learned, there is more to life than contemplation. After my stillness, I began to journey. I have only recently ceased my wanderings. I exist in the Albion Isles for this present span of time. One day, I may begin the journey anew. Perhaps we will journey together, you and I, with our dragons, openly and without fear.

"You may sit. You may ponder. You may gain some understanding in this state of contemplation. Yet the time is slipping past us, and the world is rapidly shifting."

Tasa breathed in deeply and exhaled slowly. "I believe that there is more to understanding than just sitting. I have long believed I will have to one day go and see things of this world to help gain perspective. It is what I was doing with the library and the books. It was a journey without motion. It was the seeing of a map, but I am finding the journey is far different. It is a different world by far than what I once believed was truth. I must live a long time if I am to understand it all."

"Then live long, Tasa. As for a journey through the world, why wait?"

34

I of Stone and You of the Forest

IT IS ONE THING TO MAKE A DECISION. "Take a journey," Brigid said, and Tasa knew this was the right thing to do at this time. She felt it deep inside.

"Take a journey with your friends," said Brigid, and this would become a time-consuming activity wherein many hands and voices would feel obliged and entitled to give direction. Had it been only herself and Torin, Tasa knew that leaving Albion could be accomplished in a matter of days. She was of a mind to separate herself from the many who once guided her. In their guidance it seemed they had also withheld truths. This hurt her more than angered. She did not feel obligated to the Mothers of Penthe House in the way she once did. Yet, she cared.

She could not simply take her leave of Albion without speaking to them about her course. She also could not leave without speaking to Mariel. Or Torin. And the dragon must be first for she knew he would not easily stay in the shadows. His size might be small for a dragon, but he was too large for much of the thick woods they walked about in these days.

****

Tasa and Torin had spent the last two days in one another's company after Brigid departed. Away from all others, so she could think and adapt to her new reality.

"We are being asked to do something in the world. I am not certain of the course. It seems simple enough and if it were you and I then we might be off already, if you agree to travel with me." It was a late-night conversation, and these became normal for them. Torin wrapped around her, and she leaned against his side as his breath moved gently. It felt to her like an embrace, like when she rocked slowly to and fro with one of the Hearth House children. It felt like the sea in a boat on a calm summer day.

Often, she would set a fire. Torin could provide such a thing with ease, but Tasa asked if she could follow her strength and he agreed. He often agreed with her. "I do agree to travel with you. There are others that would do so as well."

"Yes." Tasa spoke slowly, letting thoughts become words as she breathed. "Others that will have to know of your existence. Is it really so necessary that you remain in shadows?"

"Once, my mentor and I disagreed on this point. I have come to see the longer vision and his ways are now closer to my sight. It is not something I feel is correct, but it is something that I see as necessary. Especially should we leave Albion."

"Mariel first then. We must tell her. You will like her. She is funny, like you."

"Kamir is the first of your friends to know. Then Karia. Will this be a problem for Mariel?"

"Hmm...no. Maybe. Probably. A little. But she'll just give Kamir a hard time for a while and get over it."

"With you? Will she also give you a hard time? You said, 'No secrets.'"

This silenced Tasa for a long while. "She will be upset. But I didn't keep you secret. You were a secret to me as well, right? They, the Dragon Council, kept you secret. I don't understand that, Torin. We were placed together by...who did that anyway?"

"I myself am unclear of the sequence of events. I only know that my mentor was involved, and I believe it was all...not exactly against the wishes of the Dragon Council, but...separate from their knowledge and awareness. They are not pleased with the bond, but they also are not angered."

"So they...what? Like us? Are neutral about us? Never think about us? Are we restricted somehow? I will not like that, and I think you also are unwilling to be restricted."

"I have felt their restriction for too long. My mentor is wise in how he guided me. I am wise enough to know that I likely need more guidance, but if

Penthe is asking us to travel and Brigid brings such a message, then perhaps we need less guidance than we might believe."

"Master Amir…" Tasa grew quiet again, then said, "My father spoke of knowledge as good, but experience as being necessary for wisdom. I do not feel all that wise. I could use some guidance, but I am reluctant to ask. In the past, I feel that we, you and I, should have been close and aware of one another. We would be…more than what we are now."

"I agree. Wollston says that I am the only dragon he knows who has regrets. Perhaps if others also felt regret there might be more forethought and less mistakes made. We, you and I, should be more than we are now, but we are together, and I am not of a mind to allow that to ever change again, Tasa."

She reached out and stroked his forearm. Her slender fingers slid easily over his deep black scales. The firelight played tricks with his coloring, casting an orange and red glow across his surface. Each scale was firm and thick but flexed beneath her fingertips. They overlay one another and where she leaned against him he was pliant and comfortable.

Torin raised his forepaw and ran a slender claw through her long dark hair. The firelight also cast the orange and red glow across her black hair. In the deep dark cloak that she wore, the one given to her by Blade, Tasa faded into near invisibility against the dragon's body.

"With you I feel complete." They spoke the words at the same time. Tasa smiled, as did Torin. They lay quiet for a time. Perhaps they slept.

"Your mentor's name is Wollston," Tasa said, and Torin nodded affirmatively. "I remember a time when we talked. It was near the water and I thought you were a rock. I thought I was dreaming. Mother said as much. But it was you, I know."

"I recall. It was a pleasant moment for me and I remember it exactly. I can bring our minds together and we can see it once again if you wish."

Tasa pondered that, then said, "That may be nice sometime, but I recall it quite well already. What I want to know is, did Wollston ever know about that?"

"If he did, he never said. I think he knew. It was shortly after that I was brought to the warm lands of Amen." In her mind, Tasa could picture a dragon, large and light brown, like the sand that surrounded the dragon. "I was apart from you then, but we had been together that one time and our bond was stronger for it.

"In Amen's lands I learned much. My thoughts were often engaged. I like Amen. She is wise and pleasant. She did not judge my thoughts nor my heart. Nor does Wollston, but it is different with him. He makes everything a lesson. He looks to recall every event in history and apply the lessons in a great tumble. It is fun sometimes. Amen allowed me to relax. We talked about many things. She did not hold me in place, except that she made it interesting to stay in place. You grew up without me close to you in this way."

"But I heard you sometimes."

"Yes. It is not an easy thing to speak in this way to one who is not trained to hear thoughts. It is also not easy to speak to one untrained without having to be somewhat loud about it all. Others can hear when thoughts are intense. I fear sometimes I was mentally shouting to get your attention. I slipped away to private places when I could."

"It did not sound like shouting to me. It sounded like…"

"Guidance?"

"Friendship. When I arrived at Albion I was empty. I felt that there was nothing to me inside. That I was somehow without substance. Mariel helped with that. I felt appreciated or needed or…something."

"Loved?"

Tasa smiled. "Yes." They each drew a long, slow breath. "Do we love each other, Torin? Do dragons love one another?"

"I do not know the answer to this, Tasa. I feel close to you. Our energies mingle, our life force intertwines. Are our hearts also together? I sense how you are with Mariel and see that we are not the same, you and I. This does not sadden me. I see Brigid and Penthe and they are like us. I hear Brigid speak of Epimetheous and sense that she and he were like you and Mariel. My mentor does not speak much of love, though I suspect that is because he knows little of the subject. In my own sight, I feel there must be many levels to love, many variations. It is what Gaia would do, create a diversity of experience for her children."

"Are we children of Gaia? What about being of the blood of the dragons?"

"It sets us apart in ways, but we belong to Gaia, you and I, and all the dragons now alive, and all those of the blood of the dragons. I believe that once the dragons did not belong to Gaia. Now we are a part of her, but the Ancient Dragons do not yet see this as truth, even though they were born to the earth. The Aeonics, they came from the stars. Or so says Wollston."

"I have many questions about such things, Torin. But I am not of a mind to either ask them now or explore such lofty histories. We, you and I, must choose to leave or stay. I believe we have already chosen."

"The path of experience is the path to wisdom. Who will join us?"

****

"Mariel, you need to learn something about me." Tasa was rehearsing this conversation. She was not exactly afraid of Mariel's reaction, but also not comfortable with how she would perceive the new situation. One day they were friends running in the wood. The next day one of them had a dragon for a brother. She tried another opening. "Mariel, remember when your Da said something about me being a child of the dragons?"

No, that wasn't right either. Tasa wanted this conversation to go well. She felt that Mariel, her closest companion and friend, had been left out of what is probably the most important thing in her life. She felt quite awful when she imagined how hurt Mariel might be.

She spoke into the wind. "Mariel. I would never intentionally hurt you. You are in my heart, and I wish that you had been close when Torin first appeared to me. I wish I had trusted my own perceptions enough to trust you with the weirdness in my own head. I wish…I wish you were here right now and I could just see you and you could see me and maybe you would just know that I love you and whatever else is happening I only want you by my side." She felt better for having spoken the words. Her heart opened, and she knew that Mariel would be her friend no matter what, even now that there is a dragon in her life. *Their* life, she mentally corrected herself.

Watching the sea, Tasa sat on a rocky ledge just a short climb below a rocky point and out of the steady wind. Torin had flown out to gather fish for her dinner. The water was mostly calm today with just some wind-driven waves throwing spray playfully into the sky. She knew that it was a short crossing to gain the continent. She wondered if the Sir Robin could make it across the channel and if she had the skill to pilot them safely. It would be nice to gather Mariel and Torin and just set course away from Albion. Get on with it all. Kamir too, she thought. He was a better sailor than she, and Mariel would not be much use in that much water. Maybe Karia too. They could use her wisdom and she could talk to people better than Tasa. In fact, why did Brigid not ask Karia to go on this journey? Why her? Wouldn't it be better to remain on Albion with Torin? Could Torin carry them on his back? Would that tire him out? And how would they get about? Torin was good in the air and also upon the water, but while they walked about he made too much noise not to be noticed at a distance. He needed training and she needed training and anyone who traveled with them needed training and all in different things. How was this all going to happen?

So many questions. Tasa resolved to approach someone older, someone she trusted, but who?

****

The days lengthened, warming and greening. Mariel scented the fresh spring leaves. Enough had been enough and she wanted to be where Tasa was. One could only hang about Beach House just so long. This was better, tracking Tasa was a fine pastime. Mariel could tell from the trail that Tasa had made camp in her usual clearing north along the coast past Karia's temple, along a rocky cliff amidst some twisting pines. That part was easy. Then it became peculiar. Large tracks, large marks, large passage through the trees and all accompanied by Tasa's smaller prints. Something abnormal, not within the bounds of Mariel's expectations. What was this? Mariel quieted her mind and allowed the earth to speak.

No violence. No fighting. Tasa and a giant, near a small fire, one that Tasa made, and they had spent the night. The next bit gave her trouble. Rocky and windswept, there was little that allowed for clues to Tasa's passing. Did she climb higher, up the wind-scoured cliff? There was no trace of her just beyond the wide expanse. The forest closed in there and Tasa may have taken to the trees. Mariel would have, had she gone that way. Mariel again stood still, allowing the wind to blow information to her senses. She closed her eyes and reached out.

They parted, Tasa and the giant, but there was more. A puzzling area just within the wood's edge was matted down. Larger than a giant would leave. The forest grass would have sprung back in a short time had it been a bear or a boar or anything like that. She walked about, scratching at the flattened grasses and found...she wasn't sure, but she suspected that Tasa must be with Brigid. And Brigid must be with her dragon for there in her hand was scale. Black and shiny.

Mariel did not know what color Penthe was said to be, but she felt proud of herself having deduced Tasa's companions thus far. Only...

The dragon did not seem to leave with Brigid. Rather, its tracks, for Mariel saw them clearly now, led off to the south a bit, the same as Tasa's. Mariel would scold her for being so obvious when they met up, but for now, she felt concerned. It did not occur to her to question the existence of the dragon. The evidence was there, a reality beheld and now to be believed. Giants? Well, there was Karia. And Forge Mother. Why, Mariel wondered, had she never thought of them as giants before, when they clearly were? Dragons? Well, they were spoken of in all the stories from the past as being real. Even if they were no longer present in number, that didn't mean they ceased to exist.

This dragon was certainly not hard to track. In fact, he left large swaths of crushed grass and broken branches. Mariel quickened her pace. This wasn't tracking, but it was fun. The dragon's path wove in and out of trees and brush. It appeared it was attempting to be less obvious in its movement. Tasa's tracks stopped occasionally, and Mariel could tell she was standing still while the dragon moved about. Was Tasa trying to train the dragon?

A quick burst of speed and Mariel came to a clearing. There in the center stood Tasa staring at a rock and though the wind blew the words away, Mariel could tell she was talking aloud.

"Tasa, you appear to be talking to a rock." Mariel stood off a bit, just at the edge of the forest. From her perception, her friend was attempting to get words from a stone.

"He's not a rock. He's a dragon and he walks through the woods very noisily. He will need to learn to be more stealthy if he is to travel with us." Tasa acted quite perturbed, looking like she may kick the rock any moment.

"If you kick the rock, you will hurt your foot." Mariel felt foolish for stating the obvious, but Tasa was acting very much not like Tasa at the moment.

"If I kick the rock hard enough I may knock a few scales loose." Her tone was tense. Her hands were curled in tightly balled fists and planted firmly on her slim hips.

"If you kick the rock, it will not enhance the rock's forestry skills," the rock said as it opened one eye. Tasa turned to look at Mariel. Her face held an "I told you so," look, but Mariel was not in sight.

"She went up into the tree," the rock said, and Tasa looked upward. There was Mariel, wide-eyed and wary, balanced on a leafy branch. She appeared to be a little embarrassed as she met Tasa's eye. Lithely dropping down to the base of the tree, she attempted to regain her composure.

The rock gradually became more dragon-like and stretched its wings and forearms. Mariel forced nonchalance in her steps as she moved towards Tasa. Her hand rested on the hilt of her knife.

"A dragon. A real dragon. Not a story, not a legend, but a real dragon. And you were going to kick the dragon." Mariel walked up to the once-upon-a-time rock. "Tasa, you are way more interesting than any other friend I have ever had."

"Mariel, this is Torin. Torin, Mariel. Mariel, Torin is a complete oaf in the forest. He is very graceful in the air and the water and, as you can see, quite adept at sitting still. If he is to travel with us, he needs to gain some knowledge from your expertise in the forest."

Mariel removed her hand from the knife hilt, looked at Torin and stroked her whiskers. "Hiding in plain sight. That was great! You completely fooled me and I'm pretty good at spotting things," Mariel boasted and complimented simultaneously. "Can you teach me to turn to stone? I mean, really, that is great!"

"High praise from you, Mariel of the Green. If I was successful at foiling your prodigious powers of perception, then I must have been at my very best." Torin spoke in a low voice and Mariel noted that she heard him inside her head more than out. "I will attempt to teach you the look of stone, but we, you and I, are beings of differing elements. I of stone and you of the forest."

"And I will attempt to show you the paths of the green, Great Torin!" Mariel bounced up and down and a smile grew naturally across her face. "You probably won't get as good as me, but I'll get you as good as you can get! Let's start!"

Mariel beckoned to Torin and moved toward the forest. Torin turned to face Tasa. She shrugged and stretched her arm towards the woods and Mariel. Torin gave an audible sigh and approached the edge of the forest. Mariel was already talking.

"First you have got to think like the forest. What does a leaf actually do? Do the same thing and you will be as silent as a falling leaf. When a tree is silent there is no wind, so if there is a wind you can sound like a tree because it is an expected noise. But if…" Tasa watched them wander into the forest. She noticed that Torin made no noise as he slipped into the dappled shadowy realm of green.

Tasa turned and looked upward. There Karia sat high on a rock observing the exchange. She had come at Tasa's invitation, but also helped set up this seemingly accidental meeting with Mariel. When Torin vanished into the wood, the giantess took three graceful leaps down the escarpment.

"That went better than expected."

"Mariel is pretty practical. Not much seems to take her by surprise." Tasa looked up into the tree at the branch that Mariel so recently perched upon. "Not for long anyway."

"The more people that know a secret, the less a secret it is," Karia said. "Now you and I, Kamir, and also Mariel know of the dragon's presence. I believe it will be necessary to also speak to Bria about the dragon."

"Torin," Tasa corrected. "His name is Torin, not 'the dragon.' He and I are…" Tasa had not gotten to this point before. Trying to speak aloud her new reality, her new truth, to someone else was difficult. What words should she use to help them understand? Torin, it seemed, always existed with her. Even when she was unaware of his actual being, he somehow *was*.

"You are bonded," Karia said. "It is what happened in the past. It does not happen now. It complicates matters."

"Well it is what is, and I am his friend. We will travel together and deal with what arrives."

****

"So, you are of the line of Amen?" Mariel did not understand the question. She also did not understand where the question came from. Her eyes snapped about as she scanned the area. Torin had become very good at hiding. They had wandered a distance away and Mariel said he should attempt to track her. That way he could see how she crept through the woods undetected. She thought she was alone. But there was Torin in her mind.

"We can be together like this, if you wish." Torin's voice came to her clearly, just not through her ears. "We can be close, because you and Tasa are close. But only if you wish. It will be good to be close in this way for the journey we are going to take together."

Journey? Tasa had said they would travel together, and Mariel only thought of the Sir Robin and the fact that they would need a bigger boat if they were to be ferrying a dragon. "What journey?" she thought and pictured Torin.

"Very good!" Torin's voice returned to her and yet the woods remained silent. "I heard you quite clear. It may take some time, but I feel we will become very adept at this form of communication.

"I am not altogether graceful in knowing what to say or when to say it, however. Perhaps I have overstepped my boundaries in mentioning the journey. Perhaps that was for Tasa to speak of first."

"No." Mariel again pictured the dragon. "She'll be alright with it if it comes from you. Although she has a lot of questions to answer about all this, we are strong together, Tasa and I."

"She herself has many questions and is desirous of your companionship. I see that you are indeed strong together. It is my hope that you and I will also be strong in this way. Tasa is important to both you and I.

"Would you like me to tell you what I know of the journey?"

"Yes," thought Mariel, "and don't forget, you are supposed to be tracking me."

"I have not forgotten."

The thought came to Mariel that she was going to sea. Not just a thought but an image of the sea and the boat beneath her feet, rising and falling with each wave. She began to feel queasy.

"Whoa..." she said. "Whoa...wait a second." Her stomach wobbled. "I thought you were just going to tell me about the journey."

"My apologies. As a dragon I am used to communicating with all senses. I forgot that you have fewer than we, even though you are of the blood of the dragons."

"And of the line of Amen," Mariel said, recovering her composure. "Whatever that means."

"Yes. Well, it appears that there are many questions for the three of us and we will have time on our journey for all of them."

"So, this journey is a sea voyage?"

"It's not so bad really. You have excellent balance and your ancestors sailed a great river." This time the voice was no longer within her head but sounded clear and deep in the thicket where she had been hiding. She whirled to and fro. The voice was so close. No one could have snuck up on her like this. Not even Tasa.

"You are really very good in your craft. Is that the proper term? Your woodcraft? Your forestry? Tasa learned much from you. I am impressed. Because of my size, I was concerned about my ability to learn and become effective. Yet you are an excellent teacher. We will need stealth on this journey. I am certain of this fact. Only a small portion will be crossing the sea. Much will be on land."

Mariel's sense focused on a pile of rocks in the shadow of the forest edge. The rocks looked at her. It was unnerving but thrilling at the same moment. It is one thing to hear fables and tales told and to say you believe they may be true. It is quite another for the tale to come true right in front of you.

"I am good at being still and not seen," Torin said aloud. "But we, you, Tasa, and I, will need to be unseen while in motion. I cannot always risk flying, especially in daylight, and I do not expect you and Tasa to travel in the dark, even though you are excellent at it, from what I hear. It would be good to be invisible, but that is not something a dragon can do."

"You have to believe you can become invisible," Mariel said.

"Ah! Belief! It is something my mentor and I speak of regularly. Do you believe in dragons?"

"Yes, I evidently do. So…you and Tasa…you know each other well?"

At that moment Tasa came into view from the wood. She stood between Mariel and Torin.

"So…" she said. "You two are pretty easy to track, yakking away like this."

****

In the deep of night Tasa and Mariel lay against Torin's side, his tail wrapped around them and the small fire Tasa crafted. The girls were snuggled together, their cloaks covering them as the early spring day became crisp with winter's last breeze. The wind off the sea was fresh and chill and left their faces red.

"This trip, this journey, will it be a long one?" Mariel asked.

"I don't think so. We just go over there and find as many people as we can. People with the blood of the dragons."

"The ones with the light in their eyes. That light that you see, but not me."

"Yes. It should be easy. And I think we are supposed to visit with King Kane."

"Well that should be fun. I hear stories that say he has a castle. On a mountain."

"He knows dragons, so Torin should be welcome in his lands at least."

"So…you have a dragon," Mariel said, punching Tasa hard in the arm.

35
Gathering

DEAR SISTER,

I send this letter for one reason and only that one. I need to give Mariel a task. She pouts about Beach House. She sits in glum silence upon the little boat they privately call the Sir Robin. She wanders the halls of the rooms she and Tasa stay in during inclement weather, sighing like one no longer of this world but having refused to cross into the next. I shall have to endure Mariel's long, mopey days if we do not find a purpose for her while Tasa journeys with Brigid.

Thus, Mariel arrives at your door and I am shifting the problem your way with the full knowledge that our niece will return here as soon as she can to wait at the docks pining for her friend like the girls pine for their sailor boys.

Should you have any clues as to how to facilitate this issue, please send them along in a note with Mariel. This will give her purpose, and me an excuse to send her back with reply. I am designating this missive as one of high import and stating to her that only she carries my trust to get this letter through the soggy spring lands. Only her skills, I tell her, will enable this to arrive in an appropriate time period. "Be safe," I tell her, so she takes no foolish risk, but also swift and direct.

"Wait for reply," I have instructed, and you may concoct your own fable to gain her attention.

My dearest Marageth, are we doing the right thing by Tasa? In my thoughts I know we are, in my heart I doubt. There is not a day, not an hour, that I do not second guess my own choice in this matter.

I do believe it is beyond us now. Tasa is gone to the north islands, along with the dragon Torin. There they train and commune with Penthe and Brigid and I confess I am a little envious of Kila's daughter for that closeness to our founder.

The reports from overseas do not lessen in intensity. We at Beach House train in weaponry daily. Karia is a great fount of knowledge in this regard and fearsome, where she once was calming. Is this what we will become?

In all things, sister, I am lovingly yours,

Marion

✳✳✳✳✳✳✳✳✳✳✳✳

It was spring and warmer in the south, at Penthe House. Trees and flowers bloomed and grew lush. Verdant fields carpeted the land and the scent of life and vitality carried on swift cool breezes. Bees and birds sang their songs of a land awakened from winter slumber.

However, far north along the fierce and jagged western coast of Albion, where Tasa and Torin were, ice continued to crust upon ancient rocks. Waves sprayed in the wild wintery winds off the gray northern sea. Caves were damp and cold. Boating was perilous. Water washed the sides of their little craft constantly and there was never a moment when they were warm and dry while at sea. It was everything that Tasa should hate. It was the opposite of her island home of Solaine. And she loved every second.

When the little voyages were done, when Brigid felt Tasa and Torin were sufficiently trained for that day, they returned to her island home, a vast cavern that went deep into a mass of rock in the midst of the mad sea. Carved by the water over millennia and now some distance above the cresting wave tops, it remained relatively dry.

Small pockets of stone held pulsing dragonfire. Torin's flame had gotten stronger over the months, warmer and steadier, casting a brighter light and fading slowly. He no longer needed to give it constant attention. His larger fires left something to be desired, and he and Penthe spent long hours practicing upon the sodden stone islands that endured the battering waves.

Penthe and Torin were just returning to the cavern. They carried large fish within their claws and Brigid accepted the food with gratitude. Tasa wondered if she would ever see a vegetable again. A potato or carrot. Just one.

Wood gathered from the tossing waves formed a spit above practiced dragonfire and with keen, bone-handled knives the two women set to work preparing the meal the best they could. The dragons, having taken their fill before they returned, now lay quiet and still at the mouth of the cave. Their bulk prevented some of the storm winds from entering.

****

Tasa marveled at the cloak she wore. It was her gift from Blade. Well, not exactly a gift. Blade provided it before their training began and merely left it behind when she vanished. There was no emotion attached to the giving. Still, Tasa liked it and the cloak, deep and dark, warm and strong, was her constant companion along with the sword, Quiet Edge.

The sword hummed to her now and she whirled and swung about as Brigid lay into a series of thrusts. Tasa parried as best she could, backing to the end of the cavern. It was dark here and Brigid was a large shadow against the dragonfire of the front of the cave. The giantess drove her massive sword near Tasa's torso, but the girl slid away to the left. Faster than Tasa could imagine, Brigid swirled her sword point in that direction, following Tasa's movement.

The cloak continued on its way to the left as Tasa dropped and rolled right. Brigid thrust again, but too late. The cloak now became entangled about Brigid's blade and she needed to withdraw to clear it of the cloth. Tasa was behind her now and slapped the flat of Quiet Edge hard against Brigid's knee.

The giantess quivered and staggered. She tried to turn to face Tasa, but the lithe girl had slipped from sight. Brigid only knew where she was by the next burst of pain. Her elbow spasmed and she clutched her sword hard in order not to drop it. And then again, she felt the flat of her pupil's blade against the other side of her head.

Tasa's voice echoed in the cavern as she shouted, "Blade!" and again struck Brigid's sword arm, this time at the wrist. Brigid did drop her weapon and Tasa came at her from the front. She was a blaze of images in Brigid's sight. The giantess spun and parried, her forearms clad in thick leathers and metals. All to no avail.

Her fallen sword continually was spun away from her grasp. Tasa was relentless in her drive. Brigid found herself effectively backed up into black dragon scales. Torin looked at her over his shoulder and said, "I think Tasa wins this round."

Catching her breath, Brigid said, "I think Tasa is as ready as she can be."

36

The Leavings

NEW EXPERIENCES WERE ALREADY TAKING THEIR TOLL on Tasa. She had a headache. Never, ever was this something she experienced, and she did not like it at all. It made her crabby and snippy. She wanted everyone to be quiet and go away so that she could close her eyes. Everyone.

"Tasa, we can't carry all this," Mariel whispered for the dozenth time and Tasa wanted to scream. Except that would make her head hurt more. Mother Stone had shields for them. Big Huge Metal Shields. Bria could barely shift hers, let alone lift it.

"I'll train you," Forge Mother was saying. "You'll be strong enough in no time. If you carry the swords on one side and the shields on the other they will balance each other just fine."

Mother Marion looked at the shields and said, "Now Forge Mother, we want them to be inconspicuous, remember?"

Tasa was grateful for the intervention of Beach Mother, but she had her own additions to their already overflowing packs. Fishing equipment, complete with nets and small cooking pots with utensils and cloth to wrap up the metal pieces so they did not clink together, and several types of cooking knives, and even a small table, which she now conceded was too much to carry, but at least, she insisted, they must carry the little folding stools.

"Ye be correct, Beach Mother." Mother Stone acknowledged the point. "The shields be overlarge. Well, I'll make some smaller ones tomorrow." Tasa's left eye began to twitch.

"Tasa," Mariel whispered again, "we can't…" She let the thought trail off when she noticed Tasa glaring at her with one eye shut. In that moment Tasa looked a bit like Forge Mother when things were irregular.

Poor Bria stood in a huge leather vest which reached well below her knees. Gloves with gauntlets made her look quite comical. She was well protected but could barely move. Her sword hung at her hip and dragged on the ground. She looked at Tasa and Mariel and they could see tears in her eyes.

Gathered at Beach House, Tasa and her crew made ready to get underway. The Mali stood still in the bay. She gleamed bright and looked beautiful with full rigging and new sails. Master Amir insisted that he be the one to take them on the first leg of their journey.

****

Amir and Tasa had met again shortly after Tasa's first conversation with Brigid by the fire in the forest.

"You are my father." Tasa was determined not to be angry.

"Yes and happy about this fact. Are you angered that I have not been present in your life?"

"How long have you known of my existence?"

"Only a few short years. When I brought Ikara to Solaine to meet with your mother. Kila did not readily admit that you were my daughter. She feared losing you to the sea."

Tasa laughed a bitter breath. "She was almost right." A deep breath then, cleansing and calming, for she felt her chest and heart tightening. "I am angry. I do not know if I am angry at someone. You. Mother. The Mothers at Penthe House. The dragons. I feel that so much of my life was kept private…no, *secret*. And it was secreted away from me. My life! Yes, I am angry!" Tears welled.

Amir laid a strong hand on his daughter's shoulder and said, "Anger is not a fault, not a weakness. It is human. Let it come out and then be rid of it all. Today is not tomorrow. Your mother managed to hold her anger for a very long time. She is powerful that way."

They were sitting next to each other in the wood near the river's end. Sir Robin was tied at the dock. Somewhere, Mariel had made herself scarce. Torin was near, Tasa could sense that, but she asked him to be…apart from her thoughts? Silent?

She still did not have a full pattern of thought about their communication. He was present in her mind most always now and it was pleasant. But they did have a two-way conversation that others could not hear. It was confusing and Tasa caught herself answering Torin while talking with someone who did not know he was there. She spoke sentences out of context, making no sense to people, and they just looked at her as if she was odd. And she was odd. She believed she was the oddest person in Albion.

"I want to say fatherly things to you, Tasa, but I do not feel I have the right. I respected your mother's wishes, commands really, to remain private with this information, but in my heart I could only see you as a daughter. I am long lived, but you are my first child. I regret the love lost to the time passed. I do not know if we can be a parent and child. Not like Kamir and I. He loves you deeply, by the way." Amir smiled at that and looked at Tasa to see her reaction.

She did have a reaction and it surprised her. She felt Kamir's love then, and Karia's. She felt her mother's love and even Amir's. She sensed then that there were many who loved her, and she felt very sad. For she did not know if she was loving towards them. She had long felt empty, incomplete. So often she was deep within her own mind, questioning herself, her existence, her worth. So often she compared herself to others and found lack in herself. Yet others found value. Others sought her out. Others found reason to love her and yet she did not fully love her own life.

"Poor Kamir," she said. "Just a boy. Karia always called us little brother and big sister. She is wise and told me the truth in her own way. I was too small in my sight to see that truth."

"We all have our truths and they serve us at different moments. The trick is to make your truth malleable, flexible, so that when you learn something new, you do not break or harden so that others break against you." Amir shifted so they could see one another. Tasa did the same.

"The truth, my truth, is that I am scared. What once looked like a life of fun and forestry is now turning into something bigger. The beast men, how dangerous are they to Albion? Do not lie to me, Amir. Do not protect me with soft truths. Tell me what you see. I would see the world through your eyes." Without thinking, Tasa took his large hand in hers.

"Truly? You wish to see through my eyes?" Amir was very still and let his fingers curl about Tasa's slender hand.

She knew that there was something different about to happen. She need but say "Yes" and Amir would…

"Yes. Through your eyes, Father." And the vision came upon her in a rush of images. The Mali was beneath their feet, but it was not the Mali, it was a dragon and they were in flight. They flew above water and islands and she recognized them from maps she poured over as a child. Some of the islands glowed with that same green light she witnessed with Torin.

In her mind, she heard Amir speak. "Those are lands where dragons have laid their eggs." Some of the glow was pale, weak. "Those are eggs that may never hatch or spark to life. The dragons are in stasis. Only a few remain active. Not enough to spark their children to full power." Amir's voice was rich and strong within the vision. Tasa felt his hand gripping hers and returned the grasp. Mali banked away from the islands and descended.

"She is not *the* Mali, not the seafaring craft," said Amir. "Rather she is Mali, the dragon who granted me the fire and scales to create the craft. She is an Ancient Dragon who lives high in the mountains. I journeyed there and was in attendance to her as she went into stasis. She gave me part of herself. She also gave me the crystals that allow the ship to move along the ley lines around the earth. In this way I assist the dragons to communicate while they slumber. Here now, do you see this island? Do you know this one?"

Below, a wasp-waisted island appeared beneath wispy clouds. The north was green with forest and a tall mountain. The southern half was rocky and dry. A port town lay at the center on the eastern side and she did know this place. Solaine. Her home.

"You make me proud with what you know of the sea and the earth, Tasa. Not many read the world well. You are a sojourner in your heart." The words made Tasa happy. Praise from Amir, from her father.

The dragon Mali drew close to the water and leveled off, skimming the wave tops. Tasa wondered, if Mali was in stasis, how then were they flying upon her back? Amir's voice came to her again, only this time it felt there was another voice joining his. "It is an image. We are in dreamtime. You have been here before. It is why you hear my voice before you ask your questions. Within this state we are blended in our life energies. We share sight. What I see, what I image, you also witness and know."

The island approached at gentle speed. The dragon Mali flew so smoothly, she was so large, her wings spread such a great span, it felt as if they were still and the earth moved beneath them. "Different than being aboard the ship?" Amir spoke and laughed.

The village came into view and Tasa traced the familiar sights of her home, only now she observed things in a different way. The village lay upon the slopes to the north of the bay. There was the main house of meeting, white with a white door. There was a house near the dock, still white to reflect the brilliant sun, but with a blue door. Further up a little hill, sheltered by a grove of trees, stood a house with several smaller dwellings around it in a semi-circle. Each of these buildings was fronted by red doors. A stone fence enclosed the area and children played within.

Above the village, the building that had become the library stood sheltered by trees. A violet door was clearly visible in the shaded courtyard in front of the building. The door opened and a man in white robes stepped outside. Caraphino looked directly at them and smiled.

Mali veered a bit and then floated higher. Her mother's house came into view. Though far up the hill and away from the bay, it still was fronted with a blue door. Tasa could see that it was positioned quite nicely to observe the whole of the bay and also some distance out to sea. In a way, the view reminded her of the one from Karia's temple.

Nearby, amidst groves of trees and vineyards, many smaller houses were scattered around her mother's. The smaller houses had green doors. Women and children walked from them to the trees. They carried cutting tools and baskets. They gathered ripened fruits or trimmed branches.

A woman clad in blue stood up from working the vines and looked into the sky. Others did not seem to see them, but this woman took off her broad-brimmed hat and looked directly at Tasa.

"Mother!" Tasa said and felt herself slipping from Mali's back. Amir gripped her tightly about the waist and held her in place.

"Tasa?" Kila asked the sky. "Tasa!" she called out and reached upward. Those women working nearby looked up and then looked at Kila.

"They do not see what she sees, Tasa. You long to go to her, but that is a dangerous thing just now. To leave dreamtime in this manner can cause a being to become lost. Some are trained to it, not all can take this action."

Yet Tasa felt herself slipping away to the island, to her mother. She recalled slipping away from Torin when she saw Brigid. "You must stay with me for now, daughter," Amir said, and again tightened his grip on her. She relaxed into his arms at the word 'daughter' and they flew on past Kila and north, away from Solaine.

They flew high and faster now. Tasa felt wind in her face, but her hair remained unruffled. Passing over water and then over land, the region below grew mountainous. Great green forests covered the high mountains only to a certain level. Then peaks of snow and ice emerged, some climbing above the cloud lines.

Occasionally there would be that same glow of green in some deep vale or shadowed mountainside, but this sight lessened until it was no more. The peaks and mountains became ever more jagged and dark. Tasa noted small red glows here and there.

Amir's voice answered her unasked question. "The firedrakes are something like dragons, but without reason. They are growing. Few are seen in the day. They tunnel up from beneath the earth. People fear them when they emerge, for they breathe flame and cause destruction without purpose or mercy. Men once armed themselves against the beasts, but then…they began to become beasts themselves.

"Over time the energy of the blood dragon Tepes pervaded the land around the mountain where he was restrained. The fire drakes were sparked to a weak, mindless life and left to grow untutored and wild. They in turn cause a shift in humans, those who carry none of the blood of the dragons, the true dragons, Tasa, for there are such things. As there are true humans. And yet, each has their own truth."

Mali arced westward and followed a great blue river. Settlements along the banks and ships plying the waters were alight with fierce red glow. The dragon Mali stayed high, but Tasa could hear screams, cries of pain or pleas for help. "I cannot see the green glow of those of the blood of the dragons," she said aloud.

"It is diminished. It is failing against the rising tide of the beast men. This then is what we face, what the world faces. This is what I see, daughter. It is what you are being asked to enter into. In my heart I feel I cannot allow such a thing, yet a part of me is proud that I have a child that others deem skilled enough, wise enough, to accomplish such a duty."

In the distance Tasa gazed at a mountain. It seemed to rise where few other mountains rose. The glow was strong here and the light radiated from the peak out and away across the land. "What is this that you see?" It was Amir's turn to question his daughter.

The green light poured forth to the eastern land of darkness and angry red. "Father, I do not know what I am seeing. It feels like potential, a future that may yet be. It also does not feel true, not yet."

Mali banked about and circled the mountain, spiraling closer, ever closer. At the peak a vast complex of buildings carved from the stone of the mountain itself lay exposed to the constant snows and ices. A wide expanse, flagged in stone and encircled by short walls lay below them, large enough, thought Tasa, for Mali to perhaps land and be comfortable.

One lone being, a giant, a man, stood impervious to the elements around the mountain peak. He was looking to the east. Fierce winds pulled and pushed his long, curled red hair. Icy particles rimed his great ruddy beard. The giant turned as they approached and watched impassively.

Mali circled slow. Tasa caught the giant's eye as they circled. In those eyes she saw the same strong light of Brigid as she appeared in her dreamtime travels with Torin. Briefly the giant looked away to Amir and then the dragon Mali. Looking back once more to Tasa, he nodded once, then turned and strode between huge columns and into his castle.

"Kane," said Amir. "King Kane. You must make your way to him, Tasa."

"And then what, Father? I am a girl. A child to one such as he."

"You are wise, Tasa. Speak your truth to him. He knows you now."

Tasa shivered with those words.

****

The world had grown dimmer as twilight came upon them. The vision was ended. Tasa and Amir sat close, his strong arms about her shoulders. She leaned towards him, her face tight against his chest. Her sight went wispy, as if the vision sought to return. She let her eyes grow soft and saw Mali flying above Albion. Rising from the southern forests, Torin joined her and they circled high into the air. Torin looked small next to Mali, like a child, thought Tasa.

****

"We will listen to them. We will nod and agree. We will say 'Yes' and 'Thank you.' Then we will leave this land and make our own decisions." Tasa spoke as the Sir Robin drifted. Mariel was at her side on her left. Kamir was on her right. A'Tienne sat with Kianna. Bria sat alone, a small furry something in her hands and a little bird upon her shoulder.

"They care for us," Tasa said. "They only want our safety. They know that we are going into danger and I want you all to know this same thing now. We face, not just the unknown, but the unimaginable. I have seen it in a vision. I have fought it on our shores. There is activity that we have only heard hints of and seen briefly. We will be required to fight; I feel it. If this is not something you can do, I will understand, and I will tell the Mothers that they are to allow you to remain without loss of honor."

Tasa expected Bria to take this offer. Beautiful, gentle little Bria, the healer and caretaker of injured and orphaned animals. She rarely even held a weapon, let alone wielded one. But she did not look away. Instead it was Kianna who raised her hand.

"This is a difficult decision for me, Tasa. I only recently took the oath of Wisdom House. I am drawn by their serenity. A'Tienne and I have been partners for many years now and we spent long hours making this decision together. She was to go to the northern lands and join the hunt, while I went inward. She now travels with you, and I am left with the other half of the decision. Though I am skilled in forestry and the hunt, my calling is elsewhere. When Mother Meg asked us to travel with you, she did not know of our choice. Together, A'Tienne and I have chosen the path of Wisdom House for my future." Kianna gripped A'Tienne's hand.

A'Tienne looked about the boat and settled her gaze on the captain. She said, "I am still willing to go on this journey, Tasa. My bow is strong." A'Tienne stroked it with one hand as Kianna loosened her grip. It lay across her lap, polished and shining. It was the gift from the boy across the sea, the one from the emerald isle. "With the loss of Kianna, do we need to balance our party? If yes, then Ni'all is one I might suggest as a worthy companion." Kianna smiled and ducked her head.

Tasa nodded and said, "It is a loss, but I respect your choice, Kianna. As to this Ni'all, let us discuss this amongst ourselves and allow the Mothers to be free of that decision." All on board smiled. They were becoming a single unit with these small decisions and private discussions and Tasa guided the thoughts well. Amir spoke to her of leadership and decision and the ways to be strong and gain respect. None of which was going to work with Mariel, Tasa knew, but there were other ways to handle her.

"We will be leaving on the Mali in the next lunar turning. Though we still have report of winter conditions on the mainland, it is well into spring and the weather should be warming and more welcoming. We will be able to travel lighter. Even with the 'smaller shields' provided by Forge Mother." Again, they laughed together. "We will leave them aboard the Mali. Amir is in agreement with that course. He is our ally in these matters. If you have concerns or need counsel, he is open to all of us."

"But you are captain, right? We follow you, right?" Mariel was trying to make a point and Kamir squirmed a bit. "You are captain not because Amir is your Da, but because we all followed you first, before all this stupid, 'Go find people' and 'Go visit King Kane' stuff, right?"

Tasa was quiet at that, knowing that this was coming from somewhere else and knowing that Kamir was feeling some level of confusion about matters. Well, he would need to get over things, figure them out and get on with the next day. Already Tasa questioned the wisdom of taking him along. Were it up to her, she and Mariel would go with Torin and that would be that. The others were along to give a better sense of security to the Mothers.

"I have known Tasa for a long time," Bria said. She so rarely spoke at these meetings that everyone turned to her now. "She only looks to do what is best. She takes the lead naturally and is good at it. Mother Meg and Mother Marion recognize this and even Forge Mother likes Tasa. I mean she LIKES

Tasa, not just the work she turns out. And Brigid spoke with her, and she has a dragon. We've all met Torin. It is no little thing that we are being asked to accompany Tasa on her journey. It is ours too, I know, but Tasa would go whether we went or not. No one here can say that they would go if Tasa did not lead us, not even Mariel.

"I am afraid. I am not a fighter. I am a healer. I speak to the animals. I begged to be allowed to go along. If Mother Marion and Karia had not agreed, I would have stolen away and gone anyway. I want to be on this journey, and I want to follow Captain Tasa. No one else." Bria finished her speech without looking at anyone but Tasa.

"So…" Mariel said, looking everyone in the eye, "Captain Tasa, right?"

37

Handfasting

BEFORE THE DAY OF LEAVING THERE WERE MANY THINGS that felt necessary to accomplish. Much supplying of the expedition was in the hands of others and, in the eyes of the crew, these ones failed admirably. In an effort to cover every single contingency, those ones failed to take into account how exactly the crew of young folk would carry all of the supplies deemed necessary by the Penthe House Mothers.

These were practical matters that the crew left aside, for there were more personal things, matters of the heart, that they gave priority to. For Tasa, there was the matter of Mariel. Mariel needed to be comfortable with Torin as well as Tasa. Fortunately, Torin seemed to understand the new dynamic of friendship that was to be instilled between the three of them and effortlessly wove Mariel into the mixture.

From Tasa's perspective, Mariel showed no sign of being open to Torin's thoughts in the same way that Tasa was. She simply did not seem to pick up this form of communication. Speaking to Torin in person was no obstacle, and Mariel seemed content in the matter. She also did not seem to feel left out when Tasa would mentally commune with Torin, even in Mariel's presence.

"You don't tell him everything we talk about, do you?" Mariel asked one afternoon, while they were gazing at "portable" tents that, even wrapped at their tightest, still stood a head taller than Tasa. "I mean you can if you want, but I think a dragon would be bored by some of the sillier moments you and I share."

Mariel stood Tasa up against another pack. The girls did not know what it contained, but it was even taller than the tents. Mariel moved her hand from the top of Tasa's head to the pack. She just shook her head as Tasa turned to observe that the pack was indeed taller still than the ungainly tenting.

"This," Tasa mused, "must be a jest."

"Have they even seen us?" Mariel asked.

A voice from the forest floated in the girls' direction. "They believe I will act the beast of burden." Torin was quiet and sounded amused.

Mariel looked at all the packs collected in the center of a glade and said, "No offense Torin, but some of these seem even bigger than you. Even if you wanted to, I don't think you could carry all of these supplies. You might as well just carry all of us. We'll get this journey finished quick that way."

The trio stood in silence for a moment before Mariel said, "Do you suppose…"

"No," Tasa said. "We do not ride each other, Mariel. We will not be riding Torin. We will not even ask to ride Torin. We will not even say anything at all to anyone about the idea."

Torin said, "I can and will carry either of you, but understand that flight takes effort, and a dragon must remain light within and without. In case of danger or injury I will gladly make such an effort for either of you." His head was near the girls and they turned together towards him.

"I am sorry for even letting the thought cross my mind, Torin." Mariel reached a hand out as if to pet the dragon. She hesitated. She had seen Tasa touch Torin in a familiar way, but this suddenly seemed…intimate? Was she allowed to…

Torin moved his head towards the girl and at the same moment reached forward with his right forearm. Patting the top of Mariel's head, he said, "Nice little Pucelle," then he stroked her whiskers on the side of her face with one outstretched claw. Turning to Tasa he said, "Shall we all agree not to treat one another like we are pets?"

It was Tasa's nature to be quiet and she rarely laughed aloud. The stunned look on Mariel's face released that laughter. Mariel, overcoming the shock of being petted by a dragon, soon found herself laughing as well, first nervously, but soon, the trio all reaching for the tops of each other's heads to pet one another brought the mirth to her voice and throat as well.

As the moment passed, Mariel said, "So dragons can laugh then?" and together they reached for one another in embrace.

****

Ni'all was a surprise to the crew. Kianna brought him from the docks, where he had sailed his own little coracle across the sea at the written invitation from A'Tienne. The invitation was signed by both young women.

Not so tall as either A'Tienne or Kianna, he was broad at the chest and shoulders and wore a kilt that exposed muscular legs. Leather boots rose up to his mid-calf. It appeared that much of his clothing contained sewn-in sheaths. Hilts of knives, small and large, showed at his waist, wrist, shoulder, and at the outside of each boot. At his side hung a small sword, too long to call a knife, Mariel commented later to Tasa in private. Broad leather belts crisscrossed his chest, one attached to a well-stocked quiver and the other to a long pack that buckled at the top and had at least two sheaths for two more blades. His long bow arched, and he carried it strung.

Dark hair curled down about his shoulders and the pale skin of his face held bright blue eyes. He did not smile when meeting everyone but grinned broadly when A'Tienne arrived. "M'lady!" he spoke by way of greeting and doffed his cap, bowing slightly, but never removing his eyes from A'Tienne. His voice was higher than Tasa and Mariel expected, they agreed later when they compared notes, and he did not say much in the course of their first days together. In this way he was different from Kianna and the girls mused that he and A'Tienne would be good companions if stealth were necessary.

Kianna introduced him around to the crew. Ni'all spoke a greeting to each. "Kamir, son of Karia and Amir? Good lineage, boy." And, "Bria, good with the wee beasts then? Makes hunting easier when you can talk them into the nets." And, "Mariel. I hear of your forestry. We can compare our styles. Learn from each other then."

Tasa stood back observing and Kianna led Ni'all to her at the last. Ni'all nodded and again removed his cap. This time he did bow low and allowed his eyes to drop below her gaze. When he rose, he said, "You're being the clanswoman that leads us then? Ye have the trust of the lady A'Tienne. Ye have my blade and bow."

In private, Kamir spoke to Tasa of how he did not wish to be called "boy" by this stranger.

Bria commented to Tasa later in that first evening that she did not wish to use her gifts to bring her animal friends to their deaths.

Mariel wondered aloud in the late evening what this person thought he could teach her and why he felt worthy enough to be instructed by Mariel of the Green.

A'Tienne approached everyone the next day and simply said, "The ways of the tribes to the north and on his island are different than we are used to. He will learn our ways. I will teach him." She did not ask for patience.

The day was one of preparation, but not for the journey. Kianna spoke with the crew when A'Tienne and Ni'all were off on an errand. "They are to be handfasted on the morrow," she said.

Kamir scratched his head and said, "I thought you and A'Tienne were handfasted?"

"A year and a day, yes. And we have done so five times now. Five fine years," she said wistfully. "But she is with you on the journey, and I remain to follow a differing path. Ni'all is a good man and will make a fine companion for all of you. Ni'all is a different sort of person than I. He has my respect and trust that he will care for A'Tienne. They love one another, and I love A'Tienne enough to wish for her happiness. They have gone off to see if Karia will perform a formal ceremony."

****

In this way then, a final community event came about. A cause for celebration and happiness rather than sadness at the leaving of the crew. A buoyant lifting of spirits rather than dark fears of what may come to pass.

All came together swiftly. Flowers and wreaths were garlanded and woven. Feasts were prepared. Musicians arrived from all about Penthe House. Tasa was surprised at the attendance and participation. Mariel was not. "A'Tienne is a strong huntress. She provides well for all the houses. It will be a loss for Penthe House when she is gone."

Tasa grew pensive at this thought. She did not fully realize the scope of importance that A'Tienne held for their community and so sought out Karia for counsel. "How can we take her along? She is much more useful for the greater number, Karia. We have Mariel, and Kamir is a pretty fair hunter. I do okay myself, Karia, and we have…" Out of habit Tasa hesitated speaking Torin's name, but the reality was that many people seemed to have at least a passing awareness of his existence.

Karia laid her large hand upon Tasa's slender shoulder. "It is because she is important to the community that she travels with you. She is not just a huntress, Tasa, but also a fierce warrior. She and Ni'all will provide strength and support in battle if necessary. She will bring you all back safely, at least that is the thinking of Mother…well, of many of the Mothers of Penthe House."

Tasa smiled, for she knew that Karia nearly said Mother Stone. Out of all of the Mothers of Penthe House, she was the one most interested in the martial needs of the crew. "Will we really need such skills, Karia?"

"It is best to have the tool and not need it than need it and not possess such a thing. You have spoken to Amir and he has, at my behest, been honest with you. I grant you my vision now. Your path has not always been easy, but it is not one I would consider difficult. You have had support and willing trainers. Now you go out alone with peers. The situations you will encounter we cannot prepare you for, because we do not know what they will be. We hear tales. We have seen the beast men attack our shores. The stories increase as more refugees seek our shores. The skills you possess and those of your crew are balanced, and we can only hope and believe that you will each rise to whatever occasion occurs. I see that you are heading to a dangerous place on the earth.

"Dear Tasa, I would shield you all from this were it possible. It is your choice, and each member of the crew chooses to be with you and follow your lead. Even Ni'all. I know his tribe. They are fierce and do not lend their loyalty lightly. If he is willing to pledge to you, I feel many times more confident in the safe outcome of the journey. It is not that I do not possess confidence in you and Mariel and the others. It is that together you are stronger.

"We have hunters aplenty. We have only one crew that we feel capable of accomplishing such a mission. Stealth, discernment, insight, and the ability to see the spark of the blood of the dragons within others, these are the strengths you bring. The crew is bound to you because of who you are, not by command. Do you see the why of things clearer now?"

"And there is Torin," Tasa said.

"There is Torin," Karia agreed. "You are being asked to embark upon a twofold quest. It is not solely the seeking of those who will strengthen Penthe House by their presence. It also to seek my uncle, the one called King Kane. He may be a valuable ally in the securing of the world from the beast men. He, like my father, are ancient beings. They have walked with dragons, if the legends are true. Make no mistake, I do believe the legends.

"The dragons, they are missing from our lives, and we are told by these ancient ones that it is the will of Gaia. Torin belies that tale in some manner. There is a difference in the world now and with what came before. There is a delay in making a decision to take action. King Kane may have a change of heart in certain matters should he witness a dragon traveling together with a girl. Make your way to his lands, Tasa. Seek an audience with him. You are of the form of human, but Amir has given you the truth that you are more than such beings ever can be. You are like many in Albion. You are elven, and as such carry great connection to the earth and Gaia.

"Brigid will say that this does not make you superior, only different. It is a conversation that she and I have shared, and no agreement is yet arrived upon. In truth, I believe my aunt does not share her own voiced sentiments but speaks in principle. My father and uncle also speak in such ways. I speak more directly, Tasa. It is not always the path to agreement.

"You *are* superior. You always will be. Do not waste your gift on those unworthy. Send only the ones that can benefit and strengthen our purpose, for it is Gaia's purpose that we seek. Stay safe and be wise in your encounters. There are times when my sight is clear regarding the portents of the future. This is not one of those times. I seek evidence that you will all return safe to the shores of Albion. I see aught but mist."

****

Later, as the sun set, Tasa spoke with Torin.

"I am an elf." Her words sounded odd, but correct.

Torin sniffed at the top of her head. "With some giant and a small amount of human." He sniffed again and said, "On your father's side."

"You can tell that?" Tasa screwed up her face in amazement.

"I am getting better at this ability. My mentor is quite excellent, though I do feel that he sometimes is guessing more than knowing. Still, a guess backed with great knowledge can open up a path of thought that may be fruitful. In this matter of your lineage, I do not guess."

"My mother then? What of her? Giant, elf, human, or something new? And what do you mean calling Mariel a Pucelle, and a child of Amen? If Amen is a dragon, is Mariel part dragon? I mean, I can see clearly the shine she carries, but…is that even possible? Is anything not possible?"

Torin replied, "I cannot speak to what is possible or no. I only know that some things are, and that if you place belief in some things that seem impossible they can start to take on energy and form. It is what Karia does and she calls it magic.

"The Pucelles, as I am told, come from a point where the Ancient Dragon Amen befriended a family of cats, a mother and her kittens, sheltering them from a fierce storm. All her days, the mother took it upon herself and trained her children to protect the Ancient Dragon. These small beings willingly put themselves between much larger beings and their friend Amen. This, despite the fact that Amen is quite large in the physical realm and in no true danger. Amen was amused and charmed by their loyalty.

"The cat clan lived long, as do all beings who dwell near dragons. A tribe of elven beings wandered near to Amen in her warm desert and they founded a society there, carving a river with Amen's assistance. The cats and the elves began to take on one another's characteristics. Amen decreed the cats be treated as equals to her own great self. What should be impossible then, became reality to them.

"The great Port of Amen's Child grew up at the mouth of the river on the Ringing Sea not far from our home island. Eventually the mingling of energies faded as Amen herself went into stasis at the behest of Gaia.

"The Pucelles took to the sea reluctantly, and many of their journeys were one way. They arrived in Albion some generations past.

"Hence, Mariel is both a child of Amen and a Pucelle." Torin finished his tale and waved a forepaw about.

Tasa pondered a moment and said, "Hence she is whiskered and stealthy in the woods, a daughter of a dragon and a kitten to a family of cats. The world is a big place, Torin." She paused again. Together they looked out from the edge of the cliffs near Karia's Temple. Ocean waves, endless and constant, wore away stone and rock below. The sound of such power was distant, despite their proximity. The last light of the day faded to deep indigo and then to night black. Stars arrived.

"Are the beast men some combination of dragon and animal?" Tasa asked. "Are they a natural bonding of beings like Mariel? We talk about them as if they are unnatural in some manner, but they exist on Gaia's surface the same as we. Can they be wrong, and we are somehow better? How can we know what Gaia's will is truly?"

"They are an aspect of a dragon's death." Torin spoke slowly as if listening to a faraway voice and then responding. "I confess that I do not fully understand these things, Tasa. But what I am told is that once, a dragon, Tepes by name, chose to kill any and all beings at his own will. The dragons of that day were closer to the Gaian consciousness. They could hear her voice more clearly than we do today.

"This Tepes, they called him the Blood Dragon, would destroy life at will and not always for sustenance or purpose. He seemed to relish the destruction of Gaia's life forms. He brought others to his way of thinking and became the cause of a great battle and tragic deaths, giants and dragons both. The desert of Amen once was fertile, but now stands as a reminder of the release of dragonfire in the cause of anger and destruction.

"It is in this time of history that Brigid lost her dragon mate to the murderous actions of the Blood Dragon Tepes." Torin choked on the words and was unable to continue. Tasa felt a wave of great sadness encompass them both and reached her arms around Torin's neck, pulling herself closer to him. He too reached a black scaled arm about the young girl.

They held each other long into the dark night. Finally, Torin spoke. "I was with you and without you, Tasa. Now that we know one another well, I cannot image a life separate from one another. Our journey is not safe, and I am to be hidden. But I will not allow your death at the sake of some misbegotten ruling from a council of Ancient Dragons that are themselves separate from Gaia's life. Serve her they may, but I too serve in keeping you safe.

"The beast men are not in alignment with this outcome. They are treacherous and deliberate in their seeking to destroy those who carry the blood of the dragons within their core vitality. It is why they seek to attack Albion. They will hunt you and I. As a group, we go to seek those who desire refuge. As a dragon, I go to cleanse Gaia of parasites. They sought to take you away once. It shall not occur again."

Tasa leaned against the dragon, listening to the beat of his great heart. "We cannot," she began, "swiftly judge others." The thoughts formed as she spoke. "We are asked to accomplish much. But we need to remain true to ourselves as well. I do not desire to be an executioner and I do not wish you to willingly take such a responsibility either. I will not back down from such a battle. I expect you to take appropriate action as well. We must make our choices but let us be wise.

"Are these beast men solely the result of this blood dragon? Or are they First Men, humans that may be Gaia's life forms like we are? Let us be cautious that we do not act against Gaia's true will. Let us be cautious that we do not easily accept others' perceptions as our own. We have, you and I, been compliant with others' will for too long, Torin. Let us act of our own accord during this journey.

"You and I will meet with King Kane, or so say the Mothers of Penthe House. In my vision with Amir, the dragon Mali showed him to me, and Master Amir…my father, said the King now knows me. I do not know what our reception will be in his land. Yet, King Kane has walked with dragons, and I wish for you and I to walk openly into his kingdom. We are the future, Torin. He is the past. He may carry wisdom, but we carry the new ways of the world."

****

In the late morning of the next day, in the center of the temple, surrounded by marble columns and high upon a dais, Karia stood resplendent in her robes, glistening white with a deep violet sash. Ni'all waited near Karia on one knee. He wore a long white shirt and loose trousers. Hair combed and temporarily tamed from the wild curls of his windy existence was bound loosely with leather strips braided neatly down his back. His sash was black, gold, and green plaid, the colors of his tribe. One belt and one hilt, visible in a leather sheath, were the only remnants of what had become the common vision of the well-armed young man about Penthe House.

Tasa smiled as she realized the white clothing he wore once belonged to Kamir. Loose on Ni'all, Kamir had long since outgrown the outfit. Tasa glanced at Kamir and saw a secret smile on his face. He stood near Ni'all and his mother, looking quite regal and tall. He also wore formal attire, but this in the yellow and green colors of an apprentice of the Order of the Southern Gate. Ni'all had no members of his tribe to stand with him in the ceremony and had humbled himself a bit to request that Kamir be his groomsman. Tasa noted that there was more man to Kamir that day than boy.

Tasa also wore the colors of the Order of the Southern Gate. She artfully tied the scarf, the gift she had received from Captain Troylis, about her slender neck. Troylis was there as well as Amir and several of the crew of the Mali. Many of the young women in attendance were paying far too much attention to the journeymen, when they should have been watching the ceremony unfold.

Mariel stood next to Tasa. Her forest-green-hued clothes clean, brown leather belts neatened, hair combed free from twigs and leaves, face scrubbed free from dust and dirt, new leggings with no holes or patches, and, to the wonder of all, she also wore shoes. Tasa smiled broadly at the sight of Mariel when she walked into the temple that day. "What?" Mariel snapped, tugging at a crisply pressed shoulder, then a too stiff hem, and finally a cuff that did not seem to be capable of bending.

"You are beautiful," Tasa said, and laid her hand on her friend's cheek. Mariel's whiskers softened and drooped as tears formed in her deep brown eyes.

Tasa herself was clothed in greens, the color of Forest House. Her skirt loose and long, flowing in layers about her knees and ankles, brown boots rising up her calves and showing new leather lacing, her dark black hair combed and brushed to a deep shiny luster, hanging straight down her back and held in place by a few artfully braided plaits from both sides of her pale face. Mariel raised her hand to Tasa's face as well. "You think I am beautiful? Remind me to get you a mirror after all this fuss is over."

Together they smiled and laughed but became quiet as Karia raised her staff. A strumming of harp and lute sounded quietly in the distance, gentle notes meandering about the gathering. Tasa looked around from her position near the front of the circle. In accordance with the new rules, not all the House Mothers could be in attendance at a single event, but she did spot Mother Meg and Mother Stone towards the back. Many faces were familiar, and she realized how many lives circled and touched upon others without her knowledge of the connections.

A shadow beneath a tree off to the cliff side of the temple environs caught Tasa's attention. Brigid! And deeper still, she was certain she could see Penthe herself. Silently she sent a mental phrase to Torin, only to be surprised to see him become visible to her sight within those same shadows, so near to Brigid. Tasa nudged Mariel and nodded in their direction. Mariel squinted and whispered, "Was that pile of rocks always there?"

The soft notes faded. A strumming began, stronger and with more purpose, calling the audience to attention, focusing the community's mind upon the reason for their gathering. Tasa smiled at the embracing nature of the music. Red Robin. She glanced at Mariel and saw a smile on her face as well. He really was quite good, and here in this space of love they could drop all the teasing and nonsense and simply acknowledge and admire his skill.

From the back of the crowd in the temple came a rustling sound. Robin's music quieted as all eyes turned to glimpse, first Kianna, lean and lovely in her violet robes, and then A'Tienne, moving smoothly, as if she floated. Her long gown, white and bright in the late morning sun, carried the glow into the shade cast by the circular temple roof. A sash of green and another of red showed her affiliations to both Forest and Hearth House. Tasa noted a slender woven cuff that also carried the colors of Beach, Forge, and Wisdom House each on a field of pale white, honoring the entirety of Penthe House.

Few had ever seen A'Tienne's hair released from her normally long and tightly braided state. Now, all marveled at the rich, deep auburn mane that freely fell well below her waist. As she approached the center dais where Ni'all awaited, Kianna stepped to one side and held her hand out. A'Tienne took her hand and smiled. The smile wavered and tears began to flow.

The two young women had been nigh inseparable for over five years. They now were going separate ways and by mutual agreement supported one another's choices. Soft sobs and sorrowful gasps floated from the congregation at the moment. Tasa felt Mariel's hand grip her own and she returned the grasp. They leaned in to one another.

A pang of guilt rose in Tasa's heart. Would Kianna and A'Tienne be making such a choice if it were not for her impending journey?

Karia, cool blue eyes sparkling with tears, reached down and clasped both women by their hands. She guided them together up to the dais.

"In as much as this is a ceremony of a new binding, we must now also recognize what has gone before. Kianna, do you at this time, willing and from a place of love, release your mate A'Tienne from your partnership?"

Kianna found a short breath and gasped the words, "I do so release my friend A'Tienne to her future. I do so with love and a deep desire for her continued growth and happiness."

Karia turned to A'Tienne and said, "Do you A'Tienne, at this time, willingly and from a place a love release your mate Kianna from your partnership?"

Openly weeping, A'Tienne said, "I do release Kianna from our partnership, but never from my heart and my love." She turned to Kianna and said, "Be strong for us." Kianna nodded and stepped down from the platform, slowly letting their hands slide apart.

Karia allowed a few moments of silence and A'Tienne regained her composure to some degree. Through all of this, Ni'all remained on one knee, patiently awaiting his moment. A'Tienne now turned to face him. She smiled, and tears again began to flow. "I am sorry," she whispered, but the dome of the temple allowed the sound to flow to the crowd. "Thank you for being patient with me, Prince Ni'all."

He reached for her hand and said, "I will be patient always for you. You are a woman of your own heart, and I am blessed for the times we have spent together. That you chose me to be present with you, this day or any other, lifts me above what I am alone."

Karia indicated with a wave of her hand that he should rise. "Family and friends, I bid you welcome on behalf of the couple, A'Tienne of the Green and Ni'all, Prince of the Tribes of the Black Pool."

Karia took command of the ceremony then, speaking in firm tones, sensibly raising thoughts and practical matters regarding the arrangement of two people who chose to live as one. Tasa listened intently to the discourse, all the while Mariel remaining tight against her side.

Finally, Karia said, "Now we turn to the couple and ask: 'Do you vow to uphold one another exclusively? Do you vow to craft and dream a life together that acts for the good and growth of one another? Do you vow to be faithful to one another and also to support the will of Gaia in your lives?'"

Together they said, "We do so vow."

Taking a golden cord from each of them, Karia began to wind them together. She reached for their wrists and, using the twined cords, loosely bound A'Tienne and Ni'all. Karia continued speaking. "As a cord is stronger when it becomes a twofold braid, so do you now become stronger together. You will be tested by life. Remain true to your heart's vision. Remain strong. Remain in the presence of love. Love does not fail." The priestess took a breath in preparation for the conclusion.

Before she could continue, Ni'all raised his unbound hand. He held a third cord, silver in color, and looked at Kianna. "I ask you to join us, Lady Kianna." She hesitated a breath and then mounted the dais to stand with the couple. Ni'all said, "Lady, you have been a great part of A'Tienne's life and I am loathe to think that you should be apart from her. You are a deep part of her heart and I can never, nor shall I try to, supplant that love. She and I will journey from these lands, true, but I request that you remain bound to her and accept me as a member of your continuing partnership. Despite distance, I ask you to always seek us out with your heart and send us love and strength in our life's journey. We shall return to you and, if you accept, we shall be one." Kianna and A'Tienne stared at Ni'all for a moment before turning to each other. Smiles broke out and hugs ensued.

Karia took the silver cord and wound it above and about the golden cords, binding Kianna's wrist to A'Tienne's and Ni'all's. "Do you vow," she spoke again, "to seek Gaia's will in all things? Do you vow to support each other as long as you all shall grow together?"

The trio replied, "We do so vow."

"So mote it be," Karia pronounced, and applause broke out amongst the gathering. Red Robin struck a lively tune and the rest of the musicians joined in as the three descended from the dais to be greeted and hugged by everyone.

Tasa and Mariel were in the front of it all and they were the first to reach out to the trio, hugging each in turn. Karia and Kamir also descended the dais and took it upon themselves to create some space for the trio.

As the entourage passed them by, Mariel and Tasa found themselves pressed close and face to face. Mariel spoke first and said, "As long as we both shall grow together."

Tasa said, "I do so vow."

Together they said, "So mote it be."

38

Salt Water

"SO, YOU LIKED ME RIGHT AWAY, RIGHT? Or were you afraid of me because I startled you? For my part, I thought there was something a bit magical about you the moment I saw you carrying all those tools all by yourself. You did like me right away, didn't you?" Red Robin was spinning slowly as he spoke, his arms stretched out, head tilted back. The stars arched above them, and the fire burned low. The scent of pine smoke filled the air and the spring night had seemed cool and warm at the same time. Tasa sat quietly on a large log at the edge of the forest watching the world turn. "You did! I knew it! I can always tell! You did like me right away!"

"I thought you must be simple." Tasa let the words float away from her to be absorbed by Red Robin. He stopped spinning as the words took hold of him. The smile dropped off his face in the darkness. "You dropped out of the tree unannounced, called me a master smith or some such, started touching me without introducing yourself or even asking my name, and you had that foolish grin on your face all the while. I thought you were simple. I felt bad for your mother for months until I found out that you were just bold and foolish."

Robin sat down across the fire from her. He looked like he had just been struck in the back of the head. "Simple?"

"I was happy to know you were not, if that helps." Tasa wasn't smiling outwardly, but she recalled Mariel's words about Red Robin being full of himself. The truth was she did like Robin, well, now at any rate, and she was happy that he had asked her to watch the moonrise with him.

She was initially dismayed to find the two of them were the only watchers, but then recalled that Red Robin could be a gentleman when he had to be. So far, he had just been silly, trying too hard to be suave when he was clearly nervous. Tasa went on saying, "I'm telling you this because I want everything to be honest between us. Always. I've seen how you are around other girls and I've seen how they act around you. It may be fun for awhile, but I am not that way."

The fire flickered red and orange and Tasa watched the play of light upon his face. Right now, the light was missing from his eyes and she was sad about that for she did not want him to lose that inner brightness on her account. "I do like you," she offered. "I like when you sing. Everyone does, but I like you when you are just you also."

"How do you know?" Robin's voice lost its timbre and depth. He sounded like a young man. He sounded like what he was.

"Because I have watched you when you thought no one was looking. Because we walked together to Beach House, and I heard you writing a song. Because we slept out under stars and I heard your breath as it flowed easily and peacefully, not controlled and not monitored and paced, just breathing." He was looking directly at her. It may have been the reflection of the firelight, but there were sparks in his eyes again. "I know you because I look into your eyes and I look deeper than the others do." The moon rose, and they talked deep into the night.

Red Robin loved only Tasa from that moment on.

****

Forge Mother fussed with the buckles from the scabbard on Kamir's belt and fiddled with the handle of Tasa's Quiet Night. "I wish you would carry the larger shields. I wish you would give me more time to arm you better." She gave a quick tug on a buckle. "I wish you weren't going," she said so quietly that it was barely a sound. Her eyes glistened with tears.

"Grandmother, I must go to protect Tasa." Kamir spoke boldly, but Tasa knew his doubts. It had been a slight surprise when she learned that Karia was the daughter of Forge Mother. It was a guess as to who her father might be, but Tasa felt it was a good guess. She had shared the section in her scroll of passage that Grandmaster Nicholaus had written. Karia had cried then, and also smiled. Tasa would share the scroll with Kamir once they were underway.

A'Tienne now stood with Kianna. They were silent in these last moments together. It was a loss of certainty and they had little experience at dealing with such a thing. They had always been there for each other. Separation was difficult. A'Tienne gently stroked tears from Kianna's check.

Mariel was already aboard and stowing gear and packs and food and canteens and skins and all manner of extraneous material that the House Mothers came up with at this last of last minutes. Mariel kept as busy as she possibly could. She was nervous as a cat about going to sea and could not believe that Tasa would actually want to, and aboard the same vessel that she was nearly lost in.

"It wasn't really that bad," Tasa told her. "You'll do alright. I'll be watching you."

Little Bria was cheerful and looking forward to the trip. She hovered about Amir and Troylis asking endless questions and showing a surprising understanding of the workings of the stars and weather.

Tasa looked about at all the well wishers that had come to see them off. Mother Meg and Mother Marion stood close together talking in low tones and second guessing the decision to allow this journey. Tasa knew that Brigid herself had spoken to them and that was an endorsement that few would go against. Tasa had not yet completed her third year at Penthe House. Special dispensation was given and certain of her studies had been accelerated. Brigid herself had taken Tasa on a short voyage about the Albion Isles, giving her personal instruction. This alone placed Tasa far ahead of any adepts.

Many others stood about, friends and classmates, and there was an air of subdued celebration in the gathering. Laughter was scattered about, along with the tears, and the farewells were heartfelt. There was much that Tasa would miss. In a few brief years Penthe House had become home and this was her family she was saying good-bye to. No, not good-bye. Brigid had given her another phrase.

****

They had been on Brigid's island in the far north. The wind swept down from the ice cap and cut through the warmest of clothes. They had stepped out of Brigid's cavern. Inside it had been warm and dry, and the walls and floors were smooth. They were wet constantly in their little boat. It was barely big enough for the two of them and their packs. Brigid called back as they pushed off.

"Fare forward, dear Penthe! Fare forward, my friend." The ancient dragon had then stepped outside her home, two younglings at her side, both a beautiful blue.

"And you, sister! Fare forward!" The dragon's voice was heard deep inside their hearts and Tasa drew strength from the feeling. They pushed off and turned the prow south with Torin wheeling above. "Fare forward," she heard him say.

****

Now Master Amir whistled them all to attention and they began to move towards the swift craft Mali. There were more passengers than just Tasa and her friends and she lingered a bit giving final hugs and shedding final tears with the three House Mothers. She could see the glow of light clearly in each one of them.

Amir's voice came clearly over the noise of the crowd. "Captain Tasa and crew, report to the bridge for your assignments!" Tasa grinned and saluted. She hugged Karia as she came down the gangway when Tasa went up.

"We'll all come back, Karia," she said.

"How can you be sure, Tasa? It is a beautiful world, but it is not a safe one." Karia looked towards Kamir as he swung his new sword about, a late gift from his grandmother. The giantess let tears fall from her ice blue eyes.

"Because I believe it," Tasa said, "and you must believe it also.

"Do you believe?"

****

Red Robin stood at the docks and recalled the words he shared with Tasa from three nights past and the few brief moments he had with Tasa over the last few, fast years. He wished he had one more day with her. One more hour. She was embarking on a journey and he did not know when he would see her again, if ever.

He thought of her last words to him.

"I do like you and if I stay, then we have something, you and I. I believe that you will do your best with me. If I go, then the world may have something bigger than the two of us, and better. If I return, we may still have something or maybe not. I do not expect you to wait and I want you to know that I will live my own life fully, just as I expect you to do. It is a different path that I take now and not one that you can walk with me. Walk your path, Sir Robin. Sing your song. Be true to who you truly are." She kissed him then and he kissed her.

"Fare forward, my friend," she said to him, and he had no words.

He watched from a distance as Tasa leapt aboard Amir's swift craft and stood at the rail with her companions. She raised two fingers as the ship sailed from the harbor.

The sun set that night and Robin still stood watching, eyes to the sea. Within his eyes pooled tears of loss, salty like the sea. His green eyes.

Addendum
Penthe House

PENTHE HOUSE IS CALLED AFTER THE ORDER OF THE DRAGON of Albion named Penthe. Penthe is an Ancient Dragon, the daughter of Tethys, the legendary dragon of the peaceful sea. Penthe has a direct lineage to the Aeonic Dragon Tiamat and thus carries the energy of the Tablets of Destiny with her to the Isles of Albion.

The founding of Penthe House and the subsequent orders within is based on the belief that all life works together for the betterment of Gaia. This tenet is the primary one and in all decisions the question is asked, "Will this action be to the benefit of Gaia?"

From the beginning, and as time has gone on, the House of Penthe has been a predominately female-based discipline, though there is plenty of opportunity for males to be involved. It is rare, however, for a man to sit as a Keeper of the Words.

The main body of Penthe House is based in a literal structure with five equal walls. Placed in each wall at its precise center is a door. This has given rise to the name, The House of Five Doors. The wall to the north runs east to west in a straight line. The south is pointed to by the joining of the walls of the yellow and the green doors.

Each door corresponds to a path.

Each path has its own house where the followers live.

Each path is assigned a color. The adherents and adepts of a path wear robes or clothing the color of their path.

Each path is viewed as equal in importance.

Each path is based on one of the five elements, as viewed by the old ways.

The *Red Door or Red Path* is one of fire, and the followers live in Hearth House. It is here that the sacred skills of family care and family building are taught.

The *Yellow Door or Yellow Path* is one of stone and metals, and the followers live in Forge House. It is here that the sacred skills of tool making and use are taught.

The *Green Door or Green Path* is one of earth, and the followers live in Forest House. It is here that the sacred skills of planting and harvesting are taught.

The *Blue Door or Blue Path* is one of water, and the followers live in Beach House, also called the Boat House. It is here that the sacred skills of riding and harvesting the seas are taught.

The *Violet Door or Violet Path* is one of air, and the followers live in Wisdom House. It is here that the sacred skills of spirituality and healing are taught.

Penthe House is the White Path. It is where all paths come together, and it is from here that all paths radiate out into the world.

Traditionally, acolytes spend two lunar cycles within each house learning and acquiring life skills. After two months, they move on to the next discipline. An acolyte traditionally will spend two years touring each of the five houses in turn, with two lunar cycles also spent within Penthe House proper, learning the White Path of vision and leadership, community and education. Rare exceptions are made to this pattern.

The acolyte living at Hearth House wears a red robe with a yellow sash, signifying their movement towards Forge House.

The acolyte living at Forge House wears a yellow robe with a green sash, signifying their movement towards Forest House.

The acolyte living at Forest House wears a green robe with a blue sash, signifying their movement towards Beach House.

The acolyte living at Beach House wears a blue robe with a violet sash, signifying their movement towards Wisdom House.

The acolyte living at Wisdom House wears a violet robe with a white sash, signifying their movement towards Penthe House.

The acolyte serving a position within Penthe House wears a white robe and a sash the color of their primary discipline. If a primary discipline has not been decided upon, they wear a black sash. If the acolyte's primary discipline is of Penthe House, they wear a black robe with a white sash. For some, their primary path is the acolyte path. There is no command to become an adept.

All acolytes of these houses are female.

There are three orders that border Penthe House. These orders are predominately male. The mature members of these orders are often travelers and are called journeymen. The senior members are housed in collectives where they instruct the younger novices, called apprentices. While in the collective, they are identified by a band or scarf worn on the wrist, arm, or neck. This can be worn outside of the collective as well, but is not required.

The Eastern Order of the Sun is a discipline of sciences of the planets and the sun and the moon. It is of measuring and building and geometries. The Eastern Order supports Wisdom House, Hearth House, and Forge House. The scarf of the Eastern Order is violet, red, and yellow.

The Order of the Southern Gate is a discipline of trade and travel and commerce. The Order of the Southern Gate supports Forge House and Forest House. It also supports directly the Life House of Five Doors. The scarf of the Order of the Southern Gate is yellow and green with borders of white.

The Order of the Western Grove is a discipline of nature and the earth and the seas. The Order of the Western Grove supports Forest House, Beach House, and Wisdom House. The scarf of the Order of the Western Grove is green, blue, and violet.

Men have been known to serve the Violet Path of Wisdom House. This position is usually one of a traveler, or as a builder of a new community of the Penthe Path. While a community is being physically created, such a man is in charge. When the community is completed, he will step aside, and a woman will take the name of Mother or Mater of Penthe House. She will most often be of the Violet Path. On assuming the role of Mother, she will wear robes of white with a sash of gold. She will also be known as "The Keeper of the Words."

The Mother of Penthe House will have five who act as her liaisons between the other houses. These five will wear white robes trimmed at the cuffs with the color of their house and a silver sash. They are called Mother by each of their houses.

The leader of each of the Orders of the East, South, and West are sometimes referred to as Father or Dagda. Generally, this is done only when in a session at Penthe House. They hold an equal say in the actions of the community and each Mother and Father has one vote when the time for a decision arrives. The voting is open and spoken aloud. All members of the Houses and Orders are in attendance if they wish. Acolytes and apprentices are welcomed as space permits.

It is from the Order of the Western Grove that the tradition of the Oakmen emerged and the Father of the Oakmen is and always has been Nicholaus.

It is from Penthe House that we have the great traditions of the Women in White, the Red Lady, the Green Lady, and the Marions, who are originally of the Blue Path. Also, the Kelle De who, in times that were dark, took the structure of the House of Five Doors and turned it into a circle for learning the crafts of each house.

From this tradition, we also have the families of the Greens and the Robins, who follow, logically, the Green Path and the Red Path. Out of the family of Robin grew the Goodfellowes' Croft which seeks to help those who have little means.

Primarily a building croft and one of young apprentices led by a journeyman, the Goodfellowes' Croft has expanded and includes many young acolytes that follow Mater Moira, daughter to Marian and Robin A'Green. These, then, craft dwellings and shelter and clothing for those that find themselves displaced or in dwindling power due to age.

Many are the Orders and Houses that follow one aspect or more of the original Penthe House and we leave it to you to discover those paths or begin your own, asking the question, "Will this action be to the benefit of Gaia?"

AUTHOR JEFFREY J. MICHAELS is a Gemini. As such he is deeply involved in whatever interests him at the moment.

Currently he is polishing a sweeping fantasy series of interconnected tales collectively known as "The Mystical Histories." It is varied enough that he may even finish most of the stories. He likes to think of his work as "metaphyictional," combining fantasy and humor with metaphysical elements.

In his real life, Jeff is a well-respected creative and spiritual consultant.

Tasa's Path is the first book in the Tasa's Passage Trilogy. Watch for *Tasa's Journey* and *Tasa's Home* coming soon!

www.jeffreyjmichaels.com

www.ingramcontent.com/pod-product-compliance
Lightning Source LLC
Chambersburg PA
CBHW051101030726
47504CB00006B/1733